Sherryl Clark has been writing crime fiction for many years; her first crime short stories were published in the Artemis Press anthologies, as well as 'The Age Summer Reading' and in high school texts. In 2018 she entered her novel *Trust Me, I'm Dead* in the CWA Debut Dagger and was shortlisted. This led to Verve Books UK publishing three books in her Judi Westerholme series. *Trust Me, I'm Dead* was longlisted for the CWA John Creasey New Blood Award and the NZ Ngaio Marsh Debut Novel Award.

Find out more at sherrylclarkcrimewriter.com

WOMAN, MISSING

SHERRYL CLARK

FICTION
HQ

WOMAN, MISSING
© 2024 by Sherryl Clark
ISBN 9781038915443

First published on Gadigal Country in Australia in 2024
by HQ Fiction
an imprint of HQBooks (ABN 47 001 180 918), a subsidiary of HarperCollins Publishers
Australia Pty Limited (ABN 36 009 913 517).

HarperCollins acknowledges the Traditional Custodians of the lands upon which we live and work, and pays respect to Elders past and present.

A catalogue record for this book is available from the National Library of Australia
www.librariesaustralia.nla.gov.au

Printed and bound in Australia by McPherson's Printing Group

For Mum and Dad –
and librarians everywhere

CHAPTER ONE

Whop, whop, whop. The sound of my runners hitting the road was comforting, as always, like a metronome that sends a signal from feet to brain. *Whop*, peace, *whop*, calm. I loved these shoes. Loved their beat.

The rain had cleared and the streetlights cast orange blurs on the shiny road. I stopped for a moment and inhaled. Wet asphalt, soaked grass on the nature strips, oil and diesel, dog shit, the cheese factory, and the gardenias in the gardens I passed, tiny white ghosts among dark leaves. Nobody but me out at 2am. An occasional car that passed with a swish as I veered onto the footpath, but no one tooted or shouted to harass me, even though it'd be obvious I was a female.

I was alone, just the way I liked it.

I was headed for the river, where I'd run along the bike path and back up over the bridge, then home. Back in my little box. My legs burned, but it felt good. I took it easy down the slope to the river, then sped up a little, wary of the dark shadows under the walls. I could take care of anyone who tried it on, but I'd rather not have to. Up to the bridge, a glance at the dark, smelly water. The entrance to my building was ahead, lobby light out as usual.

I stopped at the door, bent over, breathing hard. Sweat dripped off the end of my nose, plopped onto the concrete. It was time to go in and shower, then lie awake for a few hours until it was time to go to my new job. I gritted my teeth and told myself it was going to be fine. I might even enjoy it.

Once upon a time, I would have been itching to get to work, to put on my police uniform and get out there on patrol. That time had gone, and I had to get over it.

CHAPTER TWO

I stepped out of the creaking lift on the third floor and pushed through the heavy wood and steel door that said *PMI—Paul Marshall Investigations.*

'Hey, girlfriend.' Gang beamed at me over the top of his massive central computer monitor. His round red-framed spectacles reflected colours and figures from all three screens. 'First day—gotta be a bit exciting!'

I'd met Gang last week and wondered how a geeky, cheerful Asian computer whizz had ended up in a private investigation firm rather than some big conglomerate, but I had a feeling this place was actually perfect for him.

'Hi, Gang. I'm trying to restrain myself.' I smiled to take the edge off my sarcasm.

His beam faded a tiny bit. 'You can have that desk over there.' He pointed to the one behind me that held a computer and two pens. 'I need to go through the systems with you first, but Paul messaged me to give you a job.'

I nodded. Maybe starting behind a desk would give me a handle on how this place worked. It wasn't going to be like a suburban police station, that was for sure.

Gang set me up with a password and email address, and went quickly through the basic software and search tools I'd be using, then handed me a file. 'It's a missing person job. This woman has left her husband, apparently, and he did report her missing, but then he told the police she'd run off with someone. Well, that's his story.'

'Story?'

He shrugged. 'Police haven't been able to find her, and our clients are her parents. They don't believe the husband. There are two kids and they reckon she would never leave her kids like that.'

'Do I need to talk to them? Get more details?'

'Not yet. Paul did the first interview with them and the notes are here. We have a process to follow—the checklist is on top. Start with her phone and bank activities, and some other things on the list. There's an electronic version I've emailed you as well.'

'Right.' I thumped down on the office chair behind the desk. Paul had warned me I'd be doing a lot of computer work as an investigator, and I was about to find out what that meant. On the screen were links to all the databases and websites PMI used to find out stuff about people. They included the police ones I used to know well, but not the police LEAP system. Of course not. That would be hacking. I glanced at Gang, who had his headphones on, bopping along to loud techno music, the kind I hated. He was already making me feel like his granny.

I'd spent Saturday night having drinks with my police detective mate, Kayla. The stories she'd told me about her cases in Serious Crime made my teeth ache with envy. I hadn't told her about my job with PMI, but I'd have to confess sooner or later. Unless I got fired first, which was always a possibility.

I checked the summary paper file, then called it up in my emails on the PMI system and stared at the screen. Diane Paterson. Left her house over three weeks ago and hadn't been seen or heard of since. Police were notified within twenty-four hours, but according to the husband, Justin, they'd had no success tracking her down. I stuck a pen in my mouth and started chewing on it while I made some notes on a pad I found in the top drawer. Police would have checked international flights, probably domestic flights, too. Also checked all her bank and phone stuff, but I would have to do it all again.

Paul's report included copies of the police file—or rather, what had been provided to the husband. He'd handed it over begrudgingly when Diane's parents employed PMI, along with her passwords to various things online. 'To prove I'm not hiding anything,' Justin had said, according to the file. That was a red flag to me straight away.

I sighed and started by pulling up Diane's bank statements, and made a quick note—*Secret bank account?*

Paul hadn't been kidding about the paperwork in this job when he'd interviewed me. 'More than when you were in the police force. Just in case you were thinking it was all action here.' He'd smiled, but I knew he knew all about me already so I didn't smile back.

'I wasn't a detective, you know.'

'I know. Cop on the beat. Surprised you lasted three years.'

I bristled. 'I was a good officer.' Until I wasn't.

He'd pointed at Gang through the open door. 'We have Gang to wrangle the computers. He's a database and information whizz kid. If you get stuck, he's your guy.'

'Right.'

I knew PMI did insurance fraud, workplace fraud and theft, security analysis and some missing person work. I didn't dare complain about being bored. I needed this job. I needed a reason to get up every morning, even though I wasn't sure this was it.

I also needed to prove to my grandfather I could keep a job and do okay. Grandad had got me in here. He'd said he was worried about me and I'd brushed him off. But I could feel him watching over me, even though he lived ten kilometres away.

I worked through everything that would've already been done by the officers dealing with missing persons. Gang had explained we had to show the client what we'd done and what we'd found, set it all out clearly in a report. That's why we got paid. The police only shared what they figured they needed to. Standard procedure.

I'd just started on a dive into Diane's social media when the boss arrived. Paul Marshall himself. Ex-military police and a few years in the NSW police force before moving to Melbourne. He still wore his hair in a buzz cut and walked like he had a gun belt around his hips.

'Lou,' he said with a grin. 'How's it all going?'

'Good.' I mustered a smile and went back to searching Facebook.

Paul talked to Gang and made himself a coffee with the big hissing machine, then turned to me again. 'Lou, I need you to go and do a security check for a client. A single woman who's worried her abusive ex is stalking her again.'

I tried to stop my eyebrows shooting up, but too late.

'Yep, I know you're on the Diane Paterson case, but this client insisted that a female do the check, so you're it, I'm afraid. Should only take you two hours.'

Paul's other two investigators were both men, although I hadn't met them yet.

'Okay. Has she seen him in her vicinity?'

'Not sure. It's your job to check her house, advise if there's anything more she needs to do, and then follow up on whatever she tells you. She may even request protection.'

I went to gather up my bag and phone, but he said, 'No hurry. Gang will text you the address. She's expecting you at five. And she sounds very nervous. Just so you know.'

I nodded, thinking of the old joke: just because you're paranoid, it doesn't mean nobody is out to get you. Not so funny when you're being stalked.

Paul went into his office and closed the door. Gang grinned at me. 'First field job, hey?'

'Yeah.' I was ridiculously pleased about it. 'What's her name?'

'Melinda Moreau.' He leaned across to his left-hand monitor. 'Thirty-one. Been in Melbourne seven months. I'll text you the details now.' He tapped fast for a few seconds. 'Done.'

'Do I need to take anything with me?'

'You'll have to take notes and also photos. You can use a notebook or note app and do the photos with your phone.' He pointed to the heavens. 'Upload the photos to the cloud straight away, and then the report when you've typed it up.'

'Okay. Do you have a template for security analysis reports?'

'Of course.' Gang seemed to have a template for everything. I wanted one that detailed how to get your shit together and keep it that way.

I focused on Diane Paterson again, but I couldn't deny I was itching to get out of the office and back into the real world.

CHAPTER THREE

Melinda Moreau lived in Kensington, up the hill from the train station, and her street held a mix of older terrace houses and concrete boxes.

She lived in a two-storey terrace with stone-arched windows and those tiny, patterned tiles on the porch. The house was in darkness, but through the stained-glass door panel I could see a faint glow, probably from the kitchen at the back. I rang the doorbell and waited, waited some more, then checked my watch—5pm. I was on time.

A shadow slowly drifted towards the door and stopped. I thought about ringing the bell again, then the door opened on the chain and a small, pale face looked out through the gap.

'Melinda Moreau? Hi, I'm Lou Alcott,' I said. 'I'm from Paul Marshall Investigations.'

She looked at me blankly.

Did I have the right house? Yes, this was number 26. 'You made an appointment with PMI for a security check?'

'Yes.' The door and chain stayed as they were.

'Well, you asked for a female analyst and he's sent me.'

'Have you got ID?' It was a normal request, but she sounded overly suspicious.

'Sure.' I pulled out the new card Gang had given me, freshly laminated, as well as my investigator's licence, and showed them to her.

She peered at them for several long seconds, then said, 'All right, you can come in.'

'Only if you are absolutely okay with it,' I said. 'You seem worried. Has something happened since you called us?'

She looked over my shoulder at the street and then blinked hard. 'I'm fine. I just get nervous, you know, with people.'

I tried to sound extra professional. 'If you could open the door, I'll come in and explain to you what I'm here to do, and you can tell me what else you need.'

She didn't answer; the door closed, the chain rattled and the door opened again, slightly wider than before. She was very security conscious—not a bad thing. I slipped through the gap and let her reinstate the chain and lock.

The hallway was in darkness, and the doors leading off it were both closed. The stairs to the floor above were on my left and beyond them was the kitchen, judging by the cabinets in view. It took me a moment to work out the square of light was a glass door onto the garden, backlit by security lighting; the inside of this woman's house was like a tomb.

She stood next to me without saying a word, waiting.

'Why don't we go into the kitchen?'

'All right.' Melinda led the way and I was relieved to see the kitchen was bright and roomy. She offered me coffee or tea and I refused, then we sat at the small wooden table and I got out my notebook.

'Now, you have a security alarm, right?' She nodded. 'And window locks and deadlocks on your doors.' Another nod. 'I will check all of those. Can you explain a little more about what you need from me? What the problem is?'

For a moment, she ducked her head and her long, dark hair fell across her face. Then she looked up, her face tight. 'I moved here from Sydney in March to get away from my ex. He was, uh, violent, you know. I tried to leave him and still stay in Sydney, and he wouldn't leave me alone.' Her eyes were shiny with tears, but she blinked hard and kept going, her voice growing stronger. 'I went to the police and they were no use. I took out an order against him—an AVO, they call it.'

'That's right. Did it help?'

She snorted. 'No. I even moved back home with my father, but he just kept saying I was being silly and Nathan ... Anyway, that wasn't working. So one day when they were all at work, I packed up and came here.' She waved her hand around. 'This was my grandmother's house, my mum's mother. My mum passed away when I was fifteen. Nana left this place to me, but it had been sitting here empty for a few years.'

'It's good you had somewhere to come to,' I said. 'What's your ex's full name?'

'Nathan Gunn.' Her mouth curled down. 'Bastard.' Now she was talking about him, her anger rose to the surface, the nervousness gone. Anger was good, much better than being afraid.

'So you've been here about nine months. Did he follow you down here back then?'

'No, but I kept getting threats and these photos ... I had to change my mobile phone again.' She looked down at her bitten fingernails and raw cuticles, and I winced. 'That worked, mostly.'

'But now you think he's being a problem again?'

'Yes.' She glanced out into the backyard. 'I keep getting this feeling someone is watching me. It's stupid, because I'm careful and I check the street regularly, but ...'

'After what you've experienced, it's natural to be extra vigilant,' I said. 'Sensible, actually. Have you actually sighted Nathan at all? Or anyone that looked like him?'

'Not yet. I thought after all this time that it was okay, that he'd given up.' She sighed. 'I should've known better, I guess. He's never been the kind of guy who lets anyone else win. That's how he'd see this.'

I nodded. 'He's not the only one, unfortunately. It's like they think they own you.' Like a piece of furniture.

'Yes!' She grimaced at me. 'The thing is, I've just started my course—I'm training to be a veterinary assistant. I can't afford to mess around, and the stress of this is stuffing up my concentration.'

'I'll get you sorted out, no worries,' I said. 'Could you show me around the house? I'll check all your security and make sure everything is working. If there's extra things you can do, I'll tell you.'

'Thanks. That makes me feel a bit better. Maybe we can start upstairs first.'

In the hallway, she pressed a switch and a bank of globes above the staircase came on. I half-expected a cobwebby chandelier, but they were modern copper shades and large LEDs that sent out a decent amount of light, thankfully. I followed her up, examining her from the back as she climbed. Early thirties and small, like me, and she wore a pleated black skirt and cream cardigan. She was also wearing brand new Nikes, lurid orange and white, which made me think she was ready to run if need be.

At the top of the stairs, Melinda took me into the front bedroom. The bed was stripped to its mattress, and there wasn't a single personal item in sight, apart from a painting on the wall of a beach scene. 'This was my nana's room. I've taken out all her things and donated them, but I still couldn't sleep in here.'

I wasn't surprised. The room felt foreboding, and the thick olive-green curtains didn't help. I checked the front sash windows, which can often be easily opened if the latch is the old kind, but there were security bolts top and bottom. I took photos.

'These are good,' I said.

Melinda smiled at last, and was suddenly delicately pretty. 'Thanks, I installed them myself.'

A motion-detector unit in the top corner of the room was blinking. My phone made a sound like a cat meowing and she stared at me.

'Sorry,' I said, 'that's my phone signal for a text message.'

'I like cats, too.'

'I wish I still had mine,' I said, remembering my big black moggie who weighed a tonne and ate like there was no tomorrow. 'Excuse me, I'll just check this.'

It was from my grandfather. *Dinner at 7. Emmanuel's special.*

I made a face. Grandad never invited, he instructed. 'Just my grandfather.'

A gleam of interest lit up her eyes. 'Your grandad texts you?'

I laughed. 'He's no technophobe. Everyone gets texts from him, ordering them around.'

'He sounds like fun.'

That wasn't how I'd put it, but I didn't correct her. I followed her into another bedroom, also empty, also with the window bolted. The third bedroom was at the rear of the house and was clearly hers. It had been painted white and held dark blue furniture with a white bedspread and touches of deep yellow. Everything was perfectly neat and tidy. My feet sank into a thick blue and white rug.

'Wow, gorgeous room.'

She dimpled. 'Thanks.'

'Sure you want to be a vet nurse? You could be an interior designer.' Maybe she could come and renovate my flat.

'Ha, not likely. All of my father's business friends in Sydney who used an interior designer did nothing but whinge and complain. I couldn't stand that.'

I checked her windows, both of which were normal hanging kinds, double glazed with security catches. Nobody was getting in here either. I could see the motion-detector unit in here as well. More photos. My final check was in the bathroom, where an old-fashioned bath sat next to an ancient handbasin. The only window in here was tiny.

'That's painted shut,' Melinda said. 'The bathroom is my next reno project.'

Downstairs, the security was just as good. The small backyard had spotlights that glared brightly as soon as I walked outside. 'Do these go off often?'

'Well … I think it's cats or possums.'

I looked around the yard once more, at the high fence, the neat lawn edged with mondo grass, the lights. 'So … what do you think is going on?'

I didn't mean to sound doubting, but her face flushed and her glare was more searing than the spotlights. 'You don't believe me!'

'I didn't say that. But your security is top notch. I've never seen better in a private home. If you're inside with the doors locked, nobody is going to get in.'

Her head came up. 'I know that. I know I've created a prison here, but it's safer that way.' She walked back into the kitchen and headed for the fridge. 'Do you want a glass of wine?' She took two glasses from the cupboard and poured white into both without waiting for my yes or no.

'Thanks,' I said, and took the glass.

Melinda drank a large mouthful and sat back down at the table, looking mulish. 'I just want a normal life. I *was* starting to live normally again, until this.'

'I can understand that.' I sat down with her and tried the wine. It was really good and I checked the bottle, but couldn't read the label from here. I made my voice calm and gentle. 'Something has tweaked your radar. Do you know what?'

'It's that sense of being watched. Exactly like how I used to feel in Sydney, when Nathan was following me all the time.'

'Stalking you.'

'Yes. I'd be checking my rear-view mirror constantly and watching out the windows. Every now and then I'd spot him or his car. I had to close down all my social media.' She shivered. 'I'm so tired of looking over my shoulder for him.'

'It sounds to me like we need to check where he is, what he's doing.' I made a note and asked, 'What's his address and phone number?'

She gave them to me. 'If he's still in Sydney, maybe he's paying someone to watch me. Like I'm paying you.'

'That is possible.' I finished scribbling and asked, 'Have you heard from him at all since you bought a new phone and SIM card?'

'I did get a couple of texts. One of my so-called friends gave him the new number.' Before I could ask, she said, 'I deleted them straight away without reading them and blocked his number.'

She looked so defeated and small that I leaned over and grasped her hand. 'We'll sort him out, I promise. For good, this time.'

She blinked hard. 'Thanks. I'd just started to, well, feel like I could meet new people again, you know?' She let out a funny laugh. 'Even tried a dating app or two. Maybe I'll give up for a while.'

'There's nothing wrong with trying to make new friends. It must get pretty lonely in a new city.' It gets lonely anywhere, but I was keeping that gem to myself.

'Yes. My course is good, though. There are some really nice people, even though a lot of them are younger than me.' She smiled. 'One of them even asked me if I knew how to crochet. I wasn't going to admit that I did. Nana taught me.'

I laughed. 'I can't crochet, but I'm very good at ironing.' The memory of pressing creases into my uniforms made my throat go tight for a few moments. I coughed and said, 'We'll get onto checking out Nathan first thing in the morning, and make sure we nip it in the bud.' I felt awkward making promises to her, but on the other hand, wasn't that the main reason why I'd agreed to take this job at PMI? To try and fix things I couldn't in the police force? Or was I living in Fairyland?

'How long have you been doing this work?' Melinda asked, after swallowing the rest of her wine.

'Not long,' I said, feeling guilty at the little fib. 'But I do have other experience.'

She smiled doubtfully. 'Don't you have to do training or something?'

'I was in the police force for three years, so that was kind of my basic training for this.'

'You were a detective?' Her eyes were huge again. 'What did you investigate? What kinds of cases?'

'I was only a constable. Out on patrols, driving around in the divvy van, all that stuff. I wasn't in CID or anything.'

'But you went to domestic situations?'

I grimaced. 'Yes.'

Her gaze sharpened. 'What does that mean? Your expression.'

I drank more wine while I thought about how to answer. 'We dealt with lots of call outs, lots of fights, women assaulted. I grew to hate how little effect we had sometimes, and how often we went back to the same places. I felt like I'd ... failed.'

Melinda didn't answer but her brow furrowed. After a few seconds, she pulled up the sleeve on one arm to show a series of puckered circular scars. 'Cigarette burns.' She touched the side of her face. 'I had to have my cheekbone reconstructed. I've got some missing teeth. Cracked ribs a few times.' She shrugged. 'But I survived.'

I looked at the scars on her arm and anger rippled through me. 'You're bloody brave.' She was. Underneath the wispy exterior I sensed a core of steel now, and it made me warm to her even more. It took a lot of guts to not only survive but to come out of it stronger.

'Not really. In the end, I looked back and wondered how I could've been so stupid in the first place.'

'Hey, it's not stupid to want a relationship and someone to love.' I leaned forward and touched her hand. 'They never start out that way. Some guys are very good at charm and romance and being Mr Perfect. Until they aren't. I've met quite a few women whose husbands were fine until the wedding night, and then all hell broke loose.'

'I know.' She blinked hard. 'I've met some of those women in a support group, and more than one of them has ended up dead. Why is it—why don't the police do anything?'

'They try,' I said. 'But to be honest, in my experience, a man who's convinced that his girlfriend or wife belongs to him, and he can do whatever he likes to keep her in line ... the only thing that stops them is jail.'

Her mouth twisted. 'And then the woman has to move away and change her name and hope to God he doesn't find her.'

'Like you.'

'Yes, I was lucky that my grandmother left me this house. But it has meant that Nathan knew where I'd moved to.' She shook her head. 'Some days I feel so paranoid.'

'Nothing wrong with that, you know. Use it like a safety shield, Melinda. If you have a hinky feeling about some guy, take notice of it. Too bad if you're wrong. It's your life and your safety.'

'Thanks. I'd just love to meet someone nice, you know? Have dinner, talk, laugh. Have someone care about me. I've tried ...' She trailed off.

Her words echoed in my head and I blinked hard.

She stared down at her glass for a while, then heaved a big sigh. 'Guess it's time for you to go.'

I sat up and checked my watch. 'Yes, I have a report to write and things to action in the morning.'

When I left, Melinda gave me a hug. I don't do hugs, but I ended up hugging her back. She needed one. 'You take care,' I said. I meant it. I hesitated, then I pulled out my phone and got her to swap numbers with me. 'Call me, all right? If you need anything, are worried about anyone or just want to talk.'

She thought for a moment, then her lovely smile flashed again. 'Okay, I will. Thanks.'

As I got into my car and edged out into the street, I had a feeling I'd be seeing Melinda again.

CHAPTER FOUR

I arrived at Grandad's house just before seven. He was a stickler for punctuality. The gate opened as I pulled up and I drove in, leaving the streets of Altona behind me. I entered into what I'd come to realise over the years was a fortress.

I guess that's what you live in when you're a crime boss. Not that Grandad would ever use that phrase. 'Legitimate businessman' was his preferred moniker. It was my mother who'd told me when I started asking questions about how come the men that worked for Grandad all carried guns, and why couldn't I have one, and why couldn't I talk about Grandad in front of my father.

Back then, my father, Jeremy Alcott, was a police sergeant on the way up. He loved the uniform and the power it gave him, and he wanted more. To my father, Grandad was a total embarrassment. Once, I heard my father tell Mum that if he'd known Hamish was a crim, he never would have married her. She'd replied, 'Pity I didn't tell you then.'

In those days, Mum had plenty of guts. Before my father crushed them out of her.

I loved my grandfather to bits, and my nana, too. Nana died just after my mother did. Grandad said she died of a broken heart. He's never forgiven my father. Neither have I. So Grandad and I have a lot more in common than just blood.

I quickly uploaded the photos I'd taken at Melinda's to the PMI cloud, then got out of my car. The front door opened as I walked up the steps.

'Ah, cara, I'm so happy to see you!' It was Emmanuel. He'd been Grandad's 'every man' for longer than I could remember. Chef, butler, housekeeper, confidant. And he was like a much-loved uncle to me. He stood there with open arms, waiting to hug me. Emmanuel is the exception to my hug rule.

'Come in, come in. Your grandfather is waiting with a large bunch of questions.' He winked at me, his dark eyes sparkling. 'Just tell him to stop being so nosy.'

'Ha, as if that ever works,' I said.

Emmanuel shooed me ahead of him and went on to the kitchen. He made the best martinis ever. In two minutes, I'd have one in my hand.

Grandad was out in his garden, feeding his koi. When I was little, I called them 'water tigers', with their flashing orange and white stripes and patches. Nobody was allowed to feed them except Grandad, not even me.

'Good evening, Louisa,' Grandad said without turning around. 'How is your new job going?'

Straight to the point, as always. I guess it got the difficult stuff out of the way first. 'It's fine. Looks like it'll be a lot of paperwork, but Paul did warn me.'

One last sprinkle of food, then he brushed his hands and turned. 'Any interesting jobs yet?' His blue eyes were sharp under his shock of white hair. He stood as straight and tall as ever. I couldn't see Grandad ever stooping or leaning on a stick.

'First one today. I went to see a woman who needed a security check and I had to find out what her problem is.'

'And?'

'Violent ex who seems to be unable to let her live in peace. He's either followed her to Melbourne or is paying someone to watch her.'

He grunted. 'Nasty.'

Emmanuel came out onto the patio behind me. 'Martinis are served, signorina.' He presented the tray to me first, so I could pick the glass with the biggest olive—he'd put two in for me and I laughed.

We all took a cocktail and toasted Nana—'To the best!'—then sipped the cold liquid. The martini was brilliant, as usual. Emmanuel went back to the kitchen after assuring me that we were having my favourite, his own special lasagne, which I happened to know was Nana's recipe. I watched him go, his neatly creased trousers under his white apron, a blue bowtie at his neck. He never changed. Thank God.

'Are you going to stick at this job, lassie?' Grandad asked.

'If I like it.' I'd drifted for a long while after leaving the force, working mostly as a waitress in a restaurant owned by a friend of Grandad's, Noddy Wells, but also as a security guard, which was excruciatingly boring; standing around in a shopping centre all day. I'd had a go at house cleaning, too, and lasted one day.

'You will,' Grandad said. Like it was a given and he wouldn't hear any different. 'Of course, there's always a job waiting here for you.' He grinned, knowing what I'd say.

'No, thanks, Grandad. No offence.'

He wouldn't take any. But he'd been hinting, ever since I stopped being a police officer, that I could take over the 'firm' from him one day. Yeah, right. For a start, I wasn't nearly tough enough. And even though he had a lot of legitimate businesses these days, I was sure his criminal dealings hadn't entirely disappeared.

Grandad started telling me all about the cricket on the weekend, the English team and the Ashes tour coming up, and I tuned out. He was a cricket nut, and to me it was like watching paint dry. It was a relief when Emmanuel came back to tell us dinner was ready. Grandad had another martini and poured me a sauvignon blanc, and I thought I'd better stick to water after that. The last thing I needed was a drink-driving conviction.

Halfway through dinner, I realised Grandad had stopped talking and was looking morose. That was unusual for him. He could look grumpy or commanding, or crack a joke and make me laugh, but morose was unsettling.

'What's wrong?' I asked.

He shook his head. 'Arr, lass, nothing for you to worry about. Just a business thing getting out of hand.'

Out of hand. I'd never heard him use that term before. 'What does that mean? Are you in trouble?'

His bushy white eyebrows shot up. 'Me? In trouble? Not bloody likely! I'll sort it out, don't you worry.' He leaned forward. 'Now, what's next for you? How's your little flat going?'

He wanted me to move into something bigger with more security, but the flat in North Melbourne suited me. It was an anonymous block with a parking spot and friendly neighbours. No garden to worry about—I couldn't even be bothered with pot plants. 'It's fine, really it is. All I need right now.'

'You let me know when you're ready to move, lass.' He nodded to himself as if he had it all planned already, which he probably did. 'Got a nice row of new condos, and I reckon one of them's got your name on it.'

'Righto,' I said. 'One day.' Like in about ten years, maybe.

I wasn't taken in by Grandad's assurances. After I'd said goodnight to him, Emmanuel walked me to the door and I whispered to him, 'What's going on? Who's upset Grandad?'

Emmanuel's face dropped and he crossed himself. That sent a deep chill through me.

'Emmanuel?'

He shook his head. 'He won't like it if I tell you. You know how he hates anyone knowing his business.'

'Yeah, but this is me.'

'Sorry, cara, you will have to wait until he decides to tell you himself.'

So I had to drive home with the worry gnawing at my guts, overshadowing my disquiet about Melinda. 'Getting out of hand.' I didn't like that one bit.

CHAPTER FIVE

In the morning, my phone alarm woke me, reminding me I'd planned a run, and I cursed. I'd thrashed around in my bed half the night, alternating between worrying about Melinda and trying to tell myself she'd be fine in her secure house, and fretting over Grandad and who might be causing him so much trouble. It was totally unlike him to admit a 'business' problem.

The whole three years I'd been in the police force, I was nervous that someone I worked with would find out I was related to Hamish Campbell. It wasn't a good look to be the granddaughter of one of the biggest crime bosses in the state. Especially when Grandad had been so disappointed I'd joined up in the first place. He'd thought I was doing it to prove something to my father. As if. At least Grandad had kept his promise and not let on to anyone that he knew me.

I hauled myself out of bed, peed and washed my face, then dressed for the run in old sweats and my favourite runners. I was moving like a zombie. But an hour later, after a run along the Maribyrnong River to Yarraville and back, I felt almost human again.

In the PMI office, I typed up my notes from Melinda's house inspection and the information on Nathan Gunn, then googled him to obtain a recent photo. Nothing came up. I emailed the report to the cloud for Paul, to join the photos I'd uploaded last night.

Paul called me into his office to ask more about Gunn. 'Do you think it's possible he's come to Melbourne to harass her again?'

'I've learned to assume the worst about these guys,' I said. 'The obsessed ones never give up, they just bide their time. The question is: how obsessed was he?'

His eyebrows twitched. 'You think she's exaggerating?'

'God, no! If anything, women in her situation underestimate what men are capable of.'

'Hmm. I know she only asked for a security check, but we need to do a bit more work on Gunn, I think. Find out more about him, would you? So we know what we're dealing with.' He'd fanned a half-dozen photos across his desk and frowned down at them. I thought they were something to do with Melinda and leaned over to peer at them, but they were surveillance photos, mostly of a man and woman inside a house. Even upside down, I recognised the woman.

Paul looked up and caught my stare. 'You know her?'

'I, ah, I think I've seen her before. A couple of years ago, when I was ...'

'Still a cop.' He smiled. 'What was she arrested for?'

'Prostitution and assault. In St Kilda.'

'You would've seen a lot of those. Why was she so memorable?'

'Oh, she wasn't really. But I …' I didn't want to sound silly, and the more I thought about how to describe it, the sillier it sounded. But Paul said nothing, just waited. Perfect interrogation technique. I cracked.

'I remember faces. Like, a lot more than normal people.' My own face was burning.

He looked like cogs were turning inside his head. 'So you're a super recogniser.' His tone was astonished.

My hackles rose. 'Yeah, I guess that's the term, but I don't think of it like that. I just remember faces, that's all.'

'It's a valuable skill, Lou. Australia is still behind in this stuff, although the UK police are keen on it. They're even putting their super recognisers into nightclubs to ferret out rapists and crims. But it won't stand up in court here. Yet.' He gazed at me for a few seconds. 'It's still an asset, though. Did you use it when you were in the force?'

'Not really. I did nab a shoplifter once that I'd seen operating before, but like you said, testifying about that in court might not have gone my way.' I gestured at the photo. 'Is she a client, too?'

He laughed. 'No, she's the "mistress" in what is likely to be an expensive, messy divorce. Our client is the wife. Interesting that this woman—' he tapped the photo, '—used to be a prostitute. Perhaps that's where the husband met her.'

I shrugged. 'Stranger things have happened. Much stranger.'

'Yes. Unfortunately, we deal with problems that are far too common.'

I remembered my initial concern when Grandad suggested maybe this job meant I'd be spending a lot of my time watching naughty husbands. 'Does this agency do much husband-and-wife stuff like that?'

'Not these days. Insurance and corporate stuff, and missing persons. We get some industrial espionage, like what Billy is doing. You haven't met Billy yet. Gang's tech abilities have expanded the range of what we can take on.' He grinned. 'Divorce work not to your liking?'

'It's not a problem.' Except a friendly divorce was as rare as pink diamonds.

He let a small silence fall while he gathered up the photos and returned them to their folder, then he said, 'Can I trust you, Lou?'

A bunch of thoughts ran through my head—how he knew my grandfather so well, for a start, and I'd said nothing about how I considered this a trial run until I worked out whether it was for me or not.

I gripped my fingers together in my lap. 'Yes. Why?'

His eyes pinned me to the chair. 'PMI is not the police.' He rubbed at a small mark on the desk. 'Client confidentiality is paramount. And sometimes we do go the extra mile for people, especially women in trouble. Even if it means we cross the line.'

I had an instant, wrenching flash of a hammer smashing down on a hand and jerked back in my seat. 'What's this about? Are you jumping to conclusions about what I might be prepared to do for you? Because of Grandad?'

Paul's eyebrows shot up like they were on springs. 'Shit, no. I'm not going to cross Hamish.' He pressed his lips together hard. 'I just want to be straight with you. PMI often helps women in abusive relationships. We get them out, hide them, move them interstate. That kind of thing.'

'Okay, that's fine with me.' More than fine. Where was he going with this? 'That's not illegal.'

'No, it's not. Well, actually sometimes custody of children is involved, which does cross the line. So it is very confidential. I've found it's better not to trust anyone with this stuff, not even police officers.'

I contemplated that for a few seconds. Imagining someone had whisked my mother and me away to hide in sunny Queensland. I wish. 'Okay, I understand.'

Finally, he nodded. 'Good. Now, what's happening with Diane Paterson?'

I handed him the file and he skimmed the printed pages and asked for a verbal report.

'No sign of her yet. No use of her credit cards, no bank withdrawals, her phone hasn't been used either.' Gang had printed out the phone records and we'd identified all of the numbers. 'Up until she left, she'd only been calling friends and occasionally family, mostly her husband or his parents.'

'Not her own parents?'

I shook my head. 'Maybe once or twice in the last few months, that's all.'

'Odd.' He closed the file. 'What do you think?'

I'd been biting at the side of my thumb and it was bleeding now. I hid it down the side of my jeans and said, 'If she's left him, she's done a really good job of setting up another life somewhere. She would have had to create a secret bank account—'

'Plenty of women do it.'

'Yes, especially if they're being assaulted by their husband.' I frowned at him. 'Do you think that's the case here?'

'Not so far. It's something you can ask her parents.'

'It looks like her husband and his family have got money and some social standing,' I said. 'If she'd met someone and was having an affair, and it was someone wealthy, he'd have enough money and power to make it easy for her to disappear.' I frowned. 'You've talked to the husband. What did you think?'

Paul closed the file and pushed it over to me. 'Only by phone. He wasn't happy her parents had brought us in, that's for sure, but he provided all of this information readily enough.' He stood and went to the window, folding his arms and gazing out. 'He seemed genuinely puzzled and upset. But some men are very good actors. Time we moved this one along more. I've arranged for you to visit him at his house at three this afternoon. I want to see what you think of him. Sus him out in person.' He turned to regard me with a deep frown. 'What's going on with Hamish? Has he said anything to you?'

The change of subject threw me. 'Just that he had a bit of business trouble. You know Grandad. All he would say was it was getting a bit out of hand.'

'If it's what I think it is …'

Paul definitely knew more than me. 'What? He wouldn't tell me anything.'

'It's probably nothing. A bit of ancient history come back to bite him. He'll deal with it, I'm sure.' He gave me a long look, his mouth working like he wanted to tell me something, but in the end he just said, 'I think you need to stay alert. Watch your back.'

That only made me feel more edgy and curious. 'Yeah. Sure.' I picked up Diane's file and left.

CHAPTER SIX

Justin Paterson was a charmer. Dark curly hair, twinkling blue eyes, great smile. He was solidly built, on the shortish side, and welcomed me into his house like a long-lost friend. 'You're Louisa Alcott. Very nice to meet you. Pity it's under such …' He made a sad face.

'Just call me Lou,' I said. I'm not keen on charmers but Paul expected objectivity, so I had to put my biases aside and do this properly.

I followed him into the large, open-plan living area. Everything was expensive and immaculate, with a large portrait photo on the wall of a blonde woman I guessed was Diane. It was so arty that I couldn't actually see her face properly. I accepted Justin's offer of coffee, and even ate one of his crumbly, delicious shortbreads. 'Very good,' I said through a mouthful of buttery wonderfulness.

His face fell. 'Diane made them. She's a brilliant cook. Look.' He spun around and pulled open one door of the stainless-steel freezer. Row after row of plastic containers filled with different coloured foods. 'Curries, stews, casseroles. She made them all. Left them for me and the kids.' He sucked in a breath and winced like it was hurting him to keep breathing. 'I just want you to find her.'

I stared at the stacks of food containers. Three weeks plus and he'd hardly touched them, by the look of it. 'Has she cooked for you like that before? Did you see her preparing all that food?'

He shook his head.

'No sign she was planning to leave? No fights or arguments? No note?'

'No. We loved each other. The kids ... I just don't understand ...' His grip on the edge of the kitchen bench was turning his knuckles white. He noticed me noticing and straightened, shoving his hands in his pockets. 'The police have been hopeless. It's been three weeks and nothing. They think she's left me for someone else, so they're not taking it seriously.'

Except Gang had said that's what Justin had told the police. 'Do *you* think she was having an affair?'

'No!' he said sharply. 'I'm worried that somebody has ... maybe ...'

'You mean you think she's been abducted?' I didn't dare say 'murdered', but his face had gone all pale and sweaty. He was definitely thinking it.

He shook himself, like he was getting rid of the idea. 'No. I don't know. I just wish she'd come home, safe and sound.'

'You know that her parents have asked us to investigate?'

'Yes, they would,' he said grimly. 'They've never liked me much. I wish they'd leave it to the police.'

But he'd just said the police were hopeless. He was upset, sure, but contradicting himself didn't sit right with me.

I took a breath. 'If she has just left, do you think she could have another credit card? And phone?'

'Why on earth would she? I told you, we were happy.' He rubbed his face hard. 'Look, what about social media? She didn't like it much but ...' He gave me her Facebook and Instagram logins. I wondered how many husbands knew their wife's passwords to everything.

When it came to what Diane did while Justin was at work, he was rather vague. 'Books, I guess. Cooking. The gym. The kids. We've got a cleaner, so ...'

So she could've been having an affair and he wouldn't have known.

The two kids, who were eight and nine, were with his parents and had been told Mum had gone on a holiday. 'Diane's parents live on the other side of town,' Justin said. 'Honestly, they might have put you up to this as some kind of weird smokescreen. If she's there, please do tell me,' he begged. 'I'll do anything to fix whatever she thinks is wrong.'

I nodded and pretended to write something, but his dislike of his in-laws was palpable. Did he really think this was all a ruse on their part?

Later, as I stood to leave, Justin flung open the freezer door again and pulled out three containers. 'Here, please take some. I can't bear to look at them all, let alone eat them.' The little catch in his voice sounded pretty genuine.

I emerged from the house, my body zinging with the two cups of strong coffee, but with few helpful answers. Diane had been gone three weeks. Her passport was still there, locked in the husband's safe in the study. Yes, she knew how to open it. But her phone and handbag were gone, and he thought some of her clothes were as well. He said her credit cards hadn't been used—like me, he'd been checking online. I confirmed with him that I'd done all the same checks already, and more.

'Well, I guess I'm glad you're on the case then,' he'd said, with a sad smile.

After leaving his house, I stopped next to a quiet park a few streets away and wrote up my thoughts. Impressions, tone of voice, anything a bit odd. I'd put it all in my report tomorrow morning. I glanced at the containers of food. Yes, that, too. Paul said he wanted all of this recorded before I moved on to the parents.

Next stop was an after-work drink with my old mate, Detective Constable Kayla Benson, who was enjoying a rare day off. I found her basking in the late afternoon summer sunshine in the beer garden of our favourite local pub. She'd kicked off her sensible work shoes and had her feet up on another chair. There was no gun in sight, but her tailored pants and shirt and chopped haircut always signalled 'police' to me. Probably did to anyone feeling guilty, too.

She greeted me with a wave and a 'Your shout, I believe', so I went inside and ordered two wines.

'Don't tell me,' she said when I sat down at the wobbly steel table. 'You've got a new job.'

'How did you know?'

She grinned. 'It's the little skippy thing you do when you're walking.'

'Skippy thing? What the fuck is a "skippy thing"?' But I did know what she meant. Having a puzzle to solve did make me eager and jumpy, all at once.

'So, spill your guts,' she said. 'Where is it? What are you working on?'

'Paul Marshall Investigations. Wait!' I put up a hand. Judging by the look on her face, she was about to say something rude. 'Grandad's recommendation and he put in a good word for me.'

'Okay, well ...' she said. 'I have heard of them. But really, PI work?'

I bristled. 'What's wrong with that?'

Her face closed up. 'Nothing. They seem to have a reasonable reputation. So are you on an actual case yet?'

I drank some wine and tucked away the fact that she'd avoided my mention of Grandad. Just as well, really. Kayla had been pretty shocked when she found out who my grandfather was and a bit miffed I hadn't told her. It was a touchy subject between us.

'Missing wife.' I filled Kayla in on the details about Diane, that she was a missing person, and the bits that bothered me, like Justin's refusal to believe she'd simply left him. 'Although no credit card use ... Still, she might just be determined not to spend his money anymore. Which he seems to have a lot of.'

'She'd be one in a million then. So he was the one who reported her missing?'

I nodded. 'He doesn't think the police have looked hard enough. And is pissed off at her parents for employing us. He even mentioned someone could have taken her.'

She ran her finger around the rim of her glass. 'Understandable. But pretty unlikely in Melbourne. We're hardly serial killer capital of the world. Jump past all of his guff and what her parents think of him. What do you think has happened to her?'

'She's left him and run away, probably. He seems really cut up about it and desperate to get her back.' I thought of the freezer full of food. At least he wouldn't go hungry. 'He seemed to have no idea what she did with her days. Maybe he wasn't interested enough to ask.' Through the side fence of the garden, I watched a homeless man sit against the wall across the street and set up his begging hat in front of him. His bitzer dog looked as sad as he did.

Kayla pushed out her bottom lip. 'So she could have been having an affair.'

I told her about the full freezer, adding, 'That says she's bolted, but felt guilty enough to cater for a month of meals first.'

'Wow, who does that? I'd just leave a pile of takeaway brochures on the bench.'

I seemed to remember Kayla had done just that when she'd left her husband, but I wisely said nothing. We'd done the topic of Diane, so we moved on to Kayla's news. Her team was working on some carjackings that appeared to be connected to at least four home invasions.

'Those seem to be increasing,' I said. 'Or is that the media again?'

'Bit of both. What I don't like is how the level of violence is also increasing.'

We ran out of gossip before long and sat there, tired and dispirited, watching the homeless man and his dog. Now and then, a commuter would get off the tram and throw something in his tattered hat and when we finally called it a day, we crossed the street together and each gave him five dollars. I felt I could afford to since I had a job.

Back in my little flat, I put Justin's meals in the fridge, then poured some wine and made a jam sandwich and used my laptop to do some more online searching with the supplied passwords. Diane's Facebook page looked almost empty, although she had about fifty friends. Nothing on any other social media, so I looked up her parents instead. Gary and Amanda Lewis. No result. Looked like they were too old for Facebook. Although, is anyone too old for Facebook?

I called them to set up an interview and Amanda answered the phone.

'We hadn't seen Diane in over six months, you see,' Amanda said. 'We had a bit of a falling out with Justin. But she did call me regularly. Before she went ...'

I jumped into the silence. 'Justin says the police haven't been doing their job.'

'At least he talked to you. He refuses to speak to us.' There was muffled conversation; she had her hand over the receiver. Then she was back. 'The police came to see us, but they never said what they thought might have happened. They wanted to know if she was here. I didn't ... I just—' She choked on a sob.

It sounded like they were being kept out of it, which might have been Justin's doing. No wonder they'd come to PMI.

'Can I come and see you?' I asked. 'I can tell you more, and I have questions I need to ask you, too.'

'Of course. We're here most of the time.'

I said I could come now and set off straight away, all
the car windows down so I could suck in the night sea
breeze as I headed down Beach Road. Not the fastest way
to Seaford, but the nicest. On the way, I passed Kananook
railway station, where a young woman had gone missing
more than thirty years ago. But instead of reminding me
of Diane, the dark, shadowy carpark catapulted me into
thinking about my mother, and for a few moments, I let
my brain go there.

Her pale face when my father berated her for something,
often her drinking; coming home from school and finding her passed out on the couch; the sound of her sobbing
late at night. And all my father cared about was how it
looked, and whether she could behave at police functions
where he wanted to show off. My mind started to take me
to the day I found her body, and I gave myself a mental
slap. I needed to focus on Diane. My mother was beyond
anyone's help now.

Gary and Amanda's place was an old weatherboard, three
streets back from the water, with a front garden full of dai-
sies and grevilleas hemmed by a white picket fence. Amanda
and Gary greeted me at the front door looking like they
were holding each other up. I'd hardly got my bum down
on their velour couch before their questions started, but I
held up my hands.

'Can I go first? That way, you'll know what I know, and
we can take it from there.'

They nodded and sat, holding hands. I told them everything Justin had said, that the police opinion seemed to be
that Diane had left Justin and taken off. The Lewises both
nodded at that. Then I started my questions with the last
time they saw her.

'Justin's a pushy bastard,' Gary said in a rumbling voice. 'He started out ever so nice, then as the years went on, he moved Diane further and further away from us. Bought a house in Moonee Ponds, got her to leave her job down this way, then it was all about how far it was to come down here to visit.'

'So we offered to go there,' Amanda chipped in. 'But they were always busy with the kids. The only way I got to talk to her was if I rang while he was at work.' Her lips made a thin line. 'He stopped her getting another job, too. Said she should focus on the kids.'

I didn't like the sound of that, but I pushed on. 'Did she ever tell you she was unhappy?'

They glanced at each other. 'No. If I asked, she'd just brush me off, or tell me of course she was happy. She had everything she wanted.'

'Except us,' Gary said bitterly. 'Apparently she didn't want us.'

'It's possible Justin manipulated all of that,' I said. 'The term for it now is coercive control.'

From the blank looks on their faces, they didn't understand what I meant.

'Would it surprise you if she'd left him?'

'No, I'd be happy, but where would she go?' Gary said. 'Why wouldn't she tell us?'

'It's possible she's gone off with someone else.'

'She would've told us,' Amanda said, but I could tell she didn't really believe that.

'Are there any friends you think she might be staying with?'

Gary shook his head. 'He'd cut her off from all her old friends. I see kids she went to school with and they never ask after her anymore.'

'She had lots of new friends,' Amanda said. 'Flash ones, with flash husbands and flash cars and flash houses.' Her tone was bitter.

'Do you know who any of those friends were?'

'Try Facebook,' Gary grunted.

'Where are our grandkids?' Amanda asked. 'I suppose his parents have got them.'

I had to say yes. It was probably months since they'd seen their grandchildren as well, and Diane was their only connection. I asked them to fill me in on how Diane met Justin and was surprised to hear they'd been going out since Year 10 at high school. When I asked Amanda if she had any photos of Diane, she said, 'Not recent ones. It's better if you look at our Facebook page. She's got a secret one just between her and me where she posts photos and things.'

Hmm, Diane had a secret or two from Justin after all. Amanda opened the page for me—it was under Deedee Lewis and meant she must have another email address as well—and I stared down at Diane's attractive, laughing face, lifting a glass of champagne towards the camera. 'Her birthday back in December,' Amanda said. Most of the photos were of the kids, a boy and a girl. 'Amy and Oliver.'

'So even though you haven't seen her for a while, she did keep in touch with this and send you photos.'

Amanda pointed at the most recent photo, dated over two months ago. 'She tried. But sometimes she wouldn't post a new one for weeks and weeks. I'd call her now and then, but it was hard to catch her when she could talk.'

I got Amanda to email me the most recent photo of Diane that she'd saved to her computer. It was difficult to imagine this happy woman deserting her kids, but stranger things had happened. Still, there were things that didn't add up, things that made me antsy. Logic said if she had a Facebook page and email address Justin didn't know about, she might also have a second phone.

I thanked Gary and Amanda for their help and promised to keep in touch, then drove home. I looked at Justin's containers of food in my fridge and, although I'd had no intention of eating any of it, it was way past dinner time and I was hungry. I tried to guess what was in each sealed dish, then did an eeny-meeny and picked one to heat up that turned out to be beef in red wine. Justin was right— Diane really could cook. It was as good as anything I'd had in a restaurant.

After dinner, I made a list of the Facebook friends Diane seemed to interact with the most on her main page, noting down their names, useful search information and email addresses. What people put on social media never failed to amaze me, but I couldn't complain. Even dickhead crims were known to post photos of themselves with stolen vehicles and weapons. It was how I'd found a stolen vintage Porsche once. Hadn't even needed the police tech guys to help me.

CHAPTER SEVEN

I slept badly, and felt groggy when I finally got up. But I had work to do. At the office, I searched for and then called two of the Facebook friends who appeared the most on Diane's page, explaining who I was, and that Diane's parents had asked me to find her. Had they seen her recently? No. Had they been in contact with her recently? No. Did they know anything about where she might have gone? One said Diane had talked about a trip to Bali with Justin, the other mentioned a health spa. Both sounded vague. I thanked them and tried friend number three, Dani Williams-Carstairs. She was a lawyer, and already at work.

'G'day, Dani here.'

She sounded pretty down to earth. I went through my spiel and asked the first question.

'Yeah, we had coffee a few weeks ago,' Dani said. 'She was being a bit weird.'

My ears twitched. 'In what way?'

'Dunno. She kept checking her phone, like she was expecting a call, but nobody did.'

'Can you remember exactly when you met up?'

'Hang on.' She tapped away on something. 'Twenty-ninth of October.'

Almost six weeks ago. 'You've had no texts or calls since?' Apparently not. And the police had asked her the same thing. 'She hasn't contacted you on Facebook?'

'Nah, she didn't do a lot of that stuff. Said Justin didn't like it.'

'Justin seems a little …'

'Over the top? Yeah, I know. He loves her but he can be … Like we were all at a restaurant a few months ago, and he ordered her meal for her. Didn't even give her a chance to choose something. I wouldn't put up with that.'

'You said she was checking her phone. Do you think she was waiting for Justin to call her?'

'No, I don't think so.' There was a long pause. 'She told me once she thought he'd put a spy thing on her phone, to track wherever she went.'

Yep, that might explain why her phone couldn't be tracked now. She'd probably got rid of it. 'Did you ever see her with a second phone?'

'No.'

'Do you think she could have left him? That she might be in hiding somewhere?'

'God, I bloody hope so!'

'If I give you my number, will you call me if you hear from her?'

'Well … if you're in contact with Justin, she's not going to want me to tell you, is she?'

This woman was on the ball. 'I really am working for her parents. Could you just let me know she's alive and well?'

'If I do hear from her, I'll ask her permission.'

I gave her my details and hung up. With no passport on her, Diane couldn't have flown out of the country. Although if she had made a statutory declaration that it was lost, she could have applied for a new one. It was definitely possible, but surely the police had checked that?

Next, I called Justin's parents, but they made it pretty clear they thought Diane was the scum of the earth for leaving her lovely children and just 'going off without a word'. They certainly weren't people she'd go to in a crisis. Time to report my lack of progress to Paul.

He seemed subdued and made a couple of suggestions, but didn't criticise any of my strategies so far, which was a relief. 'Don't forget, you can call on Gang if you need any help with tech or finding stuff out. He's got extra resources and he's fast.'

Back at my desk I made more notes and added more questions to my list for Justin, still mulling over where Diane might have gone and how to find out. Gang agreed that her secret Facebook page with her mum implied she'd set it up with a different email address. 'Look in the About section,' he said.

I clicked on that and every category was blank. 'How do I find out that other email address?' I asked.

'I'll give it a go, but don't hold your breath. If she set up a Hotmail account on a second phone, like you said, everything would stay on that phone.'

Gang and I both tried other databases and search facilities, but Diane's second 'life' wasn't showing up on anything. Either I was wrong or she'd been extremely careful.

I called Justin at midday, figuring I'd catch him before he went for lunch. He sounded annoyed.

'Did you have to hassle my parents?'

'I didn't,' I said mildly, although I wanted to reach down the phone and slap him. 'I just needed to double-check they hadn't heard from her.'

'I told you that already.'

'Right. I need to ask you a few more things.'

'You'll have to make it snappy. I've got work to do.' Gone was the charm of yesterday.

I asked everything on my list. Her car was still in the garage. No, of course she didn't have a second phone. Her passport was definitely still locked in the safe where he kept all the family documents. Yes, he'd checked with her friends again.

'You asked me this yesterday.' A sigh. 'Sorry, I'm just going out of my mind here … Look, I have to go. I've got a big construction job on.'

He hung up on me and I made a face at the phone. Was reporting Diane missing all an act for the kids and her family? So when he divorced her and moved someone else in, it would all look like he'd done his best? That didn't gel with the over-controlling stuff though.

Something didn't add up and I went out for a large, strong coffee to help me think. Sitting in the corner of a dark café, I inhaled the delicious smell of bacon cooking and finally gave in and bought a bacon and egg roll. I hunched over my coffee, trying to weigh up Justin's over-control and isolation of Diane from her family and friends against my tendency to see domestic abuse in every dysfunctional relationship. My parents' example had not set me up to be impartial, but

I was potently aware of that and how it affected my reactions to things. I hadn't needed the police therapist to point it out, even though she had, carefully, and tried to get me to talk about it before I cut her off.

I ran through what I knew, listed the possibilities, crossed off the most unlikely. I was still left with several options, including murder and running away with a lover, but no real evidence that pointed to any of them. There was a good reason the husband was always the obvious suspect.

No way was I ruling him out.

***

Going for a coffee had produced nothing except a feeling of growing frustration. Gang was working across all three computer screens and humming. Today his glasses were bright blue circles and he had matching blue tips on his hair spikes. He listened to my list of options.

'There's nothing that says you can't look more closely at Justin.' He peered at me over the top of his glasses. 'You're the ex-cop. What does your experience tell you?'

'That there's good cause why the partner is usually the prime suspect.'

'There you go then.'

I sat at what now felt like 'my' computer and logged in again. The desk was still clear of knick-knacks—I wasn't someone who brought photos and souvenir crap to work. I opened a new file and began doing a search on Justin. Mostly I found information about the family building and property development company. His father had started it back in the 1980s, so I'd expected it to be huge by now. But, going by the reports online, he'd overreached himself and got into trouble with some loans. Lucky to survive, really. I skipped over a lot and focused on the material about Justin. He wasn't on any social media but LinkedIn, and that site told me the most about his schooling and uni degree, as well as his work history.

He'd joined the family company only ten years ago after working as an architect for a big firm in the city. No projects that had made him famous, so maybe he'd put money first instead and gone to work for Dad. Diane's parents said they'd been high school sweethearts, so she'd stuck with him all the way through. He'd designed the home he'd shared with Diane and Dad's company had built it around the same time he'd joined it. A bribe from Dad perhaps. Some photos at company events. Justin didn't appear to play any sport or be a member of any community organisations. Pretty anonymous in today's world.

Was that why he discouraged Diane from using social media? I thought of the huge arty photo of her in the lounge room, and compared it to the various photos I had collected from the internet. If I ever saw her anywhere, I'd know her in an instant. But how likely was that?

I checked her bank accounts again, just in case something had happened in the past day or two. Her credit card account had been extremely active before she'd disappeared. Diane had used it for everything, even what looked like coffee and cake at a few different cafés. Google told me they were all within a few kilometres of her home. The smallest amount was five dollars, and that showed up multiple times in the past three months. Coffee, no cake, was my guess.

I could see that she'd been in the north of the state last October, in various places such as Yackandandah and

Bright. Last May she'd been in Bali, but the purchases were all small. Probably she was there with Justin and he'd paid for the big stuff. Bali meant she'd used her passport.

No travel tickets recently to anywhere. I made a note to check her car; even though Justin said it was at home, it was a BMW and probably could be tracked through its GPS. Every month, an amount was transferred into her credit card to clear it so it wouldn't accrue any interest. I assumed that came from Justin's account, but I made a note about that, too.

The only other account Diane had was for a Visa debit card, and the note next to it said it was rarely used. Still, it had to be checked, if only because it had a credit amount of around three thousand dollars showing. Like the cheque account, it had few purchases—a couple that matched the Bali trip, and an amount for $423 that turned out to be for school uniforms.

I flicked forward and checked through the most recent entries again and the hair on my neck prickled. Two purchases had popped up in the past two days. WTF. I tried to see what they were for or where they were carried out, but couldn't work it out, so I printed the page and took it out to Gang.

'Can you find out what these are, please?'

'Sure thing.' He peered at the entries on the statement. 'I need glasses,' he muttered.

'You've got glasses,' I said.

'Accessories, darl. I need the real thing.' He banged away on the computer on his left and went 'Hmm' a few times, made some notes and handed the page back to me. 'Not sure if that helps.'

One purchase was $124 in a toy shop, the other one was $17.50 in a McDonald's. Both in the same suburb where Justin's parents lived.

Was Diane secretly visiting her kids and buying them stuff?

No way was I calling Justin to ask—not just yet. I needed more. Gang had shown me how to log in to a reverse phone directory online that PMI had a subscription for and I'd already identified all of Diane's calls for the past three years. Almost half of the calls were to the same number—Dani Williams-Carstairs, Diane's friend. That said more than just any old friend. Dani went on my list for a personal visit. She had to know more about what was going on in Diane's life. She might even know if Diane had another bank account; what women often called their 'running away account'.

The calls to Diane's parents were all Monday to Friday, between 9am and 4pm. It bore out what they'd told me, that Justin didn't want her to have much contact with them. The calls became fewer and fewer, and after a call in June, which I knew was Diane's birthday, there had only been one more in early October. No wonder they had no idea what she'd been up to.

If Diane had a second phone, she'd kept it well hidden and I had no idea how to find it. If it was a cheapie on a pay-as-you-go SIM, looking for it was a hopeless task.

Paul put his head around his office door. 'How's it going?'

I reported what I'd found. 'Should I call Justin about the debit card?' I thought he'd say yes straight away, but he hesitated.

'Might be she gave the kids the card, going by the two purchases. Or he did. Let's wait on that one.'

'Okay. Justin doesn't figure much online. Even his LinkedIn stuff is minimal.'

He drummed his fingers on the side of the door. 'You're looking at him now as well. Any reason?'

I gripped my fingers together on the desk. 'Um, I just thought, it seemed like I should cover all the bases.'

'Fair enough.' Paul nodded and left, and I loosened my aching fingers.

As I bent over the printouts again, my phone rang. The caller ID said Melinda Moreau.

'Lou speaking.'

'Hi, Lou. It's Melinda. Are you working? Have I interrupted? I can call back later.' She sounded flustered and unsure.

'It's fine,' I said. 'What's up?'

'Oh, nothing. I ... I've got a date! Maybe tomorrow. Well, not really. Well, a drink somewhere. Do you call that a date?'

I laughed. 'I guess so. Who with?'

'A guy. One of those ... I joined one of those dating sites. Silly, eh?'

'Not really. Lots of people do it.' But not me, no way.

'I'd tried them out before, but ... He seems nice. I think. We've messaged a lot. Or a fair bit.' She sucked in a breath. 'I didn't call about that though. I wondered if you wanted to drop in after work for a glass of wine? Just, you know, if you have time.'

I hesitated a moment too long.

'Oh, I'm sorry, you must be busy. No worries, maybe—'

'I'd love to,' I said firmly. 'How about five thirty?'

'Oh. Sure. Great,' she said. 'I wanted to ask you about something. Anyway, it can wait. See you then.'

She hung up and I frowned down at my phone. Was she always like that? I thought back to what she'd told me. Perhaps, after being on her own for so long, she was finally reaching out. Me as a potential friend, this guy online for a drink. That must be really hard for her. I was glad I'd said yes.

CHAPTER EIGHT

I kept working on Justin until Gang packed up for the day, which meant I could, too. My eyes were burning and I was still frustrated. I'd found a few more mentions of Justin online, but all to do with his business dealings. The company name, Paterson Holdings, popped up over and over. They seemed to specialise in building offices and shops with apartments above, but nothing high rise. Nothing that indicated imminent bankruptcy or financial issues. I made a note to check if there was a life insurance policy with Diane's name on it. The red flags were from her parents' and Dani's comments, and I tried to ensure I wasn't being too suspicious, but if Diane had left and covered her tracks so well, she probably had good reason.

The burning question: Was Diane alive and hiding, or was she dead?

I really hoped she was alive somewhere and giving Justin the finger from afar.

My own car, an old Corolla, was parked at my apartment building, so I caught a train to Kensington. When I got to Melinda's street, I scanned the parked cars and front windows as I walked to her house. The whole street seemed deserted and there were only a few cars. People here must work late.

I opened Melinda's gate and went through, then up the steps. I was kind of looking forward to talking to her again. Maybe I was making a new friend? The house, as before, looked foreboding and dark. I rapped on the glass in the antique front door and waited, but nobody came. There was no doorbell. I rapped again, louder. Nothing. Strange. I pulled out my phone and tapped through Contacts to call her.

A phone rang with shrill insistence inside the house, repeating its trilling melody until I hung up. The silence was smothering. I rapped again, even though I sensed it was futile. I wrapped my arms around my body, closing my eyes for a few moments. *Melinda, please be in the back garden.*

Then I gripped the big doorknob and turned it. The door swung open to reveal the dark hole of the hallway. Not a single light on anywhere.

'Melinda?' Too tentative. 'Melinda! Hello! Where are you?'

As I stepped into the hallway, I knew I was technically breaking and entering, but I had grounds for concern. Big grounds. An image of Melinda lying on the floor propelled me forward. I turned on lights and opened the doors off the hallway—musty lounge with old furniture, cupboard, empty spare room, kitchen. No Melinda. I peered out into her small backyard, but it was empty.

Upstairs, there were more empty rooms and in her bedroom, her bed was neatly made, the clothes in her wardrobe were in a tidy row, and in the old-fashioned bathroom, her lone toothbrush stood crookedly in a mug.

It was now 5.45pm. Shit. Something was wrong.

I dialled her on my phone again and followed the noise to a shallow woven basket in the corner of the kitchen bench where a folded tea towel sat on top of her mobile. I glanced around the kitchen—it was excessively tidy, hardly anything on the benchtops, and I guessed the basket was part of her tidiness. I was no longer in the habit of carrying latex gloves with me everywhere, so had to use the tea towel to extract the phone from the basket and put it on the benchtop. The itch to check her calls and texts was growing by the second, but I knew I couldn't. If something was wrong, the police had to do all of that.

At the other end of the bench, which jutted out as a breakfast bar, two wine glasses stood next to a bottle of red wine that had been opened to breathe. I examined the glasses, but the only thing on them was tea towel fluff, as though Melinda had washed and dried them in preparation for the promised wine with me. In the fridge was an unopened bottle of sauvignon blanc.

The two kitchen stools at the breakfast bar were half-pulled out. Again, I didn't touch. If Melinda was still in the house, where could she possibly be? And if she wasn't, where had she gone?

I opened the back door to the garden and, too late, realised that I might have set the alarm going when I saw a small blue light blinking. But then I remembered the blue signalled that the alarm was turned off. Melinda had told me that while she was in the house, she kept the alarm on; it was segmented so that she could make sure the windows and back door were alarmed, and the front door was double locked, but she could still move around inside. So why was the house so unsecured now?

The garden consisted of a patch of lawn and borders full of low plants and shrubs. Nothing big enough for anyone to hide behind. She had no garden shed, just a hand mower and a low plastic crate for her spade and tools. All around, the fence loomed, with high, slick metal panels to stop cats or people climbing them.

Melinda had done more than secure her house to hide from her ex—she'd created a backyard that looked almost impossible to get into or out of. A discreet sticker on the back door told me she also had a security company on tap, and I photographed it with my phone.

I used the tea towel to search through the cupboards and drawers and found a pair of rubber gloves at the back under the sink. With them on, I went back upstairs and searched again for any clues as to where she had gone. Although there were no signs of a struggle, I was trying hard not to think *Has she been taken?*

This time, I searched absolutely everywhere, even in the toilet cistern, and found another phone in her wardrobe, tucked inside a shoebox with a pair of elegant red high heels wrapped in soft cloth.

I sat back on my heels and thought about the process the police would go through when I reported her as missing. They'd say at first that she wasn't missing, she'd probably forgotten I was coming and gone out. Didn't she tell me she might be going on a date? Well, then.

When she didn't turn up tonight, or tomorrow, they might say I wasn't even a friend, just a new acquaintance, so I couldn't genuinely have grounds to say she was missing. I didn't know her well enough. I could get Kayla onto it, though. I was sure I could persuade someone to take this seriously.

What if Melinda turned up tonight or tomorrow? I'd look really stupid.

But.

There was the security check she'd requested, and the reason why.

The phone left behind in the basket.

The front door unlocked. The alarm system off.

She'd called me and arranged this meeting just a few hours ago. It was after 7pm—if Melinda had run to the shops to get snacks and wine and been waylaid, she'd be back by now.

Where the hell was she?

Caught up with the Diane Paterson investigation, I'd done nothing more about checking where Nathan Gunn was, and that could turn out to be a fatal error. I needed to rectify it immediately. I put Melinda's second phone in my pocket and went to leave. There, dangling from the lock on the back of the front door, was a keyring with three keys on it. I stared at them, my skin crawling, and my hand went up to pull them out. Stopped. I couldn't imagine Melinda being so impulsive as to leave her keys like this. No way.

I thought about taking the keys, but the police needed to see them, too. To see how weird it was, given her high security otherwise.

Maybe she had got caught up unexpectedly. Somewhere. By someone. But … the phone. The keys.

If I'd had my car, I could've stayed and watched her house. Instead, I went home and fretted, ate some cereal and then drove back to her street, where I parked my little Corolla almost in front of her gate. I'd decided to stay there all night. But first I went and checked her house again. Still empty and dark, and no sign she'd been back.

My car was set up for just about anything. I knew this was odd. I wasn't an outdoors camping freak, nor was I a snack-food addict. All the same, I had a sleeping bag to keep me warm and a plastic crate of muesli bars, chocolate, water and a book of crosswords and some pens. All I needed was a little campfire. I've always just liked to be … prepared. Even more so since I started this job with Paul.

The hours came and went. I googled Nathan Gunn and couldn't see anything new—nothing to say he'd been in Melbourne. I played with Melinda's second phone, but it was password protected and I couldn't get into it. I'd leave it for Gang. Why did she have a secret phone kept in a shoebox? Maybe it was a relic from her life with her ex, but if it was me, I'd have destroyed it with an axe.

Around 11pm, my phone rang. Grandad.

'I suppose you're glued to your computer,' he growled in his nice, threatening grandad way.

'Actually, no, Grandad, I'm watching a house.'

'Whose house?'

'Nobody you know.'

'How do you know that? I know—'

'Everyone. Yes, but this is a young woman and nothing to do with you.'

He was silent for a couple of seconds. 'I need to … Come around tomorrow night, all right? It's important.'

'Oh. Sure.'

'I miss you, lass.' His soft tone was one I rarely heard. 'Don't be a stranger.'

'I won't, Grandad, don't worry.'

He did worry about me, all the time, but he'd never admit it. I'd go and see him tomorrow after work. By then, I might have found Melinda and proven I wasn't useless as a PI after all.

That set me thinking about what kind of influence Grandad had over Paul, since that's how I got the job. I was pretty sure Paul wasn't a crim. I'd seen a lot of them over the years, both with Grandad and while in the force. I hadn't recognised Paul's face at all. I used my phone to google him, this time taking advantage of some sites that Gang had shown me. But apart from the PMI website, there was nothing about Paul online anywhere. Not surprising.

Melinda's street was even quieter after midnight. Quite a few of her neighbours had been out and come home, including her next-doors, a middle-aged couple with a fluffy-faced dog that jumped up at their front window as soon as they parked their car. Maybe if Melinda had had a nice big snarly Rottweiler, she'd still be safe in her house. I wished she had a dog that tried to rip strangers apart.

I dozed off now and then, but jerked awake at any noise or movement. A couple of cars that looked like Ubers dropping people off, and then nothing until about 5am, when the street started stirring. Three joggers and two lycra-clad men on bikes, then a guy delivering plastic-wrapped copies of the newspaper.

I waited until there was no one around again, then went into Melinda's house. Still empty. Sunlight streamed through the door to the garden, lighting up the hallway. I peered at the lacquered wood floor. There were some long scuff marks, but they looked more like shoes had caused them than furniture being moved. I didn't like the look of them at all, and took a couple of photos just in case.

I didn't want to leave the front door unlocked, but the police needed to see it that way, to see the keys, and for me to tell them how secure the house was normally. At 7.30am I googled to check the nearest police station was open and went to report her as missing.

It went pretty much as I'd expected.

After a lot of protesting from me, the officer behind the counter took all the details, making it clear he thought it was a waste of his time. I almost said I'd been on the job, but kept my mouth shut. The first thing to come up if he checked out my details would probably be my father. It was unlikely the reason I left the force would be available to him. I didn't want to explain either of them.

He asked me questions about Melinda's work and family, medical conditions, age, what she was wearing—all things that I couldn't answer, which made him frown a lot. I couldn't even give him a photo, but I did tell him where she was a student. He wrote down what I was able to offer and said, 'If you hear from her, you have to let us know.'

Like I wouldn't. But I knew some people didn't bother—all was right with their world again and they never got around to it. 'Of course,' I said. 'You will send someone around to check? I mean, her front door is unlocked with the keys still in it. Someone needs to lock it. And take her phone for fingerprints.'

'Why didn't you lock the door?' He ignored the fingerprints idea.

'I don't have a key, and I wanted you to see it like that.'

I was repeating myself now, so I left. A quick shower at home and then into the office, where I presented Melinda's phone to Gang.

He did that high-jump eyebrows thing. 'Is this Diane Paterson's?'

'No, it belongs to someone who is missing.'

'Diane is missing.'

'A different someone. Melinda Moreau. I checked her house for her, remember?' I pushed the phone across to him. 'Can you get into it?'

'You have to tell me why first, and then I have to get approval from Paul.' He looked at the phone. 'It's an old Samsung so at least it won't need a fingerprint. Why don't *you* ask Paul? Save the middle man.'

'Ask me what?'

I jumped and spun around. Paul had an impatient 'I need more sleep' expression on his face.

'Melinda Moreau is missing and I found this phone.' Paul seemed to be in a bad mood, and I hoped he didn't assume I'd missed something important with Melinda.

His face fell. 'Get me a strong coffee—two of those espresso pods—and explain it to me.'

I did as he asked. To his credit, he let me tell the whole story with no interruptions. When I described the empty house, the phone in the basket and the keys in the door despite all her security, he started frowning.

'So I sat outside all night, and checked inside again this morning, and she still hasn't reappeared. I've reported it to the police, but they weren't interested.'

'Yet. Just as well to put it on the record now.'

I was glad he agreed with me. Then he began asking me questions I couldn't answer.

'The ex, Nathan Gunn, is still in Sydney as far as I know. No idea who this date is meant to be.' I shrugged. 'I'm not even sure she had a time and day for it yet. I was hoping some answers would be on this second phone I found.'

Paul gazed out the window for a few seconds. 'All right, Gang can have a go at getting into it. If she's still missing by tomorrow, you'll need to give it to the police. Apart from that, there's not much else we can do at this point.'

'Can I at least try to find out more about her Sydney life, and where the ex might be?'

He drank the rest of his coffee in one go, and the caffeine hit lit up his eyes a little. 'Not until you do a summary for me of what's happening with Diane Paterson.'

I fetched the paper file, giving Gang the thumbs-up to start working on the phone, while Paul opened the cloud version of my notes. We went through it all together.

'So no activity on anything at all, other than this debit card,' he said.

'No.'

'Give me a minute.' He made a phone call that sounded like it was to Justin, nodded, muttered a few words and hung up. 'He says it's the kids, sorry, he forgot about that one. His mother had borrowed it to buy the kids things to take their minds off their mother.'

'Riiiiiight.' Who actually handed out a debit card like that when it belonged to someone else? Oh yeah, Justin did.

Paul mouse-clicked through more pages on the computer screen and I stared at the matchbox container ships out on the bay and the streaks of white clouds on the horizon. Somewhere out there was Tasmania, and then the Antarctic, and if I kept going, I'd end up in …

'What's your opinion on where she is?' Paul sat back and folded his arms.

'Opinion? Um …' I thought of that freezer full of food. 'Everything points to her running off with someone who has enough money and contacts to help her disappear. That she hasn't used any of her cards or taken her phone and passport says she really doesn't want to be found. Which says Justin isn't as loving and nice as he makes out.'

'So a good reason to disappear. He's controlling, and now he's determined to track her down.' He made a big-thinking face and sucked his teeth. 'She wanted to get right away and not be found. That's where we're at. I suspect you're right, that she has had help.'

I cleared my throat. 'Except …'

'What?'

'You wanted my opinion.' I folded my own arms, tighter than his, ready for him to heap scorn on me. 'Something's not right. Justin was all keen to find her, filing a missing person report, providing us with all the stuff about her, then gets shitty when I do my job too well and ask more questions. And really, does anyone disappear completely like this?'

'Well, yes. Although it does take concerted effort and a lot of planning. What about her lawyer friend?'

'Yes, Dani could have helped her. She was very cagey with me over the phone. But if Diane had a rich boyfriend who made it all happen, why isn't there even a sniff of him? And why would she leave her kids?' I loosened my arms and leaned forward. 'Okay, some women do. But by all accounts, she's a loving mum. And to not even let her poor parents know? Something smells.'

He scanned the file again and frowned. 'We've done everything we can to find her.'

'Which is what Justin wanted. But it's not going to be enough for her parents.' I imagined their faces and cringed inside.

'How do you think Justin would react if we told him, sorry, our enquiries have been, ah, fruitless?' He smiled at me, a bit like a shark.

'He'll make a big fuss, tell us we're as useless as the police, and we've wasted her parents' money. And then he'll happily carry on with his life.'

'Mr and Mrs Lewis haven't got much money. I'd say we've used up the fee they paid.'

I huffed out a breath. 'So we have to drop it?'

'Not so fast. Write your report for them, but stay on Justin Paterson. A bit of surveillance might just lead somewhere.'

I grinned happily at him. 'Onto it.'

CHAPTER NINE

I spent the next two hours typing everything up, detailing the search and summarising what I'd found out in a report that was pretty clinical. The way I was feeling, I didn't want to give the Lewises false hope. I sent it to Paul and ten minutes later he put his head around the door.

'Good work. I've spoken to them and they're okay with Justin having a copy. I'll email it to them, send him a copy and then we wait.' He glanced at Gang. 'Have you got into that phone yet?'

'Not yet.' Gang frowned, which was an unusual expression for him. I was used to his cheery face behind the bright glasses. 'She's used a six-digit password instead of a four-digit one. I've dug into her online for birth dates and signposts but nothing so far that works.'

I thought for a moment. 'Can you get hold of her grandmother's details? Pretty sure it was maternal, and Melinda was close to her.'

'Leave it with me,' Gang said.

I rubbed my eyes and stretched out my fingers and wrists—I wasn't used to so much typing. I hadn't had any lunch yet and my stomach griped at me, so I went out to find something edible and healthy, and ended up with hot chips and gravy.

Back in the office, Gang had a satisfied look on his face.

'Cracked it,' he said. 'Date of her grandmother's death. But I waited for you.'

'Cool, thanks.' I pulled up a chair next to him. Melinda's phone sat on a little stand, plugged into his computer via a USB cable.

'I'm recharging it as well as checking the files,' he said. 'Only a dozen photos, all of her. Selfies.' He opened the Camera folder and showed me. 'All dressed up, different outfits, different close-ups and a couple in the mirror. In some of them it doesn't even look like her, but it is.'

I nodded. Melinda had makeup on as well, a lot of it, and her hair was styled. In one she had a low-brimmed, mysterious hat on; in another she looked like a very staid, buttoned-up librarian.

'Her browser history and apps are the most interesting.' He pointed. 'See the apps on this next screen?'

I peered at them, trying to read what they were. 'Is that flame one Tinder?'

'Yep.'

'Are they all dating apps?'

'Yep. That one is Hinge—'

'Ugh, that suggests things I don't want to think about.'

Gang laughed. 'Hinge is the one you can delete completely as soon as you have found someone nice.'

'Nice. Hmm.'

'Hey, don't knock it until you've tried it,' he protested. 'It's hard to meet good people you have something in common with.'

I wondered if he'd tried the apps himself but I didn't want to be rude and ask. 'The other two?'

'Bumble is supposed to empower women to make the first move.' He ignored my gagging noise and kept going. 'Plenty of Fish is supposed to encourage lots of talking first. Conversations about things you have in common.'

'Supposed to?'

'They all have ups and downs.' He wrote the names on a piece of paper. 'You can go into Google Play and read some of the reviews of each one. But you'll see that a lot of people think the apps are infested with bots and are a scam, or get very frustrated with matches and women not swiping them back or showing any interest.'

'Bots?'

'Fake profiles. Mainly men. And most of them are free to start with and then you have to pay a subscription.'

'Right.'

Gang took Melinda's phone back to its main screen. 'No contacts, no phone calls, no texts.'

'That's odd, isn't it?'

'It's her secret phone,' he said. 'I think she's only using it for this dating stuff.'

'I left her main phone for the police in case it had clues or texts or contacts on it.' I squirmed in my seat. 'Now I'm wishing I'd kept it, but …'

'Much better to leave it. Otherwise you get in a heap of trouble for contaminating the crime scene. If it is a crime scene.'

'I'm hoping it's not.' I wanted Melinda to be safe, but I also didn't want to get into trouble for taking this phone. Hopefully, the police techs could get into her main phone as quickly as Gang had with this one.

We sat in silence for a moment, staring at the phone. I went through everything I could remember from my conversations with Melinda. Her ex, what he'd done, her house, and then her excitement at going on a date.

'She said she was going on a date, but she didn't say who with.' I pointed at the phone. 'Can you tell from the apps if her date was through one of those? The app won't have wiped them out?'

'I'm not sure how they work,' Gang said, but a pink flush crept up his neck and into his face. 'Oh, all right, I know how Hinge works.' He gave me a dark look. 'You should try it one day.'

'Me? When hell freezes over!' I tried to imagine myself using an app and going on a date with a complete stranger. Never. Going. To. Happen.

'Okay, I'll open each one and see if she's been active. Give me a few moments.'

He tapped and swiped and tapped, and made little humming noises. I tried to keep up with what he was doing, but his fingers were too fast for me. Finally, he sat back and folded his arms.

'I don't like it. She's used all four of them.'

'Really?' My eyes goggled. 'How many dates did she organise?'

'I haven't got that far yet. But she has put a different profile on every site. With a different photo.'

I didn't like it either. 'That explains the dressing up and making herself look different. But why would she do that?

She said her last relationship had been really abusive. I would have thought it would make her more careful.'

'The apps are all different,' Gang said, 'but usually nothing happens unless you swipe. Maybe she was just looking, window shopping. See, Tinder is kind of fast and based on the geographical settings you use. Look.' He opened it and showed me. Melinda had used her mysterious hat photo and said very little about herself. Some stuff about loving animals, especially cats, her favourite foods, that she liked cooking and wearing high heels.

'High heels?'

'Bit of a signal, I think. As in "I'm not going to tell you much, but hey, I like high heels so ..."' He raised his eyebrows.

'Do you mean a signal she's interested in sex?' The Melinda I'd talked to was more the librarian type, but maybe she was waiting to see what happened.

'Possibly.'

'Can you tell how many guys she matched with?'

'She hasn't been very active. Only two that I can see, and they're old ones.'

'That geographical thing—could someone guess where you lived?'

'Yes. If the person drove around a lot while you were online, they could potentially home in on your street maybe. It would tell you the subject was a hundred metres away instead of five kilometres.'

'So if her ex found her on Tinder, he could work out where she goes?'

'Hmm, good question. She's used Mel as her name and a recognisable photo of herself. I guess if he was obsessive enough and used a fake profile.' He closed the app and opened Plenty of Fish. 'This one encourages more talking, lots of conversation.'

I peered at the screen. 'She's used a photo that's quite serious. Wouldn't that put people off?'

'Maybe that was her intention. "I'm not going to smile." Called herself Milly. She's filled out a lot more of her profile. Same stuff about animals, cats, food, cooking, but then she's added books, movies, talked about wanting to travel. All that stuff.'

'Nothing about loving walks on the beach at sunset?'

Gang laughed. 'You need to get a life.'

I bristled a bit. 'I do stuff.' *I run at 2am. That's not weird.* I pointed at the screen. 'How many matches?'

'Same. Just a couple of older ones.'

'Okay, what about the next one?'

Gang tapped on an icon of pink hearts with a large J in the middle. 'This is Jointly, one I'm not that familiar with.'

'Jointly? Sounds like a business merger.' The screen flashed a couple of times, bright pink circles winding in and out, and then Melinda's home page opened, showing her profile. 'That's a nice photo of her. She's almost smiling.'

'Interesting,' Gang muttered. 'Called herself Ms Q. Quite different profile information. See?'

I read the 'story'—it made her sound a bit vulnerable. *Looking for someone who is kind, who cares. I'd love a dog one day, so maybe you like dogs, too.* And further down—*Moving to a new city is hard.*

'Did she think this app was more likely to come up with someone nice and ordinary? That line about someone who is kind ...'

'I have no idea. Hang on.' He went to his computer and typed in a few things while I read Melinda's profile again and compared it with the others.

'It's got a reasonable rep,' Gang said. 'Not as racy as Tinder, about as talky as the Fish, similar to OK Cupid with the profile setup.'

'Where's the safety? Anyone could be harassed.'

'Like I said, nothing happens unless both people swipe or match. One on their own can't do it.'

'Oh, right, so what I said before about her ex? She's not going to do the match thing with him, is she? She'd run a mile. Same with any app, if she saw him.'

'True. But what if he used fake photos and a fake name? You're not supposed to, but lots of guys use their skinny photos, for example.' Gang scratched his head, pushed his glasses up his nose. He closed Jointly, opened the last app. 'Used a similar profile here, the thing about kind and caring.' The photo was the librarian one. He checked a few things, tapping fast. 'Looks like she had more than a dozen men who wanted to match but she hasn't replied to any of them. Last one was more than a month ago.'

'Do it slowly so I can see.' I watched the screen as he went through the replies. How 'kind' did they sound? Was that a quality I'd be looking for? If you were a police officer, 'kind and caring' wasn't in the Top Ten. 'Some of these guys are gross. Why would you reply with "What's up?" or "Bet you're hot under those buttons?"'

'Unfortunately, a lot of them are like that. They have no social skills, no idea how to chat online and make friends.'

'Make friends?' I gave him a look.

He gave me one back and then grinned. 'Isn't that how you like to start? He's nice, you like the same food, both been to Hawaii, you talk first, see how things go over a coffee, then maybe a real date.'

I must have looked puzzled.

'Lou, how long is it since you've been on a date, for God's sake?'

Heat crept up my neck and into my face. I ducked my head and found some crud on my jeans to pick at. 'Quite a while, I guess.' I couldn't remember. What I did remember about the last guy was the sex in the shower. At least we both ended up clean.

He shook his head. 'Anyway, let's go back to the app she did use a bit.'

I sighed with relief. Dodged that one.

I focused on the phone screen again as he went through the profiles. 'Slow down, it's too hard to read.'

'Hang on.' Gang pulled open a desk drawer full of cables and fittings, rifled through it and pulled out two cables that he joined together. 'Just as well her phone has a C port.' He plugged things in, hit some keys and Melinda's phone screen showed up on his central monitor.

'Wow, that's better!'

He brought up the Jointly app again. 'This is the only one she's used recently,' he said, 'and she's matched with five different guys.'

'So how do we know if she arranged to meet anyone?'

'We look at their chat and see whether they agreed to it.'

'Hang on, I want to make notes.'

'On paper?' Gang's eyebrows were sky high.

'Yeah, well, it helps me think.' I grabbed some sheets of blank paper and a pen and wrote down names and details for each male that came up. Five of them, all different. Some similarities though. Melinda had chosen mostly dark haired, some with glasses, one shaved head. They all liked travel, some read, some watched movies. She'd gone for guys who seemed a bit more intelligent and weren't afraid of mentioning books and movies that weren't *Fight Club* or war stories. And none of them were showing their abs or flexing bare arms.

I took a good, long look at all of their photos as well.

'Do you fancy any of them?' Gang asked.

'No!' I debated about explaining, chose the short version. 'I'm good at faces, that's all.'

'What, like seeing behind them? What's in their eyes?'

'No, just faces.' I looked at the last one again. Jonathan. Nice expression, half-smiling, hair not too tidy, small gold earring, open-necked check shirt. Mr Ordinary. There was something about him, but I couldn't put my finger on what it was. Probably me being suspicious that he looked too nice.

'She's matched with that one, and been chatting,' Gang said. He scrolled down through the chat window and I read as fast as I could. 'They both like Marvel movies, she's a Pixar fan, he likes *The Sopranos*, blah, blah.'

'Stop scrolling. Look at that.' We both stared at the chat.

M: I like where I live. It's nice and quiet.

J: I'm in a block of flats. The noise drives me around the bend sometimes. Where do you park?

M: I don't have a car right now. Parking in Kensington is a nightmare.

J: We could meet for coffee. Catch a tram.
M: That would be nice.

'She's told him her suburb,' I said.

'This app is like the others, though. He can see she's within ten ks.'

Gang scrolled down slowly. Melinda didn't seem to have gone for the coffee. They'd kept chatting. Every now and then, there'd be a comment from Melinda along the lines of 'Funny how we are so alike in some things, isn't it?'

'Do you notice how every time there's something they both like, she's said it first? And then he leaps in afterwards and says "Hey, me, too"?'

'You're very cynical,' Gang said. After a few seconds, he added, 'But you're right.'

Paul leaned against the doorway to his office. 'Getting anywhere?'

'Only as far as Lou deciding she'd rather die than use a dating app.'

Paul grimaced at me. 'I'm with you there. Listen, I sent your report to Justin Paterson, and guess what?'

'He's unhappy, we're useless, why can't anyone find her, it's not rocket science …'

'Yep. I think he requires a little more scrutiny.' A shadow passed over his face. 'We don't want to find out she's … Anyway, I think we can put you onto him for a few days and see what happens, all right? No charge to her parents, but I'll let them know.'

'Sure.' I pointed to Melinda's phone. 'What about this?'

'I'll get hold of one of my contacts and see what the police are doing so far. I'll let you know.' He threw a set of car keys at me. 'Take the Commodore. You know where Justin works. Keep me updated every couple of hours. A text will do unless something major happens.'

'Okay.' I wondered what Paul's idea of major was, but I'd work it out myself.

'Just before you go,' Gang said, 'look at this.'

I looked. Melinda had given Jonathan her number. Her main phone, not this one. 'That's not a good sign, is it?'

Gang shrugged. 'It's the next step, usually. You know, chat in the app, then you talk like normal people on the phone. Get to know each other's voice, tones, warmth. You can tell better if someone is up themselves or overbearing. Cutting you off before you can finish a sentence, that kind of thing.'

'Right.' I weighed the car keys in my hand, ran my fingers over the metal Holden decal. Some of the profiles had actually said whether the guy was a Holden or a Ford man. Like women would care. 'Can you keep looking? When you have a bit of spare time.'

He glanced at his other two computer monitors. 'Sure. I can run some searches while I'm doing other things.' He cleaned his glasses with a special cloth with birds on it. 'I'll find a photo or two of Nathan Gunn as well.'

I exited, still thinking about Melinda and all those dating apps. In one way, it seemed so foolhardy, with her ex possibly hovering. When a guy was obsessed like that, a woman rarely got rid of them for good, although moving interstate was a start. Maybe she felt the apps were safer than going to a nightclub or a bar. Besides, who would she go out with? She didn't have any friends here, she said. Not even people she was studying with. That was sad.

In the Commodore, I adjusted the rear-view and side mirrors and started the engine, enjoying the roar that settled into a purr. Grandad used to have an old Jag, dark green with comfy leather seats. He called the car Maud and liked to pat her dashboard. It always felt to me like we were cruising in a tank. It felt solid and heavy, like nobody would ever get near us.

Then somebody blew it up.

Grandad was incandescent. It was as if someone had killed his best friend. I never asked if he found out who did it, but knowing Grandad, he would have. And made the person pay. Those were the days when I thought the sun shone out of Grandad and I wouldn't hear a word against him, especially from my father, who was a senior sergeant in Victoria Police by then. It caused the first big dispute between me and Dad. Dad had just been promoted and he decided it was no longer appropriate that his daughter spend so much time with one of Victoria's biggest crime bosses.

Not that those words were ever used in our house, particularly not in front of my mother. She knew her father operated on the wrong side of the law sometimes. Her view was everyone was corrupt, which, when she said so once, sent my father into a rage. Again. That happened more and more in the open as I got into my teens, as if Dad and Mum both gave up pretending in front of me.

The memories were getting too sharp. I focused on the Commodore, the way it handled and the gear shift. I liked manual transmissions and this car had more than the usual under the bonnet. It was the perfect surveillance car, a nondescript faded bronze, older model, low seats, but if needed, it could keep up with just about anything on the road except probably a big motorbike. So did that make me a 'Holden woman'?

I snorted.

Gang had sent me a message with all of Justin's details—workplace, work ute description and rego number, who else worked with him. I found the street in West Preston and drove along slowly until I saw the sign—PATERSON HOLDINGS, with JNJ DEVELOPMENTS underneath—and found a good parking spot down the street a little way after doing a U-turn. I could clearly see the entrance/exit for the main building and its large steel roller door. I wasn't surprised to find a pair of excellent binoculars in the glove box, and zeroed in on the two utes parked on the concrete apron. The one covered in reddish dirt was Justin's, and it also had a canopy cover thing on the back. Maybe to keep his tools or equipment dry. Plenty of room for all sorts of things …

I settled in to watch. Surveillance isn't much fun, because it's boring and nothing happens for hours and it's too easy to nod off before you know it. I hadn't done a lot of it while I was in the force—too busy attending to the everyday police work. Maybe if I'd ever made it to the detectives, like Kayla.

If Kayla ended up on Melinda's case, I was sure she'd do a good job, but I didn't want it to become a case. That would mean Melinda was dead, instead of missing.

Where was she? I went through it again. Checked my phone. She'd called me at 2.52pm, and then I'd called her at 5.47pm. No doubt if someone was keen enough—if things got to that point—they'd find my call was made at her house. It wasn't a problem. I'd said I was looking for her, that we'd organised to meet up. She'd wanted me to … what? Help her decide whether to go on the date? Check out the guy before she went? That would mean she was having doubts about him.

I reran the phone conversation in my head. She'd sounded happy, excited, perhaps a bit flustered. Not wary. If only I'd been able to have a look at Melinda's main phone when I'd found it. If Gang was right and Melinda and this guy had moved to phone calls, his number would surely be in her contacts, or at least her phone records.

I mentally shook myself. There was nothing to say this was anything to do with him. Melinda wouldn't invite him to her house. No way. She would have met him on a date, like she'd told me, in some wine bar or café away from her house. I'd seen how nervous she was. I just didn't believe she'd let down her guard and tell a man where she lived before she'd met him at least once.

That brought me right back to her ex again. The guy with a motive and, if he'd found out where she was living, the opportunity. All he would've had to do was knock on her door. She wouldn't have been expecting him. She'd thought she was safe. And she had the double lock and chain.

I pounded the steering wheel with both hands. Where the hell was she?

I wanted to drive to Melinda's house and find out if she was there, or if the police had been and checked, maybe even locked the front door. But here I was, watching super-smooth Justin, who may or may not be suspicious.

Hang on, I was in Melinda's contacts. I'd watched her type me in. If she was home, she'd have her phone. She'd answer because she'd see it was me. My eyes were on Justin's ute, but my brain was leaping around like a demented frog. *Call and see what happens.* And if the police had her phone, at least I'd be able to ask what they were doing to find her.

I tapped on her name, tapped on the phone icon, put it on speaker and waited, listening to it ring and ring and ring. Then it went to voicemail. 'Hi, this is Melinda. Leave a message please.' My mouth opened and closed, and then I said, 'It's Lou. Can you call me as soon as you get this?' Innocuous and polite. I'd been half-expecting a police officer to answer and question me. Seemed to me that even if they had been to the house, they had just left her phone on the bench.

Nobody was taking her disappearance seriously except me.

CHAPTER TEN

Justin appeared at five thirty in a group of other people, mainly office workers who drove away, apart from one young blonde woman in a black pencil skirt and rose-coloured top, who smiled at Justin and gave him a little finger waggle. A man in hi-vis and tradie shorts stopped by Justin's ute and talked up a storm, waving his arms and looking pretty irate. Justin was doing the calming thing, shoulder patting and nodding and making commiseration faces. Maybe the guy was being underpaid or there'd been a stuff-up on a job.

The GFC had affected Paterson Holdings for a while, but then they'd gone from new homes to a big contract for a new housing development in Mickleham, and had expanded in 2015 to small office blocks. I'd found an online article just a few weeks old that said they were likely to get the contract for a snazzy new retirement village near Whittlesea: country living in luxury. If the rising prices and fixed contracts debacles had affected Paterson Holdings, it hadn't shown up in the research.

The heated discussion was winding down. Mr Hi-Vis was hanging his head, scuffing the ground with one grubby workboot, then came a slap on the back from Justin and they parted ways. Mr Hi-Vis got into the other ute and drove off, but Justin stood by his ute and called someone. He had a huge grin on his face and was pulling at his earlobe. I had a feeling he wasn't talking to his mother.

He finally got into his ute and set off. I soon realised that he was heading home, so I relaxed a bit and followed him at a safe distance, pulling into the kerb as he arrived in his driveway and the cream double roller door went up, revealing Diane's BMW inside. Justin drove in and the door came down. I waited. Five minutes later, a Mercedes pulled into the driveway and a thin woman in her sixties got out. She was dressed in cream slacks and blouse, with a dark green embroidered cardigan tied around her shoulders in that casual, elegant way only wealthy people seemed to manage. Me? My cardie would be around my waist, sleeves stretched from being tied too tight so I could get on with work. This had to be Justin's mother. Probably never done a day of work in her life, other than bringing up Justin and his brother, William, who now lived in Switzerland, according to Gang, who'd found extra family information.

I'd be the first to agree that bringing up two kids was a full-time job, not a part-time one like my parents seemed to assume. But Justin's mum still looked like she'd done it at arm's length so as not to get dirty or untidy. The back doors of the Mercedes opened and two kids spilled out, dragging their big, bulky school bags behind them, slamming the doors so hard that Grandma visibly winced and snapped something, which elicited a 'Sorry' from both kids. Then they launched themselves at the front door, fighting to get inside first, with Grandma bleating at them from behind to no effect.

Justin met them at the door, giving each kid a big hug and gaining a couple of brownie points from me. He gave his mother a polite kiss on the cheek, they chatted for a few minutes and then she left. She was still frowning when she got into the Mercedes and was pressing her lips together in a tight line as she drove past me. Grandma wasn't happy about something.

That was enough to keep me sitting there for a while longer, even though the itch to get back to Melinda's house was making me squirm in my seat. The sun had dropped below the roofs by now, and lights went on in the front room of Justin's house. He hadn't pulled the curtains so I could see through to a dining area with a kitchen island bench to one side. The bench where I'd sat when I interviewed him about Diane. I hadn't taken much notice of the dining area—I'd been looking out to the pool at the back. The kids probably lived in it in summer.

Maybe it was time to go. Justin had put cutlery on the table, and then one of the kids put out placemats. I could see four settings. Hmm.

A red Toyota Yaris came down the street and parked awkwardly in Justin's driveway, so close to his garage door that I was sure the car had nudged it. When the female driver got out, I knew immediately who it was. Ms Waggle Fingers. She carried a green box from The Cheesecake Shop, juggling it with an oversized handbag that kept slipping off her shoulder. A jab with the key and the Yaris locked, then she tottered up to the front door in her high heels. This skirt was white and very tight, the sandals were white as well, and the off-the-shoulder peasant top was a melee of reds and oranges and yellows that hurt my eyes as she waited under the porch security light.

The door opened and Justin's face was a picture of delight. Then, behind him in the hallway, I spotted one of the kids—the girl, Amy—who had a face like a summer thunderstorm. However, neither Justin nor his office assistant noticed a thing. She went inside, gave him a peck on the cheek that I was pretty sure would change to something a lot hotter later on, and the door shut.

Interesting.

Justin wasn't wasting any time grieving. I texted Paul and said I was leaving now. He texted back an *okay* and I was on my way. I wanted to drive to Melinda's house and check she really wasn't there, but I'd promised Grandad I'd call in, so Altona it was.

I caught myself speeding down Millers Road and braked, glancing across Cherry Lake at the sunset that was just a tinge of red now. I slowed and turned left at the round-about, cruising along at fifty, and spotted a figure hurrying along the footpath carrying a green grocery bag. He was too far ahead for me to be sure, but I thought it was Emmanuel. I smiled—he'd probably been out buying Grandad's favourite cheese.

As he crossed the road towards the high gates of Grandad's house, a low, dark sports car screeched out of its parking spot under a tree and headed straight for him.

He half-turned, already trying to step back, but it was too late. The car hit him and he went flying through the air and across the street, smashing against the kerb.

'Oh God, no!' I shouted, and planted my foot, accelerating towards the car.

Rather than speeding away, it stopped, there were two loud cracks, and then it laid rubber as it roared off. Instinct made me force my foot down more, chasing the car, determined to catch it. But it slowed again, an arm came out of the passenger window, there were two more cracks, and the windscreen of the Commodore suddenly had a starred hole in it.

'Fuck!' I slammed on the brakes and watched the car take off and disappear around the corner, repeating the number plate over and over to myself. Then I jumped out and ran across the street, praying I was wrong about who it was.

It was Emmanuel, and he was dead. Even if his broken, twisted body hadn't told me, the bullet holes in him confirmed it. I dropped to my knees, tears streaming down my face, and smoothed the strands of white hair off his face. His eyes were open, staring at nothing, and he still looked slightly surprised. I picked up his hand, brushed the dust and some bits of gravel off it, and held it in mine. If wishes could bring someone back, mine would have worked miracles.

I stayed there for a couple of minutes, crying, talking to him even though I knew he couldn't hear. I needed to tell him how much he was loved, how much he meant to me.

When I finally looked up, Grandad stood motionless, staring down, his face like grey carved rock.

He said one word. 'How?'

'Deliberate.' My voice cracked. 'A car went straight for him.'

'God almighty.' He dragged both hands down his cheeks and then covered his eyes for a moment. 'Number plate?'

'Yes.' Without thinking, I repeated it to him, and he laid a hand briefly on my shoulder, then turned. A man behind him stepped forward and Grandad muttered to him. The man nodded and went back through the gates.

I carefully placed Emmanuel's hand next to him and swallowed hard. 'They stopped and shot him as well. Bastards. I tried to— They shot at me, too.'

He made a guttural noise. 'You're all right?'

'Yes.' No, I wasn't, but that's not what he was asking.

'Someone will pay for this,' he grated.

'Do you know who did it?'

He shook his head. 'I know who sent them.'

My knees were hurting and I struggled to my feet, but the anger surging inside me straightened my spine. 'Is this the *problem* you were going to solve?' I snapped.

He glared at me and then waved his hand around. 'Not the time nor the place.'

For the first time, I saw the small crowd that had gathered, the vultures with mobile phones filming us; an elderly woman across the street sitting on a low wall, crying; a parent shooing their children home. I didn't bother to ask if anyone had called for an ambulance. It was too late anyway, but sirens pierced the night, coming closer, so clearly somebody had.

'I need a drink,' Grandad said, and walked back towards his house.

I gaped after him. Before I could follow him and demand to know what was going on, a police car came speeding down the street, its siren snapping off as the driver saw he'd arrived at the scene. The scene of the crime.

The scene of a ruthless, bloody, pointless murder. Why kill an old man like this? An attack on Grandad, I could understand. But if he knew this was possible, he'd left Emmanuel vulnerable.

As the officers got out of the car, I vowed to find out who'd killed Emmanuel and put him away for life. Even as I knew deep inside that my grandfather would take his revenge long before anyone could get near the killer. I couldn't deny that thought gave me some satisfaction. But it wouldn't stop there. These bloody things never did.

The two officers did all they were supposed to—questioned me, put up a cordon, kept gawkers away, reported to the detectives who arrived fifteen minutes later. Not Homicide, not yet; they'd be on the case soon. None of that was my concern. I felt numb, going through the motions, pointing out the bullet hole in the windscreen, pointing to where the other bullet might have gone that missed.

I couldn't look at Emmanuel, his poor body lying there like an exhibit in a death museum. I told myself he was no longer there. It was just his remains.

The detectives asked me the same questions as the officers, wanted to know what I was doing in this street. 'Visiting my grandfather.' I pointed to his house and they wrote it down. Neither of them knew who Grandad was, that Emmanuel lived there, too, and I wasn't going to tell them. They'd discover everything in due course. Right now, I couldn't find any more words. I just nodded when they said my car would have to stay there until the crime scene people had finished with it.

'Can I go into my grandfather's house and wait?' I asked.

It seemed that would be okay now I'd given my witness statement, as much as was needed anyway. There'd be more tomorrow. 'We'll call you when the car is released.'

'Thanks.'

I walked to Grandad's gate and blinked at the courtyard in total darkness, apart from the small lights along the driveway. Surely he hadn't gone to bed? The turning area in front of the house was pitch black and I almost tripped on a loose brick. Then the security sensor picked up my movement and the light over the door clicked on, making me squint.

Usually Emmanuel would be on the step by now, arms open to welcome me.

Tears burned again and I forced them back as best I could. I needed to be hard, to stand up to my grandfather and demand some answers. I rang the doorbell. As I waited, I stared at the large, black SUV with tinted windows parked to one side. That wasn't Grandad's usual transport. He didn't like four-wheel drives or SUVs, and had bought a new Jag after the old one was wrecked. The street was quiet from in here, despite the still-flashing red and blue lights, and the wind off the bay rustled through the beech leaves. The house felt closed off and foreign, even though the white shutters were open. I shivered.

The door opened. A thickset man with a large head and hardly any neck looked at me like I was a visiting gnome who hadn't been invited. He couldn't even say hello, he just stared and waited. If he was trying to be a hard-nosed arsehole, he was doing half the job right.

'Where's my grandfather?'

He stepped back, his hand on the door as if he was getting ready to slam it in my face. 'Sitting room. Back there.' His huge head jerked infinitesimally.

'Thanks.' Not.

I walked down the long hallway, my feet sinking into the plush carpet, and when I reached the tiles, I could hear grit grinding under my soles. Someone had been tracking dirt in. Emmanuel would not be happy. *Emmanuel won't know, you idiot.* The lights were off, so the hall and the rooms off it were all gloomy and shadowed. At the end, the doorway opened into the large room that looked out to the garden, an area landscaped with low formal hedges and a modern fountain and koi pond.

I thought Grandad might be outside, feeding the fish, as the glass doors were open, but he was sitting in his leather armchair, with a table at his elbow that held a thick whiskey glass half-filled with brown liquid.

'Lou.'

I sat in the other armchair, wincing as it squeaked under me. I wanted a drink, too, but whiskey wasn't my thing and I wasn't about to rummage through the bottles in the cabinet. Yet. 'What's going on? Who killed Emmanuel?'

Grandad's face spasmed for a moment, then he ground out, 'Never you mind.'

My fingernails dug into the leather arms and my face went weirdly numb. 'What—'

'You don't need to know.' He ran a hand over his face. I was glad to see it wasn't a shaky hand. The old man might be grieving, but he wasn't feeble.

'Fuck that.' I'd never sworn at him before, and his head jerked at the word. 'They shot at me, too. I want to know what is going on. Now.'

Grandad's jaw worked and he stared out into the garden. 'Know thy enemy and know yourself; in a hundred battles, you will never be defeated.' He grunted softly. 'Seems like I took this one for granted.'

'Whose bullshit line is that?'

'Sun Tzu.' He didn't react to the scorn in my voice.

I wasn't going to back down. 'And who's this enemy that's just murdered your best friend? And don't try to fob me off.'

Grandad turned his gaze on me, his steel grey eyes like silver. 'This is not what you think it is. Some kind of gangland tit for tat.'

'Isn't it? Aren't you already planning your payback?'

'Again, that's not for you to know.' He lifted the glass, hand steady, and swallowed a mouthful.

His stubbornness made me even more determined, but I knew directly butting heads with him wouldn't work. 'Have you eaten?'

He shook his head. 'Not hungry.'

I needed a drink if I was going to stay here and try to wheedle or trick the information out of him. I went into the kitchen, poured myself a large glass of pinot gris from the fridge and buttered two thick slices of sourdough bread. Their solid bulk would fill the hole in my stomach at least. As I went back to where he was sitting, I saw the large, neckless man patrolling the garden.

'Who's he?'

'Sammy. Emmanuel's nephew. He's taking it hard.'

He was taking it hard! 'Where are the rest of your guys?'

'Out there.' He pointed around the house. 'If you didn't see them coming in, they're doing a good job.'

'The gate is still open.'

'It won't be now.'

'Grandad, why won't you tell me who did this?'

He let out a huge sigh. 'I should have been protecting you, protecting Emmanuel.'

He was damn right about that.

His head bowed and he fumbled in his pocket, bringing out a large gingham handkerchief and dabbing his eyes. Then he straightened and the granite face was back. 'I've had threats. I should've taken them more seriously.' His fingers curled into fists. 'Yes, Emmanuel is my bloody fault. And you're right. You do need to know, in case they go after you.'

There was a long pause and I said, 'I'm waiting.'

He sniffed. 'As impatient as your grandmother.'

I drank more wine and tried to stay quiet while glaring at him. It was an old ploy from my childhood, and it had always worked. So far. This time I wanted to know a lot more than what Grandma was planning to buy me for my birthday.

'Do you remember Antony Fayed?' I shook my head and he continued, 'Yes, before your time. He's been inside for nearly twenty years. Got out four weeks ago.' The hankie twisted in his hands. 'Antony has never liked losing. While he was inside, he continued most of his operations. Except the ones where I was involved. I cut him out. I refused to give his son protection as well, and his son ended up dead on a street in South Melbourne.' He pressed the hankie to his mouth for a few moments, then said, 'Pretty much the same way Emmanuel was killed tonight.'

My mouth dropped open and a sick dread coiled through my guts. Grandad never usually revealed this much about his business dealings to me. We'd always worked on the premise that the less he told me, the less I'd be at risk. Especially when I joined the police force. He said he didn't want to put me in a bad position. Never mind my father, the big cop, and his reputation. In Grandad's eyes, I was my mother's daughter and that was all that counted.

I sorted through what he'd said. 'Fayed is after you. And he's made it personal.'

Grandad nodded. 'By going after Emmanuel first.' His fists clenched and opened, clenched and opened. 'It has to be dealt with. I can't lose you, too.'

'Does Fayed know about me?'

'I'm sure, but he would also know about your father. That's probably keeping you safer than I could.'

Shit. That was a bit hard for me to swallow. 'Look, maybe I should move in here, help you out.'

'No.' His reply was sharp, almost snarly. 'That would make you a definite target. You watch your back, that's all. Until I get this sorted out.'

I didn't want to have to watch my back. I wanted to be doing something about this bastard. Fixing this bloody Fayed once and for all. I ground my teeth, watching Sammy patrol past the back patio again, his huge arm muscles catching the light.

Grandad nodded at Sammy. 'I can put him with you as a bodyguard.'

'No way.' Imagine that tagging me everywhere. 'If I need help, I'll talk to Paul.'

'Good plan.'

We sat in silence for a while, drinking, probably both thinking about revenge and what it did to people; I refilled our glasses and then persuaded him to eat a sandwich. I asked him about Emmanuel's family and he said Emmanuel had never married, but had two sisters, so it was all nephews and nieces.

Grandad changed the subject. 'Tell me about your cases so far. Now you're not in the cops anymore, you can tell me, right?' He frowned at me.

'A little bit, I suppose.' Even when I was in the force, he'd still insisted on hearing what I'd been doing, who I'd arrested, what my days were like. I made sure not to name names, making it all anonymous where I could. The truth was, on the worst days, Grandad had helped me a lot. I'd never had the fantasy I'd make the world a better place by being a cop, but I'd tried to pretend I was making a difference. Every day, I was arresting drug dealers and prostitutes and an awful lot of people who had mental health and drug issues. I kept seeing the same faces. It had started to get me down, like no matter how hard I tried, I wasn't making the slightest bit of difference to people.

When I'd cracked at last and smashed the guy's hand with the hammer, the one person who hadn't been surprised, who'd had my back and said he understood, was Grandad. Unlike my father, who had gone totally ballistic and ranted and raved about how I'd shamed him and his name was mud and he was a laughing stock and … Yeah, it was all about Dad.

It had been a family violence call, a house we'd been to three times already. This time, the boyfriend had hit her with a hammer, knocked her out. She lay on the floor, unconscious, her head in a pool of blood, and he'd insisted it was her own fault for 'talking back, mouthing off'. He was drunk, waving his hands around, and I grabbed the hammer, pulled his hand onto the kitchen table and whacked it. I managed to get in three good hits, heard bones crunching, and all I could think was, *I've got gloves on so you won't find my fingerprints*. Stupid of me—no way was my partner going to lie for me. Not in an incident like that.

I still wasn't sure who'd got me off with an agreement to resign and go quietly and never darken Victoria Police's doors again. My money was on Grandad. My father would probably have urged them to prosecute me.

And it was Grandad who insisted I stay with him for a few weeks, who got me the job at his mate's restaurant, who got me back on my feet. And wouldn't accept a word of thanks. I'd never forgotten it, though. Any of it.

I told him about Diane's disappearance and the ways I'd been trying to track her via the internet.

'Justin Paterson,' he said, gazing into space. 'Father is James? Builder?'

'How did you know?'

He laughed shortly. 'I know everyone, lassie.'

Over Grandad's shoulder was an array of framed photos of him with just about every famous or infamous person in Melbourne. Even Bert Newton, for God's sake, at a charity event. I knew Grandad had been running a construction industry protection racket years ago, although I'd never mentioned it to him.

'James was all right when he started,' Grandad said, 'then he got a bit big for his boots. Owed a fair bit of money for a while there.'

No doubt some of it to Grandad. I didn't interrupt.

'Then a few words in the right places and he traded his way out again. Slippery. Bet his son is the same.'

'Well, he thinks he's clever, that's for sure.'

'Where do you think his wife is?'

'Probably in a deep hole on a building site somewhere,' I said. 'Under a tonne of concrete.' I was only half-joking.

'You could be right.' A sip of whiskey, a sharp glance at me. 'So what's really bugging you?'

'Not an official case. It's a missing woman.'

This time it was Grandad who held back from interrupting.

It didn't take long to explain about Melinda, and how the police seemed to be waiting. And how something was telling me it was serious.

'And Paul agrees?' Grandad said.

'So far. He's letting me use the agency resources to find her.'

'Dating apps,' Grandad scoffed. 'In my day, we went to social dances and church things. Met decent girls, got married, made a family. How can you work out what a man is like if you can't look him in the face, look him in the eyes, for God's sake?'

Had Grandma looked him straight in the eyes? What had she seen? I bet she'd never seen an intelligent criminal mind ticking away. But Grandad had spent years doing a great job of pretending to be a legit businessman. Maybe he'd fooled Nana as well, but it was too late to ask her.

'I agree,' I said. 'I thought Melinda would be more careful, after what her ex did to her.'

'We all want love,' Grandad said. 'The trick is to find someone who knows what that is. Not many do these days.' He sighed. 'You need any help, just let me know.'

I said I would, but despite his claim to know everyone in Melbourne, somehow I felt this would be one case Grandad couldn't help me with.

CHAPTER ELEVEN

As I left Grandad's house, the little bubble of family strength I'd felt from being around him popped and all the shit crowded in again. A man in black stood by the front gate, checking the street, making sure I departed without any hassles. The cordon was still there, of course, and I had to walk past it all to get to my waiting Uber. The Commodore was being examined by forensics officers. Thank God Emmanuel's body was hidden by a forensic tent. And the journalists and news services were mostly gone. Even the helicopter had flown away.

I wondered how Emmanuel's sisters and families were feeling tonight, whether they blamed Grandad. It would be devastating to lose their brother in such a violent way. Maybe all these years, Emmanuel had kept who he worked for secret. I dreaded what they would see in the news tomorrow.

An anonymous Uber, a dark Toyota SUV, dropped me at my apartment block, and for once I was glad the lobby light was still broken. Out of the car, I suddenly felt like I had a target on my back and whipped around to check the parking area and the street beyond, then above and around me. Nothing.

First thing tomorrow, I'd talk to Paul about the situation. Not that he could do anything. Grandad would be determined to sort it himself. I needed to know, though, how much danger he was in, whether some kind of war was about to break out. Emmanuel's murder made a statement that Grandad wouldn't—and couldn't—ignore. Despite his armoured front, I knew he'd be hurting deeply about Emmanuel; be grieving and angry. I was grieving and angry, too, and was going to do some research on Fayed as soon as I was able.

I'd also have to let Paul know the Commodore would be towed to a panelbeaters in Altona North for an urgent windscreen replacement, courtesy of Grandad.

I climbed the stairs to my flat, trying to guess what my neighbours had eaten for dinner. Ground floor was definitely something with garlic, and the Sudanese couple across the hall from me always cooked things that smelled divine. Tonight it was some kind of curry, maybe lamb. My stomach rumbled.

The guy in the flat behind me was quiet tonight, just a TV murmuring instead of his stereo at full volume. If it annoyed me, I'd bang on the wall and he usually turned it down. I pulled open the sliding glass door onto my small balcony and groaned. The couple upstairs were quiet for long periods and then something would set him off and he'd get drunk and shout. A lot. He assaulted her as well. Tonight he was shouting at the TV, from what I could tell. Better that than his partner. I'd called the police on him once already, about two weeks ago. It hadn't helped.

I closed the balcony door and turned on my TV, kept it low while I called Melinda. Voicemail again. I didn't leave a message. I stood up, I paced. No way I'd sleep tonight until I'd been to her house and checked. Checked what, I didn't know, but I had to go. Besides, every time I stopped for more than a few seconds, I kept seeing Emmanuel flying across the road into the gutter. Trying to sleep with that in my head was pointless.

I went down, jumped in the Corolla and was at Melinda's house in under twenty minutes. The street was quiet. I couldn't find a parking spot so ended up near the far end. That suited me. I slipped along the footpath under the trees and through her front gate, up the steps to the door. Using a couple of tissues, I tried the door. Locked. For a moment, relief whooshed through me, then … Police? Melinda? Someone else?

I tried her phone again, thought I could hear something faintly ringing, but I wasn't sure and then it skipped to voicemail yet again. I hung up. Had I imagined the phone ringing? If it was where I left it on the kitchen bench, there was only one way to check.

With the help of my phone map, I worked out which house backed onto hers and headed for the street, jogging, thinking it was about time I did a proper run. My calf muscles were tight. The house I wanted was in darkness but when I crept through the garden towards the back fence, I discovered there were lights on in the kitchen at the rear. A quick reccie—a couple sat on a couch with their backs to the window, watching TV. It was a risk. Their back fence was a bonus—a high, wooden-slatted construction with vines and a creeper rose covering most of it. I kept to the side in the shadows, climbed the fence carefully and only snagged my hand on the rose thorns twice.

At the top, I could see into Melinda's kitchen, which was in darkness. I kept my phone screen hidden in the crook of my arm and called her. From here, I still couldn't hear the ring tone clearly, but I could see something on the bench light up. Her phone, right where I left it. Why hadn't the police taken it?

No matter what they thought, Melinda was definitely missing. Every nerve ending in my body screamed it, so loud I almost fell off the fence. I'd have to go to the police again. I'd have to call her father—Gang would find him for me. No matter what had caused them to be estranged, surely he'd be worried?

I climbed down even more carefully than I went up and sneaked back towards the street, keeping low. The couple were watching *The Walking Dead* and she was clutching his hand so tight he was probably wincing in pain. True love.

It was after twelve by the time I got home again. I put on shorts and a light hoodie, my favourite runners, pulled the hood over my head and set off for the river. I stuck to the back streets, dodging wheelie bins and often running on the road, the pounding of my feet echoing against the brick walls. The Maribyrnong was dark and oily tonight, barely a ripple showing, and any boats or fishermen had long gone.

The mindless rhythm of my feet allowed my brain to focus, sometimes in ways I didn't want it to. Grandad and Melinda jostled for a place at the front. Grandad was adept at solving his own problems; all the same, I was deeply worried that this time, he wouldn't prevail. Emmanuel's murder was a huge, sudden escalation. Like killing a family member. Grandad wouldn't accept help from me and I hardly knew where to start to be useful.

Back to Melinda. Missing, missing, missing. In a way, I barely knew her. In another way, I knew her so well it was unnerving. That sense of a beaten woman, a terrified woman, who had run and then fought her way back. I had seen so many like her while I was in the force. Every single day. Domestic violence sucked up half of our time, more than half of our energy. Women who called for help and then were too scared to follow through, who went back time and again, often for no reason other than the alternative was homelessness and starving kids.

Melinda had got out, had even got away from a violent stalker ex. Still, she lived alone in a house that felt like a prison, and would rather risk online dating than venture into a pub or club.

Everything pointed towards the ex. He'd found her again, had kidnapped her and taken her somewhere. Why else would she have left her phone on the bench?

I had to find out if the police were doing anything. From what I'd seen so far, they'd managed to lock her house and that's all. I had to find out where her ex was. First thing in the morning, I would call Kayla and then Melinda's dad. Until then, the night ahead was full of mindless TV and staring at the ceiling.

***

Kayla was easy. I called her while I was sitting outside Justin Paterson's house in the Corolla. Ms Waggle Fingers' car had gone. Probably not an overnight stayer then. Not quite so soon.

Kayla was a bit reluctant to help out, given her search would be on the record, but she finally agreed. 'Spell her name for me?' I heard a keyboard tapping. 'Yes, she's been reported as missing. Yesterday. By … you.'

'Yes, I went to her local station,' I said. 'They took details. They've locked her house, which means they unsnibbed the door and pulled it closed. But they're not doing anything, are they?'

'Hmm.' More keyboard taps. 'She hasn't been turning up at her TAFE course. There's no record here of family members they've contacted though. Yet.'

Yet. 'I think her father is in Sydney. He probably has no idea. They weren't really speaking.' I sucked in a breath, rubbed an eye too hard and blinked the liquid away. 'Shit. She was assaulted and then stalked by her ex in Sydney. That's why she moved here, to get away from him. To hide.'

'You think it's him?'

'That's where I'd start.'

'You need to go back to the station where you reported her missing,' Kayla said. 'Give them more details. It's been well over a day now. Not turning up to class is a red flag.'

'Yep, will do. Thanks, mate.'

I would, but first I wanted more information. I wanted to be able to say who Melinda's father was, who her ex was and what he did. I needed Gang's help. Justin emerged from his house with his kids, loaded them into the work ute and dropped them at school, then I followed him to his business. It didn't look like he'd be going out to any sites. He was dressed in dark pants and a white shirt and tie. Probably meetings all day.

I managed to get a better parking spot outside Paterson Holdings under a tree, then wrestled with the payment via the app.

I'd just settled in to my seat and was thinking about coffee when my phone pinged and an email arrived from Gang. It was the information I'd asked for about Melinda's dad and her ex. I called Gang.

'This is great, thanks.'

'Clearly you haven't found her yet.' He sounded anxious. 'The information on the ex came up because he'd had an order out against him. Are you going back to the cops now?'

'I want to, but I have to follow Justin Paterson.' I squirmed around and checked the Paterson carpark. 'His ute has another car parked behind it. Space over there is obviously at a premium. I assume he's going to be in there for a few hours, but he also could leave at any time.' A familiar figure walked across the street and into the building. Today's outfit was a figure-clinging dress with a little fluttery skirt that wouldn't have looked out of place at the Melbourne Cup. 'Look, he's bonking the secretary. She was at his house for dinner last night. She's just arrived.'

Gang whistled. 'I see. Hey, Paul's here. Might be a good idea to update him.'

I agreed and was soon transferred, giving Paul the Justin updates and then Melinda.

'You're sure Melinda's phone is still sitting on her kitchen bench?'

'Her main one, yes. Gang has still got her other phone.'

There was silence on his end for a few long moments. *Hurry up, Paul.* A sense of desperation and fear was seeping through my limbs and I wanted to rush back to Melinda's house again. Surely there'd be something else there to tell me what had happened to her?

'All right,' he said finally. 'Justin can wait a little while. Get down to the station with that information first, then call Melinda's father. If you've provided the police with his contact details, then you can call him as her friend and ask him some questions. The police might be slower, but you've done things in the correct order.'

'What do we do about the ex?'

'Nothing. Gang said his stalking and assault were both reported to the New South Wales police so they'll be on record there, and give police here a good reason to track down where he is. If he's in Melbourne, they'll find out.'

'Find out when? When she's dead?' I heard the hysterical note in my voice and wished I'd kept myself under control, but it was too late for that.

'Hey, take it easy,' Paul said calmly. 'We're lucky you spent time with her, enough to know something is wrong now. If you hadn't, she'd be missing and nobody would be any the wiser. We're moving on it.' He paused. 'I heard about Emmanuel. I'm really sorry.'

I gulped and my voice came out husky. 'Yeah, thanks. Worse for Grandad.'

'He said you were there, saw it happen?'

'Yes.' My throat closed up. I couldn't add anything more. Paul probably had access to information about it anyway.

'You know what this is about?'

'Yes, Grandad told me.' I swallowed. 'You know this Antony Fayed?'

'Unfortunately. Watch your back. Don't worry about the Commodore. It'll be back in our parking spot this afternoon. You can use it any time you need a different set of wheels.'

'Thanks.' Pause. 'Okay, I'm going to the police again. Bye.'

I started the Corolla, did a fast U-turn out of my parking spot and sped off towards the police station. I knew I had to do the right thing, follow the processes, but I also knew from experience that those processes could be slow and bogged down with red tape. I'd follow Paul's orders and file more details for the missing person report, but my priority was finding out where Melinda's ex was.

The speedo needle bounced up over eighty and I slowed. Last thing I needed was a ticket. As I reached the police station and parked, I decided to enlist Gang's help again and sent him a text.

Can you do some research for me on Antony Fayed? I'll owe you.

I wanted to know more about why I had to watch my back.

CHAPTER TWELVE

The same constable was on the counter when I went into the police station and he remembered me. This time I peered at his badge—Constable Colombo. I made sure I kept a straight face.

'She's not turned up then?' he said.

'No.' I showed him the information from Gang on my phone, pushing it close to the glass barrier. 'These are her father's contact details in Sydney. Have you been onto him yet?'

He raised his thick eyebrows at me. 'Did you have these yesterday?'

'No.' I tried to make my voice sound reasonable, when I wanted to scream, *No, you dickhead, of course I didn't!* 'I've only just found them out.' I pointed to the other details. 'This guy, Nathan Gunn, is her ex. He was charged with assaulting her and then stalking her. There was an AVO against him.'

'We'll check our database—'

'That was in Sydney. New South Wales. She came down here to get away from him.' I left my phone on the counter so he could type in the details. 'I think he's followed her, found out where she lives. She said he's a nutcase.'

'Hmm.' He tapped away, squinting at the screen. He probably needed glasses, but he didn't want to admit it.

The door opened behind me and I caught a waft of rank body odour, stale tobacco smoke and wet dog. An old man shuffled in, followed by a dog that looked like a cross between a Shetland pony and a Yeti. The dog looked up at me with watery, sad eyes.

'Billy, you can't bring the mutt in here, you know that,' Colombo said. 'Go on, take him out. Tie him to the fence.'

'He's not doin' any harm, Dave,' Billy wheezed.

'Out! He pongs.' An unspoken *And so do you* hovered in the smelly air.

'Fer fuck's sake,' Billy muttered and turned to the dog. 'Never wanted, are we, Ringo? Come on then.'

Colombo gave me a look. 'Billy will have some kind of complaint about where he lives. Mostly he just wants a chat.'

'And a shower?'

'Yeah, that, too.' He sighed. 'How long since you were last in contact with Melinda?'

'Two days. She called me. We were meeting up at her house.'

'Ah, yeah, it's here.'

Of course it was—he took the bloody report! 'So you need to contact her father, right?' I leaned further across the counter. 'And see where her ex is? Because if it's him—'

'Don't worry. I'll escalate it now. I'll pass it on to someone in CIU upstairs.'

'You will tell them she could be, you know, hurt or tied up somewhere, or ...' I didn't want to say it.

'I bet she's fine,' he said with a fake smile. 'We've got your contact details, Ms Alcott. We'll let you know if we find her.'

'And if you don't?'

'Er, well, we'll ... keep you updated.' He gave me a brisk nod and went off behind the security door. It closed with a loud bang and I jumped. Then I smelled the reappearance of Billy and turned.

'You're a bit nervy, girlie,' he said. 'Lost yer cat or somethin'?'

'Yeah, something like that.' I forced a smile and escaped.

Outside, I paced near my car for a few minutes, then spotted a café up the street and bought a coffee. When fifteen minutes had passed, I sat in the Corolla and called Melinda's father.

'Good morning. Moreau, Philpott and Scanvia.'

The polite female voice threw me. 'Oh, right. Um, can I speak to Mr Moreau please?'

'What is it about?'

'It's about Melinda, his daughter.'

A sharp intake of breath. 'I see. One moment.'

I sat with blank silence that went on so long, I thought we might have been cut off. I checked my phone. No, it was still connected. To someone.

'Yes, this is Phillip Moreau. How can I help you?' He didn't sound like a loving father, he sounded wary and a little annoyed.

'This is Louisa Alcott, Mr Moreau. I'm calling from Melbourne, about your daughter, Melinda.'

'Yes. And?'

I wanted to pierce the polite wall he was putting up. 'She's missing. She has been for two days and I'm worried about her. Have you heard from her?'

'Who are you? Not your name, I heard that. Who are you to Melinda?'

'A friend. A recent friend. But I'm worried, like I said.' He didn't respond, so I ploughed on. 'I believe she left Sydney to get away from a violent boyfriend, is that right? Do you know where this guy is? Nathan Gunn?'

'Why would you want to know that, Miss Alcott?'

A strange answer. 'Do you know where your daughter is then?'

'No.'

'When was the last time you spoke to her?'

'Two months ago.'

'Why?' I meant why so long but he answered with the minimum.

'She called for my birthday.'

'Are you not close then?'

'Why are you asking all these personal questions?'

I stretched my neck from side to side, hearing a crack. Tension. 'Melinda is missing. I am trying to find her. I was hoping you could help.'

'I'm sorry, I can't help. I haven't heard from her.'

'Don't you care? Something might've happened to her! This guy, Gunn, might've tracked her down again.'

Another silence, shorter this time. 'Have you reported this to the police?'

'Yes, twice. I'm still waiting for them to get off their ... chairs and do something to look for her.'

Two men in suits came out of the police station—detectives, I could tell. Maybe they were going to Melinda's house. I wanted to follow them, just in case. They got into a car angle-parked nearby.

'I will ask someone to check if Melinda has called here recently,' Mr Moreau said. 'And I will let you know if she has. That's all I can do right now.'

'Okay, thanks. That will help a bit.' No, actually, it probably wouldn't help at all. Cold bastard. I thought of one more thing. 'Do you have a photo of Nathan Gunn, by any chance?' Expecting him to say no.

'There may be one—I will ask my secretary to check for you.'

'Thanks. Bye.' I couldn't get off the phone fast enough. Phillip Moreau's clipped, heartless tone reminded me too much of my own father.

I dropped my phone onto the console and started the car, edging out and tailing the detectives. They were chatting, taking their time. No urgency then. They might be going to get some lunch, but I doubted it. Sure enough, they turned into Melinda's street and were soon at her front door with a set of keys I recognised. I guessed the patrol who checked and locked up her house had taken the keys to the station.

They disappeared inside and I tried to wait, but it was impossible. I jumped out and went to the half-open door, pushing it wide.

'Hello?'

One of them came out of the kitchen, holding Melinda's phone. I was relieved to see he had gloves on. 'Are you Melinda Moreau?' he asked.

'No, I'm her friend. The one who reported her missing. You are?'

'Detective Sergeant Scotcher,' he said shortly. He reminded me a bit of Mark Wahlberg, without the smile and with fewer muscles.

The other detective, whose horrible blood-red tie hung skew-whiff across his paunch, emerged from the laundry. 'Have you heard from her at all? Seen her on social media?'

'Nothing. Have you tracked down her ex yet? The one who assaulted and stalked her?'

They looked at each other and Red Tie pursed his lips. I couldn't read what was going on between them, but it irritated me all the same.

'This is serious, guys. Come on.'

Scotcher held up her phone. 'You on this?'

'Yes. She put me in her Contacts. She called me the day she went missing.'

'And said what?'

'We were meeting here at five thirty for a glass of wine.'

He glanced down at the phone. 'It's locked. Do you know the pin code?'

I opened my mouth and hesitated. 'No. I suppose I could make a guess.' My mind had gone blank. I'd seen the numbers Gang had used to get into her secret phone, but now I had no idea. 'But I might guess wrong.' I didn't want to call Gang; they'd demand to know who he was.

'Is it her birth date or something like that?' The phone beeped and the screen dimmed. 'Bugger, it's nearly flat. Do you know where she keeps the charger?'

I shook my head.

'Right, wait here, would you?' He went to the kitchen doorway. 'Hey, have you found a charger for this thing?'

'Hang on.' Drawers opened and closed with a series of bangs. 'Here, this might be it.'

They were both in the kitchen, so I edged forward until I could see what they were doing. The phone was now plugged in and its screen was bright again.

'You want to try the obvious?' Red Tie asked.

'One-two-three-four? Could do.'

'Nah, wait. It's set for a fingerprint, I think.'

'You know how to override that?'

'Nup. We'll have to take it to someone in IT.'

Maybe that was why whoever had taken Melinda had left her phone—without her fingerprint there was no danger of anyone else getting access to it. A chill rippled over me—but that would mean he was expecting to get rid of her body. Or her hands. Or put her in a barrel of ... I scrubbed at my face, trying to get rid of all the stupid thoughts I was having.

My phone meowed with a text message and I glanced at it. Moreau Investment Advisors, two words—*Nathan Gunn*—with an attachment. Must be the photo he promised me.

'You need to leave, Ms ...' Scotcher said, trying not to sound impatient and failing.

I held up my phone. 'I've been in touch with Melinda's father and he's just sent me a photo of her violent ex. Do you want to see it?'

He glanced at Red Tie and shrugged. 'Sure.'

I opened the attachment. The photo had been taken at a business function of some kind, judging by the suits and ties and large marketing banners behind the trio of people. I squinted at the logo and name—Moreau, Philpott and Scanvia. A man of about thirty stood between two older men, both of whom had grey hair and lined faces. Neither of the older men was smiling. They wore that bland, pleasant look that people in power put on for photos and PR things: 'I'm powerful and rich, but I don't want to look too up myself.' The younger man, however, was grinning. It made him look avaricious, shark-like, and the dark hair flopping across his brow gleamed like vinyl.

They all held glasses of champagne, so were celebrating something big. This was Nathan Gunn. Mr Moreau hadn't said Nathan was his employee, but that's what it looked like. It explained how he'd connected with Melinda.

I held out my phone and the two detectives took a long look.

'He doesn't look familiar,' Red Tie said.

Why would he? 'He's in Sydney.'

They glanced at each other again. 'So why do you think he's responsible for your friend disappearing?'

'He was stalking and harassing her up there. There was an assault charge and an AVO. She came to Melbourne to get away from him. He could easily have come here and grabbed her.'

Sceptical looks took up residence on their faces. 'Long way to come to cause a bit of trouble,' Red Tie said dubiously.

'You should know that—' I bit off the sentence before it ran out of my mouth. 'I mean, I'm sure you've had cases of obsessed exes before. I understand that the time after a woman leaves her abusive partner is actually the most dangerous for her.' Nothing like a quote from the statistics, which were common knowledge anyway.

Scotcher let out a huge sigh. 'Yeah, that's true. Can you forward that to me?' He gave me his mobile number and I sent it on.

In a few seconds, his phone made a barking noise and he flushed. 'Doggies fan.'

'Me, too,' I said. Football—it unites the strangest people. My bet was that Red Tie was a Carlton supporter.

'Anyway,' Red Tie said, stretching his neck inside his shirt, limbering up. 'We need to do a search of this place. So, Ms Alcott, you'll need to make tracks.'

I ignored him and nodded at Scotcher. 'Let me know if you find her? Please? You've got my number now.'

'Sure.'

I think I believed him. All the same, I'd be calling him tomorrow and checking on progress. I let myself out and drove the Corolla back to the city, found a parking spot after circling the block four times, and went up to the office. First job was to report in to Paul on Melinda.

He leaned forward in his chair, frowning. When I told him who Melinda's father was, his jaw dropped, just a little bit.

'That Moreau? Shit a brick. And he couldn't protect his own daughter?'

I'd gone through the information Gang had given me on Gunn and I showed Paul the photo on my phone. 'Nathan Gunn is still employed by Moreau. I checked. Why would you continue to have someone in your company who has assaulted your daughter and made her life hell?'

'Couple of reasons,' Paul said. 'One reason is that Gunn is high up in the company and too good at what he does to lose him.'

'That's a piss-poor reason.' I huffed out an angry breath. 'So his company and its shareholders are more important than his daughter.'

Paul lifted one eyebrow. 'Not uncommon. The other reason is that quite possibly Moreau didn't believe his daughter. That she was exaggerating, or making it up. Gunn looks like a pretty clever young man. He'd know how to cover up. "She was drunk and fell down the stairs." Mount a campaign against her that totally undermines her and then destroys her, makes her look like she's unhinged or making stuff up. Gaslighting supreme. Then stalk and harass her with burner phones and fake social media accounts.'

I wanted to argue but I knew he was totally right. 'Fucking bastard.'

'I know.' Paul rubbed his face. 'These guys …' He straightened in his chair, took a breath. 'Right, stay on Melinda and keep hassling those detectives. The squeaky wheel … And have you spoken to Hamish yet? I tried to call him but he didn't answer.'

Grandad. I knew he wouldn't want me hovering, but I should have called first thing. 'I'll try him now.'

I got voicemail as well. I sent a text. *Call me, please. No excuses.*

Paul handed me a printout several pages long. 'Have a look through this—Gang's intel so far on Fayed.'

It confirmed everything Grandad had told me, but in much more detail, including the names of two men who were known to me from my time in the police force. Both suspected of murder, both had been inside for GBH, armed robbery and more. Nephews of Fayed. Also suspected of dealing in illegal firearms.

The feeling of a target painted on my back bloomed again.

Paul scratched his jaw and stared out of the huge window towards Altona, past the swoop of the West Gate Bridge and the Newport Power Station smokestack, to the bay at Williamstown, dotted with tiny white boats of all sizes. If I'd had a top pair of binoculars I could probably see Grandad's walls, but maybe not the house. For the first time, I thought of those walls as a prison, rather than something that created peace and privacy and meant Nana could grow virtually anything she wanted, even avocadoes.

'You say he's got his men all around?'

'Yes. And an SUV with what looks like armoured glass.'

He shook his head. 'Emmanuel had been with him for so long ...'

I stayed silent, my throat aching.

He glanced at me. 'Have there been threats against you?'

'He says not.' My mouth twisted around the words. 'My father being a top cop seems to guarantee I'll be left alone. But I feel so helpless about Grandad—no matter how many times he tells me he's going to sort it out.'

Paul smiled. 'I'd back your grandfather against Fayed any day. But I'll let him know he's got my help if he needs it.' He pointed a finger at me. 'Stay alert. If Fayed's got this much of a hard-on for Hamish, your father won't mean shit to him.'

My father doesn't mean shit to me.

CHAPTER THIRTEEN

I agreed that it was past time for me to go back and watch
Justin again, even though I could guess it would get us
nowhere. I took the Commodore this time, putting the
Corolla in the PMI slot, and parked near Justin's business
in almost the same place as before, noting that his vehicle
was no longer boxed in. If he'd gone out while I was away,
too bad. It was now mid-afternoon and I'd missed lunch.
There was a café on the corner behind me, so I grabbed
food and coffee and settled back in. Nothing happened.
The upstairs windows of Justin's workplace were tinted so
he could well be looking out at me, but I doubted it. I had
a feeling he thought it was all over now. He'd ticked all the
boxes, Diane's parents had received their report from PMI,
and now he could go on with his life and get cosy with his
new friend.

Except ... where was Diane?

I finished the meatball roll without dropping any of it down the front of my T-shirt—a miracle—and sipped on my lukewarm coffee. Surveillance was boring, and I needed to avoid thinking too much about Emmanuel's murder and Grandad being in danger, so I mentally ran through all the information I'd dug into about Diane: phone, bank, social media, friends. With Facebook open, I checked her page again, which had nothing on it since before she went missing, and then looked at the secret one she shared with her mother, which Amanda had given me access to.

There was only a desperate message from Amanda, begging her daughter to contact her: *Any way, any time, even just a couple of words. Please, love, let us know you're okay.* And a photo of Diane with her parents at the beach, all of them laughing happily while waves splashed behind them. It looked about ten years old, and it set off an ache in my chest that was hard to push away. I had a similar photo with my mum, the two of us arm in arm, walking along the beach at Lorne. A friend of hers had taken it and sent it to us. I'd had it printed out and framed. It was hidden away in my wardrobe now. I couldn't bear to look at it.

Grandad had said he couldn't bear to lose me, too. God, if he was killed …

I couldn't stand thinking about that, so I focused on Diane's photos again.

I knew it was possible that Diane had met someone capable of hiding her. That person could be someone exactly like Paul, whose experience and knowledge of secret paperwork and how people disappeared would be very handy. A high-ranking police officer. An ASIO operative. Maybe someone in the CIA she'd met in Bali.

Stop being ridiculous.

The other options—that she'd managed it herself, that she was merely hiding for a few weeks and then she'd come home, that she'd had a mental breakdown and killed herself somewhere remote—were very unlikely. The last one was possible, but someone would have found her by now. She'd need a car to get to the remote place. Even if she'd used a rental, that would have raised flags. Credit card, for a start.

That left me with murder, the option I didn't want to be left with. But it was why Paul and I had agreed I would tail Justin for a while. Because he was the obvious suspect and, despite him thinking he'd been clever, he'd actually made us more suspicious. I didn't need to note any of this on my phone. It was all stuck in my head, on constant replay.

Like Melinda's house and those keys in the door. Her father's cold tone on the phone. Emmanuel's body crumpled in the gutter. I blinked hard and rubbed my face, then turned on the car radio and made myself listen to someone pontificating on the ABC. It only helped a little bit.

At 4pm, a few staff left, and then at five, the rest of them ambled out. Looks of relief, of tiredness, two women giggling and heading off together, probably for a wine or two. Justin on his own, climbing into his ute and backing out. No sign of the friend. No, there she was, head down over her phone, reading. Then she looked up and waved at him just before he drove away. Little waggle of the fingers as usual. Maybe it was code for 'bed later'.

I started the car and followed Justin, Ms Waggle Fingers just a dot in my rear-view mirror. This afternoon, Justin went to a wine bar near his house and met two other men. Luckily, there was a garden area at the side where they sat, drinking a bottle of red between them and talking. All three wore business shirts and pants, their ties tucked away and top buttons open. Friends, then, not a business meeting. There was a lot of raucous laughter as the bottle emptied. Then they stood, shook hands and slapped each other on the shoulder a lot with more laughing, and everyone headed to their cars.

Justin simply drove home, into his garage. Mum was already there with the kids—through the windows, it looked like she was doing some serious talking to Justin, who listened, head cocked, expression disgruntled. My guess was she was sick of picking the kids up every day and was telling him he'd have to sort it out. He nodded several times, then a few minutes later, she left.

I waited, expecting Ms Waggle Fingers to arrive, but instead Uber Eats turned up with two bulging bags of plastic food containers. Justin wasn't eating Diane's freezer meals then. Maybe she'd known he never would. He'd probably toss them in a few months when he needed room for ice cream or a pork roast.

I settled in for a bit more boredom. But what kept me patient and calm was my conviction that Justin was telling lies. And sooner or later, I'd find out what the biggest one was.

It didn't look like Justin was going out tonight, not if he had the kids to look after. But while I was waiting, just in case he called in a babysitter, I made some calls. First one was to my new police detective mate, Scotcher.

'No,' he said shortly, 'still no sign of her in any of her usual places.'

At least they now knew her usual places. 'What about the ex?'

He let out an exasperated sigh. 'Are you going to call me and hassle me every day now?'

'Probably. But if you find her, I'll stop.' *So please do your damn job.*

'I get that you're worried, but can you let us do what we need to?'

I grimaced at the phone. 'Sure,' I snapped. 'Talk to you tomorrow. Bye.' He'd probably block my number, but I'd find a way to keep on his case, because it was my case, too.

Then I called Grandad, and he answered. 'I only talked to you yesterday, didn't I?' he said.

'Don't be a smartarse, Grandad,' I said. 'It's not a nice habit for an old man to develop.'

He hmphed. 'If you were here right now …'

'Seriously, are things okay? No sign of trouble?' I doubted he'd tell me anyway, but I had to ask.

'All good.' He paused. 'Did you tell Paul I was having problems?' His tone had hardened.

'He already knew. And Emmanuel's murder was on the news and in the papers.'

'Ach, it's fine. It'll blow over.' He was trying hard to sound unfussed, but it wasn't working.

I knew my grandfather. Murdering Emmanuel was not something he'd allow to 'blow over'. He was planning revenge now, big time, and Paul agreed, but we had to tread carefully. Grandad didn't like interference, no matter how it was framed.

'Well, you let me know if you need anything,' I said. 'Like a decent meal or a proper martini.' *Or for me to come over there with a sub-machine gun.* Not that I had one.

'You found your friend yet?' he asked.

'No.' I huffed out a breath. 'The police can't find her either.'

'You want me to do anything?'

'No, it's fine.' Melinda was unlikely to have been taken by someone Grandad knew. 'There is someone you can have a look at for me, though.'

'Just give me his name, lass.'

So I told him all about Nathan Gunn. 'I just want to know if he's been in Melbourne in the last few weeks or not. Or if he's got someone else to watch her or give her a hard time.'

'Righto, got all of that. I'll be in touch.'

It was time to go home to my little flat and chill out. Mostly I wanted to eat. The bags of Uber Eats had started my stomach rumbling, reminding me I needed some of that as well. Maybe I'd eat another Diane meal and think about Justin a bit more.

At home, I took out the second container and reheated it—meatballs in a garlic and red wine sauce on spaghetti. It was amazing, and I inhaled the aroma several times before tucking into it. Maybe I could sneak back to Justin's house and grab a few more meal boxes. If he preferred Uber Eats, he probably wouldn't miss a dozen dinners.

If he preferred the secretary, he wasn't missing Diane either.

As I ate and thought, a loud thump echoed through my ceiling. I turned the TV down a little and heard drunken shouting along with another couple of thumps. They sounded like someone either moving furniture or kicking it. Or kicking a person. I held my breath. When my upstairs neighbours started fighting, sooner or later I'd hear her screaming. When my windows were open, I could make out some of what they were saying. It was mostly him, shouting and cursing, and her protesting.

I ground my teeth. The meatballs had lost a lot of their allure. Sometimes the couple went for a few weeks without a disturbance, then it'd be several nights in a row. I hoped like hell this wasn't the start of a string of violent evenings. I couldn't stand that right now. I hated it at any time, but right now …

My neighbour against my back wall had had enough as well. He turned up his stereo and Adele sang her heart out, trying to blot out the thumps and shouts from above. A door slammed and footsteps banged down the stairwell, along with a shouted, 'Fuck youse then!' Peace came back to the building. I hated to think what it would be like in some of the cheaply built apartment towers in the city, where the person above you in high heels sounded like a stampede of Great Danes with long toenails.

I finished the meatballs and rinsed the container, added it to my recycling bag and headed for bed. I wanted to be up early and back at Justin's house, following him to work, making sure where he was. Then I'd check Melinda's house again as well, before going in to the office.

I have no idea what I dreamed about. Thankfully, not Emmanuel. My brain was giving me a rest. A fragment of the dream was me dressed in the same clothes as Ms Waggle Fingers and not being able to walk in the high heels. I woke up with a start and lay there for a while. Something was niggling at me and I knew some quiet staring at the ceiling often helped.

This time, though, it was like grasping threads hanging from a skirt hem. If I pulled on them … Nothing fell into my brain to enlighten me, but there were hanging threads all the same. When I went to the office, I'd work with Gang on those dating apps again. Try to save a record of all of Melinda's activity, because maybe it was time to hand her secret phone over to Detective Scotcher. Although how I would explain having it was going to be a problem.

Justin went jogging this morning, white wireless earbuds tucked into his ears and tanned legs pumping. It was harder to follow someone who was running, especially along quiet streets, but I had to in case he was meeting someone. Nup. He went to the park two blocks away, ran around it seven times and ran home again. Around 8.20am, he took his kids to school and drove to work. I waited for a while, but it seemed he was there for the day.

I'd planned to drive past Melinda's house, but what was the point? It would be locked up and I was sure she wasn't there. Neither was her phone now.

I marched into the PMI office, ready to get stuck into the dating apps.

Gang grinned at my request. 'Already done, girlfriend.' Today's glasses were square black frames and the lenses were …

I peered at him. 'Are they real glasses?'

He blushed. 'Don't tell anyone. My cousin informed me I was squinting all the time. Putting wrinkles on my face. I'm not happy though.'

'Why not? They look ultra cool.'

He pouted. 'But now I'm stuck with one pair. Can't afford different ones anymore.'

I kept my mouth shut on that one. 'So what have you copied? Can you copy her dating apps?'

'Yep, but I've also done screenshots of a lot of stuff. I did that first.' He handed the phone to me. 'Wasn't hard with the cables. It's all on my computer now, as well as our internal secure network and the cloud. I'll show you where to find it.'

A few minutes later, I was sitting at my own computer, looking through Melinda's photos and profiles. Nothing stood out to me. She was playing with personas, that's all. It didn't seem to have worked very well.

'Hey, is it normal to have so few guys interested? These photos of Melinda look nice.'

'It's like I said—a hundred men might give her a swipe or a tick or whatever. Doesn't mean anything unless she does it back. I've only saved things where she has connected.' His eyebrows wiggled. 'You should sign up for one of them and see how it works.'

We'd been down this road before. I shook my head and focused on the guys that Melinda had actually been in further contact with. Using her phone, I was able to go into each of their profiles and have a look at them. Nobody seemed to say much about themselves.

'Hang on …' I said. 'Weren't there five guys in this Jointly app that she connected with?'

'Yes, why?'

'One of them has disappeared.' I checked my notes. 'Jonathan Black.'

'He's probably deleted his profile,' Gang said.

'Isn't that a bit sus? Wasn't he the one wanting to meet her?'

'For coffee. There was nothing in the chat about a date. Definitely not dinner.'

'Hmm, okay.' I checked the time. 'Better go. Justin might leave work early.'

'Good luck.'

I grimaced. Luck wasn't what I needed with Justin. What I needed was concrete evidence. I just didn't know what that might be. An affair made him look bad—and sus as well—but it wasn't a crime. I drove to his workplace, in the Commodore this time, and sat across the street again. His ute was there, so I hoped that meant he was, too. This all felt a bit half-arsed, but the case wasn't a paying job anymore. It was only because Paul had a nagging feeling about Justin as well and that would wear off as soon as another important—paying—case came in that he wanted me on.

Five past five and there Justin was, backing his ute out, heading home. Same old story. Ute into his garage and the door down. It astonished me that he never seemed to twig that I was following him, but I thought that he'd surely notice after another few days. If he was up to no good, that is, and watching out for someone like me. The police had done their job and still not found Diane, but just in case something new had happened, I called Kayla.

'Is it wine time?' she asked straight away.

'I think it is,' I said. 'But can you please check something for me?'

'Lou, you know I can't look in the system again for you.'

'But you'll know the detectives whose case it is. I only need to know if they have found anything. Pleeeease?'

After a few seconds, she sighed. 'All right, but it's the last time.' She noted Diane's name, said, 'See you at the usual,' and hung up in my ear. I'd have to have a word with her about how rude that was. After she'd given me the information I wanted.

CHAPTER FOURTEEN

Kayla was late, so I bought the first round and chose a table in the back of the public bar, away from the trendy types who gathered in the beer garden, sounding like a tree full of mynahs. I'd nearly finished my glass of wine by the time she arrived. Her face was pale and she had deep lines I'd never noticed before.

'Hard case?' I asked, pushing a glass of red in front of her.

She swallowed half of the glass in one go and rubbed her forehead with her palm. 'Cases plural. Three shootings in two days, all around the Campbellfield area. Gang members. I dunno, the public always says it's a good thing when these guys knock each other off, but this is building into another war.'

A deep chill ran through me. 'Who's responsible?'

'Initially we thought it was a payback for the bikies' murders, but now there's evidence that something else is going on.'

I gazed across the bar at the three old guys who had undoubtedly been sitting there all afternoon, nursing their pots of beer and gossiping. One of them had dropped his walking stick and was having trouble straightening up. I had a flash of Grandad sitting in his armchair with a martini, Emmanuel bringing him a refill.

'What kind of something else?' I wasn't sure I wanted to know.

She gave me a sharp look. 'What do you know?'

'Nothing. Not about that. I promise.' And I didn't. It was just a guess.

'This is not your grandfather, is it?'

Kayla had always been sharp, and good at reading faces and eyes. I made my face go as still as possible. 'Grandad keeps pretty quiet these days.'

She scoffed. 'Yeah, sure he does.' She'd known Grandad as long as she'd known me, even been to his house before she found out more about what he did. 'Hey, I heard about Emmanuel. I'm really sorry.'

I grabbed my wine glass and gulped some down, then was able to say, 'Thanks.'

We sat in silence for a few moments, then I changed the subject. 'Did you ask about my missing friend?'

'Melinda Moreau? Yes. Nothing. No sign of her.' She drank more wine, rubbed her forehead again. It wasn't getting rid of the worry lines. 'How do you know her again?'

I explained. 'So I haven't known her long, but there is definitely something wrong.'

'Yes, I agree.'

'What are they doing about it?'

'Why don't you call Scotto yourself?' She grinned at me. 'He knows who you are.'

'Er, really? What does that mean?'

'Said he'd met you at the house, and you were like a terrier at his pants leg.'

'Ha ha, very funny.' I pushed my empty glass across the table. 'Your shout.'

While she went to the bar, I did as she suggested.

'Oh, it's you,' Scotcher said.

'I thought you were looking forward to talking to me. Kayla said you were.'

'Oh, for— What do you want?'

'Where are you up to with Melinda?'

'Nowhere. No sign of her and nobody has seen her. Even her neighbours don't know who she is. She's been like a hermit since she moved there.'

'With good reason. Her ex.'

'He hasn't left Sydney for at least two months.'

I weighed up my options, and went with the one that would get me into trouble. 'Did you know she was using dating apps?'

There was a long silence and I almost thought he'd hung up. 'Why didn't you tell us that before?'

'I didn't know myself until …'

'What?'

'She had a second phone, a hidden one. The dating stuff is on that.' I braced myself for the shouting.

It was louder than I feared and I held the phone away from my ear. Kayla had come back with our drinks and she made an astonished face at me, mouthing, 'Who's that?'

I tried the phone nearer my ear, caught some words.

'I want that phone right now. Where are you?'

Lucky for him, I had it in my bag; Paul had agreed I had to hand it over. I told Scotcher the name of the pub and this time he did hang up, after snapping, 'You'd better still be there in fifteen minutes.'

I was hoping he'd be on his own, and between Kayla and me, we could calm him down, although when I told her about the phone, she was mad at me, too.

'You should know better than that!'

'When I found it, nobody was taking any notice of my missing person report,' I said. 'Yes, I should have told Scotcher and his mate, but ...' I shrugged. I didn't have a good excuse, other than I'd wanted to do some investigating of my own. Who said ego is not a dirty word? Perhaps this wasn't the time to quote it.

I changed the subject again and we talked about Kayla's family for a while, until the pub door swung open and I sat back in my chair, watching Scotcher and Red Tie march across the bar. Except this time the tie was dark blue with stripes. Neither of them were smiling, and both exuded 'angry cop' vibes. More than one drinker in the bar slipped out through the side entrance.

Scotcher stopped in front of me and held out his hand. 'Phone.'

I pulled it out of my bag and gave it to him.

He looked at it and made a hmphing sound. 'Has it got a password on it?'

I gave it to them on the sticky note Gang had given to me. Scotcher handed both to his mate, who shoved them in his jacket pocket.

Scotcher glanced at Kayla. 'If she wasn't your mate, I'd charge her with obstruction.'

My mouth dropped open and anger fizzed up inside me. 'If it wasn't for me, you wouldn't even know she was missing!'

'Have *you* found her?'

'No. Not yet.'

'Shut your mouth then.'

They wheeled around and marched out again. I thought maybe they needed a soundtrack, like the marching music from *Peter and the Wolf*.

I slouched down on my chair, drank some wine and grumbled into the glass to myself, then looked at Kayla, expecting her to still be mad at me, too. Instead, she was trying hard not to burst out laughing, and failed. Little bits of spit landed on the table as she totally cracked up.

'Oh my God, your face!' she gasped. 'I think they were lucky you didn't attack them with a chair.'

'Yeah, well … How do you stand working with dickheads like that? And don't tell me the police force is no longer a pit of sexism.'

'It's improving,' she said. 'Somewhat. And a lot of the guys are good to work with. Better than some of the women even.' She pulled out a notebook and flicked through some pages. 'That reminds me, I heard something today that you might want to know. Diane Paterson.'

I sat up fast. 'She's been found?'

'No, but we have had a sighting. Noosa. Someone said they saw her in a restaurant there.'

'Verified? Someone who knew her?'

'No, a stranger who'd seen her photo in the media after she first disappeared. Swore it was her with a "rich-looking dude with grey hair and a tan". Said she looked happy and full of life.'

'A stranger. Could have been someone Justin paid to plant a false sighting.'

'Lou!' Kayla shook her head. 'What are you on these days? I thought I was cynical.'

'Yeah, well …' I decided to leave it at that. I'd have to tell Paul though, and he'd probably pull me off surveillance of Justin. Shit. I'd tell him tomorrow. Tomorrow night. I wanted to give Justin one more day, then I knew I'd have to move on. At least it would give me more time to look for Melinda.

Kayla decided to call it a night earlier than usual, and I was relieved she hadn't asked me about Emmanuel. I doubted she would be anywhere near his murder. But since she'd been a detective constable, she'd become more secretive about her cases and more tight-lipped around me generally. We used to drink wine and swap horror stories and she'd tell me all about her latest puzzle case or something she was trying to investigate, and I'd offer suggestions. Sometimes silly ones, just to wind her up, but mostly I found myself keen to contribute, to feel like I was part of it. Maybe deep down I wished I was still a copper. Maybe this was why working for Paul felt good, better than I had expected.

I suspected that if I wanted any more information or favours from Kayla, I'd better give her something back—quality intel or better suggestions or shout a round more often, now I was earning decent money. I'd been a waitress and bartender at Noddy's restaurant for too long. Used to living on leftovers from the kitchen and drinking too much at the end of my shift. Noddy was an old mate of Grandad's. He'd been in jail for ten years on robbery charges, and when he got out, Grandad staked him to open a restaurant; while he was inside, Noddy had done both a chef's course and a business course, and had discovered a talent for putting together gourmet dishes. I never asked Grandad why he'd put money in—no doubt there was a favour owed some-where. Favours made the world go around for those guys.

Which reminded me that Grandad had offered to set his bloodhounds onto Nathan Gunn. I'd call him later and check. For now, I texted Gang a reminder to look at the dat-ing apps again—maybe we could work out together what was bothering me—and headed home.

I was tempted to eat the third Diane dinner, but decided to save it for another day and made do with a toasted cheese and Vegemite sandwich and another glass of wine. My stocks were getting low so I mentally pencilled in a trip to the bottle shop.

So Diane had been sighted at Noosa. I didn't give that any credence at all. For every genuine sighting of a missing person or a suspect, there were another ninety-nine duds. I couldn't help thinking of the poor woman who'd lived at Avalon many years ago, and whose teacher husband had told everyone she'd left him. Someone had insisted they'd seen her up the coast on her way north, verifying his story that she'd caught a bus. It took an investigative podcast to ferret out enough evidence to indicate he'd killed her and finally he was charged. I wasn't sure if they'd ever found her body, although the police did a lot of digging around their swimming pool foundations and the house over the years.

I slumped down on my old couch and stared unseeing at the TV while I mulled over similar cases, ones I'd been involved in and ones I'd read or heard about. I knew I shouldn't. The result was that something inside me started to burn, like I was stirring embers that I should leave well alone.

Upstairs was quiet for a change. I went to bed and set my alarm for 5am. It was time for some self-directed therapy.

CHAPTER FIFTEEN

The gloves were big and fat on my hands. The insides felt greasy, the sum of my sweat and my punching, and I clenched harder. Right, left, right. Solid thunking, the bag swayed, punched again, the chain above twanging. The bag's black surface was impervious. It didn't care who I was, why I was punching, what my shit was all about. It absorbed the pounding, swayed and swung, like it had a deep, secret smile it refused to show me.

If I tried, I could hear it laughing.

People imagined I was hitting someone, visualising a face and smashing it. My father maybe. He wasn't worth the energy. And punching a bag wasn't the same anyway. Even if I'd taped his face in front of me. That'd give him power over me. Why would I do that?

I stepped away, wiped my face, flexed my hands. Stepped in, punched again, over and over and over. It would be better if the bag wasn't on a hook and chain. If it was solid and unmoving. It felt like it was always moving away from me. Always just slightly out of reach. I hated that.

I followed it across the floor, grabbed its bulk and rested my head against it. There was nobody else there, nobody I was fighting, nobody I was imagining. It was me and the bag. The bag was me. I was fighting who I'd become, who I didn't want to be. Fighting against the fire burning inside. Wanting a hose, an extinguisher. Wanting to stop the fire.

And yet not wanting to stop it.

Wanting to let it rage.

I clenched my fingers hard and started punching again.

CHAPTER SIXTEEN

Outside Justin's house this morning, I parked further back, wanting to make sure he wouldn't notice me. I was sure Paul would pull me off this surveillance today, but I might just continue to drop around now and then, if he did. I'd been told I had a cop's instinct for wrongness, but I didn't believe that. I suspected everybody of doing something dodgy—it was just a matter of how much. Justin kept zapping my dodgy meter bigtime.

No run this morning. He was late, or else the kids had made him late. There was a bit of shouting as they raced to the ute in the driveway. The kids looked sulky, dragging their feet, but he literally pushed them both towards the back and slammed the doors shut as soon as their legs were in. The ute roared off down the street and I followed him to the school and then to work. He was dressed in khaki work-wear today, as well as boots, so I guessed he was planning on site visits. Once he had parked at work and gone inside, I called Paul and used my speaker in case I needed both hands to start the car quickly.

'I'm outside Justin's business. He looks dressed for going out to building sites.'

'Diane has been sighted in Noosa.'

I sighed. 'I know. I heard last night. But you know how rarely those pan out.'

'Still …' There was a long pause. 'Give it one more day, okay? Then I'll have to put you onto something else.'

What I'd predicted. It still grated on me. 'Yep, okay.'

'Nothing on Melinda?'

'I handed the second phone over to the detectives last night. They weren't happy.'

'Let's see what they do with it, eh?' Paul's tone was hard to read.

'You think they'll find her?'

'When you couldn't?' He laughed. 'You've got more motivation, Lou. Don't worry, I'll get Gang onto it again today. He's saved all of the stuff off the phone. I'll let you know if anything comes up.'

'Thanks. I'll report in later.'

I hung up and settled down in my seat, but a gnawing dread spread through my guts. I couldn't think what else to do, so I called Melinda again. On her main phone she'd left in the kitchen. To my great surprise, someone answered.

'Melinda Moreau's phone. Who is this, please?'

It was a male voice, but not Scotcher.

'It's Louisa, her friend. Is she there?'

'Please repeat your phone number to me, Louisa.'

I did so. 'Who is this?' I'd kind of guessed already.

'This is Tye from Forensics. I've been working to open this phone and then you called. Can you stay on the line, please?'

'Why?'

'It was locked and I wasn't getting very far gaining access. Do you know your friend's password, by any chance?'

'Not for that phone, but surely the detectives gave you the password from her other phone?'

'No ... Do you know where the other phone is?'

'It should be with you as well.'

'Okay, hang on.' There was a faint clunk as he put the phone down and then various rustling and tapping noises. I waited, making sure the speaker volume was the highest it could go. I wanted to know what was on Melinda's phone, too.

'Hello?' I called. 'Are you having any luck?'

'Yes, I've retrieved it. It's just come in.' His voice faded away and then I heard him humming. 'Yeah, that's what I want. Mmm-hmm.' And more humming. Then he was back. 'Thanks. She used the same for both. There was hardly anything on this first one.'

'Oh. Can you tell me what you found? Please?'

'I can't, sorry.'

'But ... just tell me one thing. Are there dating apps on that phone?'

Silence. 'Um ...'

'Come on, please. She's my friend and she's missing. That's all I want to know.'

'Well ... no, there aren't. Like I said, there's hardly anything.'

I let go of the steering wheel I'd been gripping so hard that my hands ached. 'Okay, thanks. I'm hanging up now, all right?'

'Yes. Thanks for your help. Bye.'

I flexed my fingers a few times. Nothing on that phone. Yet it seemed like it was her main phone and the other one was for the dating stuff. Compartmentalised life. Did that start before or after her relationship with Nathan Gunn?

I sat there all morning, my brain jumping from Diane to Melinda and back again. It was getting me nowhere. I saw Ms Waggle Fingers get a tray of coffees at the café on the corner and a few people from her office bought lunch. I'd packed the last Diane dinner container in a cooler bag for a handy meal, but I wasn't in the mood for it so I bought a sandwich and coffee for myself at the café and hunkered down again. I got desperate for a pee and sneaked into the toilet at the petrol place a bit further up, racing to get it done and splashing water all down my front. No more coffee for me. Maybe I'd have to buy one of those things women use to pee into when they're travelling. I resorted to listening to talkback radio until I found myself shouting at people and switched it off.

When Justin came out of his building around 2pm, my sigh of relief nearly lifted the roof off the car. He was probably doing site visits, but following him would mean a change of scenery at least.

Except he drove to his own house. Early afternoon get-together with Ms Waggle Fingers? But then why wasn't she in the ute with him?

I parked further up again and used the binoculars. He opened his garage door and reversed in, then lowered the door again. Maybe he was having an afternoon nap without telling anyone. I debated going for a little walk and looking for movement inside, but there wasn't a good reason to reveal myself. I stayed put.

Fifteen minutes later, the garage door rolled up and Justin's ute emerged. The door went down and he headed off in the opposite direction. Not going back to the business then. I tapped my phone to call Paul on speaker and set off after Justin.

'Lou. What's happening?'

'Probably nothing.' I told him the latest.

'Right, keep following him. Let me know if he does anything weird.'

'Will do.'

He was doing site visits indeed, white safety helmet on his head. Starting in Flemington, moving out to Caroline Springs, back to Tarneit and then north again to Sydenham. It was getting late in the day, I was starving again, and it seemed Justin was just doing his job. He even got his hands dirty a few times, lifting bricks and lengths of timber to check things. After watching him walk inside a construction site at Sydenham that looked like it was going to be a small office block, I decided to eat quickly. I pulled the cooler bag up from the passenger seat foot well and opened it, taking out a fork and the plastic container, wondering what today's gourmet offering would be. As soon as I took the lid off, my mouth watered, even though the food was cold. Kung Pao chicken, it had to be.

It was amazingly delicious. Diane should have been a chef. I sighed in ecstasy and wondered if I could get Justin to give me all the containers in the freezer that he didn't seem to be interested in. I finished the chicken in record time and was being disgusting, trying to lick the inside of the container, when I noticed something on the bottom of it.

I turned it over and there was a tiny printed label. *Proudly made for you by Golden Peacock Restaurant.* I knew the Golden Peacock. It had won awards.

My stomach had stopped rumbling, but my brain whirred into action like a super computer. Why would Justin lie and say Diane had cooked all these dinners for him and the kids if he'd bought them from a restaurant? Or had Diane lied and been buying them all along?

I grabbed my phone, googled and then called the Golden Peacock, asking for the manager. It was urgent, I said.

'This is Mr Lu. How can I help?'

'Mr Lu, I'm ringing for Mr Paterson, Justin Paterson.'

'Ah, Mr Paterson wants to make another order?'

'No, I mean yes. Kind of. When did he order last?'

'Only a few weeks ago. He said for a big party. He's having another one?'

'Not right away,' I said. 'I'll let you know.'

I hung up and googled other restaurants close to Justin's house. One French, one Italian, a few other bistro-type places. The meals in the other containers Justin had given me matched dishes on the online menus of the French and Italian places. The Italian restaurant was famous for its meatballs, apparently. What had been my first thought when he'd showed me the freezer full of food? That she'd cooked it all to make up for the fact she was leaving him and the kids.

No, hang on. *He'd* told me that.

Ahead of me, Justin strolled out of the office building, taking off his hard hat and swinging it from one hand as he chatted to the foreman. There was a fair bit of back slapping and guffawing, which made me wonder about how well built the construction project was, and then Justin waved and hopped into his ute. It was well after 5pm by now, which was why there were no workers left on site. Avoiding overtime payments to them, no doubt.

I expected Justin to head for home, but he didn't. Instead, he turned left and right a couple of times, ending up on Kings Road heading north. I stayed back a little bit as we got close to the Calder Freeway interchange, thinking he might be heading to the Tullamarine Freeway as an easy way back to the city. But he turned left onto the Calder and accelerated.

Shit! What was out this way? Housing developments galore. I racked my brains. Sunbury. Diggers Rest. New Gisborne. He was bloody keen if he was visiting sites now, long after the workers had knocked off for the day. Unless he suspected someone of theft or dodgy building and he was doing a secret check.

But he kept going. I checked my petrol gauge, worried I'd run out. I estimated I'd be okay as long as he didn't go further than Bendigo.

The sun wasn't due to set for a while, and the longer Justin drove, the harder it would be to follow him without him noticing me. But the wind had risen and dark clouds were filling the sky. We could hit rain soon. As if he'd noticed, he turned his headlights on, but I kept mine off. Finally, past Woodend, he took an exit ramp and turned right at the top. This was the road to Lancefield. Foreign country to me.

It wasn't long before I saw the signs for Hanging Rock, and the huge rock formation looming against the grim sky.

Justin turned left again and put the boot in, speeding along the narrow road. I'd done enough country driving in my younger days to see he was taking a risk. Anyone who knew anything didn't speed around this time of night. If a roo bounded out on the road, stunned by his headlights, there was no way to avoid it.

Justin must have had the gods on his side. He kept going, heedless of roos, sliding into the sharp turn at Newham and accelerating again. I was well back now, not willing to take the risk he'd twig to being shadowed. I tried to follow his headlights instead. Surely he'd stop sooner or later.

We came into Lancefield, slowing for the town limit, down the main street, me staying even further back as there were streetlights here. When I got a bit too close for my own comfort, I pulled over and parked, squinting along the wide main street, watching Justin's tail-lights as best I could. Pub? Milk bar? Petrol? Nup. Justin turned left at the highway and disappeared.

I roared down the main street, praying nobody would stagger out of the pub and get in my way, and swung left, grateful the highway was empty. There were two sets of tail-lights ahead of me and I had no idea which one was Justin's. Across the little bridge they went, one going straight ahead, one turning left. I accelerated harder and the Commodore leapt forward, catching up a bit.

At the turn-off, I peered again at the vehicle that was heading up the road to my left. The one going straight ahead was gone. I had to decide. The one on my left was white and big. I turned and followed, soon finding myself on a road going up between an avenue of looming gum trees. Burke and Wills Track. Two explorers who had died in the out-back somewhere. Not a good omen.

I spotted the tail-lights ahead of me, then brake lights. The Track was winding here and a bit steep. I followed, not at all convinced I was after the right vehicle, but it was too late to change my mind. And I couldn't risk getting too close. Besides, if Justin had gone the other way, where the hell would he be going at this time of night?

That thought didn't help. If this car was him, the same question applied.

Bend after bend, more looming trees with black trunks, an occasional house. Then the tail-lights disappeared.

I slowed right down, my heart flapping like a mad bird. He couldn't have gone off the road, could he? Had he had an accident? Then I saw it. A track off to my left, a bent road sign. By then I was past it, but I was sure I'd seen faint lights and something white down there. I pulled into the next driveway a couple of hundred metres ahead, did a fast three-pointer and drove back slowly. Fifty metres back from the track, there was a pull-off area marked 'School Bus'. I turned in and parked.

I couldn't just sit there. I wanted to know what he was doing. I debated calling Paul, but I needed to get down that track and check first if it really was Justin. It was almost dark now, the sky thick and heavy, wind thrashing the gum trees above me. It smelled like rain in the air. I walked in along the track, taking it slowly, unable to use my phone torch to see where I was going because it would alert him. Once my eyes got used to the gloom, it wasn't so bad, but I seemed to walk for ages before I finally saw the white ute ahead of me. Hot relief rushed through me.

The ute was parked in an area bordered by logs that looked like something the council environment people might construct to stop people hooning off down the bush tracks. I hid behind a tree and watched but there was no sign of Justin and, when I pushed past the bracken under the trees to look in the driver's window, the cab was empty.

Where was he? I didn't dare try the doors of the ute in case I set off the alarm. The back canopy had Perspex windows and I peered through them, but all I could see was a large, rumpled tarpaulin. I walked a little further from the parking area and circled around, searching for signs of him, but there was nothing. It was as if he'd disappeared into the bush forever.

I had no idea what he was doing here and there was no sign of which direction he'd gone in. There were four or five tracks that were possible, all starting from the parking area. The paranoid-suspicious part of me said he was burying Diane's body. The less paranoid-suspicious part said he was meeting someone or doing some camping to get away from it all. Unlikely to come here at night though. I found a spot behind a dense patch of bracken from where I could still see his vehicle and settled down to wait, glad it wasn't the middle of bloody winter. I sent Paul a fast text, explaining where I was, then muted my phone and pushed it deep into my bag so I wouldn't be tempted to look at it and alert Justin with the light. The wind made a sound through the trees like waves crashing on the sand, but thankfully the rain held off.

About half an hour later, Justin came back, swinging a torch with a strong beam and carrying something. I thought it might be a spade but it was the wrong shape, more like a large, long-handled pickaxe. He put it in the rear of the ute and got in, then drove back down the track. Even if I ran, there was no way I'd make it to my car before he'd disappeared.

I sighed and unmuted my phone, and immediately it rang, showing an anonymous caller.

'Hello, Lou Alcott.'

'Hello, it's Diane Paterson.' Her voice was warm and friendly.

What the fuck? 'Oh, yes?' I was struggling to sound normal.

'I just wanted you to know I'm fine. I've gone away for a while. Up north. You don't need to look for me. Everything's fine.'

'Right. Um … did Justin tell you to call me?'

'No, a friend thought I should call, to save everyone trouble.' She paused for a moment. 'All right?'

'Sure. Thanks for calling.'

'No problem. By-eee.'

If that was really Diane Paterson, I'd eat my Julia Gillard T-shirt. I called Paul and filled him in.

'You think he's buried her in the bush there?'

'He's just tried to put everyone off the scent by getting some woman to call me, pretending to be Diane. Could be his girlfriend from the office, or a friend. Why would he do that unless he was up to no good?'

'Do you know where he went with the pickaxe?'

'No idea, and I don't have a torch, other than what's on my phone.'

'Hmm.' He paused, obviously thinking it through. 'Can you stay there? In case he comes back? Right now, there's no point both of us being out there. I'm going to stake out his house.'

'I'll find somewhere to park here and sleep in the car.' That meant a long, uncomfortable night, but at least I could pee behind a tree. 'I'll go looking as soon as it's light. When I find out what he was doing here, I'll call you, okay?'

'Okay,' Paul said. 'I'll call you if he leaves his house. Check in with me now and then. There's a box of phone chargers in the boot if you need one.'

'Good, thanks.' I disconnected, went and collected the Commodore and drove down the track to the parking area. I doubted Justin would return—it was more than an hour's drive to his house and he'd have kids to sort out. A bit later, Paul texted me to say Justin was home, and he'd let me know if he left again. It was an uncomfortable night, and I was cold and hungry, wishing I was in my car with its sleeping bag and snacks, but I suffered it, impatient for the sun to rise.

As soon as it was light enough, I set off along the faint path where I was pretty sure I'd seen Justin.

It didn't take as long as I'd thought. There was a lot of leaf litter around and, in the dark, Justin had thrown a bit of it over his refilled hole, but not enough to cover up the freshly turned darker soil. I'd brought rubber gloves as well as latex, but I only had the small pinch bar I'd found in the tyre-changing kit. It was enough to move the soil aside.

I found her handbag first, black leather, its buckles clogged with dirt, and lifted it out carefully. The top was unzipped and I could see a phone and some bits of makeup and tissues. I laid it aside and kept scooping out the soil, but I could already make out a large object wrapped in plastic.

Too small to be a body though. Maybe it was clothes. But when I'd brushed more dirt off and could see into the hole properly, I realised. Diane might have tried to walk away from Justin, but she hadn't got far—and here were her legs to prove it.

I screamed, once, long and harsh and throat-rasping. Birds scattered above me, and a few gum leaves drifted down. I stayed bent over for a few seconds, muttering as many four-letter words as I could think of. None of them came close to describing Justin Paterson. How I wished I'd caught him here so I could have smashed him over the head with my steel bar.

None of it was enough, it'd never be enough, but it let out some of what I was feeling so I could reach for my phone and call Paul.

CHAPTER SEVENTEEN

'I found Diane,' I said to Paul, and had to clamp my teeth together to stop the tears.

'In the bush?'

'Yep.'

'You have to call it in.'

'Thing is ...' I sucked in a breath, closed my eyes against the plastic nightmare. 'It's only part of her.'

'Fuck.' He made a strangled sound. 'So there could be other parts all over Melbourne.'

'Yep.'

'All right. You call it in now, normal channels, make it official since you're first on the scene. I'll give you ten minutes, then I'll call someone I know in Homicide and get them onto it. They need to jump fast. He might already be setting off to bury another part somewhere.'

I shuddered. 'Okay. Call me back when you're done talking to them?'

'Sure.' He paused. 'Are you all right, Lou?'

Was I? No. But. 'Yep. I'll cope.'

'Good on you.'

Paul disconnected and I dialed 000, asked for police and then told the dispatcher what I'd found. 'If you pass my number on to the police officer at Lancefield station, they'll know where to come and then direct other officers.'

'So it's not a complete body?' she asked. 'Ambulance not required?'

'Er, no. Just police and forensics.'

'Stay on the line, please.'

I waited, talked some more, then talked to the senior constable at Lancefield.

'Describe where you are, please.'

I told him about the track, the turn-off by the bus stop, the parking area. 'You'll see my car. The bush track I'm on is the one that exits the parking area at the opposite end to my car.'

'Why don't you come back to the parking area and meet me?'

I didn't want to. I didn't want to leave Diane alone, but I knew I was being a bit silly. And the longer I stayed here, I'd probably contaminate the scene even more. 'Okay. I'll walk back now.'

Fifteen minutes later, the senior constable arrived in his white four-wheel drive with the blue-checkered markings. No lights or siren needed. He parked outside the parking area, stepped out, gave me the once-over, shut his door and came across to where I sat on a log.

'I'm Senior Constable Shane Alexander. You found the body and called it in, I presume.'

That was stating the obvious. 'I'm Louisa Alcott.'

'How did you find it?'

'I'm a private investigator.' I ignored his instant bristle and showed him my licence. 'We were asked to investigate the disappearance of a woman, Diane Paterson, by her parents. I've been following the husband for the past few days. He led me here last night. After he left, I waited until it was light and walked where I'd seen him go. I saw evidence of digging.'

His face had flushed bright red. 'You dug up the body? You should have left it alone!'

'He could have been burying anything. Money from his business. Her possessions. Evidence he'd killed her. What I found was her legs.'

The redness faded rapidly and he swallowed hard. 'Her legs. Shit.' He looked around. 'Right, I'm going to check what you've told me. I'll try not to create further contamination, if you're telling the truth. Then I'll call it in.'

'My boss …' I didn't want to get further offside with this guy. 'Never mind. I'll have to call him soon. Or he'll call me.'

Alexander nodded and pointed to my car. 'You'd better wait over there. This could take a while.'

If Paul had already got onto Homicide, it would take less time than Alexander imagined, but I wasn't going to offer any more information than I already had. I watched as he followed the track I'd pointed him to, walking along the side of it, out of sight. I sat in a bit of a daze, felt someone watching me and realised it was a large kookaburra on a branch, eyeballing me. Eventually, it got bored and flew away.

Alexander came back, walking fast now, on his phone. As he talked and gestured, he scanned the parking area, avoiding any tyre marks showing in the softer earth, and then proceeded to cordon off the whole area with crime scene tape, sealing me inside. I'd guessed it was going to happen, so I didn't protest.

Just as he'd finished tying off the last knot in the tape, my phone rang. Paul. At last.

'Hi, how's it going?'

I described Alexander and his procedures so far.

'Homicide is on its way. Plus they've got someone watching Justin now, so I can go home.'

'You've been there all night?'

'Yeah, he came back about nine thirty. It's nearly time to take the kids to school, so they can follow him and see what he does.'

'He'll probably go to work like nothing has happened.'

'You said he came home before he started his site visits?'

'Yes. He was only there about fifteen minutes.'

'Long enough to get what he wanted, probably from the freezer.'

I gasped, swallowed and coughed. 'You think the rest of her is still there?'

'It's very possible. If he put a lock on it, he wouldn't have to worry about the kids or anyone looking inside.' Paul was trying to be calm and business-like, but I heard the small break in his voice.

'He really is a clever bastard, isn't he?' I snarled. 'He deserves bloody life for this.'

'He'll get it, don't worry. Thanks to you.'

'Me? I just followed him.' Again, I wished I'd followed him right to the burial site and got rid of him permanently. Except that would only be my kind of justice.

'It was you who convinced me to stay on him, that he was up to something.'

'Yeah, well …' I let out a huge sigh. 'Too bloody late to help poor Diane.'

'I think she was dead long before her parents came to us,' Paul said.

'Yeah, I know.' They were going to be gutted by this.

'Can I leave you to deal with the police stuff? You might be there for a fair while.'

'I expected that. I'd kill for a coffee and a bacon and egg roll though.'

'Let me know how you're going later this morning. You might have to wait for food. Can't imagine there's Uber Eats in Lancefield.'

I hung up and my stomach grumbled loudly. I searched the car just in case. I found half a bottle of water under my seat and a squashed KitKat bar in the glove box. Saved. I couldn't care less about who'd drunk the first half of the water.

Just as I shoved the last bit of KitKat into my mouth, Alexander came over to my car, circling around the parking area behind the logs and coming up on my right. He tapped on the window, which I let down.

'I need to take a quick statement from you before Homicide gets here,' he said.

'Sure, fire away.'

He asked a few questions, but I basically repeated what I'd told him before.

'What did you use to dig up the, er, body?' He winced.

'Pinch bar out of the boot. It was all I had.'

'Right. Where is it now?'

I had to think about that. 'I left it by the hole. Crime scene techs will want it, I guess. My fingerprints and DNA will be on the system.'

A few seconds of stony silence where he assumed the worst.

'I was in the police force for three years,' I said.

'Right.' He scribbled a bit more. 'Louisa Alcott, you said?'

'Yep.'

'Any relation to Assistant Commissioner Alcott?'

I turned and looked at him; he was smiling. For a moment, I almost said yes, just to see the grin wiped off, but old habits kicked in. 'No, no relation.'

'All right then. Homicide ETA is apparently five minutes, as long as they don't get lost. Someone had notified them already.'

I nodded and he went off to his four-wheel drive, stowing his notebook in his pocket and checking he had enough crime scene tape. He'd have to do the whole track as well as a wide cordon around the burial site.

The first of the Homicide team arrived, a man and woman who climbed out of a BMW. I got out of the Commodore and stood by the door, waiting. They spoke to Alexander for a few minutes; he read a few things from his notebook and there were several assessing glances at me. Then the two of them trod carefully around the back of the logs to where I stood.

'Ms Alcott?' the man asked. I nodded. 'I'm Detective Sergeant Mike Collins. This is Detective Constable Mary

Costa.' She gave me a half-smile. 'You were following the man who buried the body?'

'Yes, as part of my job,' I said.

'You work for Paul Marshall?' Costa asked.

'Yes.'

Collins frowned. 'You told Senior Constable Alexander that there was no need for an ambulance?'

'There's not a whole body there.' My face felt suddenly hot and prickly. Poor Diane, reduced to this. That fucking bastard. I rubbed my eyes and refocused. 'There do seem to be a few of her—Diane's—possessions thrown in there, too. A handbag, at least.'

'Okay, I'll make a note of that.' He gazed around the clearing and then up into the gum tree canopy. 'Crime Scene are nearly here.'

Sure enough, a white van appeared at the far end of the gravel road, trundling slowly towards us and stopping behind Collins's car. Two techs in uniform got out and came to the crime scene tape, scanning the parking area, us and the bush. One of them came over to us, following the path around the logs. I went through what had happened and agreed they should photograph my footwear soles and tyres first so I could leave.

Once that was done, the crime scene duo put on their white suits, gathered a mountain of gear and skirted the parking area again. The second tech took a number of photos of the half-a-dozen tyre tracks on that side, then they set off down the track, keeping to the edges and taking photos of any footprints, numbering the clearest ones as they went.

Collins came back to me. 'Paterson is being watched now. What put you onto him?'

'Small things. He was too pushy. And too charming. Then he just switched it all off. It was weird.' I folded my arms tightly. 'Do you think you'll find the rest of her?'

'I hope so,' he said grimly. 'These guys ... what goes on in their heads ...' He huffed out a sharp breath.

When the second tech came back to get them, Collins said I could go and went to suit up. Costa was already in hers, and pulled the hood over her curly black hair. They left me there and set off down the track, again keeping to the sides. They probably didn't have enough stepping plates to do two hundred metres.

I got into the Commodore and went to the Facebook page that Diane shared with her mum. The photo of her laughing with her two kids sent a stab of pain through my chest. How the fuck did you tell someone their daughter was cut up into pieces and buried in different places? Or that bits of her were still in a freezer? Her mum and dad probably wouldn't even get to see their grandkids. The tight-mouthed woman—Justin's mother—would keep them to herself, no doubt, backed up by his father.

It wasn't bloody fair. It made me want to scream. Again.

I pushed the button to turn off my phone screen and threw it onto the passenger seat, trying to remember what Paul had said, and trust that he'd be monitoring whatever the police were doing closely. He had better contacts than me. Time I got out of there, if only to find food and coffee and refuel my body.

Alexander gave me a one-finger wave as he lifted the tape for me, and I was soon in Lancefield, buying an egg and bacon roll and strong coffee, and then finding I had no appetite for either. I forced them down all the same and then headed back to Melbourne, choosing the Romsey-and-airport route this time.

As if my brain couldn't stand thinking about Diane anymore, it zeroed in on Melinda again. At the airport viewing area, I pulled in and watched a few planes howl overhead and land ahead of me, their wings tilting and righting like seagulls coming in on a beach. I wanted to call Melinda's phone, but I knew I'd be wasting my time.

I'd waste some of Scotcher's time instead.

CHAPTER EIGHTEEN

'I'm going to block you from my phone,' was Scotcher's opening line.

'Did you hear about Diane Paterson?' I countered.

'Who? Oh, the missing woman. Yeah, they found part of her up in the bush.' It took him a couple of seconds. 'Wait, that was you? You found her?'

'Yep.'

Silence.

'Hello? You still there?' I said.

'Yes, unfortunately,' he said dryly.

'No need to be rude.' But I was smiling, just a little. 'Any news on Melinda?'

'No, sorry.' He took the phone away from his mouth and there was a lot of muffled talking that I couldn't make out. Then he was back. 'It's been confirmed that Nathan Gunn never left Sydney. Hasn't left Sydney for at least two months.'

I sighed loudly. I'd been hoping they could zoom in on Gunn and make him confess. 'How are you going with the dating apps?'

'We're following up the last of the guys she connected with.'

'There's one that deleted himself.' I bit the inside of my cheek. What had I said that for? Was I trying to impress him? For fuck's sake.

His tone was chilly again. 'I suggest you get that information over to me ASAP.'

'I'll do that when I get back to the office.'

'Good.' And he was gone.

I scowled at the screen. 'Dickhead.' But I did as he asked, giving Gang his number and the request when I'd finished checking in with Paul, who told me to take the rest of the day off.

'I'll need a report, Lou,' he said, 'but it can wait. I assume you'll have to give the police a full statement?'

'Tomorrow.'

'Nothing on Melinda?' His tone was sympathetic, and I steeled myself against it.

'No. They're following up on all her dating connections now.'

'Okay. See you tomorrow.'

I wanted to be in the office, because I knew otherwise I'd just sit at home and stew on things. So I went to the boxing gym and spent an hour on the punching bag, which tired me out, but it didn't slow down my whirring, agitated brain one bit. Then I went for a long walk along Williamstown Beach and through the wetlands and coastal park, called Jawbone Reserve for some reason, and back. That didn't help much either. But it filled in enough hours that I could pick up fish and chips and wine on the way home, and try not to think about those fake dinners I'd had in my freezer and eaten so greedily.

Back in my flat, I pulled the curtains in both rooms rather than have to look out at the scenery, which was the rear of the building next door. The fish and chips were soggy and I washed them down with more wine than was sensible—according to my swimming head—so I resorted to several cups of tea and then several trips to the bathroom for a wee.

Three hours later, I was watching a weird science fiction series on Netflix and trying to stop thinking about Melinda's disappearance. I'd been over and over everything. The dating apps offered the most, but that was Scotcher's job now. Still, where was she? Every now and then, I got a flash of the grave where I found Diane's legs, but instead it was Emmanuel I dug up. And it was his body like I'd seen it in the gutter. It was worse than a nightmare—I was still awake. The flashes sent my heart racing and I stared at the TV screen, trying to replace the picture with their talking heads and spaceship gadgets.

When some alien thing reached out of a machine and skewered a woman, that was the final straw. I grabbed the remote and turned it off.

A woman's scream came from somewhere above me and I shot out of my armchair, head spinning, hands over my head. At first I thought it was a loud TV, then I realised it was the couple on the next floor again. That was all I needed. I'd hoped they'd settled down. There were scuffling feet, a couple of thumps and another short scream. Then she started sobbing. Another short scream and a loud gasp, like he'd kicked her in the guts.

I ran into my hallway and then stopped. What was I doing? *Don't interfere.* Yeah, sure. Like I was going to stand down here and listen to more of that, until she was either unconscious or dead. No fucking way. I rang 000, like I had before, but this time I made it urgent.

'She's either dying or dead,' I said. 'He's hurt her badly before. She needs an ambulance, pronto, and he needs to be arrested and removed.'

The dispatcher tried to go through the standard questions, I gave my name and address quickly and added, 'I'm going up there. Tell the ambulance and cops to hurry up, or her death will be on their heads.'

I disconnected, shoved my phone and door key into my pocket and let myself out, closing my door quietly. I knew nobody else would be out on the stairs. They'd all be turning their TVs up louder so they didn't have to hear what was going on.

The front door of flat 11 showed signs of being kicked and punched. I put my ear to the panel and listened—she was crying in big gasps, and then he shouted, 'Fucken shut up or you'll get another one.' Then he must have kicked or hit her again, and she went quiet.

I looked at the flimsy door. One good kick and it would probably give way. I badly wanted to force my way in and give him some of his own punches and kicks. But my record—

What did it matter? Against her life?

I listened again. No sound from her, but there were thumps. I couldn't tell if they were coming from him or her. I leaned against the door, my body aching with the desire to smash his head in, my head pounding, heart going like a jackhammer. *Don't go in there.* I might save her; I might mess up and he'd get off, like the last bastard did— my attack on him meant in the end he got off on the assault charges. My fault.

His voice rose again. 'Fucken slut, I'll fucken teach you …'

I slammed my hand on the door, over and over, shouting, 'Don't you bloody touch her, you bastard! The cops are coming!'

Silence. He'd heard me.

Then footsteps thundering up from below me on the stairs.

'Thank fuck.' I bowed my head for a second, relief like an icy shower over me.

A head, then a uniform, and behind him, another one. A stocky constable, puffing from the three levels of stairs, staring at me. 'Did you call us?'

'Yep. They're in there. She sounds in a bad way. He's drunk.'

'Out of the way. Stand over there, please, and stay there.' He pointed to the end of the landing. One big boot and the door bounced inwards. They were both armed and not taking any unnecessary risks, entering slowly, scanning the hallway and rooms. I could see them in my mind. I'd done it so many times myself.

Voices below as the paramedics arrived and climbed upwards. They checked with the officers before going in. Neither of them wanted to be assaulted. That had happened before, too. Even though I knew in my head what was happening inside, I wanted to be in there myself, helping somehow. Making sure they knew this wasn't the first time, that something had to be done. Something has to be done. I got a flash of Diane's legs in the hole, the plastic fogging and her knees, and I gagged, bending over.

The second constable, a young woman who looked like she was just out of high school, came out and found me like that. 'You okay?'

'Yeah.' I straightened a little. 'Is she going to be all right?'

'Probably. She's pretty badly injured though.'

I shook my head. 'I thought he was going to kill her this time. I just …' I sucked in a breath, blinking back tears. 'Bastard. Fucking bastard.' And I meant not just him but Justin fucking Paterson and every other man who damaged women because they believed they could. Because they thought—

I dropped my head. It was too much.

I glanced up at the officer. Her face was pale, her freckles standing out in dark splotches, her eyes glassy.

'He's handcuffed. We'll bring him out in a minute. You might want to go back to your apartment.' She understood somehow that if I saw him, I might not be able to hold back. 'Someone will come down and take your statement shortly.'

'Yep,' I croaked. 'I'll do that.' I shuffled off downstairs and let myself in, although it took three tries for my shaking hand to get the key into the lock.

When a detective finally came, I was steady again—from a strong cup of tea, not wine. I wanted to be able to give a clear account, get the bastard put away if I could. The detective was a brusque, older man who first wanted to confirm it was me who called 000 and to tell him what I'd heard. 'Does this happen often?' he asked.

'Every couple of weeks,' I said. 'I hadn't heard them for a while. This time it sounded really bad. Is she all right?'

'She's been taken to hospital,' he said, telling me nothing.

'But is she all right?' My voice had sharpened and at first he scowled at me, then he relented.

'She's serious but they said she's stable.'

'Okay, thanks.' I breathed in and out. 'That's good.' Focused again. 'I hope he's not going to be bailed this time.'

He frowned. 'Please tell me what happened.'

I related the history of violence above me, injuries I'd seen on her, then my actions just before.

'You didn't enter their apartment?'

I held up my hands. 'I listened at the door, and when it sounded like he was having another go, I banged on the door and yelled out.'

'That was taking a bit of a risk.'

'Would you rather I left her to be beaten to death?' I said sharply. 'He's too gutless to come out and tackle me anyway.'

'Right, thank you.' He scribbled again, then closed his notebook. 'I'll take it from here. Or we will. The police.'

That was the trouble. The hospital patched her up, the police charged him, let him go on bail or let him off with a good behaviour bond, and it started all over again.

I thanked him, for doing his job if nothing else, and showed him out. Then I slid down the hallway wall and sat on the floor, head in hands. For the first time, I truly regretted leaving the force. Not because of the circumstances, but because I'd just learned how totally ineffectual I was now. I had no authority to do anything except stand at a door and listen and shout.

What use was that?

CHAPTER NINETEEN

I had to go into my local station to meet a DC Singh and make a formal statement about my upstairs neighbours the next morning. I hadn't had a call to go in and give my statement to the other pair about Diane and Justin yet, so I wanted to get this one over with. I'd typed it up and printed it out, keeping it totally factual and simple. I handed it over to Singh and she read it through, said she had no other questions for now, and asked me to sign the statement in front of her.

When I got to PMI, Paul called me into his office. He sat in his black and blue ergonomic chair with its little headrest, swinging back and forth, and stared at me for a couple of long seconds. It started my heart hammering, but I wasn't going to wait for the words of doom.

'What's the problem?'

'Your grandfather.'

I jumped up. 'What's wrong with him? What's happened?'

He waved me back down. 'Don't panic. He's fine. But I've heard a viable rumour that there's going to be an attack on him.'

My guts twisted and I was having trouble breathing. I'd known it was possible, but … I swallowed hard. 'I think he was preparing for it. Have you talked to him?'

'He's brushed me off.' His frown was so deep, his eyes almost disappeared. 'You know what he's like. He says he doesn't need any help.'

'What kind of attack?' A drive-by in Altona wouldn't work. But then Emmanuel had just been walking back from the shops.

'Possibly a car bomb. That's the rumour. But I don't think they'd be that obvious.'

I gaped at him as my brain skidded around, pulling bits and pieces together. 'Car bomb? This isn't bloody Northern Ireland.' I paced across to the window and stared out past the West Gate Bridge to where Grandad's house was. 'It's still this guy, Fayed, isn't it?'

'These old scores—there's always someone who can't or won't let it go.'

Just get over it. Move on. Tread your own path. All those things that are said over and over. How many people managed it though?

'I bet this Fayed isn't doing his own dirty work.'

'Nope,' Paul said with a sigh. 'By all accounts, he's got a new breed of thugs around him, friends of his son. He's been revving them up for revenge. You know what they're like. All about proving they're king shit. I'll keep digging and see what else I can find out. Remember to watch your back. Now ... ' He checked his phone. 'When are you giving your statement on Diane Paterson?'

'They haven't called me yet.'

'They will. I've been told—confidentially, of course— that they did find traces of Diane in the freezer in the back of Justin's garage. Hair and DNA. Not the rest of her, though.'

'Bastard.' I closed my eyes, saw a flash of Diane's legs and snapped my lids open again. 'I hope he gets life.'

'Or close to it. He will.'

'Have they told her parents yet?' He nodded and my stomach twisted. 'They're lovely people. This will destroy them.'

'At least they know what happened to her, and there'll be some justice eventually, thanks to them wanting the truth.' He tapped the file in front of him. 'Your friend, Melinda, on the other hand ...'

'Still nothing, as far as I know.' I explained about Scotcher and handing over the phone, and then telling him about Jonathan Black. 'But I think Black is a fake name.'

'People usually use them on dating apps,' Paul said mildly, which made me wonder if he'd done it. I knew nothing about his private life. Didn't want to. 'Talk to Gang about it again. He's kept copies of everything. And I will probably have another job for you tomorrow, if you're up to it.'

'Of course I'm up to it!' Did he think I was wussing out?

'Uh-huh.' He regarded me again, and I tried not to squirm. 'I've asked Gang to give you the details of the counselling service we use. Good woman called Gabbie. I use her, too, on occasion. Don't try and tough it out. We all know where that leads.'

He meant the hammer on the guy's fingers. 'Yes, good, all right.' I got up. 'So I can spend the rest of the day on Melinda?'

'Yes, and keep me posted. Especially if you hear anything from Detective Sergeant Scotcher.' He put Melinda's file on the far corner of his desk and I left.

The desk opposite Gang's was empty as usual, so I sat down and tried to focus on the digital files he'd put together on Melinda, but my skin was itchy and hot and I couldn't sit still. After a couple of minutes, I told Gang I was going to get a strong coffee and some fresh air.

I ordered a double-shot latte and asked for an extra shot. I didn't need it; I was so on edge that if a car had back-fired, I would have probably peed myself. But the coffee actually calmed me down a bit, so I found an outside seat and settled in, morosely watching the passersby, all ordinary people probably leading ordinary lives. No faces I recognised, but I felt like every one of them was hiding something: a crime, a lie, a betrayal. The men especially. That guy talking too loudly, his head thrust forward. Or that other guy walking dick-first like he owned the footpath.

Fuckers, all of them.

Okay, okay, I scolded myself. *Stop being so angry and paranoid.*

I had bloody good reasons though. I didn't want to think Melinda was dead, but that's where it all pointed. And it churned up my guts and made my head explode with images of what might have happened to her. I'd seen too many real life examples of what happened to women and they were burned into my brain.

If Melinda was now a victim and, like Diane, a dead body waiting to be discovered, there was nothing more I could do for her. That thought made me squeeze my hands so tight that my cardboard cup burst, spilling lukewarm coffee across the table. It spread in a dark wave across the plastic and dripped onto the concrete.

'Shit.' I grabbed a handful of serviettes and tried to mop it up. A waste of good caffeine. A girl in a cheerful yellow apron came out with a cloth and cleaned it up for me.

'Did the cup split?' she asked.

'No, it was me, sorry.' I forced a smile. 'Could I have another one, please? Just a double shot this time.'

'Sure. I'll bring it out.'

More people-watching while I waited and brooded on Melinda. It was possible she was still alive. I really wanted to believe it. But in order to keep believing it, I had to get off my arse and find her. Sitting there like a frog on a rock, complaining because there were no flies doodling past, was plain stupid. I opened the note function on my phone.

Possibilities. She decided to go away for a while. Nup. She met a guy from one of the dating apps and was shacked up with him somewhere. Yeah, maybe, but why leave her phone in the house? And the front door open with her keys in the back? She went back to Sydney. Nup. Not if that was where Nathan Gunn was, and I knew he hadn't come to Melbourne.

Think! Gang had talked about some of the dating apps having a kind of location function, so you could see if your potential match lived near you. The messaging with that Jonathan Black guy was telling, the way he'd seemed to wheedle information out of her. A bit more sleuthing and he'd be in her street, watching to see what house she came out of.

That sparked a reactive zing. Yes. That was very possible.

And Mr Black had deleted himself from the app. Why? Because he'd been up to no good?

The coffee arrived and I no longer wanted to sit and drink it while I pondered. I paid for it and headed back to the office and Gang's help.

'Hey,' he said, 'you don't look overly caffeined out.'

'I spilled the first one,' I said. 'I've been thinking about Melinda. What about this for a possible scenario?' I explained my idea and reasons for it.

'Totally get that,' Gang said. 'But he's disappeared off the app, so we've effectively lost him.'

I drank some coffee, paced up and down, thumped down on my chair and stared at the ceiling. Gang watched, a little V between his manicured eyebrows.

'I can't believe this is the only time he's done this!' I said.

'Why do you say that?'

'She's missing.' I steeled myself to say something I didn't want to. 'I think someone has taken her.'

His eyebrows shot up. 'Oh. My. God. You think so?'

'Don't you?'

Paul's door swung open and I realised it hadn't actually been fully closed. He loomed in the doorway. 'Lou's right. It's looking more likely now, after three days. We want her to be alive. But if we assume she's dead, or in dire straits, it gives us compelling reasons to drive the police harder. And I'll authorise you both to push it to the limits here.'

Gang sat up straighter. 'Really? Cool.'

'Don't get carried away,' Paul said. 'Stay on the right side of legal if you can.'

'Right, gotcha, boss.' Gang tapped on his keyboard. 'File is open and ready to go.'

'You two get moving. Keep me updated.' He went back into his office and shut the door.

Gang pointed at my chair. 'Roll that on over and let's get started.'

I did as he said, sitting down next to him and his three monitors. Having Paul take me seriously and agree about Melinda made my head spin. 'What does the right side of legal mean?'

'Means not the police LEAP system,' Gang said. 'Plenty of other places to go, don't worry.'

A short time later, we had a pile of paper to spread out on the small boardroom table. I wished Paul had one of those super cool glass-wall screens that you could put documents onto, like sticky-taping them to a window, but that technology, Gang informed me, was way out of the budget. We'd have to do it the old-fashioned way.

Gang laid the pages out. 'Bank statements for savings and credit card. Not a big spender, our girl. Land title for her house. That's what it's worth.'

I peered at the figure—$980,000. 'I think she said it was left to her by her grandmother.'

'Uh-huh. Here are all of her student records. Dropped out of Sydney Uni, only completed one and a half years. Enrolled in Melbourne at a TAFE and is studying to be a veterinary nurse. She has completed two semesters of a Certificate IV, mostly online.'

I read the next sheet of paper. 'Has a New South Wales driver's licence. Why wouldn't she get a Victorian one?'

'Does she have a car?' When I shook my head, he said, 'It'd be an easy database to check for her name and address if you knew the right people.'

I nodded. 'Like you do.'

'Exactly, which would mean her ex could do it, too. We can't rule him out at all.'

'No. But the police say he hasn't left Sydney for two months.'

He spread out other sheets of paper. 'She's got no criminal record. Nothing else that's a red flag. Even her social media is almost non-existent.'

'Same reason, I guess,' I said. 'Too easy to track you, especially if you forget to disable the GPS stuff.' Which was why I avoided social media altogether. I totally didn't need anyone to see where I was or had been. Or what I was doing.

'We've done all the standard things to investigate her, and it looks like she's been focused on keeping her head down and staying out of sight.' Gang shrugged. 'You know what Sherlock Holmes used to say. When you have eliminated the impossible, whatever remains is where you're gonna find the answer.'

'Er … Sherlock may well disagree with your paraphrasing, but I know what you mean. We're left with the dating apps. Which looked pretty sus right from the start.' I separated all the pages that had the dating stuff on them.

'Good detecting means you look at everything,' Gang said. 'Then you eliminate.'

'Okay, yes, I agree.' I shuffled through the pages and saw the face I wanted. 'Hey, here's our Mr Black.'

'That's the screenshot I saved before he disappeared.' Gang looked smug.

'Great …' I stared at the nice face, the slightly tousled hair, the little gold earring. The checked shirt made him look a bit like a farm boy. 'Were there any other photos of him?'

'No. And before you ask, I've been on all of those dating sites again, plus ones she wasn't registered with, and there is no Jonathan Black on any of them.'

'How did you check? Without logging in properly?' I gaped at him. 'Are you blushing, Gang?'

Then I looked at him more closely.

'What did you do?' A feeling of deep suspicion crept over me as I stared at Gang's flushed face. 'Please don't tell me you registered on all those dating sites as me!'

'No!' His horrified expression was enough to convince me.

'How did you do it then?'

'There are heaps of nice photos on the net of anonymous women. I just "borrowed" a couple and did some profile writing.' He shrugged huffily. 'It's not illegal. Not really.'

'Oooo-kaaay. So who did you register as?'

'Jessica Smith. She's thirty, and Jessica was the most popular name for girls in the 1990s. Smith is the most common surname.' He produced two photos he'd printed out. 'She's brunette, like Melinda. This guy might have a "type", so we should play to it.'

'What's this "playing" going to consist of?'

Before he could answer, my phone rang, the discordant chime I programmed in for anyone calling whom I didn't know. I answered. 'Alcott.'

'Detective Sergeant Collins here. Are you available to come and provide that formal statement today?'

It was nearly 4pm, but there was no point putting it off. Besides, I'd already typed my statement up, using my notes that I'd prepared for Paul along the way. 'Now?'

'If that's possible.'

'Sure.'

He told me where to meet him and I hung up. 'I have to go and give my statement to Homicide about Diane and her evil husband. It could take a while.' I looked longingly at the photos in Gang's hand. 'But I really want to know what you've set up.'

'I can wait here for you to come back,' he said. 'Or you can come to my place. I have every takeaway menu possible.'

That sounded good to me. When I thought about it, I wasn't keen on going back to my apartment and pondering my neighbour and last night's events. 'You're on. Text me where you live and what you drink, and I'll bring the liquid refreshments.'

CHAPTER TWENTY

I caught the free tram towards Docklands and the Homicide squad in Spencer Street. I met Collins downstairs and he signed me in, taking me up in the lift to an office where Costa waited, and we settled into some comfy chairs for what Grandad would call a 'chinwag'. Collins had a bland kind of face, expressionless, which would give him an advantage when questioning someone. He probably never reacted to anything, just kept pushing. Costa, on the other hand, had eyebrows that arrowed down in a perpetual scowl. Today her hair was scraped back so tightly that it made my teeth hurt to look at her. They read the statement I'd prepared earlier, but they couldn't help asking more questions.

'So you kept following him?' Costa asked. 'Did your clients, her parents, ask you to do that?'

'I only followed him with Paul's permission,' I said. 'We discussed it, and he agreed that Justin Paterson was behaving oddly. And lying. I mean, why make a big fuss about Diane leaving all those cooked dinners in the freezer, when he'd paid for them from his local restaurants?'

That required a bit more explaining, because they obviously hadn't read my statement properly, and then Collins began to nod. 'Yeah, that was weird. Being too clever for his own good.'

'Sounds like he was doing "coercive controlling",' Costa said. 'It's a key sign of domestic abuse that leads to homicide.' She sounded like a university lecturer.

'But it's not specifically in the Victorian legislation yet,' Collins said.

They weren't telling me anything I didn't already know. At least Victoria had taken away provocation as a defence. Talk about the most misused legislation ever.

Costa was going on about the statistics, which was as boring as batshit, so I cut in. 'I believe you found more of Diane in Justin's freezer?'

Costa glared at me. 'There's no need to be crass about it.'

I glared back. 'Please do not accuse me of being crass. I'm the one who found her legs. I'm the one who sussed out what an evil prick he really was. Which one of you took on the job of telling her poor bloody parents?'

'A constable carried out that duty,' Costa said stiffly.

'Duty!' The stick up her bum was getting bigger by the minute. 'I'm sure everyone appreciated that.'

She gave me such a murderous look that I actually sat back in my chair. Maybe it wasn't a good idea to rile her up. She seemed to be the kind of person who would go out of her way to find something to hassle me with and, God knows, there would be plenty if she dug deep enough.

'We're going to see them tomorrow morning,' Collins said sombrely. 'It will have been a huge shock for them, I know.' He glanced through my statement again. 'You said Diane had set up a separate Facebook page just for her and her mother?'

'Yes, so Diane could secretly send her mum photos of herself and the kids.' I could see Costa was ready to say 'coercive control' again, so I cut her off at the pass. 'When I looked at the various ways in which Justin Paterson isolated her from family and old friends, that added to the suspicion. Although it also meant Diane had good reason to run away and hide herself as well. Which was his story, when he wasn't dropping big hints about kidnapping.'

They glanced at each other and I took that as my cue to leave. I stood and picked up my shoulder bag.

'Hope that's all you need from me for now.'

'I—'

Collins spoke over Costa. 'Yes, thanks. We'll be in touch if we need more.'

I'd walked at least a block of Spencer Street before I found an office building wall to lean against for a couple of minutes while I got myself sorted. The statement I'd given was just the first stage. I'd probably be called on to testify when Justin's case went to court, but that would no doubt be many months away. I'd review my statement and my notes when it happened, so I hopefully wouldn't be cannon fodder for the defence.

Still leaning, watching a steady stream of office workers in black and grey make their way to the railway station and tram stops, I texted Gang. *They let me out! See you soon.* I decided to leave the Commodore in the office parking space.

That way, I could drink as much as I wanted to. I ducked into a bottle shop for two different bottles of white wine, then booked an Uber and only had to wait five minutes before I was on my way to Prahran.

I'd been expecting an apartment block, but Gang's place turned out to be a tiny white single-fronted cottage with a front garden full of vegetables and an espaliered apple tree against the fence.

Gang answered the door in an apron covered in sprigs of red cherries. 'Don't say a word,' he said. 'My grandmother gave me this and it's turned out to be very useful.'

I mimed zipping my lips and followed him down a dimly lit hallway to an open-plan kitchen and dining area at the back of the house. 'Wow, this is amazing,' I said, full of envy for the space and light, let alone the little back garden and patio area.

'We like it,' Gang said.

I raised my eyebrows and he laughed.

'I share with my grandmother. We get on really well.'

'You have to care for her?'

'God, no! Po Po has a better social life than I do. She's out now, slaying a bunch of people at mahjong.' He took the bottles from me and put them in the fridge. 'I have some pinot gris, if you want to try it.'

'Sounds good, and you have to let me give you some money for the food. What did you order?'

He waved a hand. 'No need. Po Po got so excited when I told her I was having a guest that she's cooked for us.' He placed two wine glasses on the bench and poured us both a healthy amount of pinot.

I took a sip. 'Yum. Very nice.'

'Good.' He pointed to the dining table, which looked very much like the boardroom table at work, covered in paper. But this time, it was dating site printouts, with the two photos of 'Jessica Smith' in the middle. 'I've set it up here so you can see what I've done and where. I've kind of followed Melinda's path, with small bits of information, and I found another photo of our fake girl. It seems she's an aspiring model in the UK. I guess if anyone got suspicious, they could reverse google her images.' He shrugged. 'If they do, we'll shut down the profiles.'

I nodded and examined the Jessica Smith he'd set up. I had to admit, he'd done a great job. And yes, he'd followed what Melinda had done, plus put 'Jessica' up on two other dating sites as well. I pointed at them.

'Why these ones?'

'They're the biggest. I know Melinda mostly stuck to the smaller, less popular ones, but it's hard to know where this guy is looking.'

I sat down, drank some more wine and said, 'We both agree that this guy has possibly or probably done this before.' I paused. 'All the same, we can't afford to focus all our efforts on this one theory, or just on Black. It could be someone she met at TAFE, for example.'

'Look, the police aren't useless,' Gang said. 'They'll be pulling out all the stops now to find her. We don't need to duplicate what they're investigating—anyone who's seen her recently, her father, fellow students. And it may well be that they'll do something similar to us with the dating stuff. Eventually. Maybe if her body is found.'

A burning knot tightened in my chest and I had to bite my lips together hard.

'I'm really sorry, Lou,' Gang said. 'I thought you …'

'I had.' My voice was shaky and I cleared my throat. 'Sorry. I just realised I still had this fantasy we'd do this and find her before anything happened to her. I know that's unlikely. I mean, look at Diane …' A tear spilled onto my cheek and I brushed it away roughly. 'Sorry. This isn't getting us anywhere. It's just … this all makes me so bloody angry. And frustrated. And sad.'

'I know.' His face was so full of sympathy that I nearly lost it altogether.

'Right then.' I drank down the rest of the wine, took a big breath and said, 'What next?'

Gang jumped up and opened his laptop. 'This screen is a bit bigger—easier to use than the phone. And all of my Jessicas are live now, so we can see what's happening.'

One by one, we went into each dating site to check. Gang had chosen a good Jessica; the photos were of a pretty woman, but not someone amazingly beautiful. She looked like the girl next door, and I thought her dreamed-of modelling career probably wasn't likely. Still, what did I know? Gang had assured me that this woman's photos weren't easy for the average person to find unless they knew her real name.

On each site, Jessica had already had some interest. Two guys here, three there, and eight on Tinder! 'How long have these profiles been up?'

'Most went live this afternoon. I did the Tinder one last night as a practice run.' He clicked. 'No Jonathan Black anywhere.'

'No.' I felt a bit deflated. 'Maybe I'm wrong about him.'

'We'll see. Early days. Let's eat.'

I poured more wine and we filled our tummies with pork dumplings and what Gang said was beef chow fun—beef with fried noodles. It was better than anything that could have come out of Justin's freezer dinners. 'Do you eat like this every night?' I asked.

'Not really.' He laughed. 'Po Po likes to keep me healthy, she says, although if I ate everything she tried to cook for me, I'd be the size of an elephant.'

'How did you get into all the techie stuff? With Po Po at your side, you could have been running a fabulous restaurant.'

'I love finding stuff out, that's all. Computers and pro-gramming and making apps and things was what I was into at school. Hated almost everything else except maybe English Lit. One thing led to another ...' He tapped the side of his nose. 'Getting the job with Paul was my lucky break. Now I get to be nosy as well, and am paid for it.'

'So if not for Paul, you could have been a hacker?'

'No way. My mother would have come back to haunt me.'

That made me pause. 'Your mother has died?'

'Yes, cancer. When I was about fourteen. I know you lost your mum, too. How old were you?'

I thought I didn't want to ever talk about it, but I found myself saying, 'Seventeen. I didn't cope very well.'

'Oh God, Lou, who does? Were you still at high school?'

I nodded. 'Almost stuffed up my VCE, suffered through it and got into uni—only just. But it wasn't what I wanted.' I took the last pork dumpling and dipped it in soy sauce, thinking about the final subject I failed. Law in Society. It wasn't that I wasn't interested, but at the time, with my father breathing down my neck, telling me I should have studied proper law, not wussy Arts subjects, I couldn't focus, and then when Nana died, I completely lost all interest in anything to do with Dad and the police force. I went backpacking overseas for a few years instead. When I explained that to Gang, the little furrows appeared between his eyebrows.

'But you went into the police force anyway. What was that about?'

'Probably a shrink could tell you,' I joked. But I didn't know. I had been so busy still trying to find something to bury myself in, I'd never stood back and tried to analyse why. Even now, I didn't want to.

'Anyway,' I said, 'we're here to bring Jessica to life and find Melinda. Not waste time on boring old me and my twisted motivations!'

Gang wisely dropped the subject. 'We need a strategy. We don't need to swipe or click or do anything to any of these guys yet, right?'

'That'd get us into trouble. We're window shopping at the moment. But the time might come where we did want to look at someone a bit more closely. Then you're going to have to chat with them online.'

'No way. I thought you could do that bit—if we ever got that far.'

'Me?' I grimaced. 'Can't we just look at their photos and profiles and try to find someone who's also connected with Melinda?' I pointed at her dating app information and the five guys she'd 'approved'. 'Surely it's going to be one of them?'

'It's possible,' he said, 'but the police are going to be looking closely at all of those guys. Some of their information and photos are available, so the police tech experts might be able to go further. We need to look at what actually happened. She's disappeared without a trace. No struggle in the house. No calls for help.' He squeezed my arm. 'Lou, if you hadn't agreed to have a drink with her that afternoon, nobody would know she was missing.'

'Her father wouldn't even care.' I told him about the phone call.

'No wonder she came down here, if her own dad wouldn't protect her.'

'Her strategy to hide from her ex was her undoing.' I scanned the screenshots again. 'But none of these dating guys knew about that. We've looked at their chat logs.'

We were stuck again. We sat there for another hour, going through everything once more, and then tried to decide if we'd swipe or respond to any of Jessica's interested males.

'I can't face it tonight,' I said. 'Let's do it in the office tomorrow. I think that might help me keep a distance from it. You know, it'll be a job.'

I knew I was wussing out. But it was also getting late and I wanted to call Grandad. I got an Uber home and fell onto my couch, scrabbling in my pocket for my phone and finding Grandad in my contacts.

He didn't answer. It didn't go to voicemail because Grandad didn't use voicemail. He either answered you or he didn't. He had always answered me. Always.

Something was wrong.

I dithered and debated. I almost called my father. That's how I knew I was in a panic. My father was the last person who'd care about Grandad. In the end, when two more calls went unanswered as well, I got another Uber and headed for Altona, wishing I'd had less wine. As I sat in the front passenger seat, face to the side window so the driver got the hint about not talking, I tried to work out what to do. Go to the gate or get out of the Uber a street away? No, the gate. If I sneaked around the streets, I might get shot by one of Grandad's bodyguards.

What if nobody answered the gate? Would I try climbing the fence? Maybe. If everything was dark.

In the end, I didn't do any of that. Grandad's street was lit up with searing flashes of blue and red, and four police cars were parked haphazardly near his gate. Again.

I stared, unable to move and get out of the car.

'Far out,' the Uber driver said. 'I'm not going down there.'

My stomach had turned to acid and I swallowed hard. 'Yeah, I'll get out then.'

He did a U-turn and barely gave me time to clamber out and shut the door before he floored it and disappeared around the corner. Like the cops wanted him for something. There was police tape across the street cordoning it off, and I walked up to the constable standing just behind it.

She opened her mouth and started with, 'Move along, madam, thank—'

'That's my grandfather's house. I'm supposed to check he's okay.' I glared at her. 'Is he okay? What's happened?'

'I can't tell you that. You'll have to go home.'

'No, I won't. On this side of the cordon, I can do what I like. Including standing here and waiting to find out about my grandfather.' There were times when my cop experience paid off.

Her face went flat and she stared past me like I no longer existed. I understood it. Nobody wanted trouble when all you were doing was keeping the cordon clear. I still wanted to jump the tape and trample her as I ran through the gates that I could see were wide open.

A car pulled up behind me and two doors slammed. I turned and my guts went to ice. I'd been lucky since I'd left the force, but it all ran out in that moment.

Detective Sergeant Kluzman and Detective Constable Frankie Gallo. I barely knew Gallo, but Kluzman had been on my case over the hammer incident, pushing hard for me to be charged with serious assault. I'd heard a rumour that his real beef was with my father and that just made it worse. Kluzman had interrogated me for hours, leaning over me with his rank body odour and cigarette breath. Just the sight of him now brought those smells back into my nostrils.

Kluzman scanned the people standing around, most of whom had to be neighbours, and then his gaze landed on me and a smirk twisted his mouth like an oily worm. He didn't say anything to me, just pushed past and under the tape and gave his name and rank to the constable. Then he pointed at me and said to her, 'Under no circumstances let that woman past. Or else.'

'Yes, sir,' she said, and gave me the evil eye again.

That was the point at which I did something I'd vowed I wouldn't do.

I called my father.

CHAPTER TWENTY-ONE

'Louisa. Nice to hear from you.' His tone was measured and calm, as if he'd been waiting for my call. I didn't want to think what that might mean.

'Dad.' I hadn't spoken to him in almost a year.

'I imagine you're calling about your grandfather.'

'Yes. What's happened?'

'I believe there was a shooting.'

My teeth ground together and I had to summon every shred of diplomacy and keep my voice calm. 'Was Grandad injured? Or ...' I gritted out the word. 'Killed?'

'He's in hospital under police guard. He'll be charged in the morning.'

'Charged with what?'

'Murder. I doubt very much he'll be able to talk his way out of it this time.'

He hung up.

The bastard hadn't even told me how bad Grandad's injury was. He could've been dying. Not that my father would care. He'd probably pour himself another glass of Chivas Regal or some other fancy scotch and celebrate.

Why did I bloody call him? I should've known it would get me nowhere, and just give my father a chance to gloat. And fuck up my life even more. I called Paul instead, who should've been my first choice.

'What do you mean, shot?' Paul shouted.

I held the phone away from my ear and looked around. No TV crews, nobody that looked like a journalist. Two people whose phones were in their hands, but neither was filming. The police had this locked down tighter than a constipated snake. Then a Channel 9 helicopter clattered overhead, hovering, a camera trained on Grandad's house. Time for me to disappear.

'Hang on,' I told Paul, and walked swiftly away, around the corner to where some thickly canopied trees would conceal me. 'A news helicopter has turned up, so word is getting out.'

Paul had turned his TV on. 'Yes, it's on now. News flash at the beginning of the ad break.' He read off the scrolling news banner: 'Shooting at a property in Altona. Reports of injuries. More to come.'

'Kluzman and Gallo are here.'

He groaned. 'That guy is like slime on a pond.'

'I made the mistake of calling my father. He said Grandad is in hospital. Didn't even tell me which hospital or how bad he is.'

'I'm onto it. I'll call you back. You got wheels?'

'Not yet. I'll go and get a car as soon as I can.'

'Okay.'

I booked another Uber and was glad to see one was five minutes away. While I waited, I ran through all the hospitals Grandad might be in. Not Williamstown. It was closed to emergencies at night. Footscray then. Or maybe Sunshine. Or the Royal Melbourne. Or …

The Uber arrived and thankfully it was a different guy. This one was a very polite Indian man who actually knew his way around and didn't need Google Maps to find the West Gate Bridge. By the time I was dropped off at the Commodore, Paul had called back and told me Grandad was at the Footscray Hospital. 'He's got a bullet wound in his arm, Lou, but he's okay.'

'My father said they were going to charge him. What with?'

'Probably something like reckless discharge of a weapon. It won't be much. Enough to hold him and force a bail hearing.'

'I'm on my way to Footscray now,' I said.

'Keep me updated. And give the old bugger my best.'

Now that I knew Grandad wasn't dying, stretched out on an operating table with tubes and blood going everywhere and some doctor who maybe had worked a double shift already … now that I could think about it more rationally, I was able to drive without exceeding the speed limit by fifty ks an hour and get to the hospital without a drama.

The drama was all inside me.

***

Thankfully, I could bypass the Emergency waiting area for patients and go to the main desk. 'Can you please tell me where my grandfather is? What ward?'

I gave the woman his name and she checked on the screen, then directed me via the coloured lines on the floor and the lift. I walked slowly, pretending to check my phone, then headed up the internal stairs. If there was an officer on guard outside Grandad's room, I wanted to see him or her before they saw me, watch their body language, whether they were expecting trouble or just tolerating a boring job.

There were two of them, a male and a female, one on each side of the corridor. She saw me through the glass in the stairwell door and I had to come out and show myself before she got suspicious. I held my hands up.

'I'm Hamish Campbell's granddaughter, Louisa. Do you want to see ID?'

'Yes, thank you.'

I showed my driver's licence, but it didn't help much.

'Nobody is allowed in to see him. Orders from above, sorry.'

I could have pushed past her and got into the room, but the male officer was giving me a stony-faced look that said he was a wall, not a door, so I stayed where I was. I didn't fancy being down on my stomach, arm twisted back and struggling to breathe.

'Can you at least tell me how he is? Give him a message?'

Her eyes slid sideways to her mate down the hall and then she shook her head. 'Not allowed. Your grandfather is under arrest. The only person allowed to see him is his lawyer.'

I nodded. That would be Sherman Phillips. He'd been Grandad's lawyer for a million years. They'd gone to primary school together when dinosaurs were around. 'Has Sherman been in yet?' Maybe he could pass on a message from me.

'He's in there now.'

'Oh. Right.' I gestured to a chair, one she'd probably been sitting on. 'Can I wait here for him?'

'Er ...' She glanced past me again and I turned to see Stoneface glaring again.

'She has to leave. Now.' His voice rang out like a drill sergeant's on a parade ground. The female officer cringed.

'Okay, no worries.' I backed over to the lift and pushed the button.

Prick. I didn't care so much about myself, but he didn't have to act like the female officer was an idiot.

As I went down to the ground floor again, I found Sherman in my phone contacts; I'd had to use his services myself, unfortunately. I texted him. *I'm downstairs. I'll wait. Please give Grandad my love.*

A few moments later, his reply came back. *Ten minutes.*

I found a seat near the lifts and waited. I didn't have to watch the time; Sherman would be emerging from the lift in exactly ten minutes.

And he was. He looked the same as always—Armani suit, white shirt, black tie with a horse on it. His white hair was cut perfectly and he looked about twenty years younger than I knew he was. I stood.

'Hey, Sherman, how is he?'

'Grumpy. Angry. Abusing the morons around him.'

'Same as usual then.'

We both grinned.

'Have you got time to tell me what's been going on?' I asked.

He looked around. 'Yes, but not here. I need a drink. Come to my house?'

I nearly fell over. In all the years I'd known Sherman, I'd never had an invitation. We only met at Grandad's or at restaurants. 'Er, sure. Where do you live?'

He gave me an address in Williamstown on The Strand and I said I'd be there soon. In the car, I called Paul and let him know what I knew, which was stuff all. 'I'll call you when I've talked to Sherman.'

'Give him my best.' Of course Paul knew him. The network nobody talked about.

Sherman's house wasn't what I expected. From the outside it looked like one of the older houses in the street, a little tired and weatherworn, but inside it had been crafted, not renovated. Gleaming wood, thick rugs, startling art on the walls and a back lounge area that opened up to a beautiful garden, where soft lights glowed and the aroma of gardenias and other night-scenting plants drifted in. Sherman noticed my mouth hanging open.

'It suits me to look a bit decrepit on the outside,' he said.

'Your house, maybe. You, never,' I said, laughing.

He shrugged modestly and held up his glass. 'Scotch?'

'Wine, please. White.' I knew whatever he poured me would be something that had scored ninety-nine points and a bunch of wine show medals, and I'd never be able to afford it myself, so I'd make the most of it now. I sniffed and tasted from the glass he gave me and I was right. We sat across from each other on soft leather couches.

'You know the trouble your grandfather has been having?'

'Some big payback from an old criminal associate. Guy called Fayed.'

Sherman shook his head. 'Hamish wouldn't back down. Even though it threatens everything he's built up.'

'He said that Fayed blamed him for his son's death.'

'That's a big part of it, but Hamish also took over some of Fayed's territory while he was inside. He still wielded a lot of power from his cell at Barwon, but after his son died, so did his ability to control things as much.'

I drank more wine and felt a yearning for cheese and crackers. As if he could read my mind, Sherman got up and fetched a prepared platter from the fridge. I tried not to be a piggy, but I virtually inhaled half of the brie and a large amount of pâté in a very short time. Sherman watched me eat and laughed a little.

'Sorry,' I said. 'Must be stress making me hungry.'

'That's what it's there for. This Fayed …' He ate some blue cheese on a cracker and stared into his glass, then sighed. 'Hamish has been working hard to go more legit, you know.'

I did know that. I just hadn't taken much notice of it. Any sign of interest and Grandad would have started talking about bringing me in with him.

'There were two attempts on Hamish's life while Fayed was still in jail.'

I gaped at him. 'When?'

'Years ago now. When Fayed's son was killed. The stress … your grandmother didn't cope well.' He left that hanging, and the cogs in my brain turned another few notches.

'Are you saying that Fayed killed my grandmother?'

'No, no. But she was very afraid. And when she had a fatal stroke a few months later, Hamish blamed Fayed.'

I thought back to that time, the double grief of my mother's death and then my grandmother's. For Grandad, it had been his daughter and his wife. I said slowly, 'I'm surprised that Grandad didn't have the power then to get Fayed killed inside Barwon.'

'He did. But after the two attempts on his life, your grandmother had made him promise not to retaliate. She said it would never stop if he did, just go on and on, and she might finally lose him. Told him he wasn't invincible.'

I leaned back on the couch, the leather squeaking under me. For Grandad, a promise was a promise, especially to his wife. 'But now Fayed has killed Emmanuel, so the promise Grandad made is null and void.' Grandma had been a tough woman, but even she would understand that he had to defend himself. 'If he knew what Fayed was planning, how did he get shot? And why is he under arrest?'

Sherman blinked at me for a couple of seconds, like he was assessing how much I needed to know. 'Well ...'

'I'm not a police officer anymore, so please don't go all squirrelly on me.'

'Squirrelly?' Sherman's lips twitched. 'Your grandfather is under arrest for murder. I will, of course, make sure it doesn't stick. It was clearly self-defence.'

'Because he got shot, too?'

'Precisely. I believe there were three of them. They broke into his house, so charges will need to be laid by the police in that respect.'

'They've caught all three of them?'

'Unfortunately not. They did, of course, apprehend the one who died.'

I was trying to imagine what might have happened. Three guys out to kill an old man was serious business. 'I can't believe Grandad survived. Where were his bodyguards? The guys in his security team?'

'Only Sammy was in the house with Hamish. He's also in hospital.'

I gaped at him. 'Was he shot? How bad is he?'

'Critical.'

Fucking hell. 'What are the police doing about the two who got away?'

'Good question,' Sherman said, his voice suddenly steely. 'They apparently know about the feud with Fayed, and who's working for him. If arrests aren't made in the next twenty-four hours, heads will roll, I'll make sure of it.'

I ate more cheese and crackers and savoured the wine while I tried to think, but nothing useful emerged.

'Hamish wants to see you,' Sherman said.

'The police won't let me in. I tried.'

'You're assured of entry tomorrow morning. Early.'

'How early?' I asked suspiciously.

Sherman looked at his expensive gold watch. 'In about two hours. There will be a change of police guard at midnight. The new officers will let you through.'

'Right. I'll be there.'

Sherman stood. 'Help yourself to more wine and cheese, or anything in the fridge. I have some calls to make. I'll be back shortly.' He disappeared down a hallway and a door closed. I ended up eating all of the remaining brie and crackers, as well as refilling my glass, while questions ran through my buzzing mind. Seemed like the wine had finally restored some brain cells.

What happened to the six men patrolling the property? Were they paid off to silently leave? Why was Sammy the only person inside the house? And why did Grandad want to see me right now? I pulled out my phone and called Paul.

When I explained what had happened and who was behind it, Paul let out a long whistle.

'I'm glad Hamish is okay. I hope Sammy pulls through. This has really ramped up the dispute.'

'I think it's gone way past dispute. It's turned into a bloody war zone.'

'I'm going to use some of my less official contacts to find out what the situation is.'

'I can tell you what it is!' I said. 'They raided Grandad's house and almost killed him. We need to find out what happened to the men who were supposed to be guarding him. Were they paid to disappear? If so, I'll bloody shoot them myself!'

'Calm down, Lou. There will be an explanation, and I doubt that's it. Those guys are loyal to Hamish.'

I breathed in and out a couple of times, trying to believe him. 'What about Grandad in the hospital, then? Will the police keep him safe? Given who he is?' I felt like I was bad-mouthing my former colleagues, but I had to be realistic.

'Sherman will make sure of it, don't worry. If there's any issues with extra protection in there, I'll sort it out. Are you allowed in to see him yet?'

'Sherman has set up a visit after midnight.'

Paul was silent for a few seconds. 'Watch your back, Lou. I know I keep saying it, but I mean it. This is real. I doubt Fayed will simmer down once he finds out Hamish is still alive. Stay out of sight when you go there. You know where the service entrance is?'

When I said no, he explained how to find it, and said one of the guys he was sending in would be there to open it for me. 'Try not to get stopped by hospital security. Your safest option is to sneak in and out without being seen by anyone, especially someone who might be working for Fayed.'

These days hospital security tended to focus on the Emergency Department where most of the trouble erupted with guys on ice or fighting drunk. 'Okay, I'll let you know tomorrow what Grandad says.'

'No, call me as soon as you've talked to him. I'll be up.'

That freaked me out. He really was worried. And Paul was a guy who didn't worry about many things, he just got on with fixing them. I hoped that extra protection was sorted.

I hung up and finished my wine. It was close to midnight so I didn't dare lean back and take a nap; I might not wake up for hours. Instead, I went into Sherman's kitchen and made a strong coffee with two pods in his machine. The kitchen was spotless, barely an appliance or jar or tin in sight. I had no idea whether there was a Mrs Sherman or not.

Sherman came back just as I was finishing my coffee. His face was grimmer than usual. 'Hamish wants me to arrange for someone to stay with you.'

'What—a bodyguard?'

He nodded. 'Things are escalating because Hamish shot one of Fayed's men. These people are out of control.'

'What are the police doing?'

'They've raided two houses known to be associated with Fayed, but with no result. He's gone to ground somewhere, and so have the two responsible for the attempt on Hamish's life. They'll find them. It will take time though.'

I shivered. 'How long will Grandad be in hospital?'

'Two to three days,' Sherman said. 'Then I hope I can persuade him to move out of his house for a while. Find somewhere safer. Even go to the other side of the state, once he gets bail.'

I couldn't imagine Grandad moving anywhere. That house was his fortress. But now it had been breached, maybe he'd relent and take Sherman's advice.

'Do you know why he wants to see me?' I asked.

'No. I imagine it's to warn you. Perhaps to explain.' That was all Sherman would say. He saw me to the door and then watched until I drove off into the darkness. I followed Paul's directions and parked in McCubbin Street, well away from the main entrance to the hospital. It took me a few minutes to walk around to the entrance he'd described, all the while scanning around and behind me. I felt a bit silly doing it until I thought about Grandad being ambushed in his own house. That made me angry and scared all over again. Fayed's idea of revenge was like an octopus with poisonous arms.

As I got closer, the heavy door looked firmly shut, but I knocked, wondering if anyone would hear me through the steel, and the door opened. I entered a dark corridor, passed a man dressed in black who nodded at me, and the door firmly closed again. I headed to the nearest stairway door, and those stairs took me to the opposite end of the corridor where Grandad's room was—I eased the door open and spotted the guard sitting outside. One police officer. Where was the other? Or were they economising because it was night shift?

I trod softly along the linoed corridor, but before I even made it to halfway, the officer stood to face me. He was an older guy, tall with a grey buzz cut, and he rested his hands on his belt, ready just in case. His eyes were more curious than wary.

I held my hands out. 'I'm Louisa, his granddaughter. He's expecting me, I think.'

The officer surveyed me for a moment. 'Got any ID?'

'Yes.' I pulled out my driver's licence and offered it to him.

He glanced at the photo and name and then at me again. 'I need to make sure you aren't armed. And he'll have to verify he knows you.'

Good, this guy was on the ball. I put my arms out and waited as he patted me down professionally, then followed him to the door.

'Wait here.' He went in, closed the door and leaned against it. Voices rumbled inside, and then the door opened again. 'Show him your face.'

I stuck my head through the gap. Grandad was half-sitting up in bed, four pillows behind him, and he had more paraphernalia attached to him than I'd expected. It sent a long chill through me. He really could have died.

'That's her, Stuart. Thanks.'

The officer let me in and then shut the door. I walked over to Grandad's bed, my legs trembling, even though I could see he was okay. 'What—' I had to clear my throat. 'What have you been up to now, you silly old bugger?'

He blinked a couple of times and then held up his good arm that didn't have tubes coming out of it. 'Give us a hug, lass.'

I went close and leaned in against him, putting my arms around him as best I could. He gripped my back, pulled me close. Sharp relief swept through me, mixed with memories of other times he'd hugged me and held me together and I could hardly breathe. If I lost this man, I didn't know what I'd do. I didn't know how I'd survive. I squeezed him tighter, and he grunted a little, but he didn't say to let him go. We stayed like that for several minutes, in silence.

Finally, he released me and sniffed. I was gobsmacked to see his face was wet.

'Hand me one of those tissues, lass,' he said. He dabbed his face and then visibly stiffened his spine. 'Bastard nearly got me, eh? He won't get that bloody close again.' His jaw jutted.

'How did it happen? Why were you alone with just Sammy? Is he going to be okay?'

'Hang on, one thing at a time.' He gestured to the water cup with a straw poking out of it. 'Give me a sip of that, will you, please?'

I held it for him while he sucked down some liquid, then put it back on the side table and pulled up a chair. 'Well?'

'I hate to admit it, but I miscalculated,' Grandad said, his face flushing. 'Six around the outside, me and Sammy inside. Old days, that would've been plenty. Fayed's found himself a bunch of bloody ninjas.' Grandad started to chuckle and ended up coughing.

I had to fetch the water again, and I could tell he was in pain. His arm was bandaged and when he turned his head, I noticed a large dressing covering the other side of his head. Grandad was tough, but he looked like he'd been beaten as well as shot. Rage started to burn in my guts, and Grandad gave me a sharp look.

'What's the matter?'

I pointed at his head. 'How did you get that?' My voice came out tight.

'Argh.' He flapped a hand. 'Hit my head when I was shot and fell down. Probably a good thing. I think the bastards thought I was dead.'

'What are the cops doing?'

'You used the word cops,' Grandad said. 'Interesting.'

'Shut up. How did this happen? Where were all your guys?'

'Sherman didn't tell you? Shot with bloody tranquilliser darts, for God's sake.' He shook his head.

'Keep going. What happened?'

'I was watching a movie. *Die Hard*—the third one. It was up a bit loud. Sammy heard something in the garden. At least he told me before he went out to check, warned me. He got outside the back door and one of them shot him. Used a silencer, but I still heard it. Know that sound anywhere. I was behind the couch by the time they came in. Got the first bastard easy, winged the second one, but the third one used him as a shield and had a fucking semi-automatic.' He shook his head again.

This kind of attack wasn't rare, it was just rare for anyone to target Grandad, right inside his house. I'd thought he was invincible. I should have known better. But a semi-automatic? 'You only caught one bullet?'

'A ricochet off the metal window frame behind me.' He smiled briefly. 'Pays to buy good solid furniture, eh? That couch ... I suppose I'll have to replace it.'

'So they thought you were dead and took off?'

'Yes. I had to ring for an ambulance for Sammy, and they sent the police as well. I suppose they had to.' He sighed. 'Your father is probably laughing right now.'

'He wouldn't want to even crack a smile in front of me,' I said. 'Or else.'

'That's my girl.' Grandad smiled properly at me. If there was one thing that united us, it was our loathing of my father. Grandad blamed him for my mum's death. That's another story.

'I'm glad to see you're okay, old man. But I know you.' I patted his hand. 'Why am I really here? Because I didn't bring flowers or grapes.'

'You need to get out of sight, Lou. Don't argue with me. I've spoken to Paul as well.'

'I'm not a kid, Grandad,' I said hotly. 'I can look after myself.'

'Not with this lunatic, you can't.' He wagged a finger at me. 'I'm serious, totally serious. When Fayed finds out I'm still alive, which has probably happened already, he'll go after you next.'

'Me?' My voice was hoarse. 'I thought you said my father's name would make a difference.'

'Not anymore. Don't argue. Promise me.'

I opened my mouth to object again and closed it. 'Okay.' I heaved a dramatic sigh. 'But where am I supposed to hide?'

'Paul has it sorted.'

'What about you? How are you going to stay safe?' Grandad was in far greater danger than me. Anyone who shot Sammy as well as six security guys with tranquilliser darts to get to his target wasn't messing around.

'I've got that well in hand, lass, don't worry.'

'What—you've got a gun in your hospital gown?'

'Not exactly. Your bum hangs out of these things, you know. Where would I put a gun, for crying out loud?' He winked at me. It had to be under his pillow or under the blankets. 'Besides, I've got police outside the door, and two of my boys in the next room.'

How the hell he'd managed that, I don't know, but I wasn't going to ask. I yawned so widely that my jaw cracked twice. 'I'm going to grab some sleep.' I looked around. 'I could sleep here.' Even though the one armchair looked very uncomfortable.

'You need to pack a bag, quick smart, and go where Paul tells you,' he said. 'Plenty of time for sleeping when you're there.'

I'd had enough of being growled at, even if it was because he loved me. I said goodnight, checked out Stuart as I left, who was wide awake and reading a hunting magazine, and went down the stairs again. I skipped down the first flight, and then Grandad's words echoed at me. *He'll go after you next.* I stopped, looked over my shoulder, set off again.

Grandad had put the frighteners on me enough so that I checked every landing on the way, and then the corridor. At the service door, I hesitated. My heart was thumping in my ears, going way too fast. I had no way of knowing if anyone was out there, waiting. The guy who'd let me in was gone.

I walked back towards the ER and then followed the signs for the pharmacy. I was pretty sure I'd seen another exit door once when I'd been here with an injured fellow officer. The Eleanor Street entrance was lit up, but not nearly as much as the main entrance would be, or Emergency. And there were corners and shrubs outside—places to slip behind while I checked out who was around. At two in the morning, they'd be noticeable.

I couldn't see anyone, but there were a few parked cars. I kept to the darker side of the street, moving fast, scanning around me. I went the long way, down to Essex, along to Summerhill and up to Ballarat Road, running like I would

if I was doing my usual street pounding. Good exercise, if
nothing else. Back at the car, I slipped inside, drove to my
flat and parked in the street, a hundred metres away from
my building. My Corolla was still sitting in a PMI parking
spot in the city. It might be better to leave it there for a while
longer.

Paul answered my call straight away. 'How is he?'

'Ordering me around, as usual. He's better than I
expected. Lucky.'

'Very lucky. Sammy is still critical. Four hours in surgery.
They shot him twice, but not in the head.'

'Lucky twice.'

We were both silent, thinking about what luck might
mean.

'You got a bag packed?' Paul asked.

'I'm outside my place now. It'll take me about five minutes to fetch it, max.'

'You're going to be in a place in Docklands. A mate owns
it, but he's overseas for a few months so he said we can use it
until he comes back.' He gave me the address and the key-
pad numbers to get in. 'Stay there until you hear from me.'

All this being ordered around was starting to piss me off.
It was like I was ten years old and being grounded. Now
I'd had time to think, I couldn't see why this Fayed would
come after me. What would he gain from it, other than
another murder charge?

'What about my cases? What about Melinda?'

'I'm sorry, but we'll have to leave Melinda to the police.'
He made a teeth-sucking noise. 'I don't like it, but I can't
spare anyone else at the moment.'

Now I was totally pissed off, but I didn't say anything. 'Right. I'm going to get my stuff.' I hung up and got out of the car. This part of my street was always dark. Not enough streetlights with bulbs in them. As I got closer to my apartment block, I glanced up at the balconies.

Up there above me, the wife basher. No lights on. He was hopefully still inside.

Then I noticed a faint light bouncing around inside my apartment. Someone was in there, looking around with a torch.

CHAPTER TWENTY-TWO

I froze and stepped back behind the leafy hedge of next door's front garden. There it was again—a tiny flash. Then it was gone. I hadn't imagined it.

Only one person could possibly be in there. One of Fayed's guys. I wanted to barge in and deal with him myself, but after seeing Grandad, I knew that would be an extremely stupid thing to do. And besides, Grandad would 'tan my arse'. Instead, I dialled 000 and asked for police. Keeping my voice low, I said, 'Someone is in my apartment. Urgent help needed.' I gave the address and said I would stay on the line, but meanwhile I was watching the apartment block exits.

Just as a police divvy van pulled up at the front, a shadow emerged from the rear area where the bins were kept and ran behind my neighbours' cars towards the street.

As the officers jumped out of their vehicle, I approached fast, my hands up, holding the phone. 'I called it in. The guy just came out and went that way.' I pointed. 'He was running.'

One of them got back in to radio for backup, the other ran onto the street, but soon came back. 'A car just took off down there. That could have been him.'

'Did you get a look at it?'

'Subaru Impreza. Blue. Big mufflers.' He leaned in to tell his partner and the report went through to look out for the car. Then he came back to me. I noted he was a constable, and his nametag said J. Watson. 'He was inside your apartment, you told the operator?'

'Yes. I just got home from visiting my grandfather. I saw someone in there with a torch.'

'Which floor are you?'

'Third.'

He looked up, and his face changed; he pressed his lips together and twisted his neck around as if it had suddenly become stiff. 'Right. So you're …'

'Yeah, under the guy who was bashing his wife the other night.' Maybe it was him? But I doubted he'd be sneaking around with a torch.

He mashed his lips together a bit more. 'I'd be moving if I was you.'

'It's not a bad area,' I said. 'Can you come inside with me?'

'Of course, madam. That's why we're here, to check things out.' Watson glanced at me and his eyes caught the glow from the streetlight. 'There might still be someone in there, you know.'

You're not telling me anything I hadn't already thought of.
'I hope not.'

He clearly hoped not, too. He waited until his partner was out of the car and they both did a quick check of the exterior of the block, him circling around the back while the other went through the carpark.

Watson came back brushing dirt off his trousers. 'Back exit wide open. I shut it. Is it meant to be locked?'

'It locks automatically from the inside. Pays to have your key in your pocket when you put your rubbish out.'

The other officer muttered, 'This place gives me the willies,' and received a sharp look for it. Officers on patrol aren't supposed to be afraid of anything. Like that was true. We spent a lot of every night shift shitting ourselves at least a little. I had, anyway.

'Right, let's have a look inside then,' Watson said. He led the way, stomping steadily up the stairs, followed by his partner, whose nametag said P. Eastly.

When we reached the landing, I said, 'Mine is that one, number ten.'

Watson bent and inspected the lock. 'Looks okay. Anyone else got a key?'

'No,' I said shortly. I handed mine over and he unlocked the door, standing aside and pushing it back against the wall. Nothing happened.

'Light switch?'

'There.' I pointed.

He flicked it on and the short hallway lit up, as well as the kitchen. The lounge room stayed dark. Watson switched on the torch he'd brought from the car, went for his baton, paused, looked at me and drew his gun. His partner did the same.

What was that about?

I was dying to follow them in, but I felt Grandad's hand pulling me back so I waited by the door. Whoever had been in there was long gone. All the same, Watson and Eastly were thorough, doing a full search. I caught a glimpse of a shoe as one of them lay down to look under my bed.

'Fucking hell!'

'What?' Watson snapped. 'What did you find?'

'There's a fucking bomb under her bed!'

My skin went icy cold and my guts clenched. I wanted to run, but I couldn't just leave them there.

'Get out now. Carefully. Don't touch the bed.'

'Yeah, all right, all right.' Eastly sounded panicky. 'Don't you, neither.'

'Back away. Slowly.'

'Couldn't see a timer. But I didn't get a good look.'

'Never mind. Move back. More.'

'You, too.'

'I'm coming. Don't you fucking worry about that.' Watson's voice was shaky. I didn't blame him a bit.

'We have to radio it in.'

'Not yet! We don't know what might set it off.'

Their backs came first, and they jostled each other a little in the hallway, Watson grabbing Eastly's arm so that they came towards me together. I stepped right back, away from my front door, and stood against the wall at the back of the landing. When they turned to me, their faces were white and sweaty.

Watson swallowed hard and said, 'Why is there a bomb under your bed? Who are you?'

I shook my head. There was no way I could explain in a few sentences what was going on.

Watson looked like he wanted to throttle me. Instead he took a breath, pointed down the stairs and said, 'Go down there now and wait by the patrol car for us. Do *not* leave. Understood?'

Eastly had his radio out. 'Can I call it in now?'

'Next landing.'

They followed me down two flights and stopped, Watson watching me descend the rest of the way while Eastly called it in. The squawking from his radio operator said they didn't believe it either. Not at first.

By the time I reached the front entrance, I could just hear Watson say, 'We have to evacuate the whole building. Now. Bomb Response Unit is on its way.'

Outside, I stood by the car and watched and waited while I texted Paul. I wouldn't be going anywhere for a while, least of all to a nice, quiet Docklands luxury pad. Pity. I'd been hoping for a spa bath.

Paul replied after a couple of minutes. I'd probably woken him this time.

Stay there. I'm coming.

Relief trickled through me, heavy and solid like mercury. Someone had my back. I put my phone away and watched as, in ones and twos, my neighbours emerged from the apartment block in hastily thrown-on clothes, the couple from downstairs carrying their still-sleeping children and laying them in the back of their station wagon. Nobody seemed to know that it was my apartment that was the problem.

The big Maori guy from the end unit on the second floor was on his phone. 'Dunno, bro. Nah, not a fire. Heard someone say there was a bomb, but that's just stupid, eh? Nah, can't afford to take the day off work. Yeah, see you there. Might be late. Tell the boss, eh? Thanks, bro.'

He hung up and put his phone in his back pocket, then pulled on the hoodie he'd been carrying, yanking it over his big belly. Then he folded his arms and looked up. I followed his gaze, but there was nothing to see. Maybe he was waiting for an explosion to prove there was a bomb. God, I hoped not. I didn't have much, but I'd rather not have it shredded to confetti. I didn't know whether to laugh or cry. Crying got the upper hand for a few seconds, then I rubbed my eyes hard and folded my arms, too. *Let's get this over with, bro.*

A dark van pulled up, followed by another. Bomb unit. Nothing on the outside, of course, but very shortly the team started unloading their equipment and the Maori guy's mouth dropped. 'Fuck me,' he said.

By the looks on the other tenants' faces, they felt the same. It was hard to believe. Maybe we were all extras in some bizarre movie, except there was no way I wanted to be the star victim. For the first time, it sank in, right to my bones, that Grandad was right. Fayed was after me, too.

'Hey,' a voice behind me said, and Paul gave me a one-armed hug. 'You doing okay?'

'Yeah, I'm fine,' I said, but my croaky voice said the opposite.

'Bomb unit, I see.' He let me go. 'They'll soon sort it out. Do you have to stay?'

I gestured at Constable Watson, who chose that moment to glare at me as if warning me to stay right where I was. 'I've been ordered to stay put.'

'Fair enough. They'll want to know why.'

'How much do I tell them?'

He smiled. 'Tell them you're Hamish's granddaughter, and who your father is. That should be plenty.'

'I don't want to tell Grandad about this. That's why he wanted me to go and see him tonight. To warn me.'

'Good thing he did. Would you have been so careful if he hadn't?'

I thought about where I parked and skulking around in case someone was following me. 'Probably not.'

'Who found the bomb?' Paul asked.

'The two officers who were checking out my apartment. I'd seen someone inside.' I pointed at the hedge. 'From over there.'

'You said it was under your bed?'

I nodded. 'I'm lucky the officers were so diligent.' I could have thumped down on my bed a bit hard and set it off, or it might have been on a timer after all. Or set off remotely when they saw I was in the room. If I'd gone in and turned the light on … My vision blurred and my head spun. I leaned on the police car and tried to breathe evenly. 'This is really fucked.'

Paul didn't reply for a few moments. Maybe he was trying to find a way to put it nicely. 'I think prison has turned Fayed into a bitter psycho. Or more of one. But you're alive, and if they get that bomb defused, they may well find enough on it to arrest its maker, who may then rat on Fayed.'

'That's a lot of ifs and maybes.'

'True, but …'

'Ms Alcott?' The voice was familiar and I turned, already knowing who it was.

'Detective Constable Singh.'

Paul turned as well.

'I've been told the explosive device is in your apartment,' Singh said. 'Can you run me through how you knew it was there? Who might have put it there?'

There was something about her tone of voice that made me bristle, like she thought it was my fault, I'd done something to deserve it. 'I didn't know it was there,' I said coldly. 'I saw someone in my apartment and called the police. *They* found it.'

She wrote a lot of stuff in her notebook, making me wait while she scribbled, so I moved away from her to watch the bomb unit liaise with Watson as they prepared to take the robot up the stairs. Two more police cars had arrived and parked with their lights flashing, lighting up the area with blue and red. The officers in them began moving everyone further away from the building, setting up a much bigger cordon. One of them approached us.

'You need to move back down the street,' she said, her finger indicating where we should go. She glanced at Singh. 'You, too, I'm afraid.'

Singh signalled to another detective I hadn't noticed before, a tall, lanky male with a pockmarked face and shaven head. They conversed in low voices and he gave me a strange look. I could see his lips saying, 'Same woman?' and his almost invisible eyebrows went up.

Then we all moved onto the street, away from the cordon tape.

'Is this going to take long?' Paul asked Singh. 'My colleague has had a stressful night. Her grandfather, Hamish Campbell, was shot and she's been threatened.'

Grandad's name had no effect on Singh but the other detective knew. Another muttered exchange happened, and then Singh asked, 'Is this bomb connected with Mr Campbell's incident?'

'Yes,' Paul snapped before I could reply. 'Ms Alcott has had serious threats made against her and now they've been carried out. She needs police protection, not to be made to stand here out in the open, when a sniper could take her out in a second. Never mind any collateral damage.'

Singh opened her mouth to reply, but Paul talked over her. 'If you can't guarantee a safe place for this interview immediately, then I will be taking her away and you can talk to her later.'

Paul's words made me feel even more nervous. I scanned the apartment blocks further down the street, and saw faces in almost every window as people watched the commotion. A news van had parked at the end of the street and already the female crime reporter was in front of a camera with a mike in her hand. I recognised her, even from where I stood. The milling crowd of spectators and flashing red and blue made a good backdrop, but I didn't want to be part of it. I made sure my back was to her and said, 'I want to get out of here. Right now.'

'You can't hold her,' Paul said. 'She's the victim here.'

Singh stared at me, her eyes narrowed. I could almost hear wheels grinding inside her head. 'All right. But I want you at the station at 9am.'

'She'll be there,' Paul said. He took my arm and bustled me down the street, away from the TV reporter and the crowd, past the Commodore and around the corner into a narrow lane. Just past a white delivery van, he wheeled, pulling me with him, and opened the van's side door. 'Inside. Quick.'

I obeyed, clambering in to sit on a comfortable seat next to a dark-tinted window. He got in beside me and slammed the door shut. 'Let's go.'

I jumped when the engine started. I hadn't even noticed the small man in black sitting in the driver's seat. 'Where to?' the driver asked.

'I'll decide in a minute,' Paul said. 'Let's get out of here first.'

The way the van lumbered down to the corner and swung around it told me it was more than a normal old white van. It had extra metal in it for a start, probably all four sides. Behind my seat was a steel wall—who knew what was back there. Weapons?

'Surveillance unit,' Paul said, as if reading my mind. 'Sound proof. And the whole van is pretty bullet proof, although it hasn't been tested.'

Yet.

'How long is it going to take the police to arrest Fayed?' I asked. 'Days? Weeks?'

'I doubt it will matter,' Paul said. 'They'll have to find him first. Don't worry. The situation should be sorted out by tomorrow night.'

My brain was fuzzy with lack of sleep and the after-effects of discovering I could have been blown into tiny chunks of wet flesh. 'What do you mean?'

Paul's face creased and he blinked hard. 'It'll get sorted. Don't worry.'

I still couldn't make sense of it, but I kept quiet and let my brain right itself and settle as we rumbled through the dark streets of North Melbourne. Then I realised what he meant. Grandad had put the word out. By tomorrow night, Fayed would be dead.

And I, presumably, would be safe.

CHAPTER TWENTY-THREE

Paul made a call and then directed the driver to Flinders Lane. I slumped in my seat, feeling like I was in the middle of some kind of nightmare.

Within a few minutes he was nudging me. 'Come on, time to go. Keep your head down.'

We climbed out and he tucked my hand inside his arm; I staggered along, barely noting the W outside the glass doors, the extremely swanky lobby, gleaming marble and stern-faced security man in a black suit who held the lift for us and then let us into my room. It was the most luxurious hotel room I'd ever been in, and I gaped at the gold décor and cocktail bar in the corner.

'I have to go,' Paul said. 'You'll be okay here. Nobody knows where you are. Including the police.'

'That's a good thing?'

'For now. I didn't want you in Docklands on your own. There'll be someone outside your door here as well.' He gave me a hard look. 'Do not leave this room. Fayed is not messing around.'

I agreed. I was happy to hide here. It was serious luxury. I was too scared to touch anything and had an urge to wash my hands. But then I might dirty the towels. Or the basin. My boots were probably dirty as well. 'Who's paying for this?'

Paul laughed uproariously and I finally cracked a smile. 'Not me,' he said. 'Your grandfather. So make the most of it.'

I looked at my watch and groaned. 'It's nearly 5am. I have to talk to Detective Singh in four hours.'

'No, you don't. I'll get Sherman onto it. He'll let you know what time he's available and you go with him.'

All I could do was nod, say goodbye and crawl into bed. My last thought was to wonder how entwined Sherman, Paul and my grandfather actually were. The thought faded fast.

***

I dreamed of Melinda. I was strapped to a bed, screaming for help and being threatened by a ninja wielding a machete. I could see Emmanuel floating around in the distance, but he didn't hear me and drifted away. I looked over at the bed next to me and there was Melinda, tied up like me. Except she was dead.

I woke up with my mouth wide open, like I was screaming, but no noise came out. My throat was bone dry and I coughed and coughed. I staggered to the fancy bar in the corner and pulled open the fridge, reached for a mineral water and then thought, *Stuff it*. The mini bottle of sparkling wine had a fancy label—I twisted off the lid and drank the whole lot. It barely hit the sides. But at least I stopped coughing.

In the hot shower, which was a glass-sided, shiny-tiled space that could fit three people, I stood under the streaming water and let it pound the back of my neck.

Emmanuel. Why didn't he come to help me? Or was he a sign of what might happen if I didn't take enough care? Or was I over-analysing?

And Melinda. I'd let her down. I could've saved her, if only ...

For the first time, I tried to fully accept the possibility she was dead. It had been—how many days? Shit, I didn't even know for sure. Five days? I tried to count, but the dream seeped back into my mind. I pushed it away.

She might still be alive. Psychos did that. Kept women in a room somewhere and ... I didn't want to go there. I just wanted to find her in time and catch the guy who'd taken her.

I knew I was supposed to stay in the swanky hotel and be pampered and waited on while being watched over like a baby. I couldn't. I got dressed in yesterday's clothes and set off for Paul's office, grabbing a large triple-shot coffee and a bacon and egg roll on the way. I kept a sharp eye out for anyone following me.

I pushed through the door into the front office and Gang's mouth went into an O. 'What are you doing here? Are you okay? Does Paul know where you are?'

'Work. Yes. No.' I grinned. 'Any hits on Jessica?'

'I … um … I'm sorry, I haven't had time. I've been up most of the night.'

I checked his eyes. Bloodshot and red-rimmed. 'What were you working on? Or were you partying?'

'The main thing was I've been trying to help Paul find Fayed. And monitor the police reports on your apartment. And your grandfather's shooting. And the arrests. And keep your grandfather updated.' He paused. 'He doesn't do phone calls very well, does he?'

'Er, no. He likes face to face, where nobody can listen in.' I frowned. 'Is my apartment still there? Like, not blown up?'

'It's all cool, they defused the bomb.' He flapped his hands. 'Oh my God, if you had been in there and it had gone off! You were so—'

'Lucky. I know.'

Gang let out a huge sigh. 'I'll let Paul know you're here.' His mobile let out a jangling rendition of tinkling bells and he checked the screen. 'That's him now.'

'He's not in his office?'

Gang answered Paul instead of me. 'Yes, boss. No. No. Right.' He glanced at me. 'She's here.' He held the phone away from his ear and Paul's voice boomed out.

'What the hell is she doing there? Jesus Christ on a bike!'

Gang said, 'Do you want to talk to her?'

'No! Tell her to stay in the office, or it will be me putting a bomb under her. I'll be there in an hour or so.'

He hung up and Gang made a face. 'That went well.'

I knew Paul was trying to keep me safe, but I felt safer here than the hotel. And here I could do something worthwhile.

'Can you give me the details so I can log in as Jessica and see what's happening?' I said. 'I need to keep trying.

I just … I had this dream about Melinda and she was dead.'

'Hey, we don't know that for sure.'

'I bet that's what the police are thinking now.' I reached for my phone. 'I'm going to call that detective and see what they've found out.'

Scotcher answered in a couple of seconds. 'Detective Sergeant Scotcher.'

'It's Lou Alcott.'

'Yes.' It wasn't quite a snarl.

'I was hoping you could tell me if there was any news about Melinda. It's been nearly a week, and … you know.'

'Nothing, sorry. Nobody apart from you had seen her or heard from her before she went missing. Nobody has heard from her since.' He let out a huffed breath. 'She's not active on the dating sites, and she hasn't used her phones or bank accounts. She hasn't attended classes.'

That was more than I expected him to tell me. 'Did you talk to her father?'

'Yes,' Scotcher said shortly. 'He was no help. Also Gunn is still in Sydney, knows nothing.'

'Do you think she's … dead?'

'I'm not going to answer that, Ms Alcott. Anything else?'

'Will you let me know if you have any news—at all? Please?'

'I'll try. Not promising though.'

'Thanks.'

I hung up and sat, staring at the floor. How must it feel for families whose loved ones go missing and there is never any inkling of what happened to them? Not even a body? It must be the most gut-wrenching, never-ending pain. No wonder marriages broke up over it, especially when it was a child.

And yet Melinda's father didn't seem to give a stuff.

I pulled myself up in the chair. That was his problem, cold, miserable bastard that he was. Melinda still had me. And I wasn't giving up yet.

I took Gang's information and logged into each of the dating sites, checking Jessica's profile and who had her on their 'interested' list. Nobody who looked familiar, and nobody who was one of Melinda's original hits. Possibly the police questioning them had stopped them using the dating apps for a while.

I saw a few faces that appeared on several of the apps, meaning Melinda wasn't the only one who used at least two. How did these guys keep up with all their choices? I guessed, with some of them, at least, that they didn't get many swipes or ticks or whatever back, so it was manage-able. Probably there were a few guys who got sex out of it every night of the week. I grew tired thinking about it—the fake date, the chatting up, the manoeuvring into bed. Or maybe I was a prude and the girls were just as keen for some no-ties bonking.

'How's it going?' Gang asked, just as Paul came in.

'How's what going?' Paul leaned over my shoulder and peered at the Jessica page I had open. 'Ah, that. Any luck?'

'Our Jessica has had a lot of interest, but we're not respond-ing to any of it,' Gang chipped in. 'None of the guys are ones Melinda connected with.'

Paul frowned, thinking. 'But ... if there are any that look sus, or that did link back to her, how will you take it any further? Jessica can't meet them.'

Gang leapt out of his chair and came over to my desk, waving his hands in the air. 'I know! That's the flaw in our strategy. But I did have a better idea. Well, not amazingly better, but it would get us maybe a bit further …' He kept nodding at us.

Paul's eyebrows went up. I think mine did, too. Gang in full enthusiasm mode was startling.

'Is it legal?' Paul asked.

'Oh, yes, of course!' Gang smiled and his eyes sparkled, then he focused them on me and I felt a deep, uneasy stirring in my guts.

'What are you up to?' I asked. 'It'd better not be—'

Paul was already shaking his head. 'No, Lou can't go anywhere. It's too dangerous.'

'That's right,' I said. 'I have to stay here. Stay out of sight.'

Paul's phone shrilled some kind of bizarre music and he answered. 'Marshall. Yes. Really? Where? Fucking hell. That's brilliant. Thanks.'

He disconnected and gave me a wide smile. 'The police have arrested Fayed. He was in some expensive Airbnb at Sorrento. Cheeky bastard. Running things from down there.'

Gang beamed. 'Hey, you're safe now. His guys won't do anything without him.'

I wasn't so sure, but I did feel a tiny bit of relief.

Paul soon squashed that. 'It only takes one cowboy wanting to impress the boss. Hamish and Lou aren't out of the woods just yet.'

No way I was going home then. That gold minibar had a few more interesting bottles in it. I knew Grandad wouldn't mind.

'But she's safe here at work!' Gang said. 'I can set you up on those dating apps, you can monitor them for suspects, and we'll have another go at finding who took Melinda!'

'Well ...' Paul said. 'As long as it's all done remotely.'

Even my death glare wasn't enough to dissuade either of them from their stupid plan.

CHAPTER TWENTY-FOUR

Paul decided the Jessica profiles should be deleted. But he wasn't convinced replacing them with me was going to work either. 'My analysis says this guy probably has a type,' Gang said. 'We can take photos of Lou that will look like the ones Melinda used. But she'll have to dress up,' he added, eyeing my grubby jeans and top.

'More than dress up,' Paul said. 'She'll have to look nothing like herself.'

'Hey, I'm in the room!' I snapped. 'Kindly include me in this discussion!'

'Sorry,' Paul said. 'But this could possibly work. Will you give it a try? To see if we can flush this guy out?'

I thought about it for a few moments. Nothing else had worked, had it?

I sighed. 'All right.'

'You need good makeup and your hair styled,' Gang said. 'I know just the people. My cousins. They'll come here and do it, for a good rate.' He tapped two fingers against his mouth as he examined me in a way I didn't like at all. 'I'll ask them to bring some clothes, too.'

He was starting to remind me, in the worst possible way, of the British fashion guru who did makeovers on TV. Grok? Glock?

'There's one problem,' I said. 'Even if you had the photos, what the hell am I supposed to do if I get matches? I hate chatting. And most of the men are really stupid and arrogant, and all they talk about is football.'

'Gee, don't hold back, Lou,' Paul said. 'Besides, you won't be dating in person. We're sticking to what shows up online. This is an investigation.'

'It's a fishing expedition!' He had no idea how bad I was at this stuff.

'That's true,' he said. 'And I am well aware that we're using you as bait.'

I hadn't expected him to put it so baldly. 'I just don't think—'

'That it will work?' He perched his bum on the edge of the desk and folded his arms, nodding in Gang's direction. Gang was still on the phone, rounding up his cousins who specialised in makeovers. 'Gang and I had a long discussion about all of this before I agreed he could create Jessica. I didn't think it was worth the time and effort, to be honest, but the police still aren't getting anywhere.'

'Neither are we. Nobody has come up who connected with Melinda. In real life or online.'

'I know. So I was about to pull the plug on it. We have paying work to do here, and much as I know you want to find Melinda, we can't just ...' He cleared his throat. 'However, things have changed since then.

'I've been talking to a contact in Homicide who works in the missing persons squad,' he said. 'She thinks there's something going on, but there's little concrete proof. Her gut feeling is not enough.'

'We know there's something going on.' I tried to stop my voice from rising, but it went up anyway. 'Melinda is missing and probably dead.'

'No, you don't understand. She thinks—well, I think I agree with her—that Melinda isn't the first. She's got two other MisPer cases that are similar. I got Gang to research them last night.'

'Yeah, in among everything else,' Gang said, rolling his eyes, his call to his cousins finished.

'Two others?' I shivered and goose bumps rose down my arms. 'Melinda is the third? How come the police haven't picked up on this? Three is ...' I didn't want to say it.

'Classified as a serial killer.' Gang said it for me.

I stared at them, my mind jumping around, trying to make connections, but I had no information. 'Who are the others? What happened? Were they on one of those dating apps?' I sounded demanding, like a little kid. It wasn't nice.

'Calm down,' Paul said. 'Gang, can you bring up your distilled notes and photos for Lou? We can look at them on the conference room screen.'

A couple of minutes later, we were sitting around the big table while Gang ran through what he'd put together.

'Just finished this about an hour ago, so it's rough, but I think it covers everything.' He tapped a key and a photo of a young woman with long, brunette hair and large hoop earrings came up on the screen on the wall. 'Casey Freebourne. Twenty-nine. Went missing while running along Brighton Beach about 9pm. One witness walking a dog saw her jogging towards the carpark, checking her watch. She was wearing one of those fitness things that light up, which is why he noticed it.'

Gang consulted his notes. 'She lived alone. Family is up in Brisbane. She moved to Melbourne for a job and had only been here two months.'

'What dating app did she use?'

'They don't know. Her phone was, and still is, missing.'

'Then what's the connection?'

'She'd talked to her sister the night before and told her she'd signed up to a couple of the apps,' Paul said, 'and her sister went and had a look, just out of curiosity. When the police checked a few days later, following up what the sister said, Casey's profiles had all been wiped. So they thought she must have done it herself, thinking better of it.'

'Bit of an assumption,' I said.

Paul didn't answer, just gestured to Gang to move on.

Gang tapped a key and another photo came up, a little blurry, of a slightly older woman with shoulder-length dark hair and a nice but serious face. She was standing next to a horse, her hand on its neck. 'Facebook photo. This is Maria Dallas, thirty-four. Also lived alone. She was a legal clerk, only family is her mother, who has early-onset dementia and has been in a home for several years. Maria used to visit her three or four times a week, then she just stopped. She also stopped turning up to work, and her employer, a criminal lawyer, was the one who reported her missing.'

'Good for her,' I said. 'And?'

'Police went to her unit, no reply, they got a key from the property management company and went in. Nothing. No sign of her. No phone, wallet, purse. Just a nice dress and shoes laid out as if she was about to go out.'

'On a date,' I said flatly.

'That's what they think,' Gang said. 'They found her work diary in a briefcase-type bag, which mostly had business stuff in it. Meetings, appointments. For the night they think she went missing, there was an initial. A. With an exclamation mark after it, and a little smiley face. With a time—8pm.'

'What are they basing the date of disappearance on?'

'It was a Thursday and she would have been at work on Friday as usual, but that was the first day she didn't show up.'

I thought for a moment. 'Date?'

'Twenty-seventh of July.'

'Middle of winter. It'd be well and truly dark by six thirty.'

Gang brought up another photo of a row of single-storey units, taken from the street. 'Maria's was the one at the back. So someone could have knocked on her door and nobody would have noticed them.'

I peered at the photo. 'There are security lights at the front. Is that one over her door?'

Gang nodded. 'It wasn't working. When they checked, the bulb was fine, but it had been loosened.'

I blinked at the photo. 'Shit. That had to be deliberate. I think ...' My brain was clicking over so fast I forgot to talk as I ran through the comparisons and Gang's notes and what I knew about Melinda.

'Come on,' Paul said. 'What's your gut saying?'

'My gut?' I screwed up my face as I tried to sort through the pieces and put them in order. 'Was Maria on any dating apps?'

'The detective investigating her disappearance—and being hassled by Maria's boss to take it seriously, which she did—found a note in the front of her work diary. It was the letter B and then the letter T, each bracketed with what they think was a password, with random letters and numbers.'

'Bumble and Tinder,' Gang jumped in.

'Did they confirm that?'

'If she had a profile on Bumble, it was gone by the time they looked. They found one for her on Tinder, but the next day it had been deleted. All the detective had was a screenshot of her profile.'

'Damn it!' I slapped the table. 'So they have no idea who she swiped with.' I looked at Gang. 'Tinder is the swiping one, right?'

'Yes,' he said, giving me a look. 'I think you'd better let me take care of the apps. You might accidentally swipe on someone you don't mean to. And then you'd have to respond.'

Paul intervened. 'That's not going to happen. I want to make this really clear to both of you. There will be no real "dates" happening. We're fishing here, not looking for the catch of the day.'

Gang snorted loudly and then pretended he hadn't, making his face all serious. 'That's right, boss. We're looking. And we're using Lou's supersonic ID skills, right?'

'Yes. But I think …' Paul gazed at me and I could almost see cogs turning in his brain.

'Hang on. We're forgetting one thing—the women this guy targets are not gorgeous, or even noticeably attractive.' I waved a hand at the screen where a photo of Casey was still hovering. 'Do I even need the makeover? It's pretty clear he's targeting women who are on their own. Either they've moved here recently or are in a situation where they have little or no family close by. Nobody to gossip to, share the dating stuff with. Lonely women who probably find the chatting part of all this the safest. And he's enough of a smooth talker to persuade them to meet. But maybe they don't.'

'Why not?' Paul asked.

Gang was nodding furiously again. 'Because he can't afford for anyone to see them together. Restaurants and bars have CCTV, staff who remember faces, and there's dash cams in cars in the street. So he uses the chat to work out where they live, organises a date and then turns up early at their house or flat.'

'And then …' I blew out a sharp breath. 'That's the bit I don't get. Why wait for date night to grab them?'

We all looked at each other. Nobody could come up with anything that sounded even halfway logical. It wasn't even that he wanted to grab them when they were all dressed up and pretty, because one of the women hadn't managed to change into her going-out dress. Maybe it was simply a case of watching and striking as soon as there was an opportunity.

'So, the makeover?' Gang said.

'A disguise,' Paul said. 'I'm serious. I want you to give her a fake name and details as well, like Jessica. And make sure the photos you take make her unrecognisable, especially as a former cop.' He turned to me. 'Your grandfather would have my guts to string his tennis racquet if this put you in danger from Fayed's boys.'

An image flashed in front of me of my bed exploding and I shut up.

CHAPTER TWENTY-FIVE

Gang's cousins were so petite they made me feel like an
elephant and, given I'm only 164cm, that was a feat in itself.
They were also extremely fashionable, looked amazing and
managed to make me envious of their makeup and ease in
clothes. I should have hated them, but they were so lovely
and giggly, and they never once pursed their lips or looked
like I was a lost cause, so we became best friends in about
two minutes.

Their names were Lily and Blossom, and they listened
intently to what Gang said about 'disguise' and how I absolutely needed to be safe.

'Sure thing,' Lily said, with a faint American accent.

Blossom puffed out her small chest, covered in fuschia
silk. 'I have also done the special effects cosmetics training.'
She beamed at me. 'I can make you look like a corpse, if you
want me to.'

'Er, no, that's not necessary, thank you!' That was the last thing I needed. 'But I do need to look … not like me.'

'Not a big makeover,' Gang said.

'Aww,' Lily said, clearly disappointed she wasn't going to be allowed to turn me into something glamorous, or at least attractive.

I felt so bad for her. Before I could stop myself, I said, 'Maybe we can do that another time.'

Lily and Blossom squealed with excitement.

Gang rolled his eyes. 'You don't know what you have unleashed.'

Then I remembered why we were doing this. My face prickled and my eyes ached. I let out a long breath, my head down.

Lily and Blossom chattered in Chinese and Gang replied, and four small hands patted my shoulders. 'We know,' Lily said. 'Gang told us. We will help you find your friend.'

I pulled several tissues out of the box on Gang's desk and pressed them hard against my eyes for a few seconds. Breathe, breathe. Okay. 'It's going to be good,' I said as firmly as possible. 'We will do this and we will make it work.' As if me saying it was some kind of magic spell. Maybe it was. Fuck knows, we needed something.

Lily and Blossom worked on me in the conference room, where any clients coming in wouldn't see what we were up to. Gang had taken his laptop away and turned off the big screen, and I was relieved there were no mirrors in there so I couldn't see what the girls were doing to me.

I expected my face to feel like it had a thick mask on, but although my skin knew it had stuff on it, it was okay. My eyes, however, were a different story. I drew the line at the false eyelashes, because I didn't want to look like I was wearing a pair of hairy spiders, so instead I received about six coatings of mascara. And then the lipstick. Gross. And finally my brown hair, brushed and styled with a hot wand, hanging past my shoulders. It felt like I was wearing candy floss.

Then they opened two large suitcases of clothes and started trying dresses and tops up against me, chatting about colour palettes and patterns and ambience until I had had enough.

'Listen, I think we only need a few different looks, and anything will do.'

They looked at me as if I was mad.

Blossom scanned me again and said something to Lily, who pulled out a slinky black dress and handed it to me. 'This one first.'

I must have looked uncomfortable, because Blossom said, 'We are in shop changing rooms all the time. We are stylists, Lou. It's our job.'

By that, I guessed she meant 'just get your gear off, we don't care', so I took off my jeans and T-shirt and pulled the dress over my head. Lily tweaked and tugged bits of it until she was satisfied. She nodded briskly. 'Good fit. Call Gang.'

'But—'

Lily tsked. 'He's the photographer, Lou. And the judge, of course.'

'Judge?' Was I going on *Australia's Next Top Model* or something?

'If we have achieved what your boss wanted. We have to keep you safe, remember?' She patted my arm.

There was a light knock and Gang called, 'Ready?'

Blossom opened the door and let him in. He was carrying a large digital camera and a tripod, but he leaned the tripod against the wall and turned to look at me. His mouth fell open.

'Oh. My. Stars.'

'Doesn't look like Lou, huh?' Blossom said.

'I just … I don't …' Gang was floundering. Unusual for him.

That worried me. A lot. 'I need to see what you're going on about.'

Nobody knew where there was a full-length mirror. The one in the Ladies' toilet was barely the size of a piece of A4 paper.

'I can go buy one,' Gang said. 'Or I can take your photo and show it to you?'

I hesitated. It was better than nothing. 'All right, but if I look terrible, this is all coming off.' I noticed Lily's and Blossom's hurt expressions. 'I'm sorry, I know you've worked hard. It's just me.'

Another knock at the door—Paul this time. I cringed inside. This was so embarrassing. He put his head around the door and checked me over.

'Good job, girls. I doubt her own father would recognise her, and that's what we want right now. Photos, please. Let's get this show on the road.'

He left and most of my dread went with him. This was work. I could do this.

Gang positioned me in the best light and took several photos, not insisting I smile, then quickly transferred them via Bluetooth to his laptop and turned on the big screen. I couldn't look.

'Good photo, Gang!' Lily said. 'That course you did was worth it, hey?'

Slowly, I lifted my head and looked at the screen. 'Get out of here!' I couldn't believe it. The young woman up there looked nothing like me. She was serious and … kind of sexy. I felt a bit sick.

'We need some smiling ones, too,' Gang said. He smiled at me and added softly, 'Remember, this is for Melinda, okay?'

I took a deep breath and let it out. 'Yeah, all right. Let's get it over with.'

By the time we'd finished, I knew exactly what it felt like to be one of those models backstage being whipped in and out of outfits, re-polished and sent out again. But Gang was very particular about how he took the photos.

'I've looked at the three women's photos a lot,' he said. 'I want to try and recreate what their appearance was, what they wore, what it said to him. What drew him to those particular women.'

'I thought it was because they were all alone,' I said.

'Later on,' he agreed. 'But in the beginning, when he was sussing them all out on the apps, it was about appearance and vibes first.' He pulled the memory card out of his camera and waved it at me. 'You'll see.'

I helped Lily and Blossom pack up their clothes and makeup, and thanked them for their help.

Blossom handed me a packet of makeup remover wipes with a grin. 'I know you can't wait to use these. It's fine. My feelings aren't hurt … much.'

Lily wagged her finger at me. 'I won't forget you agreed to a proper session one day, after you have found your friend.'

After they'd left, and had given me a bag of makeup to use if I needed it, Gang called Paul in to go through the photos on the big screen. But first Gang showed us the few he had from the dating apps, most of which were Melinda's from her second phone. He'd made a list of key things to look for: brunette, longer hair, large eyes, photos that made the women look shy or a bit nervous. I'd had no trouble with that one.

'So he's looking for vulnerable then,' Paul said. 'Let's see what Lou came up with.'

Gang clicked through all of the photos he'd taken, one by one, and we rejected most of them. 'Too confident,' Paul said several times, which made me think I was a better actor than I thought. Secretly, I was gobsmacked at what I looked like. The woman in the images really didn't look like me at all. Dresses I would never choose to buy, poses I would never try, and some of the smiles looked almost natural. But I soon saw what Paul was talking about. Every now and then, Gang had captured me looking uncertain, solemn, a little bit afraid. Those were the photos we chose.

I was going to be Lisa—using a name starting with L meant I was more likely to remember to answer to it. I tried not to think about the fact that 'answering to Lisa' meant I might be going on some kind of date or meet-up, despite what Paul said.

This is the guy who took Melinda—you have to remember that!

Gang had my profile all ready to go, and I'd been through it and barely changed a thing. He knew what he was doing.

'Right,' Paul said. 'Let's launch Operation Melinda.'

Gang began uploading and activating my Lisa profile to the three apps we had chosen, while Paul and I watched on the screen. I folded my arms tightly and sat back, trying to look calm, but my heart was powering around inside my chest like a Formula 1 car.

Paul glanced at me and smiled grimly. 'We're going to get this bastard, Lou.'

Damn right.

I went off to the Ladies and used the wipes to clean my face. The mascara took the longest, and I refused to look in the mirror until I was sure most of it was gone. The face that looked back at me was pale and drawn, with reddened eyelids, but I liked it better.

Back in the conference room, Paul and Gang were conferring, nodding and making notes in a way that sent a tremor through me. They had action already?

Paul looked up. 'Lou, you need to check all of the ones who swipe you, at least. And as many of the others as possible. See if you recognise any of them. You just never know.'

I turned to the big screen. A blond guy with a sixpack of abs and a gold chain I could have towed a car with beamed at me. 'You have got to be kidding.'

'He's an obvious no,' Gang said.

'Gang's got it all sorted,' I said. 'So you don't need me.' The whole day had been a bit much. I'd kind of thought I could go home now and drink a few quiet glasses of wine and maybe throw a frozen pie in the microwave and forget all this until tomorrow.

Paul frowned. 'No, you have to be using your super-recogniser skills right from the start. I think it's pretty obvious he's disguising himself each time he goes onto the apps and looks for a woman to grab.'

'How would a man disguise himself?' I asked. It seemed risky just to rely on my super-recogniser skills. I wanted to know what the possibilities were.

'Lily and Blossom said there are lots of ways,' Gang said. 'Change hair colour and style, different glasses or not, add a moustache and beard maybe, smile, don't smile, coloured contacts.' He poked his own cheeks. 'Even putting padding inside his mouth to change the shape of his face.'

'But you'll still recognise him, right?' Paul said.

'Er … maybe. I hope so.' He had more faith in me than I did.

'All right, I'll leave you to it,' Paul said. 'I've got to talk to a potential client. Keep me updated.'

Gang pointed to several photos he'd printed out and laid across the table. 'These are the images we have of the possibles, based on Melinda's phone. But that one—' He tapped a photo of Jonathan Black. 'He's the one who deleted his profile almost straight away.'

I leaned over and eyeballed the five images. Yes, those were the ones. I took a much closer look at Mr Black. Good looking, dark hair, friendly eyes. I remembered his profile, how he liked Marvel movies, especially *Spider-Man*. Another photo caught my eye again—Nick Cullinan. He looked serious and his photo showed him sitting at a computer that had a coffee mug next to it. When I squinted, I could read what was embossed on it—*And just then Nick realised this was his circus and these were his monkeys*. I laughed. 'I might have to get me a mug like that.'

'Heeeyyyy,' Gang said, mock offended.

'Only kidding. But if Nick is a fake, he's gone to a lot of trouble to look legit.'

'True.' Gang peered at his screen. 'Hey, you've got quite a bit of interest already.'

My stomach did a backflip and I blinked at him. 'You're joking.'

'No, look.'

I didn't want to. 'Just tell me.'

'Well, this is Tinder, so you've had six so far, including Mr Blond Abs.' He clicked a few things. 'This app is showing nothing so far, but the third one has ... two interested.' He glanced at me. 'You need to look at them, Lou.'

This is work. You think this guy took Melinda. Get a fucking grip.

I moved around the desk and waited while Gang showed me which guys had 'swiped' on Tinder. None of them were the five who had matched with Melinda. It was the same with the other app.

'What happens now?' I asked.

'Nothing. If you don't swipe back, that's it. It just sits there.'

'Won't they know if I ignore them?' Maybe they were all waiting, a beer in their hand, planning a hot night. Not.

'Not necessarily,' Gang said. 'They might swipe right on half-a-dozen women at once. Like, every day. Maybe more. I'd guess the guys who don't do very well maybe try for lots?'

'Lots?'

He pointed at Blond Abs. 'If he swiped on ten girls, how many do you think would swipe back?'

'Girls with taste? None!'

'Yeah, but sometimes you might just want …' He looked at my face. 'Never mind.'

'How long do we have to stay here and do this?'

He checked his phone. 'It's nearly seven now. Probably another couple of hours.'

'Oh, please, no.' I groaned. 'I'm starving and I'd kill for a glass of wine.'

'There's a pizza place around the corner. We can order in and do this on the phone.'

'My phone?'

'No, of course not.' He patted my arm. 'I've set you up on a separate phone so you can't get things confused, and I can easily check how it's going. I know we said "bait", but we're not going to take any stupid risks here.'

I eyed the smartphone in his hand. No stupid risks.

And no sensible ones either, if there was such a thing.

CHAPTER TWENTY-SIX

By the time I'd drunk some not-very-good wine and Gang had downed an Asahi beer and we'd eaten our meat lovers pizza, my profile across all three apps had gained eleven new interested guys. None of them were our five. Or anyone who looked like Jonathan Black in disguise either. It was after 9pm and I wanted to go home, but I couldn't. The thought of sleeping in that bed where the bomb had been gave me the creeps.

I said goodnight to Gang, promised to keep an eye on the phone, which I promptly shoved deep into my bag, and nipped into a mini supermarket where I found one pair of undies a size too big, and added deodorant, a hairbrush and a toothbrush and toothpaste. I'd sort the rest tomorrow. My room at the fancy hotel was waiting for me, and so was the lovely big (safe) bed and the minibar.

I sat up in bed with some pinot gris and the TV going, and checked the dreaded phone. Another four interested guys. Again, none that looked like our suspects. Tomorrow was another day, I told myself as I brushed my teeth and climbed back into the bed.

I was almost asleep when the phone started making noises; Gang had activated the notifications on the apps. There were two more guys waiting for a match.

You'll be waiting forever.

I turned the phone off and went to sleep.

My dreams were not good, and more than once I woke up and froze, wondering where the hell I was, until I remembered I was in a hotel. In the morning, I staggered into the shower and felt slightly better after using the vanilla and coconut scented soap and shampoo. I didn't want to put on my rumpled clothes from yesterday, but I had no choice. I walked to the office, grabbing a large triple-shot latte and four crispy hash browns on the way. Gang, as usual, was there before me.

'How many?' he said eagerly.

'Um ... I think I had another half-a-dozen or so.'

'You think?' His eyebrows disappeared under his fringe.

'You've got a fringe today. Where are your spikes?'

'Don't change the subject.' He held out his hand and I turned the phone over to him. He powered it up and immediately the pings rang out, three different kinds. It sounded like a weird music composition. His finger flicked through the screens quickly. 'Hmm, hmm, nup, nup, I dunno, hey ...' He looked up at me. 'You'd better see this one.'

I went closer and peered at the screen. 'That's Nick Whatshisname, with the funny coffee mug.'

'Nick Cullinan. Who you could have responded to last night,' he said. 'He's on Bumble and you only get twenty-four hours.'

Like I could remember that. 'I don't have to actually meet him, do I?'

'No. You do have to swipe right though. And then say something in a message.'

My throat closed up and I coughed. 'Really?' It came out as a squeak.

'Lou, we talked about this.' Gang was trying to be sympathetic, but I could tell he was a bit miffed with me. 'This is our strategy. We're not playing games or having a bit of a joke. This is serious!'

'I know.' I closed my eyes for a second, then said, 'All right, what do I do? What do I say? And please don't tell me to be natural, or be me. I've never done this before and I have no idea what "chatting" is in these circumstances.'

'I've looked at some examples online,' Gang said. 'You just start off small, say hi, nice to meet you here. How's your day going? That kind of thing.'

'See, you could do it for me,' I said.

'No, it has to come from you. Otherwise, it'll be obvious there are two of us doing this. People can sense that in your voice. Your online voice.'

My online voice. Yeah, right. 'Okay, hand me the phone. But you have to help if I get stuck.'

'He's probably at work and won't reply straight away.'

I looked at his photo—he'd used the same one, but there were others. Nick at the beach, Nick with a mate who'd been cut out of the photo so only his arm was showing, Nick with a large tabby cat that was giving the camera a death stare. Fine. I swiped right. My heart was thumping so hard my T-shirt was pulsing.

We waited.

Nothing happened.

'Send a message,' Gang prompted.

'Oh, yeah, right.' It took me three tries to type *Hi, good to meet! How's your day going?* It was lame, but it was a start.

We waited. Nothing happened.

Paul came through the door and looked at us hunched over the phone. 'So, er … getting anywhere?'

'Got one of Melinda's swipes who's interested in Lou,' Gang said, 'but so far he hasn't responded to her message.'

Paul held back a grin. 'Keep going. No sign of our mysterious Jonathan?'

'Nup. Maybe he's lying low for a while.'

Because he was too busy looking for somewhere to bury Melinda? I shivered. No point thinking like that.

Paul went into his office and I could hear him on the phone for the next hour; dealing with clients, I assumed. Gang had work to do, so he left me with the phone while I wrote a report for Paul. I listed all the guys who had swiped my profile, their names and details. Was this an invasion of privacy of some kind? Well, it was a public platform, no different from Facebook. It was an interesting exercise in the end. By the time I'd listed them all and their various details in a spreadsheet that Gang showed me how to set up, it was clear that I had attracted a certain kind of guy, with a few small exceptions.

That's if they were telling the truth. Ha. As if.

Lots of them liked reading, quiet dinners, good movies, wine. That kind of matched what Gang had created for me. They were all between twenty-five and thirty-eight. I wasn't attracting any muscle-bound twenty-year-olds then. No rabid footy fanatics. Nobody with a V8 ute or a desire to go camping in the bush, thank God. Just the one with gold chains and abs.

Were there really that many men who enjoyed those four things? If so, I'd never met them. Maybe this online dating worked after all. For some people. So far I also hadn't attracted anyone who was just after sex. I'd sussed out the language for that—euphemistic and shaded most of the time. 'Looking for a good time' was obvious. 'Not looking for a long-term relationship' was another.

I went out to get a coffee and some fresh air, leaving the phone on the desk.

When I got back, Gang said, 'You need to have a look at your Tinder profile.' He had a funny expression on his face, like he was trying not to laugh.

'Oh, yes, what fresh hell is this, might I ask?'

'It's … interesting,' was all he'd say.

I opened Tinder and checked. 'Fuck my life.' Staring up at me from the screen, a pleasant smile on his face as he leaned against his Audi, was Scotcher. 'What's he doing on here?'

'Same as everyone else,' Gang trilled. 'Looking for leer-rve.' He grinned. 'You gonna swipe him?'

'No way!'

'But he's kinda cute. Isn't he? For a cop.'

'He hates me!' I frowned at Gang. 'Besides, I'm on here under a false name. If he looked close enough at my photos, he'd sus straight away what I was up to.'

'True.' He sighed. 'But after this is done, you could go back under your own name. You can still use some of our photos. Or Lily would sort you out again, make you look different.'

'You mean, make me look like me.'

'Yeah, I guess.' He made a sad face and I threw a pen at him.

'Get back to work, shit-stirrer!'

Nick hadn't replied to my message, and no other notifications were showing, so I emailed my report to Paul—leaving Scotcher off the list—and wondered what to do with the rest of my day.

A couple of minutes later, Paul came out of his office. 'Lou, I've just been talking to Hamish.'

Oh, shit, I should've called him. But since Fayed had been arrested, all that had gone off my radar. Apart from the almost exploding bed.

'I meant to call him. Is he still in hospital?'

'Yes. He's managed to get moved to a private place, and he's got bail on the charge. Court date will be a million years away.' Victorian courts were so far behind in getting cases heard and sorted that this was common. All right if you had the money for your bail, but if not, innocent or guilty, you were stuck in remand.

'I should go and see him.'

'Yes, well …' Paul's face creased in worry lines. 'Not yet. I've just heard they've dropped the charges against Antony Fayed. He's been released.'

I stared at him in horror. 'What?'

'One of his lieutenants has claimed it was all his idea, that Fayed knew nothing about it. He was trying to impress Fayed, that's all.'

'And the police believed that?'

'Not about believing, as you know. Gotta prove it.'

'So what does that mean for me and Grandad? Is Fayed still after revenge?' I swallowed. 'That all sounded like BS to me.'

'Me, too. So it's still full alert when you go anywhere.' He nodded at the phone lying on the desk next to me. 'Keep an eye on that, but I've got a job for you. Doing background checks for a company. You can do that from here.'

It was boring work, but it was one of the things that paid Paul's bills, so I got started. Close to 5pm, I finished the check I was working on and headed off, determined to visit Grandad, but knowing I had to be extra careful. I was in the Commodore again, which had been parked under the watchful eye of the building security company, and drove in circles at first to make sure I wasn't being followed. Using Google Maps, I found a park a few streets away from the private hospital and walked through back alleys, then went through the delivery entrance.

The place Grandad was in apparently allowed 'extras', or else he had paid them to allow his bodyguards to sit outside his room. After I'd been verified, I was allowed in. He was sitting up in bed, watching horse racing on a large TV and tapping bets into his phone.

'Thought you didn't bet on the horses anymore,' I said, after giving him a kiss.

He pointed at the screen where horses were lining up to go into the starting gates for a race at Doomben. 'See that one with the purple silks? Number twelve? That's mine.'

'You own racehorses now?' I stared at him.

'Good place to put my money and have a bit of fun,' he said. 'Besides, I get to name the foals as well.'

'Foals … So you've been doing this for a while.'

He sent me a sharp look. 'If you visited me more, Lou, you'd know these things.' He flapped his hand. 'Yes, I know, your life has been crap for a while and you've been a hermit. Not a good excuse in my book.'

Grandad never held back if he thought someone was being a dick. 'Sorry. I know. No excuse.' Well, I had several good ones, but there was no use trotting them out. He already knew.

'Watch carefully.' He pointed back at the screen and turned the volume up.

'Number twelve, right?'

The commentator was winding up ready for the starter's gun, then they were off, jumping out of the gates and racing hard down the first straight. In between all the horses' names the commentator was scrolling through, I caught one—Lucky Lucky Lou. 'Who the hell names their horse that?' I said.

Grandad grinned.

'Oh, you didn't.'

I stared at the screen. Number twelve was third from the front. Then it was second. It was a short race, a maiden, 1200 metres. Coming down the home straight, the two frontrunners were neck and neck. Lucky Lucky Lou got her head in front just on the finish line.

I couldn't help laughing. 'Hey, I'm a winner!'

'Make the most of it,' Grandad said. 'We'll hold her back a bit now. Otherwise the odds will be so low she won't be worth betting on.'

'So you're king of the race track now,' I said.

He grimaced. 'I can do it from a distance and visit the trainers when I want to. Have you been back to my house?'

'No. Is it still a crime scene?'

'They're supposed to be releasing it today.' Grandad gave me a stern look. 'You heard bloody Fayed is out?'

I nodded.

'Bastard is still determined to get me, I'm reliably told.' Now I got a finger wagging. 'That means you still need to watch your back as well. You staying in that pub in the city?'

Pub. That was Grandad all over. Five stars and it was still a pub. 'Yes.'

'Stay there another day or two, but if I hear anything, or Paul does, you'll have to move somewhere else. The only good news is Sammy is out of ICU.' He heaved a big sigh. 'Sherman was right. I shouldn't have underestimated Fayed, but I'm not letting the bastard get the better of me. I'll have to solve it my way.'

I didn't want to know what that was. I could guess. Maybe I could just live in five-star hotels for the rest of my life.

My dating phone peeped, and then my normal phone pinged from a different pocket.

'What's with all the phones?' Grandad asked.

I explained about the dating apps and Melinda.

He shook his head. 'I can't believe she's still missing. I'm sorry I couldn't help more.'

'Not your area, Grandad.' I stayed a bit longer, then as I left, realised I'd have to go back to my apartment and get clothes and undies and things. I couldn't afford a whole new wardrobe, or even a makeshift one for now. But the thought of going there made me shudder. In the car, I checked both phones, my own first. Paul had texted me some details about another job tomorrow and sent an email with a brief. I'd read it later. On the dating phone, I had a message from Nick.

Hey, thanks for connecting! Okay, that was nice. *It'd be good to get to know each other a little bit more.* He was cautious. That was a positive sign. *What are some of your favourite movies?* And he hadn't asked my star sign. Brilliant.

I hesitated. Gang said be myself, even though I was using a fake name. I typed slowly, thinking it through. *I like a good drama, so—* My brain went blank. I had to google recent movies to get some ideas. *Power of the Dog, Nomadland, Dune was okay, The King's Man. I didn't mind the latest Spider-Man, but not a huge fan of superhero movies.* I couldn't resist testing him. Let's see what he made of it. *What are your favourite books?* If he didn't really read, he'd tell me some classics.

There was no reply straight away, so I started the car and drove to my street, doing the same tricks to check if I was being followed and then parking further down. My heart was thumping in my ears. Too scared to go into my own home? Fuck, yeah. Maybe I should've called Grandad's guys for backup.

I sat there, debating with myself. The police had surrounded this place two days ago. Surely Fayed's men wouldn't take the risk of coming here again? I decided I wouldn't go in if I saw the slightest thing that jarred. I circled around the building next door and went through the carpark, checking for suspicious activity before I ventured up the back stairs. Thankfully, my door was locked. I don't know why I'd thought it might be hanging off its hinges, but I quietly unlocked and opened it and waited.

Silence.

I edged down my hallway, breathing shallowly, listening and looking. The place was a mess. I guessed that after they'd defused the bomb, they'd done a thorough search of the apartment for any other devices. That made me feel slightly better. All the same, I got down on my hands and knees and checked under the bed, the sofa, the armchair and then behind the toilet.

Cold sweat. My armpits felt soaked. I couldn't even bring myself to start tidying up. I grabbed the suitcase out of my wardrobe and filled it with clothes and underwear and toiletries. Threw in my spare runners and my boots, squashed the lid down and managed to get the zip closed. I glanced around, wondering if I'd forgotten anything. Yes, my safe. It was in the back corner of my wardrobe. I opened it and took out the contents. Passport, a wad of cash that Grandad had given me once as 'just in case' money, a tiny expensive digital camera, a jewellery box with my mother's rings and earrings and some of Nana's things. Now I was ready to leave.

The knock on my front door nearly made me wet myself. I dropped the bags and crept down the hallway. Before I reached the door, my phone buzzed with a text.

It's Joe. Sent by your grandfather to help. I'm at your door.

What the? I stood behind the door. 'Joe?'

'Yes.'

I looked through the spyhole, and recognised him from Grandad's garden patrols. He looked very serious, grim almost. I opened the door on the chain, even though I knew he could kick it open if he wanted.

'Why are you here?'

'Personal security.'

'Bodyguard?'

He flexed his shoulders. 'That's right. Mr Campbell's orders.'

God, he sounded like he'd been detailed to guard the Prime Minister.

'You think there'll be another attack?' I tried not to sound sceptical but it leaked out.

He sighed like the weight of the world was on him. Cheery Joe. 'Not like before. No more front-on stuff. Sneaky now.'

'Sneaky how?' Wasn't a bomb under my bed sneaky?

'No more bombs or house raids. So perhaps a sniper. Drive-by shooting, maybe. Maybe even a car bomb, detonated with a timer. I can check underneath.'

'I can do that.'

He grunted. He didn't believe me. 'Couple of days and it'll be sorted.'

I'd heard this twice already. 'By who? You?'

'Yeeaahh ... Better men than me ...'

I'd had enough of the macho stuff. 'Okay, but I'm fine. You can go, thanks. I'm not staying here. I'll let my grandfather know I'm tickety-boo.'

'Tickety?'

I didn't answer, simply shut the door, then called, 'You can go, honestly. I'll call Grandad, I mean, Hamish, and tell him.'

After a few long moments, Joe's footsteps sounded on the stairs. I waited five minutes, watching the clock, texted Grandad and then left. Thankfully, it seemed Joe had gone.

The hotel had valet parking, which I guess Grandad was paying for as well. I asked the guy to park the car near the basement lift. When I reached my hotel room, Nick had answered.

Cool selection of movies. I'm with you on the superhero thing. Books? Robert Galbraith, Michael Robotham, Ian Rankin, Tana French. Just for starters. I thought I'd have to google them for clues, but he beat me to it. *As you can see, I like crime fiction. A lot. LOL. What about you?*

One part of me was exasperated at having to do this chatting thing, like I'd been hoping the words 'I killed those women' would be in someone's profile. And compared to hiding out from Fayed, chatting on a dating app felt silly. Until I thought of Melinda. Another part of me was kind of intrigued. It was too early to tell if Nick was on my wavelength, and I had to remember I was a fake. But I was already thinking of how I would reply, and what my favourite books were. It was like having a penpal. I'd had one when I was a kid, a boy in France. All the other kids thought it was weird and nerdy, but we'd written to each other by snail mail and it'd been fun for the year it had lasted.

I made the most of room service, ordered a bottle of wine and four-mushroom risotto, then jumped in the shower. Ah, clean undies that fit!

By the time I emerged, the wine had arrived, and the food not long after. I finally got back to the dating phone and typed a reply to Nick with some authors I'd remembered under the shower. Then I checked all the apps, since I had a few notifications.

I left the Jointly app until last, checking Scotcher's profile on Tinder out of curiosity now I didn't have Gang at my shoulder. Apparently, his first name was Rob, unless that was an alias. Interesting hobbies. Fishing, comedy movies, long drives, car rallies. Not my type at all.

When I opened the Jointly app, there were two men waiting for my response. The first was some guy called Chuck who looked about twenty and had *Star Wars* figurines on the shelf behind him. Nup.

The other was a guy called Daniel. Light brown hair, cut in one of those trendy styles with shaved bits up the side. Hazel eyes. Rimless glasses. He was leaning his head on his hand, a half-smile on his face. Pretty ordinary. I flicked to the other two photos of him. One was him on the beach with a dog. It was a bit far away to see his face properly. I peered closer. If I had to say one way or another, it looked to me like that wasn't Daniel. Had he taken a photo of someone else with a dog and pretended it was him? Gang said guys with dogs or cats in their photos were popular. The third photo was Daniel on his back patio with a glass of wine, toasting the camera. The glass was partly in front of his face.

Something about him ...

I went back to the first photo and stared at it for a few long seconds, thinking maybe I was imagining it. No, I had to trust my recogniser abilities.

This was Jonathan Black.

CHAPTER TWENTY-SEVEN

It was like all the blood stopped running through my veins and my eyes dried out from staring too hard at his photo. I blinked a few times, shook out my limbs, walked around the vast room, stood staring out the window. Okay, this was it.

I called Paul. This was no time for texting.

'It's Black. Calling himself Daniel now. He's in the app and he's swiped me.'

'Holy shit.'

The words and the tone told me Paul hadn't entirely believed our strategy would work. Well, neither had I.

'What do I do?'

'Swipe first.' He waited while I did it. 'Now message.'

'What?'

'What did you say to the other guy?'

Oh, Nick. Right. I could use him as my example. 'Um, hang on.' I typed a similar greeting. 'I've done it. What if he wants to meet tonight?'

'He won't. If he's our prime suspect, he's cautious. He seemed to take a few days to set up Melinda and probably the same with the others. Remember that our analysis said his MO was to work out where they lived.'

'Wait. I'm still at this expensive hotel Grandad is paying for. If he geo-tracks me via the app, he'll be suspicious.'

'You can't go home.'

'I know. Grandad would kill me if I did.' I had an idea. 'Is your friend's apartment still available? If this Daniel asks, I could say I'm housesitting for a friend while I'm waiting for my place to be painted?'

'That might work.' Paul's breathing echoed through the phone. 'All right, I'll ring my mate and check. If it's still okay with him, you can move there.'

'Right. I'll text you when I see what's happening with this Jonathan-turned-Daniel.'

'Don't forget to keep the conversation going. But don't allow the locating to start yet.'

I had no idea how to stop that. Should have asked Gang. I could just say I was at another friend's. But I'd have to leave the hotel, damn it. I'd just got used to a life of luxury. Maybe Grandad would let me come back for a few days later. I called him, hoping I wouldn't have to explain too much about what we were doing.

'Are you sure this place is secure?' he said. 'Joe can come and watch you.'

No, thank you. 'I'll be fine, truly.'

Grandad growled, 'You have to have protection.' He paused, then said, 'What are you up to? I know you, Lou. Come on, cough it up.'

'It's about Melinda,' I said.

'Still no sign of her?'

'No.' I wondered how to explain, then I figured that since Paul and Grandad were so matey, Paul would tell him anyway. 'We think she's been grabbed by this guy who uses dating apps. You know what they are, right?'

'I don't live in the Middle Ages, young lady. What makes you think that?'

'Paul knows someone in Missing Persons who thinks she has identified two other women who disappeared, possibly under similar circumstances. There's absolutely no evidence or clues as to what happened to Melinda, other than these dating apps she was using.'

'I don't like the idea of you being bait.'

Grandad might've had a bullet in his arm but it sure hadn't slowed his brain down at all. 'It's not exactly—'

'Yes, it is.' Heavy breathing on his end. 'I want you to use Joe.'

'No, Grandad. I won't even see the guy in person. If we find him. It's all online.'

'Hmph.' A pause. 'I'm curious, lass. How do you know which one it is? They reckon thousands of people use those dating sites.'

'There were only five on Melinda's phone that she had said yes to. We could see which ones she had talked to and was maybe going to meet.' I didn't want to explain the super-recogniser thing. It wasn't the right time. That's what I told myself anyway.

'Hmm. Is Paul overseeing this operation?'

'Yes. I've already talked to him about it all, and he got Gang to set it all up.'

'You make bloody sure you keep in contact with him all the time then, you hear?'

'Yes, Grandad.' I made a face at the phone. Anyone would think I was four instead of thirty-four. 'I need to move now to the *secure* apartment, so I'd better go. Are you coming home soon?'

'I've decided to leave Melbourne for a while,' he said. 'Just a few days' holiday, some beach sunshine and fresh air. I'll let you know how I'm going.'

He hung up and I sat there in shock for a few moments. Grandad leaving Melbourne? I felt like I was sitting on a chair with one leg. I busied myself with packing up all my stuff again, what little I'd taken out of the suitcase. I clicked the case shut and looked around. Yep, I'd definitely come back—if Grandad could go to the beach somewhere for a few days, I could live it up in five-star luxury.

I called for my car to be brought to the front door, and left as soon as it was ready. Paul had texted me all the details again, the pin pad number for the parking garage underneath and how to get into the apartment. I went the long way to Docklands, circling through Footscray and back again over the West Gate Bridge, then into the garage.

The building was at the far end of Collins Street, and the apartment number had a five in front of it, so I guessed I'd be on the fifth floor. I was right. I punched in more numbers and when the door beeped, I pushed it open and found myself looking right through the place across the marina to more buildings. I dropped my bags inside the door and walked across a fake wood floor to the huge windows. Below me, boats sat in neat lines; on one I could see people sitting out on the deck, drinking and eating. I could be somewhere like this instead of listening to neighbours fighting in North Melbourne. Except men beat up their partners in every suburb in Melbourne.

My bedroom was the spare, smaller one, and I had to find sheets and pillowcases and make up the bed, then I ordered pizza to be delivered. Paul's mate had said help myself to wine. I poured myself a large dollop of the white from the fridge into an elegant crystal goblet and settled on the squishy leather couch, ready to check my phone.

There were two messages, one from Nick and one from our prime suspect, Daniel, who I still thought of as Jonathan. I was tempted to ignore Nick, but that'd be risky. He might not look like a real suspect, but the fact he'd been communicating with Melinda left him firmly on the list. Still, I focused on Daniel first.

He'd responded to my bland greeting with *Nice to connect. Cool photos. What do you do in your free time? You had a few interests.*

He was quite chatty and pleasant. Like Nick, he talked in complete sentences. I was half-expecting emojis and misspellings. Not sure about 'cool photos', but that might be a check that I was using photos of myself and not a model like, er, Jessica. He was a bit naïve if he thought someone would confess that straight away. I thought about how to answer and what we were trying to do. It wouldn't pay to be too pushy. I should hold back a bit.

Thanks. What sort of dog do you have? I like movies. I listed the same ones I'd given Nick. *What about you?*

While I was waiting, I answered Nick. *A crime fiction fan! I guess that means you're not a police officer ...* I deleted 'police officer'. *I guess you're not a cop then.*

Nick replied fast. *What makes you say that?*

I've just heard that cops don't like reading or watching police dramas because they always get everything wrong.

Did they ever. I'd never seen anyone in an Australian police drama go berserk and attack a member of the public. I pushed that away and tried to concentrate. More wine might loosen me up and get me into this stupid chatting better. I swallowed too big a mouthful and nearly choked, and spent the next few minutes coughing and drinking sips of water. By the time I got back to my phone, they'd both replied.

Daniel first. The bait had to keep tempting the biggest fish, right? He'd said, *Love French and Spanish dramas. Scandi TV shows. Do you actually go to the cinema?*

Not as often as I'd like to. Have you seen anything good recently?

Back to Nick. He'd said, *Yes, I've heard that, too. Same with nurses watching medical dramas, I guess. What do you do for a job?*

Oh. No way could I say private investigator. Shit, I'd have to fall back on Noddy's restaurant. If I said I was a waitress it might put him off if he was a bit snobby. I decided to lie. How surprising. *I manage a restaurant for a family friend. I'm having a break at the moment, taking some leave. How about you?*

Daniel answered my question about movies. *Nothing that really blew me away. Do you work at night then?*

I used the same restaurant lie on him. Gang was right. It was too hard to make up fake stuff for different guys. Just stick to one story. I found a notepad and pen on the kitchen counter, drew two columns and started making notes on what I'd told them both so far. This was exhausting.

The door buzzer thing rang and I jumped half out of the couch. It was the pizza delivery and I had to take the lift down to collect it. The delivery driver had left it on the seats in the entrance and gone. I figured I was lucky nobody had helped themselves. The smell made my mouth water, and I stuffed the first piece down my throat in the lift.

Back to work. After about another half an hour of back and forth with both of them, my brain was frazzled and I'd drunk half of the wine. I needed to call it a night with both guys and the wine before I said something that would give me away. Mostly I'd managed to keep my side limited to a couple of funny stories from the restaurant, without naming it, and other things like what I liked to drink and eat. I'd also divulged that I was housesitting for a friend while they were away. I told both of them I was signing off for tonight as I had to be at the gym early for a training session. Daniel said, *You must be fit! Is your gym any good?* Which invited me to tell him which one.

Nick said, *Me, too—got to be at work by 7. Sleep well!*

So. Should I answer Daniel? How soon did I want to let him know where I lived? The answer to that was—soon. No point being coy here. I debated about telling him the name of the gym, because what if he turned up to check me out?

I gave Paul a call and he said, 'How about you tell him the name of the gym, and I'll keep a watch out, make sure you're safe. What time are you going?'

'Six.'

He groaned. 'All right, I'll be outside by five forty-five.'

I sent him a screenshot of Daniel's profile, and then replied in the chat, telling Daniel, *Yeah, MaxPower in Footscray*, and said goodnight. It sent a chill up my spine. Even if we were getting ready to take this guy down and maybe find Melinda, I was putting myself in a very risky position. I didn't really know how tall or heavy he was. If he'd taken women off their doorsteps and into his car, even if he'd drugged them somehow, he must be strong enough to lift them easily and fast.

Or he could get them in the car first and inject them with whatever would knock them out fast. Paul, Gang and I had talked about this. We thought he probably got himself inside the house. He'd only have to be past the front door and out of sight—a needle straight into someone …

Paul knew all of that. He'd be there.

Then I remembered. I'd also have to make sure nobody was following me, like guys sent by Fayed. Maybe I should give the gym a miss.

I swallowed the last of the wine in my glass and took it to the kitchen to rinse. The fridge here was almost empty, just a few condiments and the remains of my pizza. I considered the gym again, and the fact that Fayed couldn't possibly know where I was at the moment. I'd be super careful, all the same.

In the end, the gym was an anticlimax. Paul sat in his car and I worked out on a couple of punching bags, imagining I was hitting Daniel, until my arms and hands and shoulders screamed. No sign of our prime suspect.

After a shower, I checked in with Paul.

'This guy is cautious,' he said. 'A sex pest would've been down here checking you out. Stay alert, all the same. And don't forget Fayed. Watch for anyone following you home. Or to the office.'

I glanced up and down the street, which was still filled with shadows and dark doorways, but nobody sitting in a car. Not that I could see anyway.

I headed for the office, stopping off for breakfast at a favourite café on the way. I was in the mood for scrambled eggs, although maybe that was a reflection of how my brain felt. I parked the Commodore and checked my little Corolla—apart from a layer of city dust and grime, it was okay. Gang wasn't in yet so I settled down at my computer and read through the list of new background checks. Before I hit the search options, I pulled out the dating phone and checked it, and then wished I hadn't.

There were notifications from all of the apps.

Thankfully there were only three more guys who had liked my profile on Tinder. I scanned each one, but none of them were from our original five. I closed that, opened Jointly and gasped. Scotcher was now on that app as well. And he'd swiped on me again! What the fuck was he up to? Did he know Lisa was really me? I put the phone down for a few moments and made myself a coffee from the machine.

When I looked at it again, Scotcher was still there, waiting. No, he wasn't. His picture was. I didn't know what to do so I took the chicken's way out and moved on to the chat. Nothing from Nick. Maybe I'd bored him silly and he'd given up.

Daniel, on the other hand, was still keen. *Hope the gym went well! I've done a mad thing—bought my first ever recipe book.* Then there was a funny upside-down face emoji. That was easy to reply to.

Very mad. Which one did you get? Julia Child? That'd test him. He would probably go—Julia who?

Ha ha, no. She's a bit advanced for me, even if I did see the movie about the blogger.

Yeah, I'd actually seen that one, even though I couldn't remember the title of it. Another message popped up.

It was a toss-up but I bought Adam Liaw—Tonight's Dinner. Now I need to use it.

I had to admit, he was very good at this friendly chatting thing. Was this leading to an invitation to dinner at his house? I definitely wasn't ready for that. I put the phone away for a while and focused on the background checks I'd been given. I was soon neck deep in all sorts of databases and when I finally looked up, several hours had passed. Gang was at the other desk and Paul's office door was closed. I hadn't had a chance to message Daniel again, and I was worried he'd lose interest and find another victim.

I messaged, trying not to be too encouraging. *Not familiar with Liaw. I haven't done any real cooking for ages.*

Before I'd even gathered up my bag to go out for coffee and fresh air, Daniel was back. *I guess you eat at the restaurant a lot.*

Yep, it's easy. And the chef cooks a lot better than me!

What's your favourite dish?

If I'd been out in a boat, fishing, I would have felt a big tug on my line right now. I'd go with the truth again so I wouldn't trip myself up.

Love Thai green curry chicken, but for special occasions, seafood. Chilli prawns, bouillabaisse, fresh barramundi. Not oysters though.

Bouillabaisse—way out of my league!

A brief pause.

I could give chilli prawns a go.

I didn't reply for a little while, thinking. This was definitely leading to a dinner of some kind, and it didn't feel right. It felt too fast. Like Paul said, this guy was cautious, so if Daniel was moving fast ... Then another message popped up.

But it will have to wait. I've got work stuff to do first.

I needed more clues about him. *What do you do?*

I'm a civil engineer. Very boring.

I doubt that!

Okay, I'd had enough for now. I was tired and achy and Daniel could wait. So could Nick, if he decided to contact me again. Clearly, being offline all day hadn't put Daniel off, so I figured I could leave him be for a while. The rest of the afternoon passed with more computer work, and I updated Paul and Gang about how the dating apps were going. Gang read through my messages.

'Is it usually this chatty?' I asked him. 'I was expecting to be more like phone texts.'

'You're having a conversation online,' he said. 'Both of them sound intelligent and open. They're trying hard to impress. Either because they like you or because they're trying to suck you in.' He shrugged. 'It's working like we hoped, isn't it?'

That didn't make me feel any more enthused. But as I kept telling myself, this was all we had right now, so it was worth the effort.

I left the office by 4pm, chose the Commodore and returned to the Docklands building after adding an extra twenty minutes onto the drive by going around back streets and watching my mirrors. I put in the garage code and parked, feeling instantly safer as the gates closed behind me, then headed for a long, hot shower. My neck and head ached and the hot water was bliss.

By the time I was in clean clothes and had poured myself a glass of wine, my dating app was showing messages from both Daniel and Nick.

Nick's said, *Maybe we could meet for a coffee some time?* My other fishing line had hooked a biggie.

CHAPTER TWENTY-EIGHT

Before I answered any messages, I pulled out the leftover pizza and shoved it in the microwave, then called Paul. He took a little while to answer.

'Listen, I've got both of these guys messaging me. Nick and Daniel—or Jonathan as we knew him first. And both are hinting or outright inviting me to meet up.'

Paul sucked in a breath. 'Both. Shit. Which one is more suspicious?'

'Neither.' This microwave had a lot of instant program buttons. I punched the one with the pizza picture on it. 'They're both chatty, and they both sound like nice, ordinary guys. Neither of them sounds like a serial killer.' Just saying the words made my skin crawl.

'Sociopaths can be very charming,' Paul said. 'Ted Bundy was charismatic, they say.'

'Yeah, thanks for that little gem.' I drank some wine. 'So do I keep them both chatting or move it along a bit?'

'Don't be too pushy. Remember your profile and your pics. You're a little shy, cautious yourself, and not in a rush. If either of these guys is our killer, the key thing is not to frighten them off.'

I was glad he was using the word 'killer'. It kept me focused on the end game.

'Nick has suggested coffee.'

'You could do coffee. But, Lou, you can't meet either of these guys unless I'm there to watch out for you.' His voice hardened. 'That's an absolutely unbreakable rule.'

'I understand. I can say yes, and I'll let you know when it happens.'

'Try to give me a couple of hours notice, at least,' he said quickly.

'Will do.'

I hung up and retrieved my pizza, which was so hot the cheese and tomato were bubbling like a New Zealand mud pool. I left it to cool and returned to the dating phone with renewed determination. Coming to get you, buddy. Whichever one you are.

Nick first. *Coffee sounds nice*, I typed.

Zip, he was back at me. *Or a glass of wine. Or beer. Or... whatever you like.* He sounded like he wanted to please. Was that a trick?

I looked at my nearly empty glass. Not tonight. I didn't want to meet either of these guys already slightly drunk. And there'd be no time to alert Paul. *Wine would be nice. Have to be tomorrow night though.*

Sure. After work? Then we can both leave quickly if we hate each other on sight!

Sounded like Nick had been burned a few times.

Let's just agree on half an hour, no strings?

Sure. Somewhere in the city?

I couldn't think of anywhere close to the PMI office. *Sounds good. You choose.*

He named a place I'd never heard of down the bottom of Collins Street.

Great. See you there at 7. I sent that message with my stomach rolling. God, I hoped Nick was a normal person. Or maybe I hoped he was the killer, then I could find out what he'd done to Melinda. And make him sorry.

Now it was Daniel's turn. If Paul was right about him being Mr Cautious, he wouldn't be into a date so soon.

His message was waiting for me.

So you like the gym. Are you into fitness? Watch any sports?

It was time to be a bit more strategic. *I run, mostly along the river. I don't play sport but I sometimes barrack for the Doggies. Not into footy that much. How about you?*

The pizza was cooler now so I wolfed down three pieces and then a nagging little voice said maybe I needed to go for a run tonight. I pinched some flab around my stomach and agreed with the nagger. A bigger nagger that sounded like Grandad said I should stay inside.

A peep from the phone and Daniel was back.

Same. A Doggies supporter now and then. Never been to a game though.

A lull for a few minutes while I searched the cupboards in case the owner had a secret chocolate stash, but there was nothing, so I had to settle for a cup of tea.

Daniel again.

I've got a meeting in Footscray tomorrow. Are you free for a coffee?

Footscray. About five kilometres away. He'd geo-checked me. Or it was a coincidence. Either way, things just ramped up a few levels. Now I could be meeting both of them. Either one could have taken Melinda. Or neither.

The pizza and wine rolled around nastily in my stomach.

But meeting up so soon didn't fit what we thought had happened with the others. That made me even more uneasy. We could be totally wasting our time. Or the killer could be speeding up.

How was I going to know? These meetings would be my first chance to check Nick and Daniel out. I'd have to be chatty and nice and at the same time watching and listening for any clue that I was talking to a cunning murderer. The thought of it sent a huge surge of adrenaline through me and I couldn't sit still a moment longer. I had to get some of it out.

I screwed up my face and made fists and screamed, then ran up and down the lounge room four times, going, 'Arrrrrggghhh!'

I needed to talk this through, and I didn't think Paul was the best person. I called Gang.

'Hey, do we have action?' he asked immediately.

'Yeah, but … they both seem like normal guys. I'm not really getting any bad vibes from either of them.'

'That's the point, Lou. Whoever is doing this seems like the ultimate nice guy. Friendly, quite good looking, chatty, no risk. A raving loony isn't going to attract anyone, right?'

'Right. The thing is, it looks like I've got dates with both of them.'

'Shit, already?' His voice was a squeak.

'Yeah, it's moved along faster than I expected. Maybe neither of them is our prime suspect.'

'Hey, stand back a minute,' he said. 'Think about this, about what we know. Daniel has changed his name and created a whole new profile. Daniel—or Jonathan—is the one we think Melinda was meeting. That's what prime means.'

'I know that! That's my take on it, too, but I can't afford to ignore Nick. He just might be a lot sneakier.'

'When are you meeting Daniel?'

'He's suggested coffee tomorrow, in Footscray.'

'Does Paul know?'

'Not yet.'

'You have to tell him now. He's dealing with other—'

'Jobs. I know. I'll text him in a minute. What about Nick? I'm having a glass of wine with him tomorrow night.'

'We can't count him out. Not yet. If Paul can't be there, I will.'

I did as Gang said and texted Paul, but he didn't reply straight away. I waited a while, then thought I needed to respond to Daniel.

I can maybe move a few things. What time and where?

11am at the Horseshoe Café?

I texted Paul again, adding in all the details with an *Is this okay?* at the end.

Thirty seconds later, he replied, *All good. I'll be there.*

Back to Daniel, my hands shaking so hard I had to correct the message twice. *Sure. See you then.*

So that was it. I was meeting both of them. Just like that. It occurred to me that I'd need the makeup and the hair curling thing. They were in the car downstairs. That'd be tomorrow morning's job.

On another page of my notebook, I wrote down all the things about my life that Daniel had likely gleaned from my answers. The gym name, I liked running along the river, I sometimes barracked for the Doggies footy team, I worked in a restaurant but I hadn't said where. Now he'd picked Footscray for a coffee. Regardless of whether he'd googled my gym, I still came back to the GPS location thing.

I was glad I was high up in a fancy box in Docklands where no one could rock up and knock on my door. For a moment, I wondered about asking Cheery Joe along tomorrow. No need. Paul would be a better bodyguard. Cheerier, too.

I took one more look at Scotcher's profile, shook my head and turned the phone off. Nup, wasn't going there.

***

The next morning, I was at the office early again. I'd put the makeup on first, wishing I was better at this stuff, and then brushed my hair out and curled it. I still had to ask Gang to make sure it looked okay before I had to venture out to my coffee 'date'. I pulled out my own phone before I left and checked it. There was a message from Kayla.

You up for a wine or two tonight?

I was about to reply when I remembered 7pm was the wine with Nick. I texted back, *Can't meet until 8. We could do dinner?* I couldn't imagine wanting to go past the mandatory half an hour with Nick.

Kayla sent back an immediate thumbs up and the words, *Sort out where later*. At least I had that to look forward to. I muttered, 'Peace and calm,' a few times, Gang gave me a hug and it was time to go.

CHAPTER TWENTY-NINE

In Footscray, I parked near the library and walked up to Barkly Street where Google Maps had told me the Horseshoe Café was. I had to assume Paul was already there, or perhaps watching from outside. The inside wall of the café was painted in a mural of horses racing in the Melbourne Cup, with what looked like a very shiny fake cup on a shelf. Grandad would like this place. I went and ordered a strong coffee and paid so there'd be no awkwardness about it with Daniel. I was early, so that gave me the opportunity to choose a table. I went for one in the back corner with a bench seat and sat down, so Daniel would have to take the uncomfortable-looking metal chair.

The café was half full and nobody was on their own, apart from me. My face was tacky with the makeup, which made me think I'd plastered it on too thick. I felt like a big hand was squeezing my guts, and I had to slow down my breathing. Box breathing was something I had started using a while ago, but right now it wasn't helping much.

I checked my phone in case Daniel had messaged me, but there was only a text from Kayla saying, *O'Brien's at 8*. Our usual haunt, where I'd be able to relax.

Then he was in the doorway, looking nervous and scanning the room. I knew it was him. Daniel, Jonathan. The eyes, nose and ears. Easier to spot in person. He turned towards me and his glasses caught the light, flashing briefly. I held up my hand and forced a smile. He smiled back and pointed to the counter to say he was getting coffee. I nodded, hoping my mascara wasn't running down my face.

God, this was excruciating. But I was here for a reason. Melinda.

Daniel came and sat down just as my coffee arrived. It helped to break the ice a little, having a waitress interrupt.

'It's nice to meet you in person,' Daniel said, his smile looking fairly genuine.

I couldn't manage another fake smile. 'You, too.' I half-shrugged. 'I guess you never know if people will be like their … you know.' I probably looked pretty ordinary compared to my glam shots.

'Yes, often they aren't.'

'I haven't really done this before.' It was no effort to look embarrassed and shy. 'Have you?'

'A bit. It's, well, hit and miss, I guess.'

We sat in silence for a few seconds that seemed to stretch out and out. I remembered my coffee and stirred it, then took a sip. It was lukewarm and the milk tasted slightly off.

'Do you come here often?' I asked, then laughed. 'Sorry, that's weird. I just meant ...'

I must have made a face, because he said, 'Coffee pretty crap, is it?'

'Yes, awful. Hope yours is better.'

His coffee arrived and he tried it. 'Nup. I was going to offer it to you instead of yours, but it wouldn't be an improvement. Sorry.'

'Oh, well.' I pushed my cup away.

'I didn't pick a very good place to meet, did I?' He grinned and made a noise like a quiz show buzzer. 'Zzzz. Fail on Effort Number One.'

'Well, it's Footscray. Not much to choose from.'

'There are some good ones around, more over Yarraville way. You probably know them better than I do.' He looked at me expectantly.

'Me?' Was this another way to work out where I lived? 'I've been to a couple.' I named one I could think of. 'I tend to buy my coffee where I work.'

'No free coffee at your restaurant?'

'Oh, yeah, of course. But sometimes you need to get out of the place.'

'I know that feeling.' He grinned again, very friendly. He had nice teeth.

All I could think of was that I was dying to ask him where Melinda was, and I knew that would be a huge mistake, but this dodging around, being all nice, when I wanted to lean across and punch the answer out of him ... And where was Paul? I didn't dare look around for him. I dug my fingernails into my palms. *Stay calm.*

'You look a bit stressed,' Daniel said. 'Something wrong at work?'

'Just an order that went astray.' I made my face into what I hoped was a cheerful expression and not one that made me look constipated. 'All fixed now.'

He lifted his teaspoon and stirred his coffee, the one he wasn't going to drink. 'You're, ah … not quite what I expected.'

Uh-oh. 'My friend helped me dress up a bit for the photos.'

'No, not that. Everyone does that.' He looked up at the picture on the wall behind me and I resisted the urge to turn around. 'You seem … confident, like you've done this before.'

'This?'

'Online dating. You don't seem nervous.'

He'd just said I seemed stressed! Was he looking for a woman who wouldn't fight back? Fuck, I wasn't sure what to say. 'It's my restaurant face.' I shrugged. 'I get all sorts there—sometimes rude or aggro, so I have to pretend it doesn't affect me. But this dating thing …' I did a fake shudder. 'It's pretty nerve-racking. Don't you think?'

'Yeah, a bit.' He'd turned dismissive and I wasn't sure why. Maybe I'd blown it. He checked his phone for the time. 'I have to go, sorry. Got to get back to the office for a meeting.'

'Oh. Okay.' I didn't have to fake being disappointed. Just not for the reason he thought.

'You're nice,' he said. 'Maybe we can do this again.'

He gave me a smile, showing me his teeth, and was gone in a few seconds. I thought I saw him almost running. I'd really stuffed that up, but I couldn't quite work out how. Except … If he had a 'nose' for a vulnerable woman, I'd done a bad job of acting a bit helpless and he'd decided I was too tough for him.

Still, we'd been at the same table for—I checked my watch—fourteen minutes. Not long to make up his mind against me. Unless he was a genuine date and had been looking for a 'spark' between us? I sure hadn't felt it.

I went back to the car and texted Paul, wondering why he hadn't been there watching out for me. Oh, well, it was only coffee. A short coffee.

Met Daniel/Jonathan. Think I put him off. He said I seemed very confident.

Paul's answer came back almost immediately. *No, he was definitely interested. Testing you a bit. Body language.*

You were there?

Old man in the other corner. LOL.

I shook my head. I hadn't noticed him. *See you tonight then? Or not see you, of course.*

Sure will. Don't look for me.

I sent him an emoji holding up a magnifying glass.

Back in the office, I gave Gang the rundown on how the coffee date went, and he frowned.

'If Paul thought the guy was showing real interest, I'd go with that. He knows what he's doing. But that means you need to be extra careful.'

I rolled my eyes. At the moment, my whole life was about being careful and I was getting tired of it. *Stop whining. A few months ago you were complaining of having nothing to do.*

The rest of the day was spent on finishing the background checks and filling out the report forms for the company who employed us. It was standard practice these days for people to have police checks done; maybe businesses were getting more wary of whether people were being honest about their CVs now.

I checked the Commodore's mirrors all the way to Docklands and was a bit concerned about a black Lexus behind me, but when I turned off for Footscray, to check if it followed, it went left towards the bridge. Still, I kept going and circled back via North Melbourne, avoiding the streets near my apartment.

A long, hot shower later and I chose jeans and a white shirt to meet Nick. I couldn't face pizza again, so I made some Vegemite toast to line my stomach and turned on the 6pm news while I ate. The first item had the female anchor putting on her serious, sad face.

'The body of a woman has been found in thick bush near Whittlesea by two walkers when one of them fell down a slope while retrieving a dropped water bottle. Police have not confirmed her identity, due to the condition of the remains, but she is believed to be a woman missing since February.' A photo flashed onto the screen and I froze, toast falling from my fingers onto the breakfast bar.

It was the first woman in our trio, Casey Freebourne.

She'd finally turned up. Dead.

CHAPTER THIRTY

A homicide detective with a severe haircut and a tie that looked like it was strangling him fronted the media, making the official announcement about the dead woman. His mouth was a grim line, his eyes hard.

'At this time, despite the media broadcasting a photo, we can't confirm who the deceased person is. We will need to await the results of DNA tests.' Garbled questions from the journalists. 'Yes, we believe the body has been there for several months.'

This time a clear question. 'Should women in Melbourne be worried that someone is a danger to them?'

Fuck, yes!

'We don't have any further information at this time.'

Same journalist. 'But are you treating the death as suspicious?'

Long pause while the detective glared at the miscreant, but finally he said, 'Yes, we are.'

Then the vision returned to the newsreader, who went on to something about speed cameras with barely a pause.

I had both of my phones on the bench, but I hadn't been in the mood to look at the dating phone. Until now. But first I called Paul.

He answered with, 'Have you seen the news?'

'Yes, it looks like our girl. One of them, anyway. Is this going to kick all three of them from missing persons up to murders?'

'Not necessarily.' Pause. 'I could call my contact, but I'm thinking it might be worth you touching base with that detective—Scotcher, is that his name?'

Like he didn't know. 'What for?'

'To see what they're doing now. So we don't stand on their toes.'

'You want me to tell him what we're up to?' I could see that going down like a lump of coal at a Greens rally.

'No, no. But … I'll leave it up to you. If you think— No, never mind.'

I'd never heard Paul be so indecisive before. 'You do know Scotcher's on one of the dating apps.'

'What? You're kidding. How would that get them anywhere?'

I cleared my throat. 'I think he's there on a personal basis.' Or maybe not. 'He has tried to connect with me … I don't think he knows it's me though.' I hope.

'Don't break cover on the apps. If you do call him, don't tell him what we're doing. He might insist you back off.'

I thought of the messages that had already bounced back and forth. I tapped the dating phone and the screen lit up, showing me I had more waiting. 'Too late to call him now. Both guys have sent me more messages, but I'm not going to reply yet. I'm meeting Nick at seven. I'd better get a move on.'

'Me, too. We'll talk later.'

I rinsed my dishes and grabbed my bag and car keys, hoping I'd find a parking spot in the city without too much trouble. The wine bar Nick had chosen was a few blocks from the PMI office; I ended up having to use our carpark, then racing to get there in time. Five minutes late, damn it. I'd wanted to get there early and be ready. Instead I was hot and sweaty and flustered, and my curls had gone flat. I stood in the doorway of the dimly lit bar and squinted. No single males sitting at a table, looking at their phones. Maybe he'd stood me up.

Someone loomed up behind me and I jumped, swinging around so fast I tipped sideways. A hand shot out and steadied me.

'Lisa?'

It was Nick, looking much more nerdy and serious than his photos. But not uglier. He smelled of some kind of aftershave, but it was a whiff, not an overpowering blast, and it was nice.

'Er, yeah. I mean, yes. Nick?'

'Pleased to meet you.' His face reddened. 'I mean, hi. Sorry, that sounded like you were my Great Aunt Mary's friend.'

I half-shrugged. 'That's okay. This is all a bit … you know.'

'Yeah. Let's get a drink, shall we? It might help.'

We went to the bar together and self-consciously paid for our own wines, laughing about it. Then we found a table near the back and I tucked my bag down next to my feet. We both took large gulps of wine and then sat there, looking around. Anywhere but at each other.

'So.' Nick took another sip, probably for courage. 'How are you finding the dating wars?'

'Pretty awful,' I said. I'd spotted a man at the bar that looked like Paul, although he stayed right at the other end where the light was the worst.

'Have you met anyone you clicked with?' He sounded a little desperate, and it made me think he was either a great actor or not our man. On the other hand, Daniel was pretty normal as well.

I shook Daniel out of my thoughts, and the little head jerk caught Nick's attention.

'That bad, huh?'

'I'm really new at it,' I said. 'I haven't had any disasters yet, but I'm expecting it.' His face dropped and I said quickly, 'Not you. I didn't mean you. It's just how this whole thing goes, from what I've heard.'

He said morosely, 'Some women are a bit weird.'

'So are some men! I mean, have you seen the abs on display?' Too late, I realised he wouldn't see men's profiles unless he'd put himself in as bisexual.

'Abs?' His eyebrows shot up. 'Guys post photos of their muscles?'

I laughed. 'Sure do. Topless photos are very common.' I was tempted to show him, but it might give away what I was up to. 'Surely you see a range of women's photos?'

'Well, there are a lot of women who seem to love the beach. And their cats. And drinking with their friends and doing selfies.' He sighed and his shoulders slumped. 'You were one of the few that looked ordinary.' His face reddened again. 'I didn't mean that to sound, you know, rude. Sorry. Shit, I'm hopeless at this.'

Was this an act? Let the woman feel sorry for you, and you're no threat at all? The hairs on my neck prickled a little, and I'd learned to take notice of them.

'I think most people are,' I said, trying to be consoling and understanding.

'Oh no, they're not.' His mouth tightened.

I waited for him to say more, but he just drank his wine and stared at the table. Okay, so I'd have to jolly the conversation along. Remembering that this was a job and not a real date made it easier.

'You looked like you were pretty good on computers. Is that part of your job?'

'Sort of. There's no use waiting for tech support when something goes wrong.' He rubbed the side of his hand and I noticed it was badly scarred, but I didn't say anything. 'I kind of taught myself the basics of troubleshooting. I use a lot of complicated software, and it works fine, until it doesn't.'

Did that mean he was also able to manipulate the dating apps to his advantage? And his photos? But I'd seen no evidence of it, and I'd seen no other photos of him in disguise. Not like Daniel/Jonathan. Or maybe Nick was very good at deleting as well.

'You don't go out in the field then? On your buildings?'

'I used to.' He hid his hands under the table. 'I had a bit of an accident last year, so I'm mostly in the office still.'

I drank more wine and was surprised to find my glass was empty. His was still half-full so I thought I'd better hold back. But he said, 'Would you like another?' He stood up. 'I'll get this one.' He drank his own glass in three swallows and headed for the bar. I hoped Paul was watching to make sure Nick didn't spike my drink.

I quickly got out my phone and texted Paul under the table. *Going okay. No real alarm bells.*

Cool. Keep it up.

I quickly put my phone in my bag before Nick came back, but he must have seen me with it. 'Meeting someone else tonight?'

'Just a girlfriend. Haven't seen her for a while. I've been too busy.'

'Oh, I thought you were on holidays.'

Oops. 'I am, but you know how you put things off when you're working. And my grandfather has been sick, so I've been visiting him.'

'Is he all right?'

'Yes, he's better now.'

Nick went to put his wallet in his pocket and dropped it on the floor.

When he'd picked it up and was sitting again, I gestured to my glass. 'Thanks for the wine. Can I ask you a question?'

'Sure.'

'Do you meet many women face to face from the app? I'm just curious, being new to it all. I wondered how many people do that chat thing and never get any further.'

He made a face. 'I think I choose the wrong ones. We chat a bit and then it stops and they disappear from my app.'

I looked at him properly, trying to assess him as if I were a real date. Would I have agreed to meet him if he hadn't been one of Melinda's five? Had Melinda chatted for a while and then dropped him? This guy didn't feel like a cunning killer, but then I thought of the charming Justin. Well, his 'charm' had put me off right from the start.

Suddenly, I'd had enough of Nick and his 'poor me' attitude, whether it was an act or not. 'Did you see the news tonight? They found a woman's body out in the bush. They think she was murdered.'

'What?' He stared at me. 'How could they know that?'

'Evidence, I guess. Forensics are pretty advanced now. Even if she was decomposing, I think you'd still be able to tell if she was strangled or bashed on the head. And it's almost impossible to fake suicide, especially hanging.'

His eyes had widened into something like horror, then he laughed. 'I remember—you read lots of crime novels, right?'

Real life beats crime fiction hands down, mate. I laughed, too, sounding a bit shrill. 'I do read a bit of it.' *Did I say that? Maybe I had …*

'Me, too. We swapped titles, remember? I like true crime, too.' His hands were back on the table and I could see the scars weren't burns, they looked like deep cuts that had been stitched. I had a nasty flash of the guy's hand I'd smashed.

'Podcasts, especially,' he said. 'Those people are like investigators themselves. Some of them have solved real crimes!'

I wished now I hadn't agreed to a second glass. I needed to stay alert, especially if I'd forgotten what I'd told him. 'I haven't listened to many podcasts. What do you like about them?'

That set Nick off on a lengthy description and the revelation that he'd like to make a podcast one day, but it would be about engineering disasters and what caused them. 'I sure have learned a lot about that,' he said.

It was seven forty-five and time for me to go. I finished my wine and gathered up my bag. 'This has been nice,' I said, 'but I'm meeting my girlfriend at eight, so I have to go, sorry.'

His face fell. 'Oh, right. That's it then?'

I couldn't work out what he meant for a moment. 'Oh, you mean this, tonight? You want to meet again?'

He bit his lip and blinked a few times. 'Well, only if you want to.'

'I'll message you, okay?'

Immediately, I could see him assume that meant he'd never see me again. 'Sure,' he said offhandedly. 'Enjoy your dinner.' He managed to sound like he hoped I'd choke on it.

I almost said, 'Don't sulk.' But I restrained myself. 'Thanks. Goodnight.'

And I was out of there, looking up at the office building across the street and breathing in the fumes of a car idling at the kerb. The lights were on in several offices and a woman with a vacuum machine on her back pushed a wand across the floor, head bobbing to the music that pumped in through her headphones.

I set off for the car and soon heard footsteps behind me. Shit, was Nick following me?

But it was Paul. 'What did you think?' he asked as he fell into step beside me.

'Yeah, maybe. I don't think so, but I'm not crossing him off yet.'

'Why not?'

'I keep thinking about Ted Bundy and the whole thing about acting.'

'I was mostly joking with you.'

I frowned and slowed. 'I know, but it's true. I'm acting a part. Probably not very well. The killer would definitely be acting like a normal guy looking for a relationship.'

'So what was Daniel like then? An actor?'

'Maybe.' I described what the coffee date had been like. 'You were there. You saw him.'

He grunted. 'Maybe it's neither of them. And we're back to square one.'

That was a very depressing thought.

'Have you called Detective Scotcher yet?'

'I'll do it tonight.' We reached the car and I said, 'Thanks for coming all the way to the car with me.'

'We're watching your back, remember? Are you going home now?'

'I'm meeting Kayla, so I'll be fine with her.'

'All right. But be careful, remember. And stay in touch.' Then he was gone.

CHAPTER THIRTY-ONE

I drove out of the parking building, which had casual users coming in for the shows and restaurants, and was forced to stop for a couple of minutes while a bunch of tourists stood in the middle of the footpath, chattering. A man further up the street was leaning against his car, texting, and glanced up at me. He turned away quickly when he spotted me looking. Young, muscled, shaved head, largish nose. I'd been intending to turn that way, but instead I went in the opposite direction and accelerated.

It was hard to do random turns in the city—the hook turns at the intersections made it tricky—but I was pretty sure nobody was following me. I couldn't find a parking spot near the restaurant we were meeting at; I ended up in a short, dark side street a couple of blocks away, squeezing the Commodore between two huge four-wheel drives. Paul's reminder had made me more cautious, so I turned

off the car's inside light before I rubbed off the lipstick
and brushed my hair into a ponytail. Then I opened the
door and hopped out; I closed it quietly and stood behind
one of the four-wheel drives while scanning the street. At
least the hulking machines were good for something. I
still couldn't see anyone who might be following me—no
one on foot and nobody cruising past in a car, looking.
All the same, I stuck to the shadowed pockets along the
streets as I headed for O'Brien's, glad it was one of those
places that was usually noisy and crowded. I could slip
through the throngs and Kayla would have a table out the
back for us.

Sure enough, she was already there, with two glasses of
wine waiting. My head was still a bit foggy, so I grabbed a
large glass of cool water to take with me. As I reached the
doorway to the back room, I stepped back into the little pas-
sageway leading to the toilets and checked the bar behind
me. Nobody following me, nobody looking to see where I'd
gone. Good. I relaxed a little and joined Kayla, giving her a
big hug.

'Whoa, some touchy-feely stuff, girl,' she said with a
laugh.

'Yeah, well. Life has been a bit stressful lately.' I checked
the menu lying on the table. 'Let's order. I'm starving.' We
both went for steak and chips—O'Brien's had the best chips
in town. Then we settled back and drank wine for a couple
of minutes, watching the heaving crowd in the big bar.

'God, how do women wear those high heels?' she said.
She stuck her foot out—as usual, she was in practical leather
lace-ups. She'd been a Doc Martens girl through and
through as a teenager. 'So what's up? Spill the beans.'

I raised my eyebrows at the abrupt change of subject. 'I guess you know about my apartment. I'm hiding out at a friend of Paul's.'

She shook her head. 'A bomb. That's seriously freaky. But it's safe now, isn't it?'

'Fayed is out again and Grandad thinks he's still after us both.'

'He's too clever for that.' She frowned at me. 'He knows we're watching him. He's got too much to lose, getting caught again.'

I felt exhausted just talking about it, but I knew that was worry about Grandad and this dating stuff, not Fayed. I couldn't tell Kayla about the dating. I doubted she'd inform the detectives on the murder case what I was doing, but she'd be torn about it and I didn't want to put her in that position. It was better if she didn't know.

My turn to change the subject. 'Have you heard anything more about the guy who killed his wife, Justin Paterson?'

'He's agreed to plead guilty. They've got him in remand, no bail. Last I heard the filing hearing was very soon, and then it'll go to committal mention. Whether he'll be sentenced by the magistrate ...' She shrugged. 'I'd think it would go to the County Court for sentencing.'

'Bastard had better not change his mind and try to plead not guilty,' I said darkly.

'Why? Because you'd have to testify?'

'Not really. I just think I'd have trouble staying calm on the witness stand.'

Kayla looked too concerned for my liking.

'I'm fine,' I told her. 'It was a horrible thing to happen.'

'And horrible for you to find her like that.'

I'd better not find Melinda like that. I gulped down some wine. 'So, did you know Scotcher, your mate, is using dating apps?'

Too late, I realised I'd let the cat out of the bag, as Grandad would say.

'How do you know?' She leaned in, grinning. 'Is that why you have makeup on? Are you on one?'

'Nah, not me.'

I heaved a sigh of relief as our steaks arrived. I immediately ate several hot chips, burning my mouth, and had to drink some water. 'Careful, the chips are straight out of the fryer.'

'Come on,' she said, after eating a hunk of steak. 'You can tell me. Which app are you using?'

'No, truly, I'm not. It's just part of a case we're working on. I got to see some profiles and I recognised him.'

'So you could still sign up yourself and swipe him, right?'

'Why are you so keen for me to hook up with him?'

She shrugged. 'I think you'd like each other.'

'Yeah, sure, except he actually thinks I'm an interfering idiot. That's very sexy, ha ha.'

'He's serious about his job, that's all.' She ate more steak, a little V between her eyebrows. 'So what sort of case involves dating apps?'

Uh-oh. It wouldn't take her long to put it together if I spilled more information. 'Just a fraud thing. So how's your life these days? Met anyone nice?'

'Truly, this is the first time I've been out socially for weeks. I was actually grateful the new case was given to another crew.'

My heart rate leapt up and I focused on my chips, savouring them one by one. 'God, these are good. So … you mean the woman's body found in the bush?'

'Yeah. Nasty one. She'd been missing for a while, too.'

I know. 'They know who she is then?'

'Yes, they're reasonably sure. DNA has to confirm it though. No close family for ID.'

'How long will the DNA take?'

'How long is a piece of string? You know what the delays are like. They're pushing for speed on it, though.'

About time. 'Why's that?' I swallowed a mouthful of wine. 'Do they have other missing women?'

Kayla had drunk enough not to notice my nonchalant, vaguely interested act. 'It's a definite possibility. Probability. I heard that MisPer has identified two others. You know what that means.'

'Yes, a pattern.' I was itching to let Paul know, but then I realised he already would have heard, via his MisPer contact.

Kayla straightened abruptly. 'Anyway, you didn't get that from me.'

'Course not.' I kept eating, hoping she wouldn't remember what I'd said to her about Melinda. If it wasn't her case, she'd only hear what was floating around her office. 'So you haven't met anyone nice? Maybe you should try a dating app.' I laughed when she poked her tongue out at me. 'Hey, you were quick enough to tell me to do it.'

'It's that whole … how can you tell a guy you're a police detective? Bad enough with people I know. Stupid bloody questions they ask. Sheesh.' She drained her glass. 'Your shout.'

I didn't want another one, but if I went away from the table for a few minutes, I could move the conversation on when I came back.

It worked, and we were soon reminiscing about the police academy, and catching up on news of old friends. It was almost 11pm by the time we left O'Brien's, but by then we'd been drinking soda and lime for a while, so my head was clearer. I remembered to check the streets, ahead and behind me, as I walked to my car after saying goodnight. Kayla had offered to drive me to the little side street, but I'd said no.

Now, for some reason, the deep shadows under the trees were unnerving and reminded me of a story I'd read when I was a kid, a fairy tale about a juniper tree and an evil step-mother. I shuddered, thinking of the boy in the story with his head chopped off by the wooden chest and the father eating him as soup.

Then I laughed at myself. God, talk about giving myself the frighteners!

I took a couple of breaths to slow my heart rate, then glimpsed something moving across the street and gasped. Was that … There was a thump and a cat yowled, running hell for leather across in front of me. My nerves felt completely haywire.

I picked up speed and turned sharply into the little side street, then slowed, scanning ahead. It was empty, and almost every house was in darkness. I got my car keys out and crossed, walking past the large white four-wheel drive parked in front of my Commodore.

I saw movement out of the corner of my eye, tried to turn to fend off the blow, but I was too late. A hand smacked my head against the Commodore roof, a crack echoed through my skull and I staggered. The hand shoved me against the door, I felt a sharp jab in the side of my neck and then I slid down to the ground, banging my face onto the bitumen.

Black runners loomed up next to my eyes, I smelled rubber and disinfectant, and then everything went to oblivion.

CHAPTER THIRTY-TWO

When I came to, I couldn't figure out where I was. My head ached badly, the pain jagging across in lightning streaks, and I wanted to vomit. I was lying down, scrunched up a bit, and it seemed dark. I tried to open my eyes properly, but I couldn't. There was tape across them.

Panic rose out of my guts, up through my chest like a hot wave, into my throat. Who the fuck tapes someone's eyes like this? I wanted to scream, but there was tape over my mouth as well. The scream was a knife in my head.

I have to get the tape off. I have to see.

It was a stupid thing to think, but it somehow stopped me losing it. I couldn't afford to panic.

I tried some box breathing while I tested what else was going on with my body. I was trussed up like a barbecue chicken, bound legs and wrists taped and attached to the front of my thighs. I was in a car boot, or maybe a four-wheel drive, because it was fairly roomy. And it was moving, stopping and starting, traffic lights probably, so we were in the city still.

What had happened? My head hurt so much I couldn't think past where I was right now. My face ached, too. Yes, I'd hit it on … the ground. When I fell. After someone hit me. Someone I never saw coming. Fayed? No, I'd be dead. Nick?

And the jab of a needle … How could I have been so stupid?

The sound of the engine grew louder and I sensed we were moving faster now. Fast enough that we were likely on a freeway, heading out of Melbourne.

On the way to my place of death. Like the woman found in the bush.

An adrenaline surge burned through me, spreading down my limbs. My fingers were starting to feel numb; I was hyperventilating and didn't know it. *Breathe slowly. Come on, count the fours. One two three four. One two three four. Focus on your body. What's going on? What can you feel?*

I tested again, trying to focus on one thing as a way to keep control. My wrists were taped together; so were my thighs and ankles. I twisted my fingers and felt thick, smooth plastic stuff. Duct tape. And my head was still pounding, the pain settling into a heavy, hot thump. I breathed again, counting, trying to will away the pain. It didn't help much.

Think! What was going on here? *So, Lou, who bashed you on the head and then wrapped you up in duct tape?*

This wasn't the work of Fayed. It was too personal and up close, especially after the bomb. Fayed would have had me shot and left for dead in the street, like poor Emmanuel.

That would be his message to Grandad, who was on a beach somewhere, knowing nothing of this. Which left Daniel or Nick. Nick or Daniel.

How had either of them known where I was?

I'd looked, I'd watched, I'd been careful, really careful. Nobody had followed me. I was ninety-eight per cent sure of that, so that two per cent …

How had the killer got to Melinda and the other two?

Come on, Lou, remember our analysis!

Click, click, click, click. Car indicator. Then we were slowing, turning, stopping. Traffic lights somewhere. Which meant there would be streetlights, maybe people around me in other cars. Not that they would see me. I tried to raise my hands far enough to signal out the back window, but taped to my thighs like they were, I had no hope.

A voice murmured up the front of the vehicle, but I couldn't make out the words. Whose voice? No idea.

I tried to remember what I knew about Nick and Daniel/ Jonathan. Was it one of them? It had to be. I hadn't swiped with any other guys. Our focus was these two.

What about my recent investigations? Justin or his dad? Not likely.

The guy whose hand I smashed? Was he out of jail? If so, would he go to all this trouble? Murder was a long way from assault. Why risk twenty years when a beating in the street was fast and simple?

I remembered being slammed against the top of the car door. Fuck, no wonder my head hurt so much. This vehicle went over a bump and I felt a jag of pain so bad I cried, but the tears had a lot of trouble squeezing out under the tape. *Stop it.* My neck stung, too. The needle. What had he used on me?

The vehicle was slowing right down now, and then it stopped. A door opened and I heard a roller door rattling up. The car door closed, the vehicle drove inside and the engine noise echoed off walls. Roller door rattled down.

Every muscle in my body tensed, ready for a fight. Which wouldn't happen. I was too well taped up. Still, I stayed like that. I had to be ready for whatever horror came next. I had to be able to give it all I had.

The rear door clicked open and lifted. Cold air swirled over me. Someone pulled me upright and around so I was sitting, my legs dangling over the tailgate. My ankle bumped against a towball. Something landed next to me with a thump. Possibly my bag.

'So, *Louisa Alcott*. The mysterious date with the fake name.'

On the words *fake* and *name*, light slaps hit each side of my head. Pain arced again, especially on the right side where I'd hit the car. 'And where's your nice makeup, Lulu? If you're playing a *game*—' slap, '—then you should feel a*shamed* of yourself.'

I couldn't answer. My guess was he'd gone through my bag and found my ID. My investigator's licence as well, probably. I was in deep shit.

'So, *Lou*, what are we going to do with *you*?' He giggled.

The rhyming wasn't funny. I tried hard to match the voice with Nick or Daniel, but he was putting on an act and I wasn't sure. I shook my head and wished I hadn't when the pain rose up and pounded me.

'You have no *idea*? Well, I'll make it *clear*. You're going on a little trip to the country, *dear*. Hope you enjoy it, because you won't be coming back.' Another laugh.

It was Daniel/Jonathan, I was almost sure. Our prime suspect. Much good that did me now. The best I could hope for was some opportunity to escape, if he ever took this tape off. Or if I could grab some part of him and get some DNA transfer.

An image of Diane's legs in the ground, plastic smeared with mud on the outside and blood on the inside, rose up and I retched, bile surging up. It had nowhere to go. I was going to choke on it.

I swallowed and swallowed, fighting a battle to keep breathing while my throat burned.

When I'd stopped swallowing and sat, hunched over, sucking in air, Daniel's voice came again.

'That was a bit silly. You won't last long that way. And I don't want my date to have vomit all over her!'

Footsteps went away and I thought about escaping, but it was impossible. If I jumped off the tailgate, my bound legs would probably trip me and I'd fall, with no way to protect my aching head. I strained to hear where he was and heard murmuring. Was he calling someone? I couldn't make out the words until he raised his voice: 'No, I want to do it my way this time!' And then it dropped to a murmur again.

He came back and I braced myself. Was this it? Murder in a garage somewhere, my blood hosed down by morning?

His fingers pressed on the tape over my mouth, making sure it was still stuck tight. 'Can't let you talk, Lulu. I think you'd start shouting, wouldn't you?'

Damn right.

Then something on my hair. Was he ... was he brushing it? He pulled out my ponytail and kept brushing. My skin crawled, goose bumps down my arms. I tried to pull away and got another head slap. On the left side, thank God.

Suddenly, his arms hooked around my waist and he pulled me around so my back was against him, then manhandled me out of the four-wheel drive and along the concrete, my feet dragging. I tried to jerk away but he easily pulled me back. His breathing increased and he grunted as he heaved me onto a seat. The front passenger seat, by the feel of it. My legs were pushed in and straightened, the seatbelt fastened across my arms. What the fuck was he doing? The door closed with a solid clunk.

Back passenger door opened, and he was behind me, pulling my hair up. The sound of … tape, being pulled off a roll. Then it was around my neck, pinning my head against the headrest. I panicked, feeling like it was strangling me.

'Mmmrrrhhh!'

'Yeah, right, not too tight, eh, Lulu? Can't have you dying too early.'

The tape eased off, but when I tried to move my head, I was still taped to the headrest. What the hell was all this for? Then his fingers scrabbled around the side of my face and the next moment, without any warning, he pulled off the strip of tape across my eyes. Half of my eyebrow hairs were ripped out and my eyelids felt torn. One eye burned and I thought the lid was bleeding. There was nothing I could do.

He fluffed my hair around my shoulders, probably to hide the tape on my neck, and perched sunglasses on my nose, the arms pushed over my ears. The inside of the lenses were covered in tape so I couldn't see anything, but if I squinted, I could see out the sides. Finally, he draped a scarf around my neck.

I was going to be driven somewhere, and I'd look perfectly normal to anyone glancing at us. People probably wouldn't even notice the sunnies. I blinked a few times and, despite the stinging, my vision cleared a little. I hoped that meant the drug he'd used was wearing off, too.

'There we go,' he said. 'My perfect date. Now we're going to dinner.' He giggled and shut my door. The back doors both closed, the roller door went up. My bag was maybe still in the rear compartment, but I guessed my phone wouldn't be.

Daniel got into the driver's seat and reversed the vehicle out of the garage. As he climbed back in after rolling down the door, a familiar noise sounded very near me. The sharp meow that told me I had a text.

'Ooh, look at that. Someone called Paul wants to know where you are. You want me to answer for you, Lulu? I could just say you're out on a date.' He laughed loudly. 'Nah, he can work that out for himself.'

He put the vehicle in gear and drove fast, out of wherever we were, banging over the entrance way and roaring down the street. There was no point me counting turns or anything—I had no idea of our starting point. All I could tell was we were still in the city, with traffic lights and intersections. When I squinted to my left, nothing looked familiar, just houses and cars. A side squint to my right, and I confirmed it was indeed Daniel who'd kidnapped me.

Bastard.

Daniel braked hard a couple of times, swerved. 'Bloody idiots. Fuck off out of my way.' We drove on.

Despite the pounding in my head, I kept trying to think of ways I could escape. Wait until he took the tape off, obviously. Or if he left me somewhere, maybe I could pull at the tape enough to get my hands free. Except duct tape was almost impossible to stretch or break. I had to hope he'd release me from being trussed up at some point. I couldn't think about why he might do that, about being stripped and raped, or tortured in some way. If I let myself think about that, I'd lose control again.

Control of myself was my best bet. All those counsellors and therapists who said rigid over-control of my emotions would be severely detrimental? If they could see me now. Control was what might get me out of this somehow.

The vehicle slowed and came to a stop. I tensed. This was it.

A rear door opened, someone got in, the door closed again.

'Hey, bro,' Daniel said.

Cold shock rolled through me, and my throat and chest ached as I struggled not to cry.

There were two of them.

CHAPTER THIRTY-THREE

The one in the back was silent. Daniel didn't have much to say either. I tried to remember any cases I'd ever had with two men attacking women, or raping them, or working as some kind of team. Nothing came to me. Only the Hillside Strangler in LA, who had turned out to be two men. They'd killed a lot of women. Had they been cousins?

I had no idea how to deal with this. Two of them meant I had zero chance of fighting and running. I might somehow knock one unconscious, but the other one would get me.

A huge black hole opened up inside me. Was this what had happened to Melinda? And the other two women? No wonder they couldn't escape.

I wanted to curl up in a ball, but I couldn't even do that. My body tried, like a reflex action, and the air in my throat was cut off as soon as I leaned forward. I had never felt so helpless in my whole life, not even when I found out my mother had killed herself. Then it was blame. I should never have believed my father's assertion it was an accidental over-dose. I should have helped her more. I should have found a way to stop her.

This time it was all me. It was my fault. I'd walked right into it.

And there was no way out.

Despair rolled through me in waves. What would Grandad say when he heard I was dead? I imagined his face, his reaction. He'd probably be mad that I'd got myself in this situation.

No, hang on. He bloody wouldn't! Grandad wasn't a vic-tim blamer. He was a fighter, and all he expected of me was to be one, too.

Fuck it, I wasn't giving up yet. Whatever it was they planned to do with me, I'd find a way to fight back.

Right now, I had to take notice of every detail, every sin-gle thing that might one day get these two scumbags con-victed. I sniffed. One of them was wearing cologne. I didn't recognise it, but I breathed it in, trying to imprint the smell on my brain.

I knew Daniel—I'd met him for coffee. I might not be able to see him clearly at the moment, but I could still iden-tify him and his voice. I knew he used disguises, and I'd recognise his face anywhere, any time, even if he donned a new disguise after this.

I had a talent these two knew nothing about, and I'd use it. If I could find a way to see who the other one was, I'd ID him in the future, too. Daniel's DNA would be on the tape, and on my clothing. Probably in my bag as well, from when he searched it. Now I just had to find a way to get the other guy's DNA on me. By fighting back. Fighting for my life.

A lump jammed in my throat. *Don't think about that. Think about collecting anything you can to use against them. Focus.*

The vehicle swung around a corner and accelerated, then settled into a steady roar. Not a new vehicle then. Older and growlier. I guessed it was an old four-wheel drive of some kind. Steady thrumming of tyres. We were on a highway or freeway.

'Hope you like the country,' Daniel said cheerily.

The guy behind made a grunting sound that could've been 'Shuddup' and Daniel grumbled, 'Yeah, yeah. Jeez,' and stopped talking.

I listened, but there was only this vehicle. I blinked slowly, and my eyes cleared a bit more; I looked left and could see rocks and gum trees illuminated by our headlights, a paddock, a hedge, flicking past and into the darkness. If I could see Daniel's side mirror, it might just show the back-seat passenger. I pretended to be trying to get comfortable and moved enough so I could tilt my face a little more. Lights from cars coming towards us lit up Daniel's face intermittently; he wore a smirk, as if he was anticipating what was coming.

Don't think about that.

More slow blinks to help my eyes and a tilt at a different angle. There—the side mirror. But instead of the passenger, the mirror was filled with bright light. Someone was behind us, someone who wasn't passing.

Daniel muttered, 'Arsehole,' and sped up. The four-wheel drive's motor was screaming now, and the guy in the back muttered something.

'This arsehole won't pass or back off,' Daniel snapped. 'What do you expect me to do?' Then, 'Passing at last.'

I squinted right and beside Daniel's window was a large black SUV, its passenger window down. The guy inside it was peering across at us.

Past Daniel. At me.

It was the guy who'd been standing outside the parking building in the city. Shaved head, dark eyes, largish nose. For a moment, hope leapt up like a spout of clear water. Was he Grandad's man? Was I going to be rescued?

Suddenly, Daniel shouted, 'Fuck, what's he doing?'

There was a bang and the four-wheel drive lurched then straightened. Another bang. Another lurch sideways.

A panicky shout from the back, 'Pull over, let him pass!'

'He's not fucking passing!' Daniel screamed.

This time the bang was much bigger, on the side somewhere. I could tell Daniel was fighting with the wheel, but the four-wheel drive was skidding, turning, tyres screeching. Another bang and the whole vehicle yawed sideways, tipped and then the front went down. Daniel screamed something, the four-wheel drive crunched over what seemed like rocks, tipped further and went down, rolling, and then a smash as it hit something big.

After the last huge boom and crack, there was nothing. Silence grew, and I thought I'd gone deaf. Or maybe I was dead. No—the engine was ticking.

Daniel was half on top of me and I couldn't push him off. I smelled petrol—no, it was diesel. I couldn't remember if diesel burned. I had to get out of the vehicle, I had to escape, I had to get Daniel off me. But I was still fucking taped up like a mummy and I couldn't move.

'Fuuuuuccckkkk!' The screaming under the tape across my mouth helped. I took some breaths, some more.

Settle, Lou. Settle. Come on. What's happening?

My head was still thumping, a thick, dull ache, and I struggled to get myself together enough to work out what was happening. We'd crashed, obviously. The sunglasses had twisted on my face, but not fallen. I tried to push Daniel off me using my shoulder, and managed to get him moving forward, more because of the angle of the four-wheel drive. He slumped against the dashboard, but it was dark inside and I couldn't see his face. The windscreen looked broken; no deflated airbags. The vehicle must be too old.

I yanked and pulled at the tape around my wrists, but nothing budged. Behind me was a lot of thumping, and the screech of a door opening against metal. Some grunting as the guy in the back forced his way out. I could just hear swishing and crackling as he pushed through shrubs or whatever bush was around the four-wheel drive.

Had anyone seen us career off the road and down the slope? Were rescuers coming? I sniffed again. A smell of hot engine oil and something meaty. Bloody. Maybe that was Daniel. I needed to see—to get out of here! I pulled with all my strength on the tape around my hands and whipped them back and forth. There was a little bit of give now, but not nearly enough.

Then my door was pulled open and cold night air drifted around me.

A rescuer! I couldn't talk, managed a 'Mmmrr', hoping they wouldn't try to rip the tape off my mouth. I wanted to do that myself, gently.

But the rescuer didn't say anything.

They cut the tape from around my neck. Oh, bliss! I could move again at last. I stretched my neck and heard things crackle. I tried to talk to my rescuer. 'Mmmrrr.'

No reply. Weird. A crawly feeling rippled across my skin. I knew who this was. Back-seat Man.

An arm across my body and the seatbelt sprang open. Almost there.

Then an arm through mine and I was dragged roughly out of the seat, banging my head on the side pillar. Fuck! Pain arced again, white lights flashed in my eyes, and I groaned. I could hardly stand, hands still taped to my thighs, and my feet prickled with pins and needles.

He put his arms around me from behind and started half-dragging me and I stumbled, smacked in the face by a bush with sharp twigs and leaves. My cheeks stung and I was hauled up again. He continued to pull me with him, away from the four-wheel drive, further into the bush.

This couldn't be happening. No. This bastard wasn't taking me again. I bent my knees, jack-knifed and went down, pulling him with me. I curled more, head down, elbows in. He let go, then kicked me hard in the ribs, winding me. I couldn't breathe. Couldn't get air.

A pinch of light. A voice. 'Hey, anyone down there? Are you in there?'

'Go and look, Les!' a woman yelled.

Witnesses. I tried to shout or scream. All that came out was a muffled roar.

The guy who'd pulled me out gave me another kick, connecting with my thigh. Pain seared down my leg, my thigh bone felt on fire. Then he crunched away through the scrub.

Another pinch of light. Someone back there had a strong torch.

'Les, over there, by that tree. No, there!'

'Shit, she's been thrown out of the car. Hey, lady, are you okay?' A man's voice from somewhere behind me. I tried to sit up, but my thigh blasted me with pain.

'Is she bleeding?' The woman.

'How the hell can I see from here, Irene? Wait a minute.' Feet scrambling on gravel, sliding. 'Hang on, lady, I'm coming. Did you call the ambulance, Irene?' His voice was closer, and I guessed he was by the four-wheel drive. 'Shit, there's a man in here, looks bad. Blood everywhere. Irene!'

'Yes!' she shouted. 'Of course I did, you idiot! You think I'm stupid or something?'

Great. We're all injured or dying here and they're having a fight about it.

The man was puffing hard, making his way towards me. 'Christ, this is steep. Hang on, lady.'

Like I was going anywhere.

When he reached me, he touched my shoulder and said, 'You okay?'

What part of okay do I look?

Flashes of light disoriented me for a moment—he was shining his torch at me.

'What's all this tape? You look …' He trailed off, and cleared his throat.

I had no idea what I looked like. I realised my hands were almost free of my legs so I brought them up together and pulled at the tape across my mouth. It was slick and slippery, but it came off at last, even though it pulled the hairs out around my lips.

At last I could open my mouth and breathe. I sucked in great gulps of night air, chest heaving. 'Hey ... thanks for stopping,' I croaked. 'That ...' I tried to gesture to where the man had gone into the bush.

'Yeah, no worries, but ... why are you all taped up, like?'

'Because ... Is that guy ...' I pulled the sunglasses off and peered up.

An older man with dark hair peppered with white tufts was kneeling next to me, his face furrowed with concern. 'That stuff on your face, was it ...'

'Yes, someone grabbed me. Taped me up.' I looked past him. Nobody there. I offered him my bound hands. 'Can you try to get this off, please?'

'Sure,' he said uncertainly. 'Are you hurt? Anything broken?'

'I don't think so.' Perhaps being taped up had saved me. That was ironic. I waited as he picked at the edges of the tape with no success. Up close, he smelled of tobacco and beer, but his hands were steady.

'Sorry,' he said. 'I can't find the end of it to get it going.'

'Les, what're you doing down there?' Irene shouted.

'God save me,' Les muttered. 'Look, I might have a knife in the car. You wanna wait a minute?'

Instantly, fear bolted through me. 'Don't leave me! Is there ... is there anyone else down here? Behind you?'

He glanced around. 'Just you.' He hesitated.

'Okay, get the knife then. Thanks.' I got him to sit me up against a tree trunk first. 'The guy in the four-wheel drive. Is he dead?'

'Yeah, I think so. I haven't tried to move him. I think I'd make him worse—if he's still alive.' Les scrambled to his feet and tried to climb the bank back to his car, but he kept sliding down. 'Shit, this is hopeless. Irene!'

'What?'

'Is the ambulance coming?'

'How would I know?'

'You should ring the police, too.'

'They've already notified them, they said.'

'One good thing,' Les muttered. 'Irene, have a look in the glove box and see if my Stanley knife is still in there.'

'What for?'

'Just do it, please.'

'All right, no need to get snappy.'

A couple of minutes later, she called, 'Here. You want me to throw it to you?'

'What, and stab me in the head? Toss it down towards my feet, low.'

Irene said something unrepeatable, and the knife clattered down and into the long grass. Then Les was back, cutting the tape around my wrists and legs. He tried to pull it off, but I stopped him.

'You can leave it like that, thanks,' I said. 'The police will want to take DNA evidence off it, I think.'

'Oh, right.' He peered at me again, but didn't actually shine his torch in my eyes. 'You've got blood on your hair and down the side of your face. Did you hit your head in the car? Do you know what happened?'

I could've explained it to him, but I couldn't think how to, and really I didn't want to draw him into the whole thing.

'Has anyone else stopped up there on the road?'

'Just us. It's not a busy road this time of night. Lucky Irene saw your headlights disappear.'

Thank you, Irene.

'And it's dark down here. I just saw your white top in the bushes. Thought you were a man at first.' Les got to his feet, groaning. 'Bloody cold ground plays havoc with my arthritis.'

In the distance, sirens whooped. Thank God.

I hoped the police were right behind the ambulance. They needed to get a KLO4 out to all the officers around the area, fast. The second guy was on foot, but I thought he was cunning. He'd not spoken in the back seat, then he'd tried to take me with him, probably to get rid of me and whatever I might say, somewhere out in this area of bush. Another smack on the head with a tree branch and I'd be dead and silent. Dogs might have found me, but in time?

The ambulance pulled up, blue and red lights flashing, lighting up the trees and shrubs around me and glinting off the four-wheel drive. Now I could see it was an old Toyota LandCruiser, almost on its nose, and it had hit a small gum tree. A big tree and we might have all been dead, wrapped around it.

Two paramedics hauled their kit bags to the top of the slope and made their way carefully down, boots sliding, leaning back into the slope.

'One here, and one in the car,' Les said loudly. 'Think he's a goner though.'

One paramedic went to the driver's side, the other one came over to me, and went through all the basic tests and questions. I could answer everything, but my response to whether I was feeling pain made her raise her eyebrows.

'Yes, my head. The vehicle's driver did it when he abducted me.' I pointed to the right-hand side of my head.

'I don't know how long I was unconscious. Five minutes maybe?'

'Abducted?' She stared at me, her large blue eyes bulging. 'Before the crash?'

'Yes.' I held up my hands, the tape still dangling. 'He grabbed me, knocked me out. But there were two of them.'

'Whoa, you'll definitely need a trip to hospital. Let me take that tape off you.'

'No, leave it. The police will want it.'

'Yes, she told me that, too,' Les said earnestly.

She glanced at him, then turned to her partner, who was inside the four-wheel drive. 'Marty? Need help?'

'Yeah, this guy's still got a pulse. Is the second team here yet?'

Daniel was still alive? I shivered.

'Not yet. Police are, though.' She used a small torch to examine the side of my head. 'Listen, I'll get you sorted out as soon as. But I need to help my partner until the others get here.'

'I'll stay with her,' Les said.

I knew they were just doing their job, but I wanted to be out of there, talking to the police and making things happen, not stay sitting here, being useless. I tried to get up, but pain jabbed through to the middle of my brain, and I thought I might vomit on Les's nice leather shoes.

'You stay still, lady,' Les said. 'You don't want to make yourself worse.'

'Can you …' I took a breath, closed my eyes for a second to try and stop the world revolving around me. What had Daniel injected me with?

'Yes?'

'Would you be able to look in the four-wheel drive for me, please? For my bag and phone?'

'I dunno. I don't want to get in their way.' He frowned at the two paramedics, who were now both in the front. It looked like they had eased Daniel back and cleared his airways. They were talking to him, but there didn't seem to be any reply.

Another vehicle stopped up on the road, a police car, its lights also flashing. It was starting to look like a summer light show up there. One officer stayed up by the car, the other made his way down to the four-wheel drive, skidding from halfway.

He glanced inside and talked to the paramedics, then came over to me and Les. 'You were the passenger?' he asked me.

'Yes.' Before I could tell him about the man who'd run off, he turned to Les.

'What about you, sir?'

'Me and the missus stopped to help. I didn't see it happen, but Irene reckoned she saw headlights all up and down from way back, so I slowed down to have a look.'

He came back to me. 'What's your name? Can you remember what happened?'

For the first time, I thought about what I'd heard, what I'd felt. 'I think we were run off the road. There were bangs and thumps at the rear end, headlights like she said, and the driver lost control.'

'So you're saying it was deliberate.' He sounded disbelieving.

'Yes.' But that didn't matter right at this moment. Back-seat Man did matter—a lot. 'Can you please call Detective

Sergeant Scotcher? This is to do with his case. He needs to know what has happened.'

The patrol officer still looked at me sceptically. 'And this Detective Sergeant Scotcher knows you?'

'Yes. Tell him it's Louisa Alcott, and this is to do with the woman's body that was found yesterday in the bush. I was nearly another murder victim.'

That smartened him up. 'Will do.' And he reached for his radio.

I leaned back against the gum tree and breathed in the faint scent of eucalyptus. I'd much rather be sitting on the damp gum leaves than buried under them.

CHAPTER THIRTY-FOUR

It took a while for them to get Daniel out of the four-wheel drive. A fire engine with a crew had arrived to help, too. By the time they had him on a type of stretcher that could be hauled up the slope, he'd been stabilised with a drip and been intubated. Half-a-dozen officers were roped in to help get him up to the rescue helicopter that had landed, which gave me the chance to look for my phone. I eased myself to my feet and over to the passenger door that was still hanging open.

I'd remembered hearing my phone meow and Daniel saying I had a text, so I knew it had to be in the front somewhere. He might've been planning to throw it out the window. I found it on the passenger side, at the top of the foot well, screen intact. I needed my bag as well, but I'd wait for that until the police released it. They'd want my dating app phone as evidence—it should be still turned off and tucked away in a side pocket. My stuff would have Daniel's fingerprints all over it. This phone would, too, I guessed, but I held it on the edges and tapped the screen with my finger through a layer of shirt.

Paul answered straight away. 'Where are you?'

I told him what had happened, including being run off the road.

'Jesus, Lou!' Paul said. 'Thank God you're alive. Are you all right?'

I laughed, but it came out as a choked sob. I sucked in a couple of breaths to steady myself. 'They're insisting I go to hospital. The way my head feels, I'm not going to argue.'

'Let me know which one as soon as they tell you. I'll come, I promise.'

Tears burned in my eyes and I just managed to get out, 'Thanks.'

'So it was Daniel. And he's still alive?'

'Just. No clear prognosis yet. But, Paul, there were two of them.'

'What?' Stunned silence for a few seconds. 'Fucking hell. Who was the other guy?'

'I have no idea. He hardly spoke, sat in the back seat. Did a runner from the scene.'

'Do the police know?'

'Not yet. The locals here are dealing with traffic control and helping the paramedics. I'm waiting for Scotcher to arrive. I asked them to call him, but no one has come other than another patrol car. I heard them say the accident analysis guys are on their way. That's all.'

'I'll get onto Scotcher right now. They've got to go after the other man. Text me the hospital—don't forget.'

As if I would. I wished with all my heart that Grandad wasn't far away on a beach somewhere. To see his face and feel his wiry arms around me and smell his Old Spice right then would have made me feel a hell of a lot better.

The paramedics were back, checking me for everything again and taking vital signs and examining my head with a torch. 'We're going to lift you up on a chair as well.'

'I'm sure I can walk or climb or whatever.'

'Not happening. That's a bad crash. You could have internal injuries, and that head wound … You said you were assaulted?'

'Yep.'

'Hmm. Can we get these bits of tape off you?'

'They're evidence of my abduction,' I said. 'You have to leave them, unless the officers have evidence bags on them.'

It turned out that a pair of detectives who had all the necessary gear had arrived. One of them slid down to where I was sitting and, since mini floodlights had now been set up, she pulled on gloves and then carefully removed all the tape, putting each piece in a separate labelled evidence bag.

I let out a *fffff* of relief when it was done, and said, 'My bag is in the back somewhere. Daniel went through it, so things in there will have his fingerprints all over them. Not sure where the hypodermic needle is he used on me, but if you can find it, it'll have my blood on it. And probably residue of whatever he used on me.'

She gave me an odd look. 'Are you on the job?'

'Used to be.' I didn't tell her I was a PI now—some police had very low opinions of them.

She nodded. 'I'll make sure we cover all of that—the crime scene techs are here now.'

The scene was starting to look like a footy melee, for sure.

I asked the paramedic, 'Do you know what hospital they're taking me to?'

'Not yet. It's a busy night.'

That meant a lot of the Emergency Departments would be on overload, with ambulances diverted here, there and everywhere. I'd have to wait and see.

They strapped me into a plastic chair with things to attach to the rope, then I was hauled up the slope, sliding over the grass and weeds, then lifted over the gravel. They put me in the ambulance, where I had to shut my eyes against the lights for a couple of minutes as they made the pain in my head ramp up again. Things got jumbled then; the detectives said something about a statement later, or as soon as, or something like that, and the paramedic said something about head scans, and then the ambulance took off, and I started to feel sick.

I tried to tell them and found a plastic thing in my hand to vomit into, which I did, so hard that I thought the top of my skull was going to shatter. Finally, I stopped and lay back, feeling like I'd been battered by a tornado from top to bottom. A tornado full of rocks and bits of wood.

The hospital stuff went on and on, and I kept falling asleep and being woken up. The head scan lulled me to sleep as well. It seemed like hours later before I was in a bed, pain-killers making me totally relaxed and almost pain free, with a nurse giving me water via a straw. I sucked it down and it tasted better than the most expensive wine in the world.

The nurse went and I was about to drift off when a familiar voice said, 'Lou, are you up to telling me what happened?'

I forced my eyes open, blinking.

Scotcher.

'Hey,' I croaked. 'Um ... I guess so. Not sure I'll make total sense.'

He looked down at me and grimaced. 'They said you have a hairline fracture of your skull. You'll be here for a few days, probably. Two cracked ribs, bruised kidney. Other bruising from your seatbelt across your arms?'

'Yeah. He strapped me in after he taped me up.'

'Ah.' He pulled up a chair and got out his phone. 'Mind if I record this?'

Another voice. 'If I think she's saying anything that is a problem to her ...'

I turned my head too fast and the room went wobbly, but it was Paul sitting on the other side of my bed.

'Hi. Didn't see you there.'

'I know.' He smiled, and then nodded at Scotcher. 'Get on with it. She needs to sleep.'

Scotcher cleared his throat, then pressed his phone to start recording, reciting day and time (6.35am) and who was present. 'Lou, do you remember how you got into the four-wheel drive that was involved in the accident?'

'I was coming back from ... um, the restaurant. O'Brien's. Met Kayla. But I was on my own.' I glanced at Paul. 'I did check the street. But Daniel was waiting, hiding. He smashed my head against the car, and then jabbed me with something that knocked me out. When I came to, I was all taped up and lying in the back of the four-wheel drive.'

I went on to describe as best I could what happened. Some of it was hazy; some of it was totally clear. 'Then another guy got in the back.'

'So there were definitely two of them?' Scotcher sounded disbelieving.

'Absolutely certain. Absolutely. Because after the accident—which wasn't an accident—the second man pulled me out and was dragging me away into the bush.'

'What stopped him?'

'These two people who were fighting.'

Scotty frowned.

'Irene and, um … Les. They stopped to help, but they argued a lot. Funny …' I remembered their back and forth sniping, but I reckoned they saved my life. 'Did you get their full names? I owe them a lot.'

'Yes. Les and Irene Egland. Mr Egland says he might've seen someone with you, but he wasn't sure.'

'I'm sure. You have to look for an accomplice.'

'But you don't know who it was, who it might be.'

'No. Sorry.'

'So you've been posing as someone other than yourself on the dating apps? Bloody risky, wasn't it?' Scotcher's tone was sharp and a bit angry.

I sighed. 'It was about Melinda. You know that. I was hoping … well, I was hoping she was still alive.'

'How did you—'

Paul cut in. 'I can fill you in on all that. It was a joint operation, not just Lou on her own. We were being careful.'

Scotcher scoffed. 'Not careful enough.'

'Look, we had Lou under surveillance every time she met one—'

'Whoa, guys,' I said wearily. 'Give it a rest, will you?' I took a few breaths—there was something in my poor, knackered brain that was struggling to the surface. 'How did Daniel know where I was? I hadn't seen him since lunchtime, and I made sure no one followed me to and from O'Brien's. Did I have a tracker on me or something?'

Scotcher and Paul glanced at each other. 'We don't know yet,' Scotcher said.

'I'm going to find out,' Paul said.

There was a silent standoff for a few seconds, neither of them giving way.

'Okay,' I said, 'you two go away and sort it out. I'm going to sleep.'

'I have more questions,' Scotcher said.

I winced. 'I've already told the officers at the scene that Daniel's four-wheel drive got pushed off the road on purpose by a black SUV. Find out who did that and why. I'd seen the guy in the SUV before.'

Paul leaned forward. He understood. 'Who was he?'

'Don't know. Look, I really need to sleep. Ask me again later.'

I closed my eyes and waited, breathing slowly. After a few long seconds, both chairs moved and I sensed the two men leaving. I waited a bit longer, then opened my eyes a tiny bit. Good, the room was empty, just a bit of testosterone still floating around, perhaps.

I lay there, going over everything I remembered, trying to piece it all together. Not for Scotcher's benefit, for my own. It had never once occurred to me that the man who took Melinda and the others might be working with an accomplice. No wonder those women hadn't had a chance.

And that had nearly been me.

I shuddered, and nausea rolled up from my stomach into my throat. I fought it back, swallowing. I couldn't bear to vomit again, painkillers or not. I wanted to get out of the bed and get moving. Maybe find out who the guy in the SUV was. Lying here like this felt hopeless, like I was a victim who couldn't fight back or defend myself.

As soon as I could stand up without getting dizzy, I was out of here.

CHAPTER THIRTY-FIVE

I eventually let myself sleep, even though I didn't want to. I drifted in and out, having weird dreams of fragments of the days before. Daniel in the café; the guy standing by his car and turning away; the bomb under my bed; Grandad with his arm bandaged up telling me to be more careful; Melinda drinking wine with me; Diane's plastic-wrapped legs in the ground.

Each time I jerked awake, looked around, then gradually went back to sleep. A nurse came in and checked me, taking vital signs and giving me more water. I told her I might need to wee and she said she'd bring a pan in a little while. 'Don't get out of bed,' she warned.

My hand ached. The cannula needle in it was attached to a long tube leading up to a bag of fluid. 'How long do I have to have this in?' I asked. The tape holding the cannula down was starting to lift.

'At least another day,' she said. 'I'll get some tape to fix that down properly.' She added that I'd receive some more painkillers in the line shortly.

That sounded good, since my head was starting to thump like a red-hot hammer was pounding on it. I had no idea where my phone was, but she said it was in the drawer of my side table. 'Not supposed to use them in here though.'

Too bad about that. I waited until she left and carefully leaned over to the drawer and found my phone. Twenty per cent charge left. It was enough to call Grandad with.

'Lou!' His voice sounded funny, like he was choking up.

'Grandad?'

A rumble of throat clearing. 'Are you all right? I'm coming back now, just waiting for my flight to board.'

'You don't have to do that.' But I was so glad he was.

'I do. I will. Don't argue. I'll move you to the private place I was at.'

'But ...' There was no point arguing. 'Okay. What about ...'

'Fayed? I'll explain when I get there. See you soon. Love you, lassie.'

I had a big lump in my throat, but I whispered, 'Love you, too, you old fart.'

He chuckled and hung up.

I pushed my phone under my pillow. When I was a bit more with it, I'd ask Paul to bring in a phone charger for me. Right then, different parts of my body were all playing different tunes of pain, like an orchestra with screechy instruments competing with each other. I gritted my teeth, but that made the pain in my head worse. I hated feeling sorry for myself, especially when this was partly my own fault, but still my eyes blurred with tears.

Through the glass in the door, I spotted someone in a white jacket. Oh, please, let that be a doctor with something potent to numb everything!

The door swished open and Dr White Coat came in, head down, reading something on a clipboard. His hair was clipped super short and his scalp looked pink. I checked his hands for drugs, but he only held a pen. Damn. Not more questions and blood pressure bands.

He came around the end of the bed and sidled up next to me, head still down. But he wasn't writing, and I glimpsed his eyes—he wasn't reading either. He was kind of squinting at me. That was weird.

He seemed somehow familiar behind the black-rimmed glasses and little goatee. I stared, blinked, tried to work out who he was.

Then I tensed just as he looked up and reached behind me. He pulled out one of my pillows, and my head fell back.

His ears, that chin. And yeah, that nose.

It was Nick.

'What are you doing—'

He slammed the pillow down on my face, pushing on it so hard my nose was squashed. And that meant I couldn't breathe. I opened my mouth instead but the pillow pushed against that, too, and I could barely get any air in.

I started panicking, fighting back, thrashing around, but the pillow stayed, and I couldn't breathe.

I was going to die.

I had to get my shit together, fast.

My hands flailed, I felt the cannula tape pull hard, the needle starting to rip out of my skin. It was my only hope. I used my last burst of strength to bring my hands together and rip the needle out. The tapes on my arm pulled off as well.

Jabbing him was a waste of effort—I'd miss. Instead, I gripped the needle tightly and raked across his hand as hard as I could, once, twice.

'Bitch!' he shrieked and that side of the pillow lifted enough to let me suck in some air. I pulled the pillow aside with my other hand, fighting with him to get it off my face.

The pillow slid away and, for a wild moment, it seemed Nick couldn't decide whether to get the needle off me or try to strangle me with his bare hands. One of his hands landed on my neck and started squeezing, the other reached for the needle, but I kept jerking it out of his reach. The pole holding the bag crashed to the floor and the cannula snapped free from the line.

I couldn't move away from him, so I went for a boxing maxim. Surprise him. Move in on the bastard.

I whacked his hand sideways off my throat, sending him off balance. As he fell towards me, I whipped the needle up and stabbed him in the side of his neck. Once, twice, three times. He staggered back, holding his neck. No massive spurt of blood so I hadn't hit anything major. Pity.

I had to get out of there.

I slid off the bed and tried to run for the door, but my legs gave way and I fell to my knees. They cracked on the hard lino and I cried out. I didn't know if I could get up, so I started screaming instead as I tried to crawl to the wall for support.

Nick was right behind me, grabbing my hair, trying to get his hand over my mouth. I twisted away and wrenched my arm back, elbowing him in the ribs. But he still scrabbled for my mouth, his fingers scratching my cheek.

I screamed again and shouted, 'Help! Help! Fire! Code!' Whatever I could think of, which was bugger all.

Just as Nick pulled my head back, ripping hair from my scalp, the door burst open and Cheery Joe launched himself, his fist sailing past my head. There was a loud smack, then another. Nick's hands fell away from me at last. I heaved for breath, got my hand to the wall and turned.

Nick was on his back on the floor, trying to get up. Joe punched him again in the side of the head and this time he stayed down. His eyes rolled up and he sagged.

Thank fuck for that.

Cheery Joe came over and helped me up, one arm around my back, the other under my arm. 'You okay? Shit, I thought you were a goner.'

'I'm alive. Breathing.' I took some breaths to make sure. Joe was about to lead me back to the bed, but I said, 'No, chair. You need to ring the police right away. This guy …' I waved my hand weakly. 'I think he's the other killer. The one they've been searching for.'

I wasn't sure, but it was pretty bloody likely.

'Triple zero will take too long. Got a name? Number?' Joe asked, pulling out his phone.

'Use my phone. Under the pillow. Scotcher. In Contacts.'

'Righto.' He made the call. 'Yeah, ringing for Lou Alcott. Some turd has just tried to kill her.'

A babble from the other end.

'Nah, mate, not in the four-wheel drive, in the fuckin' hospital. Yeah. You'd better get someone here soon as. I'll look after him until you show up.'

He hung up and grinned at me. Cheery Joe, cheery at last. I loved the man.

'Your grandfather won't be happy, eh?' he said.

'No, I guess not.'

The nurse bustled in and pulled up short.

'What on earth are you doing out of bed?' she scolded. Then she saw Nick. 'And who is this? Why is he on the floor? What's going on?'

Joe said politely, 'He's just tried to knock off your patient, nurse. And now I need something to sort him out with until the cops get here. Cable ties?'

'Oh. I … Yes. I think so.' She looked at me. 'Louisa, are you all right? Do you want to get back into bed? Please?'

I shook my head. 'In a minute. Please get those cable ties. I'm not moving until that man is restrained.' My arms and legs were trembling so much, I doubted I could get back on the bed anyway, and I wasn't going to have someone help me like I was ninety years old, even if I felt like I was.

Cheery Joe had a concerned look on his face. 'Just sit there until you come right,' he said. 'You did bloody well to fight off the bastard for as long as you did. Jeez, if I'd been a couple of minutes later …'

'Thank God you arrived when you did.' I took a shuddering breath. I could still feel the pillow jammed over my face; another thing I'd be having nightmares about.

'Your grandad's flight hasn't landed yet. He'll be ropeable when he finds out.' Joe sighed. 'And when he's ropeable …'

The nurse came back with some long, skinny plastic ties. 'Will these do?'

'Sure will.' Joe bound Nick's wrists, then put two together and put them around his ankles. Just as he finished, Nick groaned and started coming around. He wriggled on the floor, trying to pull the ties loose, but he had no hope. He glared up at Joe.

'This is false imprisonment. Let me go!'

'No fuckin' way,' Joe said.

Nick called to the nurse, who was opening the door. 'Hey, you can cut these, can't you? This man's a lunatic. I'm going to get him charged for assault.'

Never mind the gouges across his hand and the holes in his neck, still bleeding, that I was responsible for. I nodded to myself. *Hmm, good job, Lou.*

She smiled at him, and it wasn't a nice smile. 'You can discuss that with these gentlemen.' She held open the door and Scotcher and a uniformed officer came in and surveyed the scene. Then Scotcher focused on me.

'You're lucky I hadn't left yet. What's going on?'

His words made me conscious of several things at once. One was the pounding in my head, which all the drama had made me forget for a few moments; another was the blood all over my hand where the cannula had been ripped out. And then there was the skimpy hospital gown I was in. That was the one that made my face burn. I had a feeling if I got up, everyone would be able to see my bum.

The nurse came back with a blanket and wrapped it around my legs, then took one off the bed for around my shoulders. I huddled into them and started to warm up.

'We need to clean and dress your hand,' she said. 'And put another cannula in.'

I scowled. 'I'll be okay like this for a few minutes, won't I?' I asked.

She finally nodded. 'I'll be back shortly, then I really will have to fix everything.'

When she'd gone, I pointed at Nick and asked Scotcher, 'You know who this is?'

Scotcher peered at him and Nick turned his head away.

'He's another one of the five who were contacting Melinda on the dating app.' I glared at Nick and the old familiar rage ignited inside. But this was not the time to explode. 'He's been working with Daniel, or Jonathan, as he called himself with Melinda. They're a bloody tag team.'

'Where's your evidence for that?' Scotcher said.

The rage bubbled to the top. 'I'm the evidence, you dickhead! The two of them abducted me. They were both in that four-wheel drive that crashed. Ask the other one—Daniel, or whatever his name is.'

Scotcher flushed bright red and glared back at me. 'So you reckon this guy was the one in the back seat.'

'He must have been. Why else would he come here and try to kill me?'

'Kill you?' Scotcher looked around. 'How?'

'Pillow over my face.' Exhaustion suddenly felled me, and I could barely open my mouth or get my brain to function. Cheery Joe put a large hand on my shoulder and gave it a squeeze.

'Take this guy away and charge him with assault at least,' Joe said. 'I'm a witness. I came in and he had Lou on the floor, trying to strangle her.'

'I did not!' Nick shouted. 'This is all fake. This lunatic assaulted *me*.' He brought his bound hands up to his neck wounds. 'I want a medical examination. That crazy woman stabbed me in the neck. Look, you can see what she did. I came in here to check on her and she went berserk, then he did as well. You have to arrest them both.'

I couldn't believe his audacity. 'You're not a doctor!' I said, exhaustion gone again. 'You came in here to attack me. Where did you steal that white coat from?'

Scotcher's face was thunderous as he looked from Nick to me. Then he said to Nick, 'If you're a staff member here, where's your ID? You're supposed to wear it around your neck.'

'I— She ripped it off me. And threw it. It could be anywhere.'

I shook my head wearily. 'Bull. Shit. Look, my grandfather will be here soon. You need to get this guy out of here and into a police cell, then charge him.'

Scotcher stood there for a few moments, seemingly adding it all up and deciding what to do. Then he said to the officer behind him, 'Arrest this man and take him to the station.' He pointed at Nick. 'I want a full ID on him, where he works, what his movements were last night. That's for starters. Tell them to keep him in custody while that's sorted out. And you'd better get medical attention for him, too. I'll be down to interview him shortly.'

'Yes, sir.' The officer went to the door and came back with his partner, a bulky woman with tight, dark curls and a set to her mouth that told me she wouldn't put up with any crap. They cut the ankle tie so Nick could walk, but left the wrist one on, despite his protests. The female officer told him they'd see about his injuries when he was at the station: 'We'll document them as well, don't worry.'

'Do you want an officer outside your door?' Scotcher asked me.

'It's a bit late for that now,' I said wearily.

'I'll be here,' Joe said.

'Right. I can see you need to rest, Lou.' Scotcher hesitated. 'By the way, the other man died before they got him into theatre.'

'But you'll get DNA off him? Fingerprints? Did you find the needle?'

'Leave that to us.' He leaned forward and looked into my eyes. 'You do have a small amount of petechial haemorrhaging. Likely from trying to strangle you.'

'Yeah. That's after he'd tried the pillow.' I gave him a brief description of what had happened. 'Then Joe came in and dragged him off me.'

'You used the cannula needle?' Scotcher's tone had gone from sceptical to gobsmacked. 'How did you get hold of it?'

'I told you. It was coming loose and I pulled it out.' I held up my hand, smeared with blood. It was starting to throb now, in tune with the pain in my head. Right then, my stomach decided to eject whatever it could find.

I leaned forward, starting to retch, gasping, 'Sorry …'

Joe grabbed the rubbish bin and stuck it under my chin. Yellow bile and some gross stuff dribbled out, but the retching made my aching ribs feel like they were being kicked all over again.

The nurse burst into the room, pushing a trolley with her equipment on it. 'All right, everybody out. Now.'

Scotcher started to protest, even though his face looked a bit green, and she pointed to the door.

'Please leave. You might be allowed back later, if Ms Alcott has improved. That's a big if, from what I see. The doctor is on his way.'

Joe leaned down to me. 'I'll be right outside the door. Not moving a centimetre.' He followed Scotcher out and I heard him say, 'You get off to the station and sort that bastard out.'

The door closed behind them and I sagged. A paper bag filled with mashed potatoes went some way towards describing how I felt. I was happy for the nurse, whose name turned out to be Gloria, to help me into bed, and I even let her put a new cannula in my other hand, because she promised to add the painkiller stuff into the line straight away.

A small part of my brain wanted to know what was going on at the police station, making sure they didn't let Nick go, but the rest of me floated away and stopped worrying about any of it.

CHAPTER THIRTY-SIX

The next time I opened my eyes, the first thing I saw was Grandad. He was staring down at his phone and frowning so deeply that his face looked like a mini mountain range. He made a tsk sound, and tapped some words, pressed send and muttered, 'Take that, ya bastard.' What was he up to now?

'Grandad?'

He jumped slightly and a huge smile cancelled out the frown. 'Louisa! About time. I was beginning to think you'd sleep into next week.'

'I feel like I could.' The aches and pains were dulled, but still there in the distance, trying to make a comeback. 'How long have you been here?'

'Couple of hours. Took me a while to get here from the airport.' He looked around. 'Need to get you out of here.'

I didn't want to move. 'I'm okay.'

'No, we'll have you moved by tonight. Don't worry about a thing.'

'Is Joe still here?'

'Outside the door.' Grandad raised his eyebrows. 'What do you want him for?'

'I should thank him. He saved my life.'

'From what I've heard, you saved your own life. Quick thinking and all.' He took my hand and gently patted it. 'I'm very glad you're still with us, lass. Close call, eh? In fact, two close calls.' He shook his head. 'Working with Paul was supposed to be safer than being a cop, you know.'

'Yeah.' I thought of the bodies I'd seen when I was a cop. And then I thought how close I'd come to being another one, lying in the bush somewhere, maybe never to be found.

'Have they charged that Nick guy yet?'

Grandad shook his head. 'Haven't heard. I'm more concerned right now with Fayed.'

'You shouldn't have come back.'

'Makes no difference, lass. He just went after you instead, and I'm really sorry about that.' His face hardened. 'It won't happen again.'

'What do you mean?' Had there been another bomb in my apartment? Or at Grandad's house? A sniper? The hospital suddenly felt much safer than the real world. I shivered and snuggled under the blanket more.

'You remember much about that accident in the four-wheel drive?'

'Some of it. Well, quite a bit.'

'You told the police you thought you'd been run off the road.'

'Yes. Do they know …'

'I know who did it.' His knuckles cracked as he clenched his hands. 'It was Fayed, or two of his dickheads. They'd been following you. Tracker on the Commodore.'

I gaped at him.

'They didn't see what happened to you,' he said, 'but they were pretty sure you were in the four-wheel drive. Once they'd checked the Commodore was still parked where you left it, they followed the four-wheel drive instead. They thought you'd picked up some bloke at the restaurant. When they saw it was you in the passenger seat, they ran you off the road.'

A laugh spluttered out of me. 'That's fucking unbelievable. Daniel and Nick were taking me out bush somewhere to kill me. So …' My brain jumped around a few times and then stopped. 'So Fayed's guys tried to kill me, but actually they saved my fucking life?'

Grandad tsked again. 'Profanities, Lou. And yes, strange but true. I've had words with Fayed, so he knows what happened. Anyway, he's sorted.'

I glared at him. 'You haven't threatened him, have you?'

'Waste of time. He's a lunatic. It's over, that's all.'

I wasn't convinced. People like Fayed didn't agree to pleasantly stop hostilities. I figured Grandad might have something to bargain with that Fayed couldn't say no to. 'Do the police know that was who pushed us off the road?'

'Well, no, and I won't be telling them. Neither can you.' He shot me a warning look. 'It'll keep you safe that way. If the police find out through their own investigating, that's on them. Nothing to do with us.'

Except Scotcher had told me Daniel was dead, and Fayed's boys had killed him, so I wasn't sure the police would give up that easily. Still, not my problem—I'd tell them what I remembered. The main thing now was getting Nick charged and convicted.

What I still really wanted was to find Melinda. I knew the odds were bad, that she was probably dead, but ...

'Is Scotcher coming back to question me?'

Grandad checked his watch, an old Rolex he'd had as long as I could remember. 'In about half an hour.' He looked up at the glass panel in the door. 'Someone else here to see you first.'

The door opened and Paul came in, followed by Gang. Today's glasses were purple with diamantes and matched his T-shirt. Paul was in a suit.

I smiled at him. 'Dressing up just to visit me?'

'Ha ha. I've got to be in court in a couple of hours, so no. The hearing is about Diane.'

'Oh.'

'As far as I know, Justin is now pleading not guilty, but when the prick is facing the judge and the reality of it, he might change to guilty. It's happened before.'

So Justin had decided he'd fight the murder charge. Probably still trying to convince his kids he didn't do it.

Gang was jiggling with excitement and said, 'Were there really two of them, Lou? Both of them did it together? That's so bizarre. You know tag team killers are quite rare, don't you?'

I rolled my eyes. 'Gang, you're not going to tell me all about the other dual killer cases, are you?'

His face fell. 'Well, maybe not right now ...'

I focused on Paul. 'You're the one with the contacts on the inside. Has Nick confessed? Where are the other women? Where's Melinda?'

'They should be interviewing Nick now,' Paul said. 'But they're wanting to talk to you again. You're their star witness.'

'We've given our statements,' Gang said. 'And I showed them all my screenshots and the evidence I'd collected.'

'Screenshots?'

'Both of their profiles had been deleted.'

'What? How?' I tried to figure it out. 'You're not saying there was a third person in the team, are you?'

'Oh God, no!' Gang said. 'They were deleted pretty much straight after Daniel bashed you and put you in his car.'

'Wow, that was fast.' I ran the timing in my head. 'Nick must have done it as soon as Daniel said he had me. Fu—' I stopped myself before Grandad could tell me off again.

Paul added, 'We think Nick was the tech person running their profiles and deleting them. He'd taught himself a lot of hacking and extra skills, beyond his actual job, probably while he'd been off injured.'

I remembered Nick's hand. 'I bet that wasn't a work injury.'

'No, we checked this morning. His workplace said he'd done it at home with a power tool.'

Immediately I had a picture of Nick cutting up a woman's body and had to swallow hard a few times. Grandad patted my hand.

A sharp knock at the door broke me out of my dark imaginings.

'It's that detective,' Gang said. 'We can tell him to come back later?'

I grinned at my new bodyguard. Seemed I had two now. 'It's fine, truly. The sooner I tell them everything, the sooner they'll charge Nick and maybe get the truth out of him.'

'Don't bank on it,' Paul said sourly. 'I'm off to court. See you later.' He and Gang left as Scotcher and a female detective came in.

'You want me to stay, lass?' Grandad asked.

'Yes, please.' I wanted someone at my back who I knew I could rely on one hundred per cent.

Scotcher had his recorder out. 'Ready to talk?'

I nodded. Time to make sure Nick was charged. I was determined the police would find out where Melinda was.

After the two detectives had pulled up chairs, Scotcher did all the intro stuff for recording. He introduced himself as Detective Sergeant Robert Scotcher. Rob. I filed that one away for another time. It was strange to hear Grandad referred to as 'Hamish James Campbell', but he just grunted in response and sat back, arms folded.

'I'd like you to explain the setup,' Scotcher said. 'Going on the dating sites and creating a profile. Why you did that.' His tone was terse; he clearly thought our actions were all idiotic, and mine in particular.

'As I explained to you at the time, Detective Sergeant Scotcher, my friend Melinda was missing, and nobody seemed to be treating it seriously.'

'I don't think—' He broke off and took a breath. 'Carry on.'

The female detective shifted in her chair but said nothing.

I explained briefly how we'd found five possible suspects on Melinda's phone. 'Which I gave to you.' He nodded and I continued. 'Eventually we realised that the only way to properly check all five was to go into the dating apps and do it in person. If possible.'

His mouth tightened, but he managed to keep quiet.

'I had photos taken by Gang, and he helped set me up. Not with my real name, obviously. After a couple of days, and a range of interest, those two popped up and I did the swipe thing. I chatted with both of them.' I went on to explain the chatting and the two 'dates'.

'So you met both of them in person?'

'Yes.'

'How did you know they were your ... suspects? Daniel was using a different name and I've seen both profiles. He looked very different in each one. I would have said it wasn't him.'

'I, ah ... I recognised him. It's something I can do. With people. You know.'

His face creased. 'Are you saying you're a super recogniser?'

'Well, um, yes.' I could feel my cheeks burning, and that made me mad. 'I don't see why I should have to apologise for it!'

Grandad leaned forward as if to say something in my defence, but the female detective interrupted.

'Did you know you had this skill while you were in the force?' She was interested, not accusative.

'Not really, no. It wasn't something I could use in court so ...'

She nodded and looked like she was dying to ask me more, but Scotcher kept going.

'Describe the two meetings you had, please.'

I did as he asked, then said, 'I was very careful after both meetings to make sure neither of them followed me at all. I don't know how they knew I was in the restaurant with Kayla. I didn't see either of them there.'

'We found a tracker in your bag,' Scotcher said.

My mouth dropped open. 'Shit, if only I'd got Gang to check it for me.'

'If Nick had put it in there when you met him for a drink, there was no time, was there?'

'I guess not.' That's right, he dropped his wallet under our table. Another thought occurred to me. 'In that case, they had it planned already. They ...' Words failed me.

'My guess is Daniel checked you out first, on your coffee date, then as soon as Nick met you and agreed you were the next one, he slipped in the tracker. Those aren't their real names, of course.'

Grandad squeezed my hand and I glanced at his concerned face. If I'd gone straight home to Docklands after the wine date, none of it would have happened. I would have been protected. Except I'd been thinking about going to the gym early the next morning, to work off the wine and food from the pub. Following the tracker, they would've got me there, or while I was out running. I was their target. And discovering I was a PI didn't make much difference to them in the end.

'These two ... how did they team up? Find each other?'

'They went to school together.' Scotcher named a big private school in the eastern suburbs. 'Either they've been friends ever since, or somehow found each other again.'

I could just imagine Daniel and Nick at a school reunion, realising they had the same 'interests'.

'As I told you earlier,' Scotcher said, 'the man calling himself Daniel has died. His injuries were too severe. It's our belief that Nick is going to claim innocence and blame it all on Daniel, so ...'

I was swamped by the sensation of the pillow over my face again, feeling like I couldn't breathe. I gripped Grandad's hand so hard it turned white. Then a familiar burning rage bubbled through me and I steeled myself. That bastard wasn't going to get away with it. Not if I could help it.

I checked Scotcher was still recording and went through everything I remembered, from the attack and the needle to waking up taped and immobilised, being put in the four-wheel drive front passenger seat and hearing someone get in the back seat. The accident, being pulled out by Nick, then Les and Irene. Some of it was patchy, but as I talked, more of it came back. So did the fear and panic, the tight sticky tape trapping me, and I had to stop a few times to breathe slowly and calm down. Grandad held my hand, squeezing it tightly, and he felt like such a safe anchor that I had to blink hard so as not to let any tears out.

'Did Les see Nick dragging me away or not?'

'He says he thinks he did, but probably not clearly enough to provide an ID on him.'

'Surely you can get DNA off my shirt from where he was dragging me into the bush?' I clamped my mouth shut before I said something rude, then asked, 'So what are their real names? Do either of them have previous convictions?'

'Their real names are very different, but for the dating apps he used Nick all the time. We think he believed he was too clever to get caught. That explains his silence in the back seat. And why he was in the hospital, still trying to get rid of you. You are the one person who can identify him.'

So Scotcher was going to charge him, as long as I stayed alive.

'My granddaughter will be under my protection from now on,' Grandad rumbled. 'Until you put this bastard away. You'd better make damn sure you have a watertight case against him. And no bloody bail either.'

Scotcher surveyed him in silence for a few moments. 'If we could find the bodies of the other two victims, it would help. The first victim was too degraded to collect evidence from, other than the probable cause of death.'

'Which was?' I asked.

'Strangulation.' He hesitated, swallowed and added, 'There were also signs of torture and possibly sexual assault.'

'You know what direction we were headed in?'

'There's a hell of a lot of bushland out past the airport and Sunbury. We're checking to see if either of them or their families owned any property outside of Melbourne.'

Scotcher continued his questioning, and we went through the last bit of being brought to the hospital, and then Nick's attempt to smother me and then strangle me when I fought him off. The female detective looked a bit pale as she took notes. Scotcher winced at some of it, which made me like him a little better.

Finally, they were finished. But I had one more question. 'Are you going to push him to tell you where Melinda is? Where they put their bodies?' I didn't want to say the words 'make a deal'.

'Of course,' he said. 'And not just for ticking the boxes either.'

I was glad he didn't say 'for the families' sakes'. Melinda's father might regret his dismissal of his daughter, but I doubted it.

As they were leaving, Scotcher said, 'By the way, there are still a couple of journalists out there in the waiting room. They weren't allowed to hang around in the corridor. Just letting you know.'

'Thanks.'

When they'd gone, I said to Grandad, 'Journalists?'

'Ah, well, you found the Tag Team Killers, lass.' He wasn't laughing.

I groaned. 'I can guess which scummy newspaper came up with that one.' There was always someone ready to create a media scare campaign where murder was involved. As long as it was something exciting like serial killings, or someone they could portray as a 'lunatic'.

'There'll be no journalists talking to you, right?'

'No way.'

He patted my hand one more time and let it go. 'Now, they've finally agreed to discharge you tomorrow, and you're coming home with me. Joe will be there, and I've organised a nurse for a couple of days to keep an eye on your head injury.'

For once, I didn't argue. No matter what Grandad said about Fayed, I wasn't anywhere near ready to return to my apartment. I wondered if I would ever feel safe and secure there again.

'You're the boss, Grandad.'

'Damn right,' he said with a grin.

EPILOGUE

Two weeks later

I pushed open the door to PMI, trying to ignore the little tremor inside that made me question if I was really ready for this. I was ready. Time to get back on the zebra.

'Heeeeyyy!' Gang leapt up from his chair and gave me a big hug. 'So good to have you back, girlfriend. Look, your chair is waiting for you.'

I looked at the brown office chair and computer and tried not to wince. 'Great.' I didn't sound convinced, but he took no notice.

'Coffee? Double shot?'

'Please.'

Paul's office door opened. 'Good to see you, Lou. All set to go?'

I swallowed. 'You've got a job for me already?'

'Desk job for now. Insurance fraud, so lots of follow-up on the internet and reports.'

Woo hoo, I couldn't wait. Although I had to admit I was a bit relieved. Field work, well … it could wait a while longer.

'Grab a coffee and come into my office—I'll update you on a few things.'

When I was settled, with Gang in the seat alongside me and Paul swinging in his big leather chair, he started.

'You know that Nick—real name Marcus Mason—has been charged and was denied bail?'

I nodded. Scotcher had called me, a week after I'd finally been up to making my formal statement. 'His fingerprints and DNA from the four-wheel drive and on the tape around my arms and neck are enough evidence to prove he was part of the abduction and assault on me. And the attempted murder in the hospital.' I folded my arms tightly, tamping down my anger. I was getting better at it. 'But they can't charge him with murder yet. They still haven't found Melinda and the other missing woman. Or the place out of Melbourne where they were taking me.'

Paul glanced at Gang, who tapped the iPad on his lap and held it out to me.

'What's this?' I asked.

'It's an email from Detective Sergeant Scotcher,' Paul said. 'Hikers found a body in the bush near Woodend last week. The police think it's Melinda.'

A surge of something dark and unnameable rolled over me as I took the iPad and pretended to read the email. But it was all blank and meaningless—I'd known she was very likely to be dead. The reality was gutting. I'd failed her.

'Oh, Melinda, I'm so sorry,' I whispered.

'The thing is …' Paul cleared his throat. 'As you can see there, her father says he's unable to come down to identify her.'

'Bastard.'

Gang took the iPad back, as if guessing I hadn't been able to read it. 'Scotcher is going to call you. He wants to know if you can do it. The identification. You're, well, you're the only person in Melbourne they feel they can ask.'

'You're kidding!'

Poor, lonely Melinda. All she was trying to do was start again, to find her feet and maybe also find someone to love, someone who would love her. Instead she was preyed upon by two fucking psychos who were on the lookout for solitary, vulnerable victims. Women who couldn't fight back, who trusted the wrong people and who paid for it.

I wished that cannula needle had opened Nick's carotid artery.

'Yes, I'll go and identify her,' I said. It was the very least I could do.

'In case you were worried, Antony Fayed is out of the picture,' Paul said.

'I found a record of him leaving Melbourne on a flight to London,' Gang chipped in. He grinned. 'Don't ask how.'

I'd already asked Grandad what his 'lever' over Fayed was, and he wouldn't tell me. For my own good. I didn't agree. None of that felt finished.

'Are you still staying with Hamish?' Paul asked.

'Yes. But I'm moving home tomorrow.' I took a breath. 'I need to pack up my apartment and get the painters in. I'm selling up and looking for somewhere new.'

That was the other decision I'd made. It was time to get a grip on my life. Grandad had offered me one of his condos again, but I needed to think about that more. He'd also pressed me about joining him in the 'business', insisting he was almost totally legit these days.

That was still a definite no.

'Right,' Paul said, standing and stretching. 'Glad you're back, Lou. We have new clients and we need you.' We left his office and Gang handed me two new files ready to go.

'Hey, I'm really glad you're back, too,' Gang said. He gave me a hug. 'And Blossom and Lily said to let you know they're ready for your makeover.'

Just in time, I spotted his smartarse grin.

'In. Your. Dreams!' I said.

ACKNOWLEDGEMENTS

Lou Alcott burst into life as I was trying to write a short story for the Australian Sisters in Crime Scarlet Stiletto award. I'd never written a private investigator story before, but I had read quite a few, starting with Sara Paretsky's and Sue Grafton's novels years ago. However, Lou wasn't happy just solving the one case through dogged determination— she kept coming back to nag me! Especially after the short story received a Highly Commended, my first ever.

That story almost proved my undoing. It kept trying to take over the novel and I had to throw out more than 60,000 words before things started to work. Mainly the manuscript's evolution was due to some great feedback from my writing group, and a lot of thinking, but it took eight drafts to finally show what Lou was capable of.

Huge thanks to Lucia Nardo, Demet Divaroren and Kathy Mueller in my Big Fish writers' group. Equally huge thanks to Tracey Rolfe, who read the eighth draft and gave me the extra feedback and encouragement I needed to revise and polish one more time and send out the manuscript. Thanks to Fiction Feedback in the UK whose assessor gave me a lot of great advice on an earlier draft.

My thanks also to Rijn Collins and the other women who contacted me after my Facebook request and agreed to answer all my questions about their online dating experiences. None of which had led to death, fortunately. Thank you, Megan, for your online dating stories, too!

As always, thank you, Dr Sandra Neate, for answering all kinds of weird and wonderful medical questions, and Adele Romita for helping with all my paramedics questions. And I still draw on the interviews I've done with various police officers over the years, as well as a range of excellent podcasts, books, online articles and YouTube videos. Any errors will be my own. As well, I thank a former student of mine, Dijana Necovski, whose book project of interviews, *The Online Dating Jungle*, somehow stuck with me and undoubtedly contributed to my initial plot ideas. It was a great experience talking to author Robin Bowles who shared her memories of working as a PI.

I'm so grateful to Annabel Blay at HQ for enjoying my previous novels and helping Lou find a home, and shepherding me through the publishing process. Thank you, Rachael Donovan, for loving Lou and being so keen to publish (and finding me a great new title). Kylie Mason was an excellent copyeditor and tactfully pointed out two big plot holes that needed to be fixed. And many thanks to all in the HQ marketing team for guiding me through the maze.

Even though my longtime agent, Brian Cook, has now retired, I truly appreciate all of his support and advice over the years. And thank you to my new adult fiction agent, Sarah McKenzie, for her feedback and wise advice.

The support and encouragement over the years from my family cheer squad has been wonderful. Various cats have trod across my keyboard and sat on my lap while I was writing, but Sooty was the best. Miss you still.

And thank you always, Brian. Yes, you.

talk about it

Let's talk about books.

Join the conversation:

f @harlequinaustralia

♪ @hqanz

⊙ @harlequinaus

harpercollins.com.au/hq

If you love reading and want to know about our
authors and titles, then let's talk about it.